PRAISE FOR CH

Praise for *Beneath the Poet's House*

"*Beneath the Poet's House* is creepy and addictive. Carmen uses a gothic New England setting to explore art and magic and left me thinking that the things men do to women are far more terrifying than any conjuring."
—Jessa Maxwell, author of *The Golden Spoon* and *I Need You to Read This*

"*Beneath the Poet's House* is a brilliant, gripping novel filled with secrets and danger. Christa Carmen captures the haunted magic of Providence and introduces one of the most fascinating and singular characters I've ever encountered. The novel shimmers with questions of what is real and what is imaginary, helped by the extraordinary setting of a writer's house with a tragically romantic rose garden, a cemetery, and ghosts in love. Shocking, tender, and wildly compelling, *Beneath the Poet's House* will keep you racing through the pages all night long."
—Luanne Rice, Amazon Charts and *New York Times* bestselling author of *Last Night*

"With secrets as deep and dark as catacombs and lyrical writing befitting of its literary inspirations, *Beneath the Poet's House* is a truly eerie page-turner."
—Zoje Stage, *USA Today* bestselling author of *Baby Teeth* and *Dear Hanna*

"In *Beneath the Poet's House*, haunting history meets a riveting modern mystery. It's a spellbinding, beautifully told story about secrets, the supernatural, and ultimately, finding the strength to fight back against impossible odds."
—Jess Lourey, Edgar-nominated author of *The Taken Ones*

"With lush, haunting prose to rival any classic, *Beneath the Poet's House* twists patriarchal gothic tropes and gives new breath to old stereotypes in a story that is at once a historical reckoning, a desperate love story, and an intriguing mystery. Like a crooked finger beckoning the reader down a castle's winding staircase, Carmen's writing is impossible to resist. Mark my words: she will soon find her place among the gothic greats."

—Katrina Monroe, author of *Through the Midnight Door*

"Christa Carmen has cleverly resurrected the infamous Providence romance between Edgar Allan Poe and Sarah Helen Whitman in this thrilling novel set in modern times. What unfolds is worthy of a plot concocted by Poe himself. You won't be able to put this book down!"

—Levi L. Leland, creator of www.edgarallanpoeri.com and *A Walking Tour of Poe's Providence*

"Haunting and gorgeously told, *Beneath the Poet's House* brings new life to the tumultuous romance and compelling lives of Edgar Allan Poe and Sarah Helen Whitman, all within a modern psychological suspense with a riveting plot that will enthrall readers."

—Vanessa Lillie, *USA Today* bestselling author of *Blood Sisters*

Praise for *The Daughters of Block Island*

"Thrilling psychological suspense that should appeal to fans of gothic novels and the works of Gemma Amor, Sarah Waters, and the Brontë sisters."

—*Library Journal*

"Great fun for readers . . ."

—*Kirkus Reviews*

"This compelling and atmospheric thriller pays homage to classic gothic novels while still adding something fresh to the beloved genre. An easy sell to fans of the Brontës but also those who enjoy the creepy, psychological suspense of Simone St. James."

—*Booklist*

"Christa Carmen celebrates the gothic in this twisty, spooky tour de force that ticks all the boxes with panache and style! This love child of Barbara Michaels and John Harwood has written a chilling page-turner guaranteed to keep you up all night. *The Daughters of Block Island* is a top-notch read!"

—Nancy Holder, Lifetime Achievement Award winner, Horror Writers Association

"The mystery leaves the reader feeling like they are trying to escape a twisted haunted dollhouse without knowing what is real or imagined. Lovers of gothic fiction should pick up this book, which contains a wealth of nods to the genre but also discusses personal horrors like addiction, abuse, and mental health."

—V. Castro, Bram Stoker Award–nominated author of *Goddess of Filth* and *The Queen of the Cicadas*

"A tantalizing love letter to gothic fiction, imbued with rain-soaked atmosphere and scandal-ridden mysteries that unravel to reveal the dark beating heart at the center of a mysterious island mansion. Readers of gothic novels will delight in nods to classic works and the way the past continues to haunt the present in White Hall. Filled with intrigue, this book is the perfect addition to your bookshelf, tucked in beside Radcliffe and du Maurier!"

—Jo Kaplan, author of *It Will Just Be Us*

"With its lush and exquisite language, Christa Carmen's *The Daughters of Block Island* honors and explores the great gothic novels of the past, but here the rules are rewritten. Be prepared to find yourself in White Hall's spider's web."

—Cynthia Pelayo, Bram Stoker Award–nominated author of *Children of Chicago*

"Offers an atmospheric, harrowing plight of ghosts and murder. Christa Carmen paints an island of vivid and unsettling imagery, where every claustrophobic twist leads deeper into an underworld of dread. A compelling mystery, with arresting characters ready to engulf you."

—Hailey Piper, Bram Stoker Award–winning author of *The Worm and His Kings*

"Christa Carmen has long been one of my favorite horror authors, and *The Daughters of Block Island* is further proof that she's among the most important voices in the genre today. A clever inversion and exploration of gothic tropes, this is a debut novel unlike any other. A true macabre masterpiece, this book is a must-read."

—Gwendolyn Kiste, Bram Stoker Award–winning author of *The Rust Maidens* and *Reluctant Immortals*

"Christa Carmen cleverly combines classic elements of the Victorian literary canon in a fast-paced island intrigue that is atmospheric and enigmatic. A tale to rival Ann Radcliffe's *The Mysteries of Udolpho*, told in exquisite prose and embracing contemporary themes, Carmen's debut novel is a triumph of the modern gothic genre."

—Lee Murray, five-time Bram Stoker Award–winning author of *Grotesque: Monster Stories*

"Immerses the reader in the inexorable, chilling, uneasy atmosphere one hopes for in a gothic novel. Classically genre aware while still being inventive, Carmen has a compelling voice no matter which of the sisters is taking the lead. Generational trauma, true villainy, tragedy, loss, and resilience collide in a rushing tide of a powerfully wrought story."

—Leanna Renee Hieber, award-winning author of *Strangely Beautiful* and *A Haunted History of Invisible Women*

"The gothic horror novel just received a massive shot of adrenaline to its bleak-but-beautiful heart . . . In this debut novel, Carmen doesn't attempt to top the classics; instead, she subverts them in a unique manner. She embraces the tropes that made the subgenre what it is and forges an enthralling tale of two sisters, a strange town, and a cast of characters that would make the masters proud . . . If this is any indication of what Christa Carmen can bring into the world, readers will be smiling under candlelight for years to come. An exceptional new talent has arrived."

—Cemetery Dance

BENEATH THE POET'S HOUSE

ALSO BY CHRISTA CARMEN

The Daughters of Block Island
Something Borrowed, Something Blood-Soaked

BENEATH THE POET'S HOUSE

A THRILLER

CHRISTA CARMEN

Text copyright © 2024 by Christa Carmen
All rights reserved.

Published by Thomas & Mercer, Seattle

www.apub.com

Amazon, the Amazon logo, and Thomas & Mercer are trademarks of Amazon.com, Inc., or its affiliates.

ISBN-13: 9781662513275 (paperback)
ISBN-13: 9781662513282 (digital)

Cover design by Caroline Teagle Johnson
Cover image: (Stairwell) © Rob Power/Unsplash. Reproduced by kind permission of the National Trust. (Lower right painting) Portrait of Sarah Helen Whitman-Brown, (1838) by C.G. Thompson, via Danvis Collection / Alamy Stock Photo.

Printed in the United States of America

For Eleanor . . .
I love you now
As I loved you then,
When we still lived on the moon.

Prologue

Rosedale Cemetery, Montclair, New Jersey
January

It was hard to argue against death's inherent beauty in a place where stonework snaked through icy landscapes like abstract art, and ever-greens softened the spaces between tombstones as elegantly as emerald paint. Saoirse White resisted the urge to wrap her arms around her black-clad torso and tried to focus on the priest's words—something about grains of golden sand creeping through one's fingers—rather than the collection of mourners gathered around the open grave. But no matter how many statements of comfort and peace the priest offered, Saoirse remained jumpy, unmoored, and on edge.

The slightest movement in either direction found her face-to-face with yet another friend or family member of her late husband's. There was Jonathan's college roommate. Next to the roommate was the law school mentor, blotting his eyes with an endless stream of tissues. Jonathan's Princeton colleagues huddled in a group, and Saoirse recognized the president of the historical society Jonathan volunteered at, as well as a few members of his bowling league. And to her left, beside a massive arrangement of creamy orchids and indigo gladioli, were Jonathan's mother, older brother, and younger sister.

At the sight of Isabel, Issac, and Caroline White, Saoirse felt her heart tighten and her breath grow short. As panic climbed up her throat,

Saoirse's own mother took her hand and squeezed it. Ann Norman glanced down with practiced subtlety, catching Saoirse's eye, refusing to relinquish her grip on her daughter's hand.

"Got you," she whispered, and Saoirse relaxed. Her husband may be dead, but her mother was the unyielding pillar from which she'd always drawn strength. She could get through this. Her mother *would help her* get through this. Saoirse closed her eyes, and let the priest's closing remarks wash over her: boundaries dividing life and death . . . uncertainties about where one ends and the other begins.

When the last lemon-yellow lily had been thrown atop Jonathan's casket, Saoirse's mother started to lead her away. As they stepped onto the dirt path, Saoirse felt a hand on her shoulder. She turned to find Isabel, flanked by Jonathan's two siblings, her green eyes smudged with mascara and the corners of her lipsticked mouth trembling.

"Isabel," Saoirse said before her brain could tell her to wait, to see what Jonathan's devastated mother might say to her first. "I'm . . . I . . . I can't believe we're standing here."

"I can." Isabel sniffled and reached into her purse for a tissue. "I told him it was too much. All of it. The work, the charitable organizations, the students he was supervising. The"—she paused to blow her nose—"expectations he had for his home life. The things he still wanted to accomplish. What you two were trying to—"

Saoirse's mother broke in before Isabel could finish. "Mrs. White, now's not the time. Everyone is grieving. Emotions are high. There's no sense in bringing up the past"—she gestured around them—"with all these people present. Saoirse and I are going to head to the house. Why don't you let Jonathan's friends and colleagues know that anyone who wants to come back there is welcome. We'll have the food and drinks out by the time you arrive."

Isabel sniffled again but nodded. With the help of her two remaining children, Jonathan's mother retreated to where the largest group of mourners still lingered, paying their final respects.

"Thank you," Saoirse whispered to her mother, who gripped her hand harder and led her toward the limo. A sleek-feathered black bird—too large to be a crow—issued a series of croaks from a nearby bush, and Saoirse jumped. "Goddammit," she muttered. But it wasn't the bird that had her looking over her shoulder. She needed to get out of here, away from the whispers and prying eyes. Away from the endless prayers and the cloying scent of flowers and the frigid weather.

When they'd arrived at the cemetery, Saoirse had instructed the limo driver to pull away from the rest of the procession. A copse of weeping willows had provided the privacy she'd needed to compose herself before the service, but now those same hanging boughs seemed ominous, the shadows stretching out from under them creeping and curling like probing fingers. Saoirse forced herself to continue forward, ignoring her fear that she might disappear beneath those branches and never emerge.

"Go ahead," her mother offered, holding the driver's-side back door open for Saoirse.

"My bag's on the other side. I'll go around." Circling the back of the limo, Saoirse couldn't help but consider Isabel White's words: *The expectations he had for his home life. The things he still wanted to accomplish. What you two were trying to—*

Saoirse knew what *Jonathan* was trying to do, yes, and what he would have told his mother and the rest of his family he wanted to "accomplish." She cringed at the word. But had anyone been aware of her thoughts on the matter? Certainly not. Likely, the only one who knew anything close to the true nature of her and Jonathan's relationship was Aidan Vesper. Jonathan's partner in crime. Jonathan's confidant since boyhood. Jonathan's—

"Saoirse," a voice said, at the same time Saoirse felt a hand grip her elbow. She whirled around, almost catching a branch to her cheek, and found herself staring into Aidan's pale, angular face, as if her thoughts had conjured him from the air.

"Aidan." Saoirse tried to back up, but she was already pressed against the limo. She skirted several steps to the right, intent on putting some distance between them. Under the weeping willow, framed by skeletal branches and wearing a black trench coat, he looked like something out of a Grimm's fairy tale.

"Saoirse," he said again. "I've tried calling, but it goes to voicemail. How are you holding up?"

She stared at him, not answering. A sound came from inside the car. Aidan's eyes flicked past her, to where Saoirse's mother would be seated. "Can we go somewhere private?" Aidan asked. "To talk?"

Saoirse's earlier panic crashed over her in an instant. She had to refrain from bringing a hand to her chest; feeling the erratic beating of her heart would only alarm her further. Why did her husband's best friend want to talk with her?

Aidan reached into the pocket of his trench coat and came out with his phone. "I know this is not the best time to—"

"No, it's not," Saoirse's mother said. She'd gotten out and come around the back of the limo. "It's not the best time at all."

Saoirse nodded. "I'm sorry, Aidan, but I can't. Everything's too . . ." She trailed off. *Everything's too what? Fresh? Final?* "Over," she finished.

"Over?" Aidan appeared genuinely confused.

"You and I were never close. Jonathan's people were *his* people. Now that he's dead, our feigned affinity for one another . . . it's over." She sighed. "I just want to be left alone. To grieve. To—"

Aidan pursed his lips. "Listen, Saoirse, you *need* to hear what I have to say. For the sake of the investigation. For closure. It's beyond important." His tone was hard, unflinching. Gone was the friendly—or at least civil—man of a moment before, replaced with the person Aidan became when he scrubbed up and hit the hospital floor for work . . . or the person he used to morph into when he would spend time with Jonathan.

"There *is* no investigation," Saoirse reminded him. "Jonathan died of a heart attack. The autopsy confirmed it."

Flustered, Aidan shook his head. "Still, it's about his last night. The night the police say Jonathan died. Even though . . ." He trailed off, but Saoirse knew what he was going to say: *even though his body wasn't found until three days later . . . by you.*

Saoirse shook her head fiercely. "No. I don't want—"

"That's definitely enough," her mother said. "How dare you bring that terrible night up at Jonathan's funeral?"

Saoirse held up a hand. "It's okay, Mom. Let's just go." She maneuvered forward enough to open the limo door and helped her mother back inside. Saoirse had placed a foot on the running board and was reaching for the handle when Aidan shot out one black-gloved hand, stopping the door from closing with a grunt.

"You *will* listen to what I have to say," Aidan said, his voice so low, it was almost a growl. "And you will look at the text message Jonathan sent me that night, right before *you*—"

Saoirse lurched forward, knocking Aidan's hand off the door. She dove into the limo beside her mother, pulled the door shut, and shouted to the driver, "Get us out of here, please. Now!"

The driver stared at Saoirse in the rearview mirror.

"Go!" Saoirse shouted, and he hit the gas. The limo lurched forward, sending dirt and stones spraying up, where they clanked against the hubcaps. Aidan brought one arm to his face against the exhaust.

The last thing Saoirse saw as they pulled out of the cemetery and onto the main road was the black-garbed figure of Aidan Vesper walking toward Jonathan's still-open grave. She sat in silence, breathing hard, until her mother said, "What the hell was that about?"

Saoirse closed her eyes. "I don't know."

"He said something about a text from Jonathan. You don't think—"

"I don't know." Saoirse placed both hands on her knees and tried again to catch her breath. She lowered her voice to a whisper. "But I do know that I don't want to talk about this. Not ever again."

She raised her eyes to meet her mother's but was distracted by the sudden buzzing of a fly. She swatted at it, then felt another crawling across the nape of her neck, inching toward her hairline. Shuddering, Saoirse smacked the skin there, but her palm came back empty. A quick scan of the cab turned up nothing. *Had the flies been there at all?*

Her mother's eyes narrowed. "Sersh, what's going on?"

"Nothing. Listen, I'm serious, you and I are not going to speak about what happened to Jonathan. Not even to each other. Do you understand?"

Her mother nodded.

"It's the only way." Saoirse looked out the window, but caught her own reflection and turned away. She didn't want to see the haunted look in her eyes or the hollowness of her cheeks. She needed a change. She was *working* toward a change. And it was time to tell her mother.

"I'm moving," Saoirse said.

Her mother's head jerked up. "Back to Connecticut? You can stay with me if you need to—"

"Not to Connecticut. Rhode Island. Providence, to be exact. I haven't found a place yet, but I'm looking. It will take a few months to get everything together. But I think it's for the best."

To her surprise, her mother nodded again and said, "I understand."

Saoirse closed her eyes and exhaled, grateful her mother had refrained from asking additional questions. She hadn't actually started looking for places in Providence yet, but she would, as soon as she had the energy. As soon as she had convinced herself that Jonathan was gone. That the creak of wood as he crept up the stairs to where she slept would no longer pierce the gauzy fabric of her dreams.

She swallowed down something between a whimper and a sob. She would rebuild her life in Providence. Maybe somewhere near Brown's campus, in the northern part of the city. She just had to hope it was far enough away from her and Jonathan's home in New Jersey to quiet the voices in her head.

And far enough away to keep Aidan Vesper from finding her.

Chapter 1

The house smells strongly of honey-tinged beeswax and bergamot, the warm notes as distinct as a long-steeped cup of Earl Grey. Saoirse stumbles into the shadowy foyer with a sigh and a crinkle of bags. When she closes the door behind her, the lingering warmth of twilight disappears with the finality of a stone slab sliding over a crypt. She inspects the space—feathery fern on a cherrywood stand, peach settee, marble table, gold-framed paintings of an idyllic countryside—and allows herself a moment of relief as small as it is earned.

The sound of voices comes from somewhere deep within the house. Saoirse freezes, mind stuttering, then lets out a small bark of laughter and shakes her head. She's in the city now, not the suburbs. There will be noises beyond the trills of whip-poor-wills and the white-noise hum of a neighbor's lawn mower. Her nights will be backdropped by teenagers hooting on street corners, students singing on their way to parties, spouses teasing one another as they hustle to dinner reservations at fancy restaurants.

She drops her computer bag, purse, and shopping totes to the floor and pats her pockets. Empty. Her cell phone must still be in the car. Why did she time the three-hour drive to arrive in Providence so late?

She could run out again, find a Starbucks, guzzle a shot of—or maybe a double—espresso. Another perk of the city: things stay open later than 7:00 p.m. But the thought of delaying the inevitable makes her want to collapse to the floor with her bags. And she's not supposed to have too much caffeine; her doctors tell her this constantly. Saoirse pulls her hair into a ponytail and heads back outside to begin the painful process of unloading her car.

Each trek between her grime-coated Mazda and the garnet-red building that is now her home—striking even in this fading light—recalls another detail from her new landlord, Diane's, pitch. *The woodwork is mesmerizing,* she'd said on their second call, treating Saoirse's desire to rent 88 Benefit Street sight unseen as an opportunity to wax poetic. *And the front door is white as bone and just as sturdy, reminiscent of the early 1800s during which it was built.*

Saoirse had mumbled something like approval but had already decided to sign the lease. She didn't care about Federal Period architecture or the house's "storied history," whatever that meant. Still, Diane had insisted on finishing with the declaration that the property sat at the top of Church Street, overlooking Saint John's Cathedral and the adjoining cemetery. *On foggy nights,* she said, sounding more like the tour guide of a haunted house than the owner of numerous high-end properties, *the tops of the headstones cut through the fog like rows of teeth.*

At the time, Saoirse had been curled miserably into a worn wingback chair, hands wrapped around a mug of tea long-cold, and Diane's description of the nineteenth-century graveyard had done little more than unnerve her. But standing in the rose garden behind the house, peering down at elaborate stone arches and hydrangeas—melancholy blue in the haze of the streetlights—the marble crosses covering the expanse of grass like forgotten pendants at the bottom of a jewelry box, Saoirse can't help but admit that the view is thrilling, like the unexpected chords of a violin slicing up from an orchestra pit where before there'd been only silence. She shivers, adjusts her grip on an armload of sheets and blankets, and returns to the house.

She hadn't taken enough with her from Cedar Grove to warrant a moving truck—and 88 Benefit Street was fully furnished—but Saoirse's car is full of her most important possessions. Yellowed photo albums. Treasured novels. A tea set inherited from her grandmother. Piles of clothes, including a sweatshirt of her mother's that smells perpetually of jasmine and cardamom, and a Brown University T-shirt so soft, it could double as a baby's blanket. A framed copy of her and Jonathan's wedding invitation. A conch shell from their honeymoon. A photo, refrigerator-worn, of the two of them hiking Rocky Mountain National Park. Everything one might expect a grieving widow to have.

Entering the house with the load of bedding, Saoirse surveys the narrow foyer, clogged with piles from previous trips. Her heart thuds in her chest from the constant lifting, and a voice in her head sounds the alarm: *Be careful. Don't overdo it.* When she's caught her breath, she ventures farther inside to find a place in which to lay her haul.

Beyond the foyer is a living room enlarged by several Zuber panels depicting lush, jungly landscapes. Heavy hunter-green velvet drapes hang from black metal rods, the fabric an exact match to the green velvet settee along the left-hand wall. A candle chandelier casts a shadow over an ornately carved wooden table. The pink roses in the vase at the table's center are silk but look freshly picked. There are candelabras on the mantel above a tiger bust–adorned marble fireplace. The Zuber panel over the hearth shows a distant mountainscape, the glow of a sunset over an inviting, frothy-green sea.

Saoirse sets everything down on a chair by the fireplace, oscillating between exploring the rest of the house and embarking upon the last trip to the Mazda, when the sound of voices comes again. Muffled but layered, as if several people are speaking in unison. Rising in volume. A little frenzied. This time, it's unmistakable that they're coming from inside the house.

Aidan, she thinks, and freezes. But it can't be. Only her mother knows she's moved here. It must be the landlord. Though, Diane hadn't said anything about meeting her here in person. Saoirse received the keys two weeks ago by mail and had texted Diane to confirm receipt. It's someone else who's inside the house.

She creeps forward, but her foot catches on a fold of the afghan that had spilled over the seat of the chair. She stumbles, steadies herself on the coffee table, catches the vase of pink roses before it can topple. The voices pause, and Saoirse crosses the room into a hallway. She can go right, to the house's main staircase; straight, to the kitchen; or left to a short set of steps leading to the walkout basement. The voices start again. There's a rhythm to the garble, but the sound comes from above and below her all at once. Swallowing her unease, Saoirse starts for the staircase.

On the second floor—no, third; she decides the walkout basement constitutes a floor—she turns left, stopping outside a closed room. There is silence again, minus the pounding of her heart in her ears. She steels herself as she throws open the door, but the floral-papered bedroom, while dark, is empty.

Saoirse opens the other doors on the third floor—two bedrooms, two bathrooms, and an office as paradoxically sleek and cozy as every other room in the house—before climbing the next set of stairs. There is a kitchenette on the fourth floor, two more bedrooms, and a bathroom, all empty. The house is large, but she'd wanted large. Something tangible to get lost in, as opposed to wandering through her own sinuous thoughts. Diane had said 88 Benefit Street had been converted into a five-unit residence in the eighties before she'd bought it and done a complete renovation. No, that wasn't the word she'd used . . . a *restoration*, not renovation. But restored to what?

Saoirse doesn't have time to consider. The voices are back. This time they seem to be engaged in a chant. And they're coming from below her. She races down the two sets of stairs, her hand slick on the walnut wood banister—then descends farther, into the walkout basement. Even as she spins to examine the spacious, rectangular room, Saoirse is asking herself how the sound could be coming from here. But then . . .

the beeswax and bergamot she smelled upon entering the house grow
stronger.

Saoirse follows the scent toward a window on the western wall and
spins in another circle. She's about to chalk the whole thing up to new-
house jitters when she sees the corner of the braided area rug is turned
up. The voices, now a droning hum, float up from beneath it. Dropping
to her knees, she pulls the rug back farther and finds herself looking at a
groove in the floorboards. Antique strap hinges. A metal chain running
through a small square opening. It's a trapdoor.

A trapdoor that could only lead to a basement.

Do houses with walkout basements have *actual* basements? Saoirse
doesn't really feel like finding out. She considers running back to her car.
She considers calling 911. She considers collapsing in a heap and letting
dread consume her. But what Saoirse does is the same thing she did nine
months earlier, on a frigid evening in early January when she found her
husband's body. She grabs the metal chain, pulls open the trapdoor, and
starts toward what she fears.

The stairs are unfinished. The floor below her is mere dirt, patterned
with light coming from someplace beyond Saoirse's field of vision. The
honeyed scent of candles and incense is overwhelming. The voices are
no longer muffled:

> "Oft since thine earthly eyes have closed on mine,
> Our souls, dim-wandering in the hall of dreams,
> Hold mystic converse on the life divine,
> By the still music of immortal streams."

Saoirse is at the bottom of the stairs. She takes two hesitant steps
toward the light, toward the voices. Then two more. The chanting starts
again, the words both ominous and old-fashioned, the speakers male
and female, their voices lilting together.

The room is L-shaped, and she can see the edge of a table beyond
the jutting wall, a dark-clothed elbow angled out from a high-backed

chair. Saoirse grips the wall and leans forward. Sees the table is circular, draped in black crepe. Sees the innumerable candles on its surface, the Ouija board at its center, the amethyst chunks and tourmaline spears, the crushed flower petals, the oracle cards fanned like feathers. Sees the cauldron spitting smoke, obscuring the features of a woman whose head is bowed, shoulder-length brown hair parted like a knife slash down the middle.

The chanters are not teenagers bent on wreaking a little havoc; the man in the high-backed chair is silver-haired, though seemingly prematurely. They are her age. Thirty. Maybe thirty-five. And they are immersed in their séance. None of their accoutrements are cheap Halloween props; the Ouija board looks to have been hand-painted around the time Emily Dickinson learned the alphabet. Saoirse thinks she sees the board rise several millimeters and struggles not to cry out. *The candlelight. Just a trick of the candlelight.*

Saoirse takes a breath and holds it until the tremors in her hands and fluttering in her stomach lessen. Before she can lose her nerve, she demands, "What the hell are you doing in my house?"

A woman—not the one before the cauldron—gasps. The man whips around. All three of them stare at Saoirse as if she is the interloper, not them.

"*Your* house?" the man says. He looks to the woman on his right, eyebrows raised. The woman in turn levels her gaze at Saoirse, her black hair and black-framed glasses accentuating the paleness of her face. Candlelight dances over the black-ink tattoos snaking up both her arms.

"This isn't your house," the tattooed woman says calmly.

"It is," Saoirse says. "I signed the lease last month."

"No."

Saoirse is hit with a wave of unreality not unlike that which accosted her in the moments after finding Jonathan. "Yes" is the only word she can force her dry mouth to say.

The pale-faced, black-haired woman leans forward and takes something off the table. To Saoirse's surprise, the woman stands and, as calmly as she'd addressed her, approaches Saoirse. She reaches down, takes Saoirse's hand, and places the object in it.

Saoirse recoils. Then, seeing it's just a photograph, or rather, a daguerreotype, stares at the image within the oxidized gold frame. A white-garbed woman, spiral curls framed by a sheer ruched bonnet, stares back.

"This isn't your house," the woman repeats. Her voice is not unkind, but it is also not uncryptic.

"Then whose is it?" Saoirse asks. She's annoyed that her anger is tempered by the strangers' refusal to act as if they're doing something wrong.

The answer comes from the brown-haired woman behind the cauldron, words thick, as if the smoke has hardened her vocal cords into something akin to the wide pillar candles at her elbows: "It's Sarah Helen Whitman's, the poet, essayist, transcendentalist, and spiritualist." The corners of the woman's mouth turn down slightly. "And I suppose I'd be remiss not to include 'onetime romantic interest of Edgar Allan Poe.'" She forces Saoirse to meet her gaze. "We're bringing her back from the dead."

Chapter 2

Saoirse narrows her eyes at the strange brown-haired woman, a frisson of fear creeping up her back like a clutter of spiders. Just as quickly, she shakes the fear away and holds the photograph out to the first woman. "Cut the crap," she says, in what Jonathan used to call her take-no-prisoners voice. "You have five seconds to tell me what the hell is going on, or I'm calling the police."

The man pushes back from the head of the table and approaches her as if the séance worked and Saoirse is, in fact, a ghost. "Did you really sign the lease to this place?"

"Yes," Saoirse says in exasperation. She looks from one baffled expression to the next. "What am I not understanding here?"

The man reaches out and takes the photograph Saoirse is still extending. He peers down at it, then back at Saoirse. "No one's lived here for the last five years."

"So?"

"So, this is the former house of the poet Sarah Helen Whitman, like Mia said. We—Lucretia, Mia, and I—have a little arrangement with Diane's ex."

"Diane Hartnett?" Saoirse asks. Her head is spinning. She wishes she'd gone for that espresso when she had the chance, doctor's orders be damned. But at the mention of her landlord's name, something passes between the three trespassers, an uneasy acknowledgment that she might actually be 88 Benefit Street's new tenant, like she says.

"Yes, Diane Hartnett," the man says. "She's owned this property—along with two dozen others—for years, but has only been divorced from Larry the last five. Larry's the one who managed Benefit Street when they were together."

"And what?" Saoirse asks. "Diane never thought to get the key from him over the last half decade?"

The three exchange another round of looks. "Like I said," the man explains, his voice apologetic, "he took care of the place. If you know 88 Benefit, *really* know it, there are other ways to get in besides the front door."

Saoirse throws her arms out angrily. She should have finished unloading her car by now, taken a shower, and be climbing into bed. Instead, she's standing here with a bunch of nutjobs, listening to how her new house is not bound by the regular rules of leases and locked doors. Before she can say anything, however, the pale-faced, black-haired woman—Lucretia, the man called her—reaches out and takes her by the hand.

"What's your name?" Lucretia asks.

"Saoirse," she surprises herself by replying.

"Ser-shah," she repeats, drawing out the syllables. "Pretty. Listen, Saoirse, we're not a bad lot, I promise. And we can explain everything, why we're here. You've just arrived, I imagine. Where from? Do you need help unloading your car?"

Saoirse lets out a huff at Lucretia's presumptuousness, at the idea that Saoirse would want them to do anything other than get the hell out. But Lucretia continues before she can retort. "Roberto can help get the rest of your stuff inside. Mia will make you a cup of tea. After that, we'll tell you anything you want to know."

"And then we'll leave you in peace," the man adds quickly.

Something inside Saoirse lets go. She is beyond exhausted. Haunted. Hurting. Drained of every ounce of motivation. Though it's insane, she is less dismayed by the idea of having tea with a trio of occultist interlopers than by the prospect of climbing the stairs and claiming one of the empty bedrooms, of trying to fall asleep while, all across the city, museums and parks and libraries thrum with the echoes of Jonathan's memory. And by the prospect that Aidan Vesper might still discover the details of her new address going forward.

Saoirse sighs. If either Roberto or Mia had looked even slightly put off by Lucretia's suggestion, Saoirse would have returned to her original plan of kicking them out. But nothing about the strangers standing timidly on the dirt floor of her basement suggests they mean her harm, or that they won't leave at the culmination of the impromptu tea party.

"Sure, okay," Saoirse says, forcing more annoyance into the words than she feels. "But blow those damn candles out. I'm not going to be blamed for the house burning down the first night I'm in it."

The smile that suffuses Lucretia's face is wide and guileless. Likely, she's just relieved to have convinced Saoirse not to call the cops. Lucretia bounds toward the black-draped table, closes her eyes, and bows her head. Her lips move in some sort of closing prayer, an official end to the séance. A moment later, she blows out the candles. Mia unearths a black drawstring bag from under the table and slips the Ouija board inside it. The trio packs up everything with speed and precision.

"I'll come back down for the candles after tea," Roberto says to Saoirse. "By then, the wax will have dried."

"Whatever," Saoirse says, and starts for the stairs.

They climb to the first floor in silence and go to the kitchen, where Mia retrieves tea and honey from a cupboard with a quickness born of familiarity. Roberto rubs his hands together. "Okay then," he says. "Show me where you parked."

Ten minutes later, Roberto, Mia, and Lucretia are seated once again around a circular table. This time, Saoirse sits with them, a cup of steaming rooibos (she declined Earl Grey, wanting to get the bergamot smell of the séance out of her nostrils) before her. "All right," she says, using the take-no-prisoners tone again. "Start explaining."

Lucretia lifts her mug and blows on the steaming liquid, then sets it back on the table and shrugs. "We're artists," she says. "And spiritualists.

We love Providence because of its history of producing freethinkers, and Sarah Helen Whitman was one of the best. We've been coming here once a week for the last five years to, well . . ."

"To bring her back from the dead?" Saoirse finishes for her, one eyebrow raised.

Lucretia's pale face flushes. "Mia may have been a tad dramatic, putting it like that. To commune with her spirit, is probably a better way to phrase it."

"While leaning hard into performative ritual," Roberto says.

He grins rather wickedly, and Saoirse is forced to recalibrate her earlier impression of him. Maybe he isn't as stodgy as she thought. Still, he was making a joke of breaking into Saoirse's new home and turning her basement into a parlor act. She scrunches her nose. "Performative ritual? Seriously?"

"I know, I know, it sounds ridiculous." Roberto runs one hand through his salt-and-pepper hair. Saoirse thinks her earlier guess at his age was too high; despite the hair, he looks closer to thirty than thirty-five.

"On one hand," Roberto continues, "it's become something to do with friends. Every Friday night, more or less, we get together for the séance, and we each play our little roles. Sometimes we go to dinner afterward, or to one of our houses to watch a movie." He pauses, gauging the others' reactions to his assessment. When they nod—Mia, once, Lucretia, an enthusiastic bobbing that sends her black hair bouncing—he continues, "But on the other, it's a manifestation of our beliefs and our hopes for the future."

"How so?" Saoirse asks.

"We're transcendentalists," Mia says, "meaning we believe what Sarah Helen Whitman believed. And Ralph Waldo Emerson. And Henry David Thoreau. And Margaret Fuller and Ellen Sturgis Hooper and Elizabeth Peabody. That the 'divine' is here on earth among humans and nature, and that society and its institutions have corrupted the purity not only of the individual but of all of humanity. We also believe the only way to solve the climate crisis is for the world to embrace transcendentalism and give themselves back to nature."

"Though, the stuff about the climate is noticeably missing from the writings of nineteenth-century transcendentalists," Roberto adds. "We had to update the philosophy to fit the times."

Saoirse resists the urge to rub her temples and takes a sip of tea instead. "Let me see if I've got this straight," she says. "You three attempt to commune with the dead girlfriend of Edgar Allan Poe . . . to save the world from global warming?"

"Well, sheesh, when you put it like that," Lucretia says, twirling a lock of hair and looking embarrassed.

Mia scowls. "Like Roberto said, there's no single reason for performing the ritual. For example, he didn't mention that the three of us are writers and use the time during the séance to meditate as much as commune. Ways out of sticky plot points, formulating new ideas, et cetera."

"Exactly," Lucretia chimes in. Her dark eyes flash behind the lenses of her glasses. She seems the youngest of the three. Not naive, exactly, but radiating a childlike sense of wonder and fascination. Saoirse has no trouble buying Lucretia's interest in the otherworldly. "Sarah Whitman is sort of our muse," Lucretia finishes.

Saoirse scoffs, but a smile tugs at one corner of her mouth. "You're *writers*," she says, as if this puts everything that's come before it in perspective. "What do you write?"

"Mia's a poet," Lucretia says. "She's amazing. I write a little poetry, too, but nowhere near as good as Mia. I dabble in science fiction and fantasy, but my true love is horror." She smirks at Roberto. "Roberto calls what he writes *literary* horror, but that's because he's a snob."

"No, Lucretia," Roberto says, "*Publishers Weekly* calls what I write literary horror. In that starred review I got for my debut novel, remember?"

Lucretia snorts. "Where's the second novel? That'll help us figure out your genre. Oh, wait, that's right. You haven't finished it yet. Better start focusing your appeals to Sarah on increasing your daily word count."

Roberto leans over and gives Lucretia's arm a little flick. It's the gesture of an older brother; the affection the two have for each other is obvious. Saoirse can tell Roberto and Lucretia are close with Mia, too, but Mia commands respect, not affection. She wonders how they know one another, but her tea has gone cold, and she feels the stirring of a headache behind one eye. Still, there's something else she wants to say to them before calling it a night, something she hasn't said to herself in almost four years, and out loud in even longer.

"I'm a writer too." Saoirse feels their eyes on her and squirms. "Cozy mysteries. Suspense. I used to write a little poetry, too, but not since college. I had an agent, but she dropped me after . . . Well, let's just say it's been a long time since I've written anything good enough to be seen by an agent. It's been a long time since I've written anything at all."

"Shut *up*," Lucretia squeals. She wraps her tattooed arms around her torso and hugs herself, practically vibrating with excitement. Roberto smiles, but Mia's expression remains unchanged, unreadable. She drains her tea and looks hard at Saoirse.

"Of course you are," Mia says. Roberto and Lucretia turn to Mia.

"I'm sorry?"

"No one's been here for five years," Mia continues. "Prior to that, everyone who moved in left before the lease was up."

"Because it's haunted by the ghost of Sarah Whitman?" Saoirse really needs to go to bed now. Her thoughts feel like crows startled by thunder, exploding out of a skeletal tree in eight different directions.

"Maybe," Mia says, her expression still deadly serious. "You're the one who's going to be living here, so I suppose you'll find out. But at the very least, it's because Sarah doesn't want anyone but another writer living in her house." Mia's eyes lock on Saoirse's. "You know, you look like her too. Sarah Helen Whitman. Same sharp profile, thoughtful eyes, wavy brown hair."

"Same waifish Victorian figure and pale skin," Roberto adds jovially, and Mia gives him a look.

Just as Saoirse is about to make another sarcastic comment, the intensity of Mia's gaze softens. "I'm not trying to weird you out. All I'm saying is, even if your coming here means the end of our séances, it's nice to have a writer in Sarah's home."

Saoirse opens her mouth, but nothing comes out. She can feel Lucretia and Roberto studying her, the unasked question hanging over the room. "I guess . . . ," Saoirse begins, then stops. She doesn't trust herself not to make a hasty decision, doesn't want to commit to inviting these three strangers back next Friday. "I guess," she repeats, "it might be nice to get together again, maybe."

"Ooh, for a writing group?" Lucretia asks.

Roberto cheers and pumps a fist into the air.

"Maybe just tea," Saoirse says quickly. She stands and walks her mug over to the sink. "But for now, you've got to leave. I need to sleep for about twelve solid hours."

"Of course." Mia stands, and Lucretia and Roberto follow suit. Saoirse leads them to the foyer.

"I'll give you my number," Saoirse says. "That way you can call before you come over, rather than sneaking into my basement." She pauses. "How *did* you get in?"

"The white paneling on the outside of the house," Roberto says. "Right where the sidewalk starts to incline. Three of the panels are connected and swing outward—if you know where to hold them—into another, albeit hidden, entrance to the walkout basement." He smiles sheepishly. "If we're going to be back, can I leave the candles downstairs?"

"Fine," Saoirse says, shaking her head at his matter-of-fact admission and ushering them toward the door.

"But we can't take your number," Lucretia says.

"Why not?"

"We commune with the earth, remember?"

"Huh?"

"We're one with nature."

Saoirse gives her a blank stare.

"We don't carry cell phones," Lucretia says finally.

Saoirse looks from one face to the next. "None of you have phones? How do you get in touch with each other?"

"Well, we *have phones*," Lucretia says, placing emphasis on the final two words like a disgruntled teenager. "We're transcendentalists, not monsters. We just don't carry them around. Mia has a house phone, and Roberto uses an old-school flip one. I have an iPhone, but I put a bunch of content blockers on it so I can't waste time scrolling on social media." She shrugs and smiles. "You'll have to take *our* numbers if you want us to come back."

Saoirse sighs and hands Lucretia her cell phone. Lucretia enters her number and passes it to Roberto, who enters his and passes it to Mia. Mia holds Saoirse's gaze for a beat before keying in her own number. She thumbs the side button to darken the screen, but when she holds the phone out to Saoirse, the home screen reappears. Mia stares at the photo of Saoirse with Jonathan, the snowcapped mountains behind them, the healthy flush to their cheeks and giddy smiles.

Saoirse waits for Mia to ask who the man is, why he isn't here with her now, unpacking his things along with her in this house on Benefit Street. But Mia says nothing, thumbs the screen off again, and holds the phone out for Saoirse to take.

"I hope we hear from you," Mia says.

Saoirse opens the door onto the crisp October night. "Uh-huh" is all she can manage. It's not even midnight but feels as if it's three in the morning.

Lucretia squeezes Saoirse's arm as she walks past. Roberto pulls his sweatshirt hood up when he gets onto the street. "Good night," he and Lucretia say in unison.

"Night," Saoirse says. When the door clicks shut, the silence comes to life, rolling toward her from every corner of the house like water unleashed from a dam.

The silence unnerves her far more than the chanting voices of strangers in her basement.

Chapter 3

When Saoirse wakes the next morning, she is half-convinced the events of the previous night were a dream. But when she descends to the kitchen and sees the four unwashed teacups in the sink, smells the lingering traces of bergamot and honey, she knows it was real. "What a bunch of weirdos," she whispers. Dead poets. Transcendentalism. Nature as God, and God as healer of climate. But then she thinks of the way Lucretia and Roberto made her laugh, and how Mia's softspoken demeanor calmed her inner turmoil. Would it be all that bad to spend time with people from the city? And writers, no less, around her age?

She pushes the question from her mind, relieved that—with their numbers in her phone and not vice versa—the decision to see them again is up to her. She washes the teacups, places them in the drainer beside the sink, and inspects the cupboards. Aside from a few boxes of tea, the honey, and a dented box of shortbread cookies, the shelves are empty. She'll need to find the nearest grocery store if she wants any breakfast.

She grabs her phone and sees there's a Trader Joe's a mile away. She dresses, fishes her keys from her purse, and is out the door in under ten minutes. The morning is bright, but she senses a note of autumn, like a taste of earth, of fallen leaves, on the back of her tongue. Maybe she'll pass a farmers market on her way and buy a pumpkin for the front stoop.

She's halfway to the grocery store, enjoying the sunshine and the historical homes, the beech trees awash with brilliant swirls of color, when she's struck with something like déjà vu. The Athenæum is up ahead. She knows it, though it's been fifteen years since she last lived in Providence. Fifteen years since she would leave the halls at Brown where her undergraduate classes were held to visit Jonathan at his job in the two-hundred-year-old library. She doesn't want to see it. Doesn't want to recall the quiet evenings they spent there, the whispered conversations over lattes she'd fetch from a nearby café. But her feet keep moving— past the corner market, past the Shunned House of H. P. Lovecraft's famous horror story, past one of the steepest streets in the city—following an agenda at odds with her earlier desire for breakfast, toward the rusticated stone-and-pillared Greek Revival building she already sees in her mind. Toward the ornate granite fountain below the Athenæum's main entrance. Toward enshrined memories and book-bound secrets. Toward the past.

Saoirse climbs the steps between twin cast-iron lanterns, ignoring the hypnotic thud of her footsteps. Why has everything lately been reminding her of the night she found Jonathan? She passes through the entrance and stares up at the skylighted ceiling, marble busts peering at her like curious owls. It's only after she spins in two complete circles, marveling at the stacks of books eighteen shelves high, and a voice comes from her left—"May I help you?"—that she remembers she'd been able to visit Jonathan here *after* he'd secured her a membership.

"I . . . ," she begins, already knowing she will hand over whatever amount this librarian states is the cost, despite there being no allowance for pricey library memberships in her budget. She simply knows that, now here, she has to stay. Has to inhale whatever lingering essence of Jonathan remains. Because even after fifteen years, his essence *does* remain. And in a weird way, that essence helps her understand that he is gone.

Ten minutes later, newly laminated card warming her thigh through the pocket of her jeans, Saoirse wanders through the upstairs stacks, lost in a memory that gives way to another and another and another, memories like dreams that collapse in on themselves and make her dizzy with nostalgia and want and regret. She'd forgotten—until this moment—that she and Jonathan were here when he asked her to "go steady," a phrase so old-fashioned she'd almost laughed until she saw how terrified he was of her answer. He'd been so unsure of his own charm, possessed of the nonsensical belief that, because everyone at Brown was intelligent, he was unable to claim intelligence as a defining trait, at least for the duration of his time at the university. And he'd been *back* at Brown then, for a master's degree in history, having gotten his BA five years earlier. Saoirse found his lack of vanity—lack of confidence, really—strangely attractive. Until twelve years later, of course, when it was anything but. When it manifested as a need for control. For the last word. For power.

Saoirse rounds a corner. There are three shallow steps ahead, leading to a closed door with "The Art Room" carved across a piece of wood mounted above it. She doesn't see the "By Request Only" caveat taped beneath the wooden sign until she's pushed the door halfway open. She hesitates, but a glance behind her tells her no one's watching. Not entirely sure why, she slips inside and closes the door.

The muted teal of the room's walls contrasts sharply with the white bookshelves. Light fills the space from a large skylight, glinting off the cherrywood conference table beneath it and the books and papers spread haphazardly over its surface. There's a lattice window along one side, overlooking the main section of the Athenæum below. Across from the window, the subjects of seven gold-framed portraits stare unsmilingly down at her. Edgar Allan Poe sulks from within two of the frames, but Saoirse recognizes none of the others. A taxidermy raven tilts its head, beak open, beneath a glass bell jar on an ebony mother-of-pearl-inlaid table. There's a joint thermostat-and-moisture-monitoring device mounted to the wall, set to seventy degrees and 50 percent humidity.

It's vaguely familiar, this space, but less so than the rest of the library. Saoirse guesses she's been in the Art Room before but only briefly. Perhaps she stuck her head inside once or twice to alert Jonathan to her presence, back in another life. She is about to turn, her empty stomach reminding her of why she left the house in the first place, when she notices the books and papers on the conference table again, how their placement is not as random as she first thought. The tomes are open to places marked with lengths of ribbon. Various velvet-cushioned, glass-front boxes hold ancient-looking letters. Additional photocopied letters are cataloged in binders or piles, the piles delineated with little knickknacks: a ceramic raven, a brass bust, a miniature daguerreotype.

The artifacts are meant for an exhibit. An exhibit someone's been working on until just recently. And their work is not quite done.

Saoirse should leave before they return. But then she spots the photograph, a black-and-white version of one of the seven portraits on the wall. It's the same woman who was in the daguerreotype Lucretia handed to her the night before.

The poet, Sarah Helen Whitman.

She leans over, studying the image—the curly hair, the long-sashed bonnet—then transfers her gaze to the stack of letters beside it. The signature on the top page is cut off, but on the next page, a second correspondence begins:

> I have pressed your letter again and again to my lips, sweetest Helen—bathing it in tears of joy, or of a "divine despair."

The letter is signed: "Edgar." A spidery feeling that's at odds with the warmth of the room travels up her back. She's been in Providence less than twenty-four hours and been confronted twice with the tortured, enigmatic writer she hasn't otherwise thought of since high school English.

"What the hell?" she whispers, placing the photocopies on the table. She is reaching for a small navy book, the spine of which reads *The Last Letters of Edgar Allan Poe to Sarah Helen Whitman*, when the door to the Art Room swings open. A middle-aged woman with short blonde hair steps inside and looks up. She's holding a small to-go cup, and when she sees Saoirse, how close Saoirse is standing to the letters on the table, her mouth parts in a little O, and her eyes go almost comically wide.

"What are you doing?"

"I was . . . ," Saoirse starts. "I'm . . . I found this room and didn't realize . . . is it off-limits?"

"The sign," the woman says and gestures over her shoulder. "I'm working on something and have this space reserved the entire week." Her words are clipped, high-pitched. The woman isn't angry; she is panicked, as if, though everything is as she left it and Saoirse has backed away from the table, she half expects Saoirse to start smashing glass-front boxes and shredding priceless letters with gleeful abandon.

"I'm sorry," Saoirse says. "I didn't realize. I just renewed my membership and was getting reacquainted with everything." Saoirse isn't sure why she ignored the instruction on the door and why she's lying now, but she does know she was drawn to the Art Room by the same force that brought her down Benefit Street to the Athenæum.

The fact of Saoirse's membership registers with the woman; that it was a renewal seems to soften her further. "It's not a problem," she says. "I'm sure you can appreciate the historical significance of our exhibits and understand that we must exercise caution while preparing them." A bit of her earlier anxiety returns, and she leans over the table, surveying its contents. "You didn't handle any of the artifacts, did you?"

"No, no, of course not. Again, I'm so sorry. Let me get out of your hair."

Saoirse goes the long way around the table to avoid having to brush past the woman. Before she can get to the door, the woman says, "I'm Leila Rondin. Welcome back to the Athenæum, Ms. . . . ?"

"White. Saoirse White."

"Ms. White. If you're interested in Edgar Allan Poe and Sarah Whitman, the exhibit goes up at the end of the month."

"I'm—" She almost says, *I'm living in Sarah Whitman's house*, but decides against it. One veritable team of ghost hunters obsessed with 88 Benefit Street is enough; no need to add another Poe–Whitman enthusiast to the mix. "I am interested," she says instead. "I'll definitely come back to view the exhibit."

Leila smiles. "That's great."

"In the meantime," Saoirse says, and points to the small navy book, "is there another copy of this in the library? I was hoping to read some of their letters."

Leila perks up. "Of course. Right this way. I'll show you where all the books having to do with Poe are shelved."

Saoirse follows Leila, but at the door, the librarian gestures for Saoirse to exit first. She takes a ring of keys from her pocket and locks the Art Room, then returns the keys and spins on the top step, her features arranged in a way that's meant to suggest the act was nothing more than routine. *That's the last time Leila Rondin runs for a coffee without securing an exhibit prep,* Saoirse thinks.

They wind through several stacks, sunlight streaming in from the alcove windows, and cross the dizzyingly narrow aisle separating the right wing of the Athenæum from the left. Leila stops abruptly and runs a finger along the books on the third shelf of the stack before them.

"Here we are." Leila points to spine after spine displaying titles with all manner of references to Poe and his work. *The Haunted Palace: A Life of Edgar Allan Poe. Edgar Allan Poe: The Man, Volumes I and II. The Tell-Tale Heart: The Life and Works of Edgar Allan Poe. Midnight Dreary: The Mysterious Death of Edgar Allan Poe.* Then, finally, another edition of the book of letters between Edgar and Sarah.

Saoirse slides the book from the shelf, flips through it, then closes it and tucks it under her arm. "Perfect," she says. Catching sight of another title—*Poe's Helen Remembers*—she points to it. "Who's Helen?"

"The same Sarah Helen Whitman whose letters you hold in your hand," Leila says. "She first published poetry using the name 'Helen,' a fact that was convenient for Poe when he reworked an older poem,

'To Helen'—intended to evoke images of Helen of Troy—for Mrs. Whitman during their courtship."

Saoirse adds the book to the one she already holds. She might as well learn as much as she can about the two figures everyone around here seems to be so obsessed with. "Thank you for your help."

She expects Leila to bid her farewell and stride back toward the Art Room, but the woman leans in and whispers, "Do you want to see something amazing?"

It hits Saoirse suddenly that she's past the point of mere hunger. There's a headache starting behind her right eye and, after spending the morning in this place where so many memories were formed, grief has settled over her shoulders like a shroud. She wants to be alone, to walk home, climb the stairs to her new bedroom, and disappear under the blankets for the rest of the day. Instead, she forces a smile and says, "Sure."

Leila darts past several stacks and cuts right. Saoirse hurries to keep up. Three more strides and they're ensconced in one of the alcoves that run along the library's outer walls. Leila makes a sweeping gesture at the space, and Saoirse stares at the multipaned windows, the bust on the sill, the straight-backed chair pushed neatly against the empty desk. "What exactly am I looking at?" she asks a moment later.

"On December 23, 1848," Leila says, "two days before their planned Christmas Day wedding, Poe and Whitman were sitting in an Athenæum alcove when an unnamed messenger handed her a note telling her that Poe had been drinking the night before and that morning. Whitman called off the wedding and rushed to her house, where she drenched her handkerchief in ether—she did this often, on account of her medical condition—threw herself on the sofa, and attempted to lose herself in unconsciousness. Despite Poe's attempts to rouse her, she merely murmured 'I love you' before fainting away.

"The two would never see each other again," Leila continues, "and Poe was dead within a year. Whitman would live for close to another three decades, spending much of her time here at the Athenæum. Did you know the house she inhabited is on this very street, half a mile up the road? And while no one can be certain it was *this* alcove they were in when Sarah learned Edgar had broken his promise of sobriety, I like to think it was. The morning light is best in this one, and the adjacent shelves used to hold a slew of works by writers Poe admired: Coleridge, De Quincey, Byron, Shelley, Keats."

Saoirse looks around again, trying to imagine the figures from the Art Room photographs sitting in this very space, flipping through a book of poems by Lord Byron and whispering conspiratorially. "The light *is* good here," she admits. "Thank you for showing me. You're right, it is amazing." *Amazing, and, in conjunction with the last twelve hours, overwhelming.*

Leila nods fervently. "It's my pleasure."

Saoirse takes a step toward the mouth of the alcove. "I look forward to seeing the Poe exhibit once it goes up. For now, though, I think I'm going to head home." She refrains from sprinting out of the suddenly claustrophobic space. The more time she spends here, the more she feels as if she's in a haunted house. "Apologies again for being in the Art Room earlier."

"It's all right. Oh, and make sure you take an October brochure on your way out. It includes descriptions of all the events going on at the Ath this month."

"I will," Saoirse says. The books feel slick and heavy and—as if a heartbeat pulses from within them—*alive* under her arm. "Well, good-bye." She turns and walks away from Leila, sneakers thudding on the shiny oak floorboards.

Just like a librarian to go on and on about a subject they're interested in, Saoirse thinks. Jonathan, though technically more historian than librarian—at least, before he'd received his JD from Princeton University and become assistant university counsel there—was renowned for it. He could rattle off facts about textile production or the history of Gothic Revival architecture until dinner party guests' eyes grew glassy. At the thought of it, Saoirse swallows a groan, aware that Leila may still be nearby.

A fly buzzes by her head, and Saoirse stops, goose bumps rising on her forearms. *What's the matter?* a voice from inside her head asks mockingly, and Saoirse's heart rate increases. *Unsure if the little buzzy bugger is real or in your head?* It's the first time she's heard the voice since leaving New Jersey, but she hadn't held out any real hope that the move would silence it for good.

She waits, refraining from slapping at the air, but the buzzing doesn't return, and she grows annoyed for succumbing, once again, to paranoia. As she nears the stairs, however, annoyance is replaced by the distinct sensation of being watched. Instantly, she recalls Aidan slinking out from beneath the weeping willows in the cemetery but just as quickly forces the image from her mind. She keeps her head down, but the sensation persists. When she looks across the library, a bust of Poe stares back.

I don't care what I told Leila Rondin. I'm not coming back for that exhibit. She's two stacks away from the stairs, and still, the skin along her neck and upper back tingles. Saoirse glances over her shoulder, almost dropping her books in the process. This time, a different pair of eyes meets hers.

Jonathan! So his ghost resides *here*—not in their home in New Jersey—among the stacks and tomes, where history is held in alcoves and secrets lorded over by silent portraits. Saoirse swallows, resisting the urge to cry out, but as she gapes at the man, adrenaline shooting through her veins, she sees it is not her husband. She's projected his likeness onto someone who—with his dark hair and dark eyes, a face made slightly asymmetrical by the tilt of his eyebrows and the way he holds his mouth—possesses similar characteristics. Someone who, like Jonathan, though she never noticed, never had cause to notice, looks uncannily like a modern-day version of Edgar Allan Poe.

The man stares at Saoirse across the open air of the second floor of the Athenæum. His gaze is penetrating, stark, and unabashed. It leaves

Saoirse feeling exposed and vulnerable and completely unsettled. It's not just his appearance but his intensity. He's looking at her as if he wants to gaze upon her forever, to speak to her every day for the rest of their lives, to possess her. As if he *already* possesses her.

She holds the beguiling—and terror-inducing—gaze another moment, then jerks her head back in the direction of the staircase. She rounds the rail and starts down the steps as fast as she can move her feet. On the last step before the bottom, she looks up again. The man is moving away, toward the Art Room. As Saoirse hurries toward circulation, she sees the man disappear into the stacks.

Unlike her husband—but very much like Poe—the man's expression never shifted or softened. Saoirse did not see the smallest hint of a smile flash across his face.

Chapter 4

Three days after her impromptu trip to the Athenæum, Saoirse sits on the third-floor balcony overlooking the rose garden, eating an orange. She finally has groceries in the house, though she didn't get them that first morning she went out. She was too tired, and felt too haunted after her experience at the library, and spent the rest of the day in bed. The afternoon is unseasonably warm—in the high seventies—and she wishes she brought a glass of something cold out with the fruit. It's not laziness that keeps her from going inside for a can of seltzer but the paralysis that comes with crushing boredom. And, if she's being honest, this pervasive inability to rouse herself comes from being depressed too.

She hasn't been *completely* useless the past few days. She managed to unpack and to transfer the utilities into her name. She also wandered out to the graveyard to explore the two-hundred-year-old tombstones, drawn by the feeling that the cemetery existed on some other plane, that the cracked granite and other signs of age were illusions meant to deceive the casual passerby. She was disappointed to find that the lichen crumbled corporeally between her fingers, that the hanging boughs did not disguise a shimmery barrier between this world and the past.

Saoirse sighs. She *should* call her mother, longs to speak with her beyond the *Made it here safe* text she sent upon arriving Friday evening, but then she'll feel like she needs to call her father as well, and she doesn't want to do that. There's a show on Netflix that's captured her interest, but it always makes her feel more depressed to binge something in the middle of the day. Her old therapist would suggest she do a meditation exercise, or maybe make a list of all the things she can control versus those she can't, but Saoirse's done trying to implement Dr. Fitzpatrick's handy-dandy tricks of the trade, and besides, she's no longer her patient anyway. She could read, but the novel she started—well, about a month ago now, if not longer—isn't really meeting her expectations.

Though . . . the disappointing novel isn't the only reading material she has. With the sensation that she's about thirty years older than she is, Saoirse pushes herself up from the wicker chaise and goes in search of the books on Poe and Whitman she borrowed.

In the living room, she pauses to marvel at the bold colors and large windows, the damask-patterned floor and lofty ceiling. She is struck—as she has been every day since moving in—by the way the space feels both contemporary and old-fashioned, by the poetic balance between order and chaos: a double-handled vase centered neatly on a desk in one corner faces a bookcase in another, its shelves scattered with shells, fossils, the compact skull of a small animal, a bird's nest, and several pressed, dried flowers. The leather-bound gold-leaf books appear well curated and well read, the quaint daguerreotypes suitably cloudy. Who knew "fully furnished" could equate to such inspired decor?

She finds the library books on the coffee table beside the silk roses and her cell phone, and sinks onto the settee. Opening *Poe's Helen Remembers*, she begins to read.

An hour later, she's scrolling an article on her phone detailing the couple's short but intense relationship. It seems Poe had first seen Sarah Whitman in the backyard of this very house in 1845, tending her rose garden under a midnight moon, while he'd been walking with the poet Frances Sargent Osgood. Three years later, on September 21, 1848, Poe met Sarah officially for the first time, again at 88 Benefit Street. The two shared the same birthday—January 19, though Sarah was six years Poe's senior—and a love of literary criticism, and began corresponding with one another, culminating in plans for what was to be an "immediate marriage" at the end of December. Poe wouldn't spend much time at

88 Benefit Street; Sarah's mother detested him. Here, the article picked up with what Leila Rondin had relayed at the Athenæum, and Sarah's reasons for breaking off the engagement.

Amending the wording of her original search, Saoirse brushes up on the life and work of Edgar Allan Poe. She'd forgotten, since high school, or maybe from the courses she took as an English major, of the writer's marriage to his thirteen-year-old cousin, Virginia, who died of tuberculosis, and of the degree to which he struggled with substance abuse. Though, claims of Poe's dependence on drugs were apparently unfounded, propagated by a high-profile obituary published by literary rival Rufus Wilmot Griswold. The reason *Poe's Helen Remembers* even existed was because biographer John Henry Ingram appealed to Sarah Whitman for help in writing a redemptive account of her once-love. She accepted and would spend the rest of her life working to repair Poe's reputation whenever the chance arose.

Saoirse can see why Roberto, Mia, and Lucretia are fascinated by the poet. Sarah Whitman was a woman of knife-edged intellect and fierce loyalty; she was genuinely kind, independent, and unconventional. Saoirse slides farther down on the settee, considering the walls around her with new interest. Sarah might have written those letters defending Poe from this very room. Satisfied—for now—with what she's learned of the couple, Saoirse closes the browser.

Before she can think about what she's doing, she's opened a text message draft. Is it Mia who has the smartphone? No, Mia uses a landline, and Roberto, a flip phone. Lucretia is the one who admitted to enabling a slew of content blockers on her iPhone to keep her from wasting time.

Saoirse starts to type, but a floorboard pops behind her, followed by a quiet rustle on the air. Saoirse whips around, squinting into the shadows. What had Mia said when Saoirse had asked if the house was haunted? That she would find out soon enough? She stares a moment longer into the darkened corridor beyond the living room, unsure if she'd prefer Aidan to step from the gloom or a chain-weary specter. Nothing further comes, but Saoirse still can't relax.

Jumpy, are we? the voice in her head asks, and she shakes herself, then types a quick message to Lucretia and sends it before she can change her mind. The reply comes instantly, so Lucretia—if her claim that she doesn't carry the phone around with her is truthful—must be home:

> OMG, hi, Saoirse! How are you?!? Do you want to get together? Maybe do a little writing/hang out/coffee date? I'm working on something for a submission call, a short story of about 5,000 words, and Roberto and Mia aren't around, but I LOVE writing WITH another person when I have something I'm putting together on a timeline . . . so, let me know!!! It'll be so fun!!!

Saoirse winces. The thought of Lucretia watching her try to formulate paragraphs, sentences, even string two words together when she hasn't written in almost four years, causes a pit to form at the bottom of her stomach.

Maybe this is what you need, the voice whispers, and Saoirse freezes, anger rising.

"Uh-uh," she says aloud. "No way. You don't get to comment on this, of all things, when it was you that caused me to stop writing in the first place."

Yeah, well, maybe committing to a writing date will get you to stop feeling sorry for yourself, the voice offers unhelpfully. Death has not stopped Jonathan from advising—or judging, or demeaning—her every decision, though now his words come from inside her head as opposed to across the breakfast table or behind the wheel of their car. But unlike when he was alive, Saoirse has the luxury of not dignifying those words with a response. Her thumb hovers over the blank text box. *Say yes,* she thinks. *Just type,* yes, that sounds great, *find a notebook, and be on your way.* She stands but is rooted to the living room carpet, stuck entertaining the same tired justifications and whiplash pull of the past.

In the three years before Jonathan's death, no force on earth could've gotten Saoirse to write; the root of her pain was too present, the need to protect herself all too real. But since his death, she's been tortured by her inability to put pen to paper. Every waking hour since the previous January, some deep, repressed part of her has screamed for her to write. But another, stronger part—the part that's stuffed down what happened—resists. Tells her that returning to writing will expose her to her own terrifying thoughts and to the raw ugliness of her grief in a way she won't survive. That it will break her.

She types her response to Lucretia:

> Getting together sounds nice . . . but could we save the writing
> for another day? Maybe just grab coffee?

She considers adding more, explaining her reluctance, then decides she doesn't owe Lucretia anything. She hits send. A few seconds later:

> That's totally fine! Okay, yes! Awesome! Do you know where
> Carr Haus Cafe is?

Saoirse googles it. Spidery tickles of unease graze the back of her neck. Carr Haus would have her walking in the direction of the Athenæum again. Still, there's no *good* reason to suggest they go somewhere different. Saoirse doesn't know any other coffee shops in the area, though it can't be far to the nearest Starbucks. Would a transcendentalist go to a Starbucks? She sighs, looks up Carr Haus on Google Images, and types:

> The Gothic-looking place right past the old library that's part of
> the RI School of Design?

Lucretia confirms, and they agree to meet in half an hour. Saoirse wanders the rooms on the main floor, planning on going out in what she's wearing. That is, until she catches sight of her reflection in the bathroom mirror. Her hair is wild and unwashed, and her clothes are rumpled. There are bags beneath her eyes, and her skin has the same pallor as some legless, eyeless creature scooped out from under a rock. She hikes up the too-big jeans and smooths her threadbare sweater, but her efforts are futile. Saoirse trudges upstairs.

There's no time for a shower, but she alleviates the worst of her problems with a belt and a hair elastic. She fishes a slightly less worn sweater from the closet and mines a nearly dry tube of mascara for enough of a coat to promote her appearance from half-dead to merely exhausted. Slipping her phone into her pocket, she returns downstairs and grabs her bag. She doesn't bother with locking the house.

The walk goes quickly, focused as she is on keeping the Ath from luring her toward it, sucking her into its serpentine rooms. She's keeping her mind sufficiently empty, considering nothing more than the rustle of leaves and the murmur of passing cars, when her phone vibrates in her pocket.

Maybe Lucretia's calling to cancel. But no, it's her mother's name that flashes across the screen. Saoirse answers the phone, feeling both the little twinge of warmth that always comes with thoughts of her mother and guilt for not calling her first.

"Hello," she says breezily, as if everything is fine, as if the past nine months—and maybe the entire marriage preceding them—never happened.

"Hi!" her mother responds, and the concern and love in that one word make Saoirse close her eyes and take a breath. "How are you settling in?"

"I'm . . . settling," Saoirse says.

"Is the neighborhood nice? Are there any issues with the property? Do you need anything? I can do an Amazon order."

Saoirse stares up at the bright-blue sky. "The neighborhood's great, and the house is fine. More than fine, really. You'd love it. Homey and beautiful at the same time."

"And you have everything you need? Towels? Toiletries? Groceries? Blankets?"

"My husband died, Mom. I didn't lose everything I owned in a fire." She wonders if her mother is surprised she's mentioned Jonathan, but the only response is a bit of static as Ann Norman expels a whoosh of air. Saoirse can picture her, perched at the island in her kitchen, lips pressed together while one hand rests on a cup of tea and the other fidgets with the pearl-and-sterling drop earrings Saoirse bought her the previous Christmas. Photos of Saoirse, her mother's only child, would be hanging on the wall behind her, glass frames glinting, each shot curated to suggest the nonexistence of any father figure, the same way the photos in Saoirse's father's house contained only him and his new wife, with no allusions to her mother or to her.

"Fair enough," her mother says. "When can I come and visit?"

"Give me a few weeks." Saoirse has stopped walking and stands at the corner of Benefit and Angell Streets. She is vaguely cognizant of the flashing walk sign on the opposite streetlight but doesn't move. "I need to get my bearings. I've . . ." She hesitates, then says, "I've met a few people already. I'm on my way to get coffee with someone as we speak." With her father, this sort of admission would invite endless inquiry and suspicion, but her mother responds as expected:

"That's great news! I'm so happy to hear it." A pause, and then she says, "You haven't called in a while, Sersh. You know how I worry."

Guilt causes her eyes to water, clouding her vision. "I'm sorry, Mom. I'm really sorry. You know why I do it. It's just—" Saoirse's fingers are cold around the phone case, and her mouth is dry, but she manages to continue. "Even though we agreed not to talk about things, it's hard just *knowing that you know.*"

"I understand," her mother says. "I just worry about you, all by yourself in the city. And I worry that you're wallowing, letting the past remain present. You're allowed to let things go, you know. Allowed to move on with your life."

The walk sign is flashing again, and Saoirse steps off the curb. "I'm not wallowing, Mom. I promise."

"And you're taking care of yourself? Not overdoing it? Taking your medications?"

Saoirse resists the urge to bring her hand to her heart, to feel the steadiness of the beats in her chest, like she occasionally did at night before she fell asleep. "Of course," she says. "But I've got to go. Coffee date, remember?"

"Right. Okay." Her mother still sounds reluctant to hang up.

"I love you."

"I love you too."

Saoirse ends the call. Her mouth is even drier than before, and it's hard to swallow. She slides the phone into her pocket and gives her bag a halfhearted pat, but she already knows she didn't throw in a water bottle before leaving the house. When she looks up, the fountain at the base of the Athenæum looms before her. Its epitaph is direct to the point of absurdity:

COME HITHER EVERY ONE THAT THIRSTETH

The water that runs from the bronze spigot and over the granite tier looks cool and inviting. Wasn't this fountain bone-dry whenever she visited Jonathan here twelve years earlier? Feeling out of sorts from the impending meetup with Lucretia and the emotions brought to the surface by the conversation with her mother, Saoirse leans in and drinks before she can consider whether it's a good idea.

The water is colder than she anticipated and far more luxuriant, like water from a mountain spring instead of a public city fountain. She drinks great, deep mouthfuls, starts to pull away, then lowers her head again and drinks some more. When she finally straightens, she feels more sated than she has all day. Satisfied and clearheaded. She takes two steps backward and wipes her mouth with the back of her hand. A couple is coming toward her on the sidewalk, and they stop when they reach her.

The man on the left raises his eyebrows. "Wow, Julio." He lets go of his partner's hand to gesture at the granite structure. "Someone's hitting the magical Richmond Fountain a little hard today, aren't they?"

His smile is warm and good-natured. Despite her confusion, Saoirse smiles back. She glances at the fountain as if she hasn't just drunk from it, as if it burst through the concrete like a beanstalk. She returns her attention to the two men. "Magical?"

"You haven't heard the legend?" the smiling man asks. "It's from, like, the 1900s, but it's become pretty well known since the fountain was restored several years back." His voice takes on the tone of someone relaying a spooky story around a campfire. "Anyone who drinks from this fountain will return to Providence again and again. They're drawn back, by virtue of the Pawtuxet River flowing through their veins."

"That's not it," the second man, Julio, exclaims, and Saoirse jumps. "Sorry," he says, "but it's not that you *return* to Providence. It's that, once you drink from the fountain, you can never *leave*."

A fly buzzes by Saoirse's left ear, and her arms break out in goose-flesh. She swats at the air and turns back to the couple, but they've linked hands and resumed their stroll down the sidewalk. "Have a good one," Julio calls over his shoulder.

Saoirse watches them cross the intersection and turn right onto College Street. They disappear into a throng of pedestrians. Other couples, students, professors pass her in either direction. She wants to shout at them, *Have you drunk from this fountain? Have you heard the legend? Is it real?*

Instead, she takes a breath and shakes the tension from her shoulders. A shadow darkens her periphery, and she swats at the air again, but the fly is gone. Maybe it had never been.

"Get a grip," she mutters, then lifts her chin, sets her gaze on the gingerbread-house-style lattice of the Carr Haus building one block away, and forces herself forward. Behind her, the water from the curved bronze spigot continues to flow.

Chapter 5

The hostess waves Saoirse in the direction of a table in the café's back corner where Lucretia sits, reading a book. Saoirse feels as if she's on display as she crosses the room toward the slight, dark-garbed woman, though none of the other patrons—an older couple at a booth by the register, a woman with a baby, a man at a high top by the window clicking away at a sleek silver laptop—give her more than a passing glance.

"Hi!" Lucretia squeals when Saoirse reaches her, and jumps up to give her a hug. Saoirse has no choice but to return the embrace, though the display puts her even more on edge.

"I'm so glad you texted," Lucretia says as Saoirse pulls the opposite chair out and sits.

Saoirse nods awkwardly. She has no idea what to say, but the other woman fills the silence.

"How's the house? I've been thinking about you constantly, wondering how you've been doing there, if you've been getting any vibes or seen anything unusual."

The creaking floorboard occurs to Saoirse, but before she can say anything, Lucretia continues, "Even more so, I've been wondering if you've been writing! That would be so incredibly cool, if you moved into 88 Benefit and were immediately struck with divine literary inspiration. I mean, Mia is convinced it's only a matter of time, and it wouldn't *surprise* me, per se, but I'd still probably freak out, just a little."

Saoirse feels the thin smile on her face curdle into something even more pinched, and Lucretia must sense she's gone too far because she winces. "I'm so sorry. You haven't written in forever, you *said* that. I need to respect your process. Also, gosh, I am just the *worst*. A toddler is better at making friends than I am. I should be asking you where you're from, why you came to Providence, what you plan to do here."

Before Saoirse can tell Lucretia that she likes this line of questioning even less, a waitress appears. Lucretia orders a cappuccino and a blueberry scone.

"A large chai with oat milk and a glass of water, please," Saoirse says.

The waitress leaves them alone again, and Saoirse tries to steer the conversation away from herself. "Where are Roberto and Mia today?"

"Work. Roberto gives tours at the John Brown House. It's part of the Rhode Island Historical Society. And Mia . . ." Lucretia sighs in a way that suggests what she's about to say is the cause of long-standing exasperation. "Mia works for PETA. She's probably toiling away at some ridiculous, Sisyphean task, like trying to contact every Thai restaurant in the country to request they remove all factory-farmed meat from their menus."

"PETA, huh? Though, I guess I can see that. Mia seems . . ." Saoirse pauses. "A little intense."

Lucretia waves a hand. "Nah. Well, I mean, yes, she totally is. But it's just her personality. That and, well, I don't want to share Mia's personal stuff, but she was in a bad situation before. With an ex. She's a little wary of meeting new people now. Likes to keep to herself." She laughs. "Which is why Roberto and I push ourselves on her constantly. She needs us."

The waitress reappears with their drinks and Lucretia's scone, which Lucretia breaks into tiny pieces.

Saoirse blows on the steaming liquid. "What about you?" she asks. "What do you do for work?"

Lucretia groans. "Financial planning company. I hate it. It's the antithesis to everything I believe in." She shrugs and grimaces. "But, bills, you know? I'm constantly asking Sarah for guidance in finding a position that honors transcendentalism while allowing me to, oh, I don't know, maybe eat and pay rent in the same month."

Saoirse nods. On one hand, Lucretia's words sound New Agey and absurd, but on the other, she gets it. She worked for a pharmaceutical company before Jonathan's death, and while Saoirse has never been a member of an animal rights organization, she still squirms when she thinks of the activists who staged protests on her company's campus, how she always aligned more with their views than with her employer's.

"What about you?" Lucretia asks, and Saoirse's stomach gives a little lurch. This is part of it, of course, getting to know someone. She has to share *some* details of her life; she may as well lean into the innocuous ones.

"I'm not working at the moment." She summarizes her past with the pharmaceutical company as having worked "in supply chain management," and Lucretia doesn't ask any follow-up questions. "I went to school here in Providence," Saoirse continues. "At Brown. So, you can imagine how pleased my father is with my status as an unemployed Ivy League graduate."

Lucretia sips her cappuccino, eyes wide over the rim of the cup. "Is he, like, really mad? What about your mom? Is she upset too?" Worry furrows her thick black eyebrows. "Shit, is your mom around? Sorry, I should have asked that first."

"My mom lives in Connecticut," Saoirse says. "My parents are divorced. I have a bit of a strained relationship with my dad." She pauses. "But my mom and I are extremely close. She's not upset that I'm not working right now." Saoirse wraps her hands around her still-steaming cup. "Not at all." Without meaning to, Saoirse's voice has gone quiet. "She gets it. She understands. She's the best."

"That's definitely good," Lucretia says.

"Once I'm settled, I'll start looking for a job. Not sure where, or doing what, but I'm in a position where—" She stops. If she's going to spend time with Lucretia—and Roberto and Mia, for that matter—she's going to have to tell them, and while it will be miserable no matter what, putting it off will only make it harder. She exhales, takes a sip of tea. Her hands are shaking, but the tremors are so slight as to be unnoticeable, and this small detail gives her the courage to push forward. That she has at least this much control over her body is refreshing.

"My husband died," she says. "In January. From a heart attack. Well, a heart attack brought on by complications stemming from a dependence on several prescription drugs. Adderall. Ambien. A couple of others. He was forty, and he wasn't as much an addict as he was a workaholic and perfectionist." *Not to mention a control freak,* she thinks but doesn't say. "His job—assistant university counsel at Princeton—was stressful. Because of his position, his life insurance payout was decent. Between that and my savings, I have enough to live on for at least the next year."

She thinks she's in store for more *oh-my-goshes* and sorority-girl squealing, but Lucretia surprises her. "I'm so sorry," she says evenly. "That's terrible. I'm so sorry you're going through this. No wonder you stopped writing."

She's touched by Lucretia's use of the present in that Saoirse is very much still "going through this" but also struck with an almost uncontrollable desire to laugh. *No wonder I stopped writing? You have no idea.*

"Thanks," Saoirse says instead. "It's been tough, but I'm managing. And sorry if it seems weird to tell you about Jonathan's death with regard to my financial situation, but most of the time, I can only process that he's gone through the filter of things like finances and other logistics. If I think of anything beyond that, I—" Saoirse pauses, swallowing the lump in her throat, resisting the urge to blot the tears welling in her eyes with the sleeve of her sweater. She glances away, focusing on the man at the high top by the window, though, now that she's looking at him, she thinks he's a different man from the one who was here when she arrived. "It's just too overwhelming," she finishes.

"Be it life or death, we crave only reality," Lucretia says, and at Saoirse's puzzled expression, she continues, "Henry David Thoreau,

Walden, 1854. I may be obsessed with Sarah Whitman, but Thoreau was my gateway drug into transcendentalism. So many people think he's just the 'walking in the woods' guy, but his musings on death and dying are poignant to the point of otherworldly." Lucretia looks down into her lap. "My dad died two years ago, and rereading everything Thoreau ever wrote was basically the only way I got through it."

"I'm sorry, Lucretia. I'm glad you found something that helped you during such a tough time."

"Thanks." Lucretia tosses her glossy hair over one shoulder and pushes up the sleeves of her black sweater, revealing the snaking black-ink designs beneath it. "Listen to us," she says. "Talk about a morbid first coffee date. Tell me something good going on in your life, Saoirse, please, I beg of you."

Good? Pathetic half thoughts fire uselessly. Should she tell Lucretia about the prescription bottles lining the shelves in her cabinets? Or that, lately, she worries she'll find Jonathan around every corner, despite his voice in her head never quieting long enough for her to forget he's dead? Should she tell her that Jonathan's best friend may be looking for her to talk about the text Jonathan sent before he died? Or that flies whiz around her constantly, and she's not sure if they're real or a product of her overtaxed—yet frustratingly sluggish—mind?

"I'm thinking about getting a cat?" she says, and it comes out as a question. Which, of course it does, because she's not even sure where the idea came from. She doesn't think pets are allowed at 88 Benefit per her lease, but it's something safe and carefree to say. Lucretia squeals and wiggles in her chair like a kid who's just been told it's time to head out for trick-or-treating.

"That is *so* exciting! Sarah's ghost will *love* that. *Oooh*, you should get a black one—they're the hardest for shelters to place, and Mia would be absolutely thrilled—and name her Catterina, after Poe's cat! Can I go with you to pick her out? My cat, Cocoa, is with my mom in Arizona. She's a Maine coon. I miss her so much." Lucretia scowls. "I can't have animals per my stupid lease."

Saoirse should double back on her impulsiveness and agree with this last, rational statement, but the excitement lighting up Lucretia's eyes is bizarrely contagious. Besides, if Diane Hartnett can't be bothered to retrieve the keys to her property over the past five years, Saoirse can bend the rules enough to adopt a cat. Sharing the house with another living creature might offset the stillness of the rooms, the museum-like quality of the foyer, the way that, sometimes, she gets the feeling that Sarah Whitman is watching from the daguerreotype on the bookshelf, taking stock of Saoirse's every move.

"Sure," she says, and the decision—both to go forward with the idea and to invite Lucretia to embark upon it with her—is justified further by the flush of happiness she feels at her response. "I'd love the company."

Their conversation passes into an easy rhythm, with Lucretia promising to find out which shelter Mia recommends and Saoirse making plans to peruse the website for available cats and fill out an application before that weekend. When they stand, donning jackets and slinging purses over their shoulders, it's—somehow—five o'clock. The shadows on the street outside the windows are long, and the waitresses are tidying up. Besides Saoirse and Lucretia, the only patron inside the café is the man working at his computer by the window.

Saoirse's steps feel a little lighter as they move toward the door, free from that sense of dread she so often experiences. Her coffee date with Lucretia has broken things up to the point where she feels equipped to deal with the impending nightfall.

They thank the staff and step outside. Lucretia wraps her in another hug. "I'll call you tomorrow. And just so you know," Lucretia says, "there's no way you're adopting the future Catterina without Roberto. He's going to insist on coming to the shelter."

Saoirse rolls her eyes. "The three of you were my uninvited welcome committee, why shouldn't you be present for the adoption of my new pet?" Lucretia's dark eyes skitter over Saoirse's face, trying to gauge if some of her initial frustration with the trio has returned, but Saoirse laughs and pushes Lucretia's arm gently to show that she's kidding. Lucretia laughs, too, then, raising her hand in a final goodbye, heads up Benefit Street.

Saoirse pulls her sweater up around her neck—it grew cold while they were inside—and turns in the opposite direction. But before she can start forward, she senses movement, a flash of darkness in her periphery. Someone's watching her from the coffee-shop window; she feels it as distinctly as she feels the wind on her cheeks.

For a moment, she hesitates, figuring she's about to come face-to-face with a waitress wiping down tables along the café's perimeter. But the feeling is too intense to ignore, and her head turns as if on a swivel. As Saoirse's wide, frozen eyes meet the dark, asymmetrical ones of the Poe look-alike from the Athenæum, numbness overtakes her muscles like frost.

The man holds her gaze in the same way he did at the library. It's not threatening but intense, demanding she straighten up and pay attention. *He was here the whole time,* Saoirse thinks. *The watcher from the Athenæum, a mere fifteen feet from Lucretia's and my table.*

Or had he been? There *was* a man working at a laptop by the window, but had it been the same man the entire time? Saoirse isn't certain. This man sits behind a Lenovo laptop, the same brand of PC Saoirse uses at home. She could have sworn the man who'd been at the high top when she entered was using a MacBook Air. She also has a vague recollection of the man at the window wearing a thin sweater, or maybe a button-up shirt, consisting of several bright colors. The man before her is dressed in black.

Did the man from the Athenæum follow her, or is his presence here a coincidence? Could Aidan have somehow found her and sent someone to keep an eye on her? Either way, Saoirse doesn't want to stand here any longer, pondering it.

I'm sure Poe has something to say about the nature of coincidences in at least one of his lurid Gothic tales, Jonathan says from her head. Saoirse shushes him with a hiss and turns away.

Before she can turn completely, however, the man raises one dark eyebrow and nods his head. It's more than a gesture of acknowledgment: *We're just two people accidentally locking eyes through a coffee-shop window.* It's a declaration. A promise. That this won't be the last time. That they will meet again. And if the slant of that eyebrow—along with the small smirk that animates one side of his mouth—means anything, she suspects it will be soon.

Saoirse turns away from the window and starts down the sidewalk, using all her self-control not to break into a run.

Chapter 6

On Friday morning, the phone on the kitchen wall rings before Saoirse has finished making breakfast. Frowning, she wipes her hands on a dish towel.

"Hello?" Her tone is wary.

"Saoirse!" The female voice garbles the pronunciation of her name. "It's Diane Hartnett. Just wanted to check in and see how things were going. Is the house up to your expectations? Do you need anything? Have you had any problems?"

Saoirse's eyes flick to the hallway leading to the walkout basement and her mind to what lies beneath it. *If you know 88 Benefit,* Roberto had said, *really know it, there are other ways to get in besides the front door.*

What would the landlord's reaction be if she knew about the occultist writers obsessed with the house? This is her chance. If she doesn't tell Diane everything now, whatever happens going forward will be on Saoirse. Despite her coffee date with Lucretia, she still doesn't know much about the trio. If she continues letting them in—both metaphorically and physically—she may come to regret it. And what about the floorboards that creak mysteriously, and the unsettling feeling she's always just missed someone the moment she walks into a room? Should she mention that?

The seconds in which Diane's questions hang in the air stretch and bloat. Saoirse imagines she hears the ticking of a clock. "Everything's fine," she says finally and feels anticipation pop like a bubble. "The house is beautiful. Atmosphere rivaled only by location."

Diane expels a sigh of relief. Could the landlord know more about her ex-husband's "deal" with Mia and the others than Saoirse first thought? But then Diane's going on about how she's had more than her fair share of renters from outside the city who are unhappy with the more "antiquated" aspects of several of her properties, and Saoirse decides Diane is simply relieved that she won't be losing the first inhabitant of 88 Benefit in years after only a week. They chat for another minute about the annual boiler cleaning and the temperate weather. When Saoirse hangs up, she has a feeling that she won't be hearing from Diane again anytime soon.

She finishes her breakfast and washes it down with two large pills and a glass of cranberry juice. A glance at her phone informs her that it's only nine thirty. What do people do all day when they're not working, when they've gone through something like she has? How do they spend their days? How to reconcile with a clock that goes backward and in circles as much as forward? It's been nine months, and she still hasn't figured this out.

The basement beckons with the promise of time filled, luring her toward the trapdoor in the southwest corner. Saoirse still hasn't examined the paneling Roberto claimed would swing outward when you knew what to look for, granting access to the walkout. She walks to the wall and places her hands flat against it. Pressing out and down, she tries to pop the passage open, but the panels don't budge. She pushes harder, changes the position of her hands, and pushes again. Still nothing.

"Guess I'm going to have to ask the Whitman squad how to break into my own house," she mutters. She spies her new broom against the wall, grabs it, lifts the trapdoor, and descends into the gloom.

Saoirse hasn't been in the basement since the previous Friday, when she led Roberto, Mia, and Lucretia up the stairs with a demand that they explain their presence in her house. She'd forgotten about the dirt floor; her broom—the duster, any of the cleaning products she bought during last night's time-waster trip to the Charles Street Home Depot, really—won't be of any use here, though she does give each step a good sweep on the way down. Propping the broom up, she trudges across the dim space, around the corner, and toward the site of the séance. Pillar candles stretch up from the table like strange, dark anemones on the floor of a tar-black sea.

Saoirse trails a finger over a depression of wax, picks off a bit of wick. She breathes deeply, but the smell of honey and bergamot has disappeared along with the people who'd wielded matches and tiny vials of essential oils, the absence of their noise and light and vibrancy creating a void that reverberates in their very own residual haunting. She wonders if they'd be pleased with her perception, three individuals mesmerized by the possibility of lingering spirits, of messages from the dead, that their own absence carries such a palpable weight.

Saoirse turns from the black-draped table and hurries for the stairs. Before starting up them, she hears a noise behind her, something like a muffled, guttural growl. Saoirse freezes, then risks a look back across the basement, but there's nothing there. *An old boiler,* she tells herself, ignoring the fact that she sees nothing that might conceal a large steel drum.

She takes the stairs two at a time and doesn't bother lowering the trapdoor behind her. She finds her phone in the living room, tossed onto the coffee table. In the shadow of the Zuber panel landscapes, she opens the text message app, sends a response to a text from her mother asking if she'd heard from "any of Jonathan's friends," code for whether Aidan Vesper managed to contact her since leaving New Jersey (*All quiet on that front . . . and I miss you too*), then opens a new thread and adds two recipients.

> I've made up my mind. No need to change the Friday ritual. I'll see you at nine for the séance.

The responses rush into her phone like waves. Saoirse reads the *oh-my-gosh-YES* followed by dozens of emojis from Lucretia and the single *See you soon* from Roberto. She navigates to her call app, searches her contacts, presses send. Mia answers on the third ring.

"It's Saoirse. I texted the others. Come tonight. For the séance." She hears Mia's sharp intake of breath, then the clink of glass, as if Mia is setting down a cup of tea.

"Thank you," Mia says. "That's fantastic. See you then." The line goes dead.

A part of Saoirse is embarrassed by her boldness. She knows she's reached out to the trio from a place of depression, boredom, and loneliness. Another, larger part of her doesn't care. Regardless of the circumstances, the idea of people, friends, coming to take her mind off the past—even as they summon it—excites her. She smiles.

Now all that's left to do is wait.

Chapter 7

Roberto, Lucretia, and Mia arrive in a flurry of decidedly unspooky fervor, no mention of specters or tarot cards from any one of them. Lucretia *is* wearing all black, but by now, Saoirse is inclined to believe this is her usual attire. Mia is in a taupe-colored cashmere sweater, her brown hair parted down the middle and pulled into a low, Dickinsonian bun. She carries the large black drawstring bag she'd had with her a week prior. Roberto's navy long-sleeve T-shirt and jeans establish him as the least horror-writer-looking member of the group.

"I brought dessert," Lucretia says and thrusts a platter of large chocolate-frosted cupcakes at Saoirse. "They're vegan. And gluten-free."

"Oh. Okay." Saoirse looks around, unsure what to do with them. "Do you usually . . . I mean, do you want to eat them now? Or are we going right downstairs? How does this work?"

Roberto laughs. "Relax. There's no schedule. But I just had dinner. I couldn't possibly eat one of Lucretia's experimental cupcakes now."

"They're not experimental! I followed the recipes."

Roberto sighs. "Combining recipes from two different cookbooks does not mean they'll come out twice as good, Lu."

"I'm sure they're delicious," Saoirse says before the two of them can continue with their banter.

"Will you try one?" Lucretia asks.

Saoirse hesitates, but there's such childlike excitement on Lucretia's face, she doesn't have the heart to say no. She unwraps the foil liner, breaks the bottom portion off, presses it into the frosting to avoid making a mess, and takes a bite. It's good. A little bitter, but she imagines any baked good without dairy products might be.

"What's the verdict?" Roberto asks.

"They're great." Saoirse fixes Lucretia with an appreciative smile. "Thanks again for bringing them." She pushes the last large bite into her mouth. "I'll put the rest in the kitchen. Does anyone want something to drink?"

Mia shakes her head, and Roberto holds up a glass bottle of Coca-Cola.

"I'll have whatever you're having," Lucretia says. Saoirse goes into the kitchen and returns with two cans of seltzer. Lucretia opens hers, guzzles half the can, and burps quietly.

"Gross," Roberto says, and Lucretia sticks out her tongue.

"Now what?" Saoirse asks, at the same time Mia says, "Let's head downstairs." As Saoirse leads them through the walkout to the basement door, more emotions—excitement, pleasure, nervousness, a sense of camaraderie—compete for space in her body than have done so in close to a year. It's exhilarating. And frightening. Saoirse's pulse quickens, and she makes a conscious effort not to blurt out the rapid-fire thoughts in her head.

At the bottom, Mia hands Lucretia the drawstring bag. Roberto turns and looks back at the stairs. "Is it . . . cleaner down here?" His features scrunch.

Saoirse blushes. "I was bored."

Roberto raises both eyebrows. "Girl, we've *got* to get you back into writing." Then, with none of his previous sarcasm, he adds, "Seriously. I think it would be good for you."

As they cross the basement and approach the table, Saoirse's anxiety increases. "I added a fourth chair," she says, her words clipped, a little manic. Why does she feel so weird? Is she this out of practice in being around other humans? A fly slices through her periphery, and she resists the urge to swat it. "I hope that's okay. Maybe you'd prefer me to stand to the side or something? Or add the chair after the three of you start? I'm not sure how you want this to go."

"This is perfect," Mia says. "Whichever way you did it is exactly how it's supposed to be."

Roberto and Lucretia take the seats that correspond most closely to the positions they were in the previous Friday. Mia eyes Saoirse, then nods at the table. Her intent is clear: Saoirse's decision will dictate where both women sit. A little panicked, Saoirse watches as Lucretia opens the drawstring bag and places the Ouija board at the table's center.

When the planchette, too, is in place, Lucretia removes an hourglass, two small gold candelabras, two handfuls of chime candles, a brass teapot, a stack of old books, a crystal ball, the daguerreotype of Sarah Whitman, and a gorgeously ornate, old-fashioned telephone. Roberto moves to situate each item, then lights the candles. In front of one open chair is the teapot, far more sinister-looking than any teapot has a right to be; the other open chair is closest to the antique phone. Lucretia removes the final items: a jar of ink and a black quill pen, a crystal chalice, and a pendulum mantel clock. How everything fit into that single black bag is a mystery Saoirse cannot begin to solve.

Saoirse takes a step toward the teapot, then changes her mind and sits in the chair by the phone. She is unnerved by the table's contents, having prepared for the séance by envisioning last week's spread of amethyst chunks, the cast-iron cauldron, and crushed flower petals. But there's no time to worry about the purpose of these new items, for Mia has taken her seat and closed her eyes.

"Whitman House," Mia says, and Lucretia and Roberto join hands. Lucretia reaches for Saoirse on the other side, and Saoirse takes her cold, many-ringed fingers in hers. She glances at Mia, but both of Mia's hands remain flat on the black-crepe tablecloth.

"Whitman House," Mia says again. Without opening her eyes, Mia reaches for the hourglass and flips it. Red sand flows through the narrow neck from one bulb to the other like a flood of tiny carapaced beetles. "We sit within you and reach back through time to your one true inhabitant."

The second hand on the pendulum clock shudders forward. Each individual candle's small, flickering flame stretches toward the ceiling while also seeming to borrow strength from the flame beside it, and from the reflections of the flames in the silvery daguerreotype, the prisms of the chalice, the stormy, milky glow of the crystal ball. The effect is that the room appears both darker and brighter, the dirt floor and the walls behind them dropping away, while their faces, the candelabra, the whorls and coils of the latent, expectant telephone receiver seem lit by an internal—and indefatigable—source. Mia continues:

"Vainly my heart had with thy sorceries striven:
It had no refuge from thy love,—no Heaven
But in thy fatal presence;—from afar
It owned thy power and trembled like a star . . ."

Before Saoirse can fully process the inherent eeriness of the words, Roberto takes up the poem, and then, Lucretia.

When they've finished, Mia opens her eyes. Saoirse drops her gaze to the crystal ball on the table. Was the globe like one of those garden torches, designed to leach power from a secondary light source? How else to explain the growing illumination, the ethereal, infernal, exponential glow emanating from it? Despite the surrounding darkness, Saoirse sees flies in her periphery. She closes her eyes hard. When she opens them, her head aches, but the flies are gone. Without warning, Mia clutches her hand on one side and Roberto's on the other, locking them in a circle. Saoirse feels the air around them grow warmer, as if the crystal ball is emanating not only light but heat.

"We bring you a fourth, dear Sarah," Mia says, "strengthening our commitment to you. We want only to share our love for you and your work, to change our destinies by honoring yours." The words are currents of water that flow through Saoirse's mind, smoothing the banks of her thoughts, filming everything with a layer of silt, refusing to be stopped by the normal dams of rationality and expectation and reality.

"Saoirse White has taken up residence in your home," Mia continues. "Like us, she seeks to uncover the truth through words, through a lens that many never pursue, preferring to experience the world in black and white, in everyday moments without reflection. But also, like each of the seekers at this table has experienced at one time or another, she is stuck. She needs her ability to *see* restored. A cosmic rainstorm to wash her lens free from the grime of the past."

At Mia's disconcertingly accurate analysis, a blip of the old Saoirse breaks through: *This is the placebo effect, right? I'm experiencing odd thoughts and psychic phenomena because of the power of suggestion?* But *is* this the voice of reason or that of her depression, that inner monologue, which habitually sucked every last bit of fun and magic and forgiveness from her psyche over the last twelve years? Before Saoirse can decide, the voice is eclipsed by the sudden ringing of the telephone on the table. The antique, obsolete, *disconnected* telephone.

It rings once, then stops, though the discordant chime echoes in Saoirse's head, increasing in volume and chaos like a microphone picking up interference. In response to the single, haunting ring—*And had the others even heard it? For if they had, they hadn't reacted*—the air grows warmer still, and coalesces, so that the warmth becomes a physical presence, a floating witness to the impossible. As if to drive home Saoirse's intense uneasiness, a splintering sound comes from the side of the table closest to Mia.

The glass at the top left corner of the daguerreotype of Sarah Helen Whitman has cracked.

Chapter 8

Saoirse stares at the phone like it's a snake and the ring an ominous rattle from the bushes, an urgent and unambiguous warning. She's seized by the fierce desire to lift the phone's heavy-looking body, certain there will be a battery compartment underneath. But before she can, Mia follows her gaze and lays one hand on the receiver. Saoirse forces herself to focus on the faces around the table, forces the dizziness to recede. Mia's hand remains on the receiver, but she doesn't lift it.

"The Divine Poet," Mia says, then looks at Lucretia, Roberto, and Saoirse in turn, "asks us to heed her call. Over the next few minutes, pay close attention to whatever thoughts, ideas, or visions present themselves, visions that will carry us *forward* toward something we need or *away* from something we need to abandon. Sarah's done a great deal of the work for us, reaching through time and space, beyond the great divide of the living and the dead, to present us with this opportunity. It is time to do our part. To answer the call by letting go of our doubts and preconceived notions of what we might receive from this ritual. Prepare yourselves to be open to whatever Sarah shows you."

Mia stops, then turns to Saoirse. "It's a bit like meditating," she whispers. "Just clear your mind and wait until something pops into it. And it will. You just need to have patience. Do not judge yourself—or Sarah—with regard to what is delivered to your waiting mind, and be open to going in whatever direction the idea or vision takes you."

Saoirse nods. She tries to persuade herself that, with this simple act of instruction from Mia, the otherworldliness of the past few minutes has dissipated, but she cannot do it. Not completely. The warm, floating aura still lingers, as if the four of them are sealed within a gentle, temperate, *patient* cyclone, the inward-spiraling mass of air separating them from the rest of the world as completely as if a wall of stone has been erected around them.

She's distracted from her thoughts by a swirl of steam curling from the spout of the teapot. Saoirse tracks its progress toward the ceiling with disbelieving eyes and remembers last Friday, when she thought she saw the Ouija board lift off the table. It is impossible to convince herself that this, too, is a trick of the candlelight—though, how could a teapot produce steam without stove or flame to heat it up?—but everyone else appears unfazed.

Roberto leans under the table, and Saoirse hears the rustle of the drawstring bag. He comes up with a stack of four tiny teacups, teacups that might be at home in a fairy garden, set atop a birch tree stump. "Good thing I brought these," he whispers to Saoirse. "You never know through which tools Sarah's guidance will flow." Saoirse stares back at him mutely.

He pours an inch's worth of liquid into each cup and distributes them around the table. "What is it?" Saoirse asks, but Lucretia furrows her eyebrows at her and shakes her head. Saoirse stares into the cup. The liquid is tea-colored and steaming but produces no smell.

Mia raises her cup to the center of the table, one hand still on the telephone receiver. The others follow her lead, with Saoirse hurrying to meet them in the impromptu toast. None of them go so far as to touch the others' cups; they lift them toward the ceiling, close their eyes, then bring the cups to their lips and down the contents. Saoirse is a beat behind them but manages to swallow the liquid a fraction of a second after Mia lifts the receiver.

"Hello," Mia says. It's not a question but a statement. Of readiness. Of acceptance. Of carefully restrained excitement. Mia knows who will be on the other end of the line.

Saoirse returns her gaze to the table, but at the conclusion of that single word, her head is thrown back as if she's been struck in the shoulders. The bitter, burnt-tasting concoction coats her throat and tongue, and she feels the hand holding the teacup slide from the table, the porcelain handle slipping from the hook of her finger as unceremoniously as if she has released a handful of sand.

Saoirse's eyes, wide and unblinking, take in the darkness above her, the shifting shadows, as if the aura she perceived earlier is visible now, oscillating like smoke, like a murmuration, like a hungry tidal wave, lacey strands of seaweed and hard-shelled marine life appearing like cryptids in the cresting surf, disappearing as the massive shelf of water crashes. Then, the shifting, breathing, *living* aura vanishes or, rather, changes yet again, morphing, rearranging, solidifying, though that's not quite right. There's nothing solid in what Saoirse sees, nothing scientific about the electrical signals traveling through her optic nerve from retina to brain. This new image is a cloudy film reel superimposed onto the ceiling not by her mind, but by some projector on another plane of reality. It's a ghost haunting a ghost haunting a ghost.

The aura grows, lengthens, becomes an ethereal specter: Jonathan. His eyes are somehow empty pits *and* hawkishly discerning, piercing through to the marrow of her soul in a single glance. Before she can react to this terrifying vision of her dead husband, it collapses in on itself. Again, the tidal wave rises, this time containing not seaweed and skates and the limbs of a thousand spider crabs but the features of Jonathan's face. Eyes, nose, mouth, hair, ears, jawbone—each is thrown haphazardly as the wave crashes against the shore, but as the next wave rises, the features rearrange themselves. Saoirse stares in horror at Edgar Allan Poe.

At the top of the wave, the dark bags under the writer's eyes grow so concave that Saoirse feels she'll be sucked up into them. The aura undulates, stretching the writer's mouth grotesquely. He appears to be shouting at her from beyond the grave, but then the mouth disappears, a black hole that's swallowed itself. The wave falls, and Poe's features fall with it, scrambled like so many seashells, the bones of seabirds, the rotten carcasses of porpoises. Saoirse wants to scream. She wants to run, but she's pinned to the chair by whatever unseen force pins these ghostly men to the ceiling. By moving to Providence, Saoirse knows she's now a resident of the Ocean State, but the sea, the cosmic, endless feel of it, terrifies her.

A new wave rises. The features within it rearrange themselves, and the man from the Athenæum now stares down at Saoirse from the black depths—or heights?—of the ocean, from the beyond, from some hell Saoirse cannot conceptualize. Struck with fresh terror by the man's concentrated stare, Saoirse prays for this specter to pass quickly, as the others did. But the wave does not crash. This time, the revolving visions cease as if the wave really is a mere projection and someone has hit the pause button. It strikes Saoirse as somehow worse for everything to be held in suspension, for this stranger—who somehow recalls both Poe and her husband while occupying an entirely other body, an entirely other space—to be as paralyzed as she is. Summoning all her strength, all her motivation, Saoirse forces her mouth to expel a single word: "What?"

What do you want? *What* is happening? *What* am I doing here? *What* are you? The lone "what" can stand for any one of her desperate questions. She no longer feels the aura is benign, if it ever was. She'd initially believed it to be the spirit of Sarah but knows she was wrong. It is angry. Aggressive. *Possessive.* Before she can attempt to form a second word—or force out a scream—the man from the Athenæum changes. As fast as a cartoon figure in a flip-book, the image stutters, a vessel possessed and in need of an exorcism.

The man becomes Jonathan again. And then Poe. Then the man from Athenæum. Jonathan. Poe. Athenæum. Jonathan. Poe. Over and over, faster and faster, until the three faces, the three bodies, become one obscene, flickering vision of madness. The mouth opens, but the image continues to stutter, resulting in a display of horrible, unnatural movement, as if the mouth is controlled by insects that squirm and writhe in a mindless attempt to replicate speech. Saoirse's mind threatens to collapse under the weight of her terror. The flickering of the three specters becomes so fast, the mouth no longer convulses imperceptibly. It responds to her "What?" with a word of its own:

"Miiiiiiinnnnnnne."

Fear as sharp as the stab of a knife explodes in her stomach at the threat in this single word, the implications of it, what it means coming from each of the three flickering figures: the dead husband who won't stay dead; the ghost of a historical figure whose haunting has become personal; the stranger who stares at her as if he is anything but. What happens next, however, is so sudden, the word leaves her brain as quickly as it entered it. The flickering body drops from the crest of the aura-wave straight down toward her.

The figure's mouth is still open, as if it will swallow her whole. The arms are outstretched, as if to engulf her. Though the distance should be no more than four feet, it seems to take a lifetime for the falling specter to reach her. It's enough time for her vision to flash red, then blue, then red again, and Saoirse recalls the parade of police officers, telling them how she returned to their home in Cedar Grove, New Jersey, to find the house preternaturally quiet, how she'd listened at the door of each room in her quest to find her husband. Her dread had grown with each passing second, and her shoes thudded hollowly against the floorboards. The single fly that buzzed past her, a portent of the dozens more, the horror to come.

The flickering figure falls over her like a shroud. She's released from her paralysis just in time. She ducks, screaming.

The world goes gray.

Then black.

Then everything is quiet.

Chapter 9

Saoirse awakens, disoriented, though it takes only a moment to identify the hunter-green velvet of the living room settee. Someone has lit the three tall candles in the chandelier as well as the ones on the mantel. The shadows cast by the flames ripple along the walls, and Saoirse shudders, recalling the jumping, shifting aura in the basement. Nausea roils in her stomach as she remembers what the aura became. The rise and fall of the waves. The writhing mouths. The word that both extinguished all noise and sounded only in her mind.

Already, however, the memory is fading. The acuteness of the terror she felt is blunted, seems almost secondhand, as if someone else experienced it. As if it were nothing more than a nightmare.

"Saoirse," Lucretia says, worry clouding her eyes behind the black-framed glasses. She had been perched on the edge of the coffee table but now she stands, hovering over Saoirse like a fretful mother. "Are you okay?"

"Don't bombard her with questions." Mia's voice comes from deep within the living room. Saoirse struggles to sit up. "At least, not with meaningless ones." Mia steps forward, out of the shadows, until she is at the other end of the settee. Lucretia moves toward the fireplace where Roberto leans, looking uncomfortable. "The question we should be asking her"—Mia's voice is thick, as if she's an actor about to deliver a monologue that will reveal an important Shakespearean truth—"is not 'Are you okay?' but 'What did you see?'"

Irritation with Mia's perpetually nonchalant attitude reunites Saoirse with her strength. She's about to lay into her when she remembers the conclusion she reached while talking to Diane. She'd decided to keep Mia, Lucretia, and Roberto's existence to herself; whatever happens going forward is on her. Still, how to explain the visions in the basement? Had Mia put something in the steaming cup of strange tea? But everyone had drunk from the same pot; if Mia had drugged her, she'd drugged all of them. Saoirse swings her legs to the front of the settee and pushes herself to a stand.

She's still shaky, but she feels a little better. In fact, every minute that passes sees her coming closer and closer to feeling good. Maybe, inexplicably, great. Saoirse scrunches her eyes closed and shakes her head. When she opens them, she catches sight of the shelf on the opposite wall, of the tiny animal bones, and a line of poetry springs into her mind as plainly as if she were looking at it on a computer screen:

My bones were never as happy in my body as they
    are on my lover's shelf.

Saoirse freezes. Twenty minutes ago, she was terrified, certain she was going to be pulled into another dimension by a shape-shifting ghost. Now, after almost a year of grief-induced writer's block—not to mention the time preceding Jonathan's death during which her creativity was stymied by other traumas—her brain is spitting out first lines with equal parts promise and intrigue, albeit ones that are far darker than she ever produced in the past. *What is happening to me?*

"Saoirse?" It's Roberto who says it, forcing Saoirse back to the room, to the accusation she was about to make. Her fear during the séance has retreated further still, and she's finding it harder and harder to remember what she was upset with Mia about.

"I . . . I'm fine. I must have just gotten wrapped up in"—she pauses—"the *performative ritual* of it all."

Roberto flushes, embarrassed at having his own words thrown back at him.

"You're not going to tell us what you saw?"

Saoirse studies Lucretia. "What makes you so sure I saw something?"

Now it's Lucretia's turn to flush, the rising color far more noticeable in her fair cheeks than in Roberto's olive ones. "I just thought . . ."

"Enough," Mia chastises. "If Saoirse doesn't want to tell us what Sarah showed her, we shouldn't push her."

Saoirse turns to Mia. She feels positively spritely, as if she could leap over the coffee table and up to the chandelier, hang there while the three diminishing candles drip wax down her wrists and onto her hair. "What did Sarah show *you*?" she asks instead.

Mia smiles shrewdly. "I've been struggling with a new poem. It's meant to be part of an anthology of Rhode Island–inspired pieces, one of a series of five I'm preparing for submission to the editor. I asked Sarah if she could throw a few fireflies my way, maybe a will-o'-the-wisp or two. Something to light my path through the darkened thicket."

"A poignant metaphor," Saoirse says. "Perhaps the Divine Poet has already delivered."

Mia's smile grows, but Lucretia fidgets and stamps her foot. "I don't believe either one of you. I think you both saw something. Something amazing. Maybe even dangerous."

Saoirse continues holding Mia's gaze, but at Lucretia's declaration, Mia looks away and shrugs. "Sorry to disappoint you, Lu," she says.

Roberto's pursing his lips beside the fireplace, and Saoirse knows that, like Lucretia, he isn't fooled by her and Mia's playacting. She feels bad about keeping them in the dark, but more than anything, she wants the three of them out of her house as acutely as she did last week so she can hurry to the cozy antique desk in the upstairs office and expand on the line of poetry that appeared—like a bird to a feeder after a blizzard—in her head. Was it placed there by Sarah? Or—and this is far more unsettling to consider—by the flickering shape-shifter, the figure with the face of Jonathan, Poe, and the stranger from the Athenæum? Crazier still is that, right now, she doesn't care.

She just wants to write.

And write.

And write.

Saoirse does manage to take leave of the trio, declining—with exaggerated regret—Roberto's offer to move the party to his house to watch a new horror film he's been waiting to see.

"Mind if we take the cupcakes with us?" Lucretia asks. "You know, for the movie?"

Saoirse retrieves the platter from the kitchen. Roberto gives her a quick hug before stepping out onto the sidewalk. Lucretia smiles a little sheepishly, as if sorry she'd been so pushy about whatever she thought Saoirse had seen. Saoirse gives the pair a little wave, then watches as Mia makes her way down the steps and joins them on the street.

Mia nods in the direction of Roberto's apartment, and Lucretia and Roberto start walking. She goes only a few steps before she stops, turns back toward the house, and gives Saoirse a knowing smile.

"Happy return to writing," she says. "Keep Sarah's gift close. Only share it when you're ready for whatever might be summoned in response. For the power that might be unleashed."

Before Saoirse can respond, Mia turns and strides away. Saoirse shuts the door and starts toward the stairs, still planning on holing up in the third-floor office for the rest of the evening. But something pulls her down the hallway, to the walkout, through the trapdoor, and into the basement. She crosses the room to the scene of the séance, where she surveys the unlit candles, the silent mantel clock, the now-opaque crystal ball. She picks up the antique phone. No battery pack, after all. Had she really heard it ring? The daguerreotype lies face down beside the quill pen and bottle of ink. She reaches for it, careful to grasp its edges to avoid slicing her finger on the cracked glass. She turns the daguerreotype over.

The image of the Divine Poet is clear beneath the smooth, unbroken glass.

Chapter 10

Saoirse walks around the quiet house the next morning giddy with excitement, the lines of the poem she stayed up half the night completing whirling around her head like the words of a lover. That is, until her father's words eclipse them: *I've got an idea . . . how about focusing less on your stupid writing and more on finding a job?*

Saoirse sighs. She feels any prospective employer would be satisfied with the "My husband died in January, so I didn't have the stomach to continue working" excuse, but she also knows her safety net won't last forever. She tries to recall the location of her computer. She wrote the new poem out by hand, snapping a photo of it on her phone to reread later. Since the poem is in her notebook, her computer should be wherever she left it after transferring the Wi-Fi into her name.

She's on her way to the kitchen when something catches her eye. A piece of card stock on the small marble table in the foyer, propped against the wall, angled out like a cherished photograph. She walks to the table, resisting the urge to look behind her. She's alone in the house—no matter what her spooked mind tells her, no matter the presence of this flyer. She lifts the card stock and reads the words printed there. It's an invitation to a career fair, today at twelve thirty, at Brown University.

There are several bullets beneath the heading, but Saoirse's fixated on the event's location. The career fair is intended for Brown University students. She was a Brown student *twelve years ago*. How had the flyer ended up in her house?

Saoirse's eyes travel up from the flyer. Slowly, she turns to look behind her, her gaze sweeping from one side of the room to the other. Last night, in a room thick with the honey-sweet scent of candles, Mia had told Sarah Whitman that the new inhabitant of her house needed help. Had the Divine Poet actually intervened?

"Sarah?" Saoirse says softly. "Did you leave this for me to find?"

She feels foolish the moment the words are out. She will take the mysterious flyer as a sign that her luck is changing and get herself to campus. Not because it's what her father would want her to do, but because she *should* explore her options. Mind made up, she hurries to her bedroom to change, donning clothes she hasn't worn since . . .

Since when? Since before Jonathan had stopped seeing her as a person with an identity that was anything other than *his wife*? Since he'd begun speaking to her only about ovulation cycles, and what position she should lie in after sex for his sperm to have the best chance of fertilizing one of her eggs? Saoirse shakes her head violently, willing the thoughts away. Today will be about her future. Not the past. Jonathan's memory already permeates the Athenæum, the university buildings, the city. He can't have her mind. Not anymore. She'd given that to him, too, once, and it still wasn't enough.

An hour later, Saoirse enters Chafee Garden. The area at the foreground of the John D. Rockefeller, Jr. Library is abloom with powdery goldenrod and cheery helenium. Far more students than she expected mill about. Members of the Brown Band tap their drums and blow animatedly into their horns. So this career fair is a big deal. Saoirse eyes the booth closest to her, and when a pair of young men in suits move away, she steps up to the table.

"Hi there," says the woman.

"Hello." Saoirse glances at the materials spread across the tablecloth. Goldman Sachs. *Of course* it's Goldman Sachs. She makes noncommittal small talk for several minutes before thanking the woman and moving along.

The names of the tables blend together quickly. Google. Harvard. Microsoft. Does everyone want to work for a Fortune 500 company these days? Saoirse collects a modest number of pamphlets, but if her earlier optimism is a bird, it's one who's flown over a body of water too vast for its little wings to handle. After twenty-five minutes, she is ready to go.

The marching band has struck up a strangely somber tune—the horns all melancholy wails and the drums a low, pressurized thudding. She crosses the gardens, trying not to make eye contact with any of the employers positioned alongside the far-right wall as she passes. *How disappointing.* The rest of the day now looms before her, each hour threatening to last twice as long as the one preceding it. She could look for a job the old-fashioned way: inquire, in person, whether an establishment is hiring. She could go home and crawl into bed. She could . . .

She could write.

It's not the thought itself that causes her to stop abruptly, but that the thought is accompanied with neither an *Are you crazy?* nor the sudden onset of dread she's become accustomed to. She is still standing in the middle of the sidewalk when someone careens into her from behind. The binder she's holding shoots out from under her arm, and the air whooshes from her lungs. A hand grabs her by the elbow, keeping her from tumbling to the ground after the pamphlets and business cards.

"I am so, *so* sorry," a deep voice says. "Are you all right?"

Saoirse takes a breath, wincing as the muscles where she was struck twinge, then hurries to collect the various career fair detritus before it can be carried off by the wind. From the corner of her eye, she sees the man who ran into her drop to his knees to help. She wants to tell him not to bother, but he's already plucking up a piece of card stock printed with a large QR code. Saoirse grabs the last dirt-smudged business card, climbs to her feet, and shoves everything back into the binder.

She turns, and the man's hand holds out the QR code. The arm of his thick wool peacoat is black and velvety. Saoirse takes the card stock, resisting the urge to mutter to herself that she hadn't wanted any of this junk in the first place. Finally, she looks up.

Into the face of the man from the Athenæum.

"Shit," Saoirse squawks and jumps back, unable to help herself. It's not just that the images from the séance are too fresh for her not to be startled; it's that, after two previous occasions of running into this man, there's no way the third can be a coincidence.

"Are you following me?" Saoirse asks. "Did Aidan send you because I wouldn't talk to him? First the Athenæum, then the coffee shop, then—" She almost says *my basement last night*, but stops herself in time. She needs to keep the upper hand, not sound like some lunatic. "Then today," she finishes. "What the hell do you want?"

The man shows none of the unsettling intensity he'd displayed on earlier sightings, but he doesn't manage to look apologetic either. "I don't know anyone named Aidan," he says, raising his hands in a gesture of surrender. He looks in the direction of Benefit Street. "But I did see you at Carr Haus," he admits. "We could go there now? I'll buy you a coffee and exp—"

"No way," Saoirse interrupts. "I want an explanation now. Why do I keep seeing you everywhere?"

The man scrunches his wide, smooth forehead and runs a hand through hair that is dark and a bit unkempt. He looks a little like the lead in a romantic comedy who's been waiting on the stereotypically adorable but klutzy woman to clean up his act, and this puts Saoirse on edge even more than her certainty that his running into her was *not* an accident. But then his dark-brown eyes squint in a way that says he fears he's about to embarrass her.

"I was running to catch up with you after I saw you at one of the booths. I didn't expect you to come to a complete stop on the sidewalk." He squints further. "But I was running after you to ask why *you've* been following me."

Saoirse stares at him, dumbfounded. "Why *I've* been following *you*? Are you kidding?"

"You stared me down at the Athenæum so intently that, for a second, I thought I knew you," he says. He's animated now, dark eyebrows bobbing, one side of his mouth popping up between words in a nervous half smile. "Then you show up at my regular coffeehouse." He gestures at the gardens around them. "Now you're at one of Brown's career events." He pauses, shrugging his leather messenger bag higher onto his shoulder. "Are you even a student here?"

Saoirse is still trying to process the one-eighty the conversation has taken. "I'm—" She hates how shrill she sounds, having been put on the defensive. "I *was* a student here," she huffs. "Are *you*? You look old enough to be a professor."

He gives her that squinty-eyed look again, the one that says he's sorry she keeps putting her foot in her mouth. And why *had* she said that? He doesn't look any older than she is.

"I am a professor," he says. "An associate one, anyway. In my third year. I'm a member of the fiction faculty for the Literary Arts MFA program. That's sort of why I thought you were following me. I've been warned by colleagues not to be surprised if prospective students attempt to stage impromptu meetings with me, try to get a one-up on the other applicants by showing me their writing sample, that sort of thing."

Saoirse doesn't respond. She can only stare at the man who, five minutes ago, she would have sworn was stalking her, the man whose eerie resemblance to Jonathan—as if he were her husband's long-lost (and more attractive) brother, or maybe a cousin—makes her breath catch in her throat, and who she was going to go as far as accuse of following her home from Carr Haus so he could sneak a career fair flyer into her foyer four days later. Now that same man is suggesting *she* is stalking *him*. Saoirse looks away, then back, to find the man's expression has changed yet again. Now he's eyeing her like he thinks she might be a little unstable.

"*Are* you a writer?" he asks in the same tone one might use to ask someone if they had a gun.

"No!" Saoirse bursts out. "I mean, yes, but not like that." He cocks his head. "Not to where I'd be pursuing you, staging 'impromptu meetings,' or whatever the hell you said people do. Jesus, that sounds crazy. I sound crazy." She stops and takes a deep breath. "I stopped writing a long time ago. I did just start again, but I'm certainly not looking to pursue an MFA, and I had no idea you were a writing professor. I saw you watching me at the Athenæum last week and thought it was weird you were at the coffee shop a few days later. Though, I suppose you could have been there first," she admits.

He stares at her, lips pursed, but then the small smile returns to one corner of his lips. "Are you *sure* you're not a writer looking to get into the Literary Arts program? This sounds like the start of the conversation in which you ask me to review your personal statement."

Saoirse huffs out a breath of laughter, despite herself. "I suppose it does. Alas, sorry to disappoint you, Mr.—"

"Powell. Emmit Powell."

Saoirse almost drops the binder again. "Emmit Powell?"

He grins. "That's right."

"As in, the Emmit Powell whose debut novel won the Pulitzer a few years ago?"

She doesn't add, *And whose second novel was the subject of a reportedly historic auction among the top five publishing houses,* or, *Emmit Powell, the darling of the national literary scene.*

"The very same. And you are . . . ?"

"Saoirse White." Emmit holds out his hand, and she shakes it. "Well, shit," she says.

"What?"

"Not only did I come to a career fair where I found zero job prospects, a career fair that someone probably invited me to as a mistake, but I've accused *Emmit Powell* of stalking me." *And of being a pawn for my husband's best friend's vendetta,* she thinks but doesn't say. Saoirse slides her binder into her backpack, ignoring the haphazard corners of paper sticking out from every side. "I should call it a day." She holds up her hand in a self-deprecating little wave, turns, and starts down the sidewalk. "Nice to meet you, Emmit Powell," she calls over her shoulder.

"Wait a minute," he says from behind her. "It all sounds way worse when you put it like that."

She turns back, and he's smiling. Not the half smile but a full one. The smile transforms his face, and suddenly he doesn't look a thing like Poe or Jonathan. Neither, however, does he look like the handful of photographs she's seen of Emmit Powell online and in newspapers, photos of a professional, respectable author. She remembers how he watched her across the open air of the second-floor Athenæum and from behind the paned glass of the coffee shop. The intense, knowing stare; the mischievous curve of his lips. This man—somehow—seems like dozens of different men, personas he embodies, roles he tries on as easily as slipping on a mask.

He's lying, she thinks abruptly. He knows she wasn't stalking him, just like he knows he's the one who initiated this supposed run-in. No man looks at a woman like that, shows up at the same location she is on three separate occasions, without some sort of nefarious intent. Just as quickly, however, the rebuttal comes: How could he be lying? He's an accomplished writer who, if not well known outside of the writing world, certainly has a reputation worth upholding. He's a professor at one of the world's most prestigious universities. Her alma mater, no less. He's polite. He's charming. He's laid out ample reasons to be wary *of her.*

You're confused, Jonathan says from her head. *The séance last night really scrambled your brain.*

Saoirse forces herself to meet Emmit's eye. "It sounds bad no matter how I say it," she quips.

"How about we do go to Carr Haus for that coffee, then? Change the narrative."

"Change the narrative." She repeats his words slowly, skeptically.

"We're both writers." He winks. "We shouldn't have any problem with a little editing."

She hates how that wink causes a quiver of excitement in her stomach, and tells herself it's the same pathetic anticipation she felt when Lucretia asked her to go for coffee. *It's because I never go anywhere or do anything, and it's so hard to fill the hours. I'm moved by the prospect of not having to trudge home yet, not by the idea of sitting across from an intelligent and charismatic man.* Still, *does* she want to fill her hours chatting with someone she has no intention of seeing again?

"I don't know," she says. But Emmit has already started up the sidewalk, ushering her along with him, slipping her bag off her shoulder as he goes and easing the binder—which was sticking out at an awkward angle—all the way into it. He slides the bag to the top of her shoulder again and gives the strap a pat.

Again, the quiver of excitement, and again, she chastises herself for being so ridiculous. He probably feels bad for her. The unemployed, washed-up writer she's somehow become.

"Fine," she agrees. "But just for a quick cup of tea. I'm sure you have student manuscripts to critique or your own writing to work on."

Emmit laughs a little bitterly. "Hardly." He puts a hand on her back at the end of the sidewalk and guides her right onto Benefit Street. Pathetically, she thinks, *This is the most physical contact I've had with another man since Jonathan.*

As they pass the Athenæum, Saoirse keeps her eyes fixed on the sidewalk ahead. She has the notion that, should she turn toward the glass doors at the library's entrance, she'll see her dead husband, his depthless black eyes charting her progression—on the arm of another man—down a street along which they used to walk together. A ghost leering out from the broken windows of his haunted house.

Chapter 11

The café is busier than when she was here with Lucretia, but they're able to get a spot along the far wall, away from the register. For the tenth time since leaving Chafee Garden, Saoirse asks herself what on earth she is doing, but she hangs her coat over the chair and takes a seat.

Emmit rubs his hands together. "I'm going with something hot. How about you, Saoirse White, what's your pick of nonalcoholic poison?"

The waitress appears, and Saoirse orders a hot chai with oat milk.

"Size?"

"Large," Emmit cuts in before Saoirse can respond. "I'll have the same."

The waitress nods. "Is that all, Mr. Powell?"

"For now. Thanks, Jess."

The waitress flushes, smiles, and hurries away.

Saoirse refrains from commenting on the way he completed her order. If he thinks having a greater amount of tea in her cup will keep her sitting across from him longer, he's mistaken. She'll leave when she wants to. She has no intention of seeing this man—talented writer or not—after today.

"So, Saoirse," Emmit starts. "That's not a name you hear every day. Are you Scottish?"

"Irish. My father was born there. It was his grandmother's name, and my mother took a liking to it."

"Have you been to Ireland?"

"Once, when I was a teenager. It was a family trip. The last before my parents' divorce." She isn't sure why her words come out so easily, but she'd forgotten how enjoyable it could be to converse with another person without putting up walls, without going out of her way to avoid certain topics, her certainty that this relationship is casual and transient giving her the freedom to say whatever she wishes.

"I'm sorry to hear your parents are divorced."

"It was for the best." The waitress reappears, places two steaming mugs on the table, and flashes another timid smile at Emmit, but he doesn't look at her. "What about you?" Saoirse continues. "Do you have a good relationship with your parents?"

Even as she poses the question, she's trying to remember if there was anything in Emmit's explosive debut novel that hinted at a writer intimately familiar with warring parents or a turbulent childhood. She read it when it first came out, and while she knows it featured a main character with skeletons in his closet, she couldn't remember if those skeletons eventually came out and danced, tempting the reader to flirt with the idea that their genesis was autobiographical in nature.

"My father ran out on my mother, brother, sister, and me when I was a year old. My sister was a newborn. My mother died a year later, and I was raised by my aunt and uncle in Virginia."

Saoirse wishes her tea wasn't so hot; she doesn't know what to do with her hands. "I'm so sorry," she says. "How awful." Had she ever read anything about his upbringing? She doesn't think so.

Emmit shrugs. "I got to travel a lot. I lived in London for a year. My uncle and I only had one major disagreement in seventeen years, while I was an undergrad at Johns Hopkins. I wanted to drop out to pursue writing, and my uncle insisted I stayed. We laugh about it now, but at the time, I was certain he was condemning my creativity to an early grave. I became suitably melancholy, of course, as any dramatic, literary type is wont to do. I spent the entirety of my senior year in black, reading nothing but Dickinson, Blake, and Plath."

Saoirse raises an eyebrow. "You? A Goth English major quoting tortured poets from the back of the lecture hall?" She chances a small sip of tea then nods at his crisp button-down shirt and well-tailored sport jacket. "I can hardly picture it."

Emmit lowers his head, pushes his chair back slightly from the table, and leans forward. From beneath hooded eyes and long lashes, he recites:

> "Gaunt in gloom
> The pale stars their torches,
> Enshrouded, wave.
> Ghost-fires from heaven's far verges faint illume—
> Arches on soaring arches—
> Night's sin-dark nave."

He sits up straight, scoots his chair back in, and smiles like the impromptu recitation never happened. "What can I say?" he says. "He might not've been tortured, but James Joyce could pen a bleak verse with the best of 'em."

Saoirse has the unexpected thought that the old her, the one who never married, who never met Jonathan, would have laughed off this strange performance. This Saoirse, however, is mesmerized. She studies the man across the table. There is something about him. For a professor, a professional writer, he is so . . . what? Unrestrained comes to mind. So does unconventional. Free-spirited and easygoing are too trite. Whatever it is, the effect is one that renders him almost aggressively interesting. Most people who try to be different fail miserably, or else come across as shameless impostors. Emmit Powell is the real deal. But what *is* his deal? Saoirse can't be sure. All she can settle on, for now, is that Emmit is not just unlike anyone she's ever met, he's unlike anyone she's ever comprehended.

"Of the three you mentioned," Saoirse says, forcing an air of casualness, "I'm partial to Dickinson. I like how she balances her interest in death with an exploration of nature. Of light. Death certainly was one of her favorite subjects, but it never slipped into preoccupation."

"I beg to differ," Emmit says and sips his chai. "Respectfully, of course. I think she forced herself to tackle bumblebees and metaphorical mermaids because she knew death was everywhere. I mean, death *is* everywhere." His tone isn't flippant. It's sad and awestruck and full of deadly solemnity. "It's a wonder any writer anywhere ever writes about anything else."

Saoirse freezes at this declaration, knows that the shock at hearing her own private thoughts spoken out loud, at being *seen* by this stranger, is written all over her face. She tries to loosen her muscles, to arrange her features into some mixture of amusement and apathy, but it's too late. Emmit is staring at her with maddeningly genuine concern.

"Why do you look like you've seen a ghost?"

"It's just that—" Is she really going to say this out loud? *Unburden yourself,* a voice in her head says. It could be Jonathan, setting her up to make a fool of herself, but maybe not. Maybe it's her own tired mind, jumping at the chance to connect. "I've had this same thought every day since my husband died nine and a half months ago." She takes a shaky breath. "I'm the one who found him. It's why I haven't been able to write for that same amount of time."

Emmit opens his mouth, but Saoirse cuts him off. "No, that's a lie. It's been longer that I haven't been able to write, but not for the same reason. Not exactly. Before my husband died, *I* was dead. How the hell was I supposed to write about relationships or the complexities of the world or the limits of possibility when I saw Death in the mirror every day for months before I saw him in the lifeless face of my husband?" Before Emmit can ask the next logical question—*Why did you feel this way?*—Saoirse adds, "Please don't ask why. It's too much to get into in a crowded café."

"I won't," Emmit says. "But, more to the point, you're not."

"I'm sorry?"

"No, *I'm* sorry. About your husband. And I'm so sorry you're the one who found him. But you're *not* supposed to write about anything else. Not in the wake of something like that. That's why you've been blocked. Because you've refused to allow yourself to write about the one thing your mind's been screaming for. It's like denying yourself water. No, that's not acute enough. It's like denying yourself air. And I'm not being hyperbolic. You're suffocating. Believe me, I know." He pauses, takes a sip of tea, looks forlornly out the window. "I've been suffocating too."

He says this last part so softly, Saoirse has to lean forward to hear him. "*You* have writer's block? The great Emmit Powell?" As soon as she speaks the words, the first of their conversation that have been anything but naked and honest, she winces at the rift the sarcasm causes. Emmit visibly pulls away from her, pressing himself against the back of his chair and turning his upper body toward the wall. His eyebrows furrow and his mouth turns down, making the melancholic amalgamation of his features decidedly more pronounced. Saoirse's not sure how he comes across as attractive as he does; it's like the whole is far greater than the sum of its parts.

She surprises herself by laying a hand on his arm. "I'm sorry. You've been nothing but open with me since we sat down. I shouldn't have been so dismissive." She catches the waitress's eye, and when the woman walks over, asks if they could have a couple of glasses of water. It's too warm in the coffee shop; Saoirse wishes there was a window nearby they could crack.

They sit in silence while they wait for the waters, and after the waitress brings them, Saoirse forces Emmit to look her in the eyes. "Let me try that again," she says. Weird that she's apologizing for not being intimate enough with him, this man she's just met. "I think your theory has merit. I wrote last night for the first time since Jonathan— he was my husband—passed. And the subject matter was dark. *Really* dark. I think it's safe to say that, while abstract, the poem was certainly about death. So, I'll turn the question to you. With earnestness. What essential thing are you denying yourself that's causing the block, and, I suppose more importantly, why?"

Unexpectedly, Emmit blushes. "Have you ever known something was going to happen before it did?" he asks.

"Like a premonition?" She feels the spiders again, the ones that love to scuttle up her back whenever she feels nervous. "I suppose."

"I'm not talking about something small, like grabbing an umbrella on a sunny day when there's no rain in the forecast only to get caught in a downpour. I'm talking, you intuited something momentous, something soul-crushingly significant, before it happened, and both the event itself *and* the knowing of it beforehand simultaneously changed your life?"

Saoirse doesn't like the question. Not because something like this hasn't happened to her, but because it has. It's just not something that she can share, no matter how forthright she's been with Emmit up until now. "For conversation's sake, let's say I have," she responds.

"What if I told you that this happens to me all the time?"

Saoirse scrunches up her mouth. "How often do 'soul-crushingly significant' events happen to you?"

"I'm the Goth English major quoting Joyce from the back of the lecture hall, remember?" he says, and smiles. "I've got a tendency to lean toward the dramatic."

Saoirse didn't know she missed his smile until she sees it again. She's happy he's opening up to her, but she can't help but enjoy the pleasant, charming Emmit better. Both versions are intense, but this deeply philosophical one is almost unendurable, like lying on the launchpad for a fireworks display or viewing a famous painting through a magnifying glass. The emotions that her medications fill in and shave down in equal measure are now jagged peaks and dizzying valleys inside her.

"Okay," Saoirse says, "so you're good at listening to your gut, is that what you're telling me?"

"It's more than that. For example, with *Vulture Eyes*," he says, naming his debut novel, "I didn't know what I was going to write about—mainly, a man who's tortured by the things he's done in his past in order to get ahead—right up until the moment I started the book. Not just the plot, but the characters, the themes, they came to me in—and I know it's inexcusably cliché—but in a flash, like a gift from a benevolent god. Like a goddamn vision."

Their conversation has reclaimed its earlier rhythm, so she's taking a chance when she says, "But couldn't that be said of a lot of writers? Maybe you're someone to whom inspiration comes fast and furious, and you have the talent and motivation to act on that inspiration quickly."

He shakes his head, frustrated. "That wasn't the right example." He sighs and stares into his drink. When he raises his eyes to meet hers, his expression has changed. It's *the look* again, the one from the Athenæum. The one that says he knows every thought she's ever had, every secret. Saoirse resists the urge to squirm out from under that penetrating glare, to stand up and run out of the coffee shop.

To say he's making her nervous is an understatement. She wants to shrug into her jacket, to cover every inch of herself. She wants to stitch up her lips with a darning needle and heavy thread so he can never elicit another admission from her, to pluck out her eyes so he cannot read her thoughts in the movement of her lids and the dilation of her pupils. At the same time, she wants to stare into the deep pools of his dark-brown eyes for an eternity.

"Today, at the career fair," Emmit says. "I wasn't lying when I said that I thought you were stalking me. But, watching you walk along the garden paths, considering each table, making the decision to speak with someone or move on, occasionally taking the time to finger the petals of a beautiful flower, more tempted by present beauty than future prospects, I knew I'd been wrong about something. Like I said, I've been blocked. Ever since *Vulture Eyes*. And I owe my publisher the next book. They outbid everyone to work with me again, and I've already requested two extensions on my deadline, and I'm close to having to ask for a third. It's a terrifying, helpless, hopeless place to be in. But lately,

I've had the feeling the block was nearing its end. That any day now, I'd be struck with another Great Idea.

"'Something is coming,' a voice in my head told me," Emmit continues. "No, not a voice. That's too orderly. This was nowhere near that buttoned-up of an experience. This was like a drug that, once in my veins, shot to my brain and exploded over every inch of my body. I waited for whatever was going to happen. And waited. First patiently. Then desperately. And finally, despairingly. This morning, I threw a coffee cup across the room. It shattered against a bookcase. I cried myself ragged in the shower. After that, I dressed and resigned myself to returning to the brainstorming process for the new, nonexistent novel. 'I was wrong about the feeling,' I told myself. And that was that."

Emmit looks at her expectantly. Saoirse goes over every turn of the story he's just told her, but she's not sure which admission he's expecting her to comment on. When several more seconds pass, and he still doesn't say anything, Saoirse says, "I don't understand. Wasn't this supposed to be a better example of your uncanny intuition?"

Emmit smiles, and this time, Saoirse sees the specter from her basement the night before, sees Emmit's features rearrange themselves like jumping fish, his flesh stretch and reform, psychic energy doing its best interpretation of a living, breathing man. She shakes the image away.

"It *is* the better example," Emmit says. He places his hands on the table and leans forward. "I wasn't wrong. Something was coming. It just wasn't the next Great Idea, like I'd thought."

A fly buzzes past Saoirse's right ear. A moment later, she feels one crawling along the collar of her shirt. Using every ounce of self-control she possesses, she refrains from swatting the air, from slapping at her skin. "What was coming, Emmit?" she asks. Her voice is low, hardly more than a whisper. "What momentous, soul-crushingly significant thing?"

There are people in the coffee shop, but their voices have fallen away. The clang of spoons against teacups, an espresso machine whirring to life, a barista calling out an order—they are nothing more than the far-off whoosh of a passing train.

Emmit's smile widens. She didn't notice before, but his teeth are very, very white.

"It was you, of course, Saoirse," he says. "*You* are the momentous, once-in-a-lifetime thing."

Chapter 12

As if his words are the play button on a paused sitcom, the sounds of the coffee shop come roaring back. Saoirse feels more foolish than frightened, annoyed with herself for believing Emmit to be different. To be genuinely interesting. To be anything other than a creep. All his beautiful ideas and thought-provoking words, his perfectly cultivated interest in her . . . it was little more than a short-lived performance before his self-indulgent—albeit creatively executed—pickup attempt.

"Riiight," Saoirse says, and brings her mug to her lips, swallowing the last of her tea. She pushes the cup across the table, drops a ten-dollar bill from her wallet beside it, and pulls her jacket off the back of the chair.

"Hold on," Emmit says quickly, and throws back the rest of his drink too. "I know. It sounds wild. And I didn't mean for it to come across so creepy. I'm not saying your purpose is to inspire me or something. Like the universe delivered you to me. That's not what I'm saying at all."

"Really, because that's what it sounded like." Saoirse shrugs into her coat. "Thanks for the company, Mr. Powell, but I need to get going."

"Mr. Powell? Oh, come on, Saoirse, don't be like that. I didn't want to imply that my intuition, my feeling, whatever the hell you want to call it, meant that I thought we were going to *be together*. I just meant that any opportunity to see more of you, to get to know you, was an exciting prospect on par with writing my first novel. It's a compliment."

As soon as he says it, he cringes. "I'm making it worse. I don't want to be that guy, telling a woman how to take the things he says. I have zero expectations. I just hoped—I *hope*—that our impromptu run-in this morning would be the beginning of something. A friendship, perhaps. That's all! Please don't—"

He pauses and goes to put a hand on her arm, then stops himself and looks her in the eyes. "I don't have many friends. They're all in Maryland. You probably don't know this—well, of course you don't know this, but I live there. In Baltimore. I'm only in Providence half the week to teach my classes. That's how little I meant for you to take what I said as an invitation—a preordainment—for us to start dating. My whole life—aside from this teaching position—is in Baltimore." He sighs. "I'm really sorry. I guess I got excited by the prospect of having someone cool in this city I could occasionally have a cup of tea with."

Saoirse is moved in spite of herself. Maybe he didn't mean for what he said to come out the way it did. But between the admission of his strange "feeling" and the lingering memories of him staring at her from across the library, from atop her basement ceiling, Saoirse doesn't want to be here anymore. She wants to go home. Emmit may be telling the truth about wanting to make friends in Providence, but the whole interaction has taken a turn for the weird.

She's ready to bury herself in blankets, to recover from last night's excitement, the all-night writing session, the unexpected one-on-one interaction today. She's supposed to meet Lucretia and Roberto tomorrow at an animal shelter Mia recommended. This is the last evening she will be without the responsibility of taking care of a cat—or maybe even a kitten. She wants nothing more than to watch Netflix until her eyes burn and crash into bed.

"I'm not leaving because of what you said," Saoirse lies. "It's just, I have something planned for tomorrow. I need to go home and get a few things ready." She holds her hand out. Looking miserable, Emmit shakes it. He tries to give her the ten-dollar bill back, but she shakes her head. "Put whatever's leftover toward the tip."

Emmit nods once, a heavy, tired movement. "I would offer to walk you out—walk you home, even—but I have a feeling that might make things worse."

Saoirse gives him a wry smile.

"Could we at least agree that this won't be the last time we see each other? I don't dare ask for your number, but would you consider taking mine? I really enjoyed talking with you today."

Saoirse pauses, having already taken two steps away from their table. Their waitress is eyeing Emmit from the pick-up station, no doubt wondering if this is the end of a first date gone bad. *Let her wonder,* Saoirse thinks. *Hell, let her come over and pick up where I left off.* "I'm sorry," Saoirse says to Emmit. "I don't think that's a good idea."

He bites his lip. "I understand. I'm sorry I weirded you out."

His expression is so morose, Saoirse almost reconsiders. Then she reminds herself that he's already lied to her once, about his motive in coming up to her in Chafee Garden. "You did," she says firmly. "But it was nice talking to you up until then. And who knows . . ." She stares at his downturned face until he lifts his gaze, his brown eyes—so dark they're almost black—locking on to hers. "We've run into each other three times already. If we happen to meet a fourth, maybe I'll be more inclined to believe in your theory of 'premonition.'"

She walks off before he can say anything else, wondering if she's made a mistake. Providence is not a large city, and she and Emmit *have* run into one another an absurd number of times. Now if she sees him again, she'll be all but obligated to join him for tea or maybe even a meal.

"That won't happen," she whispers and steps onto the sidewalk. It is a shame. She did enjoy spending time with him, before he got all Twilight Zone on her.

She walks home quickly and, once there, exchanges her sheer blouse and tight pants for threadbare leggings and an old Brown sweatshirt. She makes for the couch, but before she can get there, the decision as to whether to finish the conspiracy sci-fi show she's been watching or start a new stand-up special featuring a comic she enjoys is replaced by another thought. Not a thought but, specifically, a sentence:

Unbroken silence turns one's soul away from the shores of discontent.

Saoirse stops halfway across the room. Another first line. An invitation to tell a story in trochaic octameter. *Isn't the best-known work in trochaic octameter Poe's "The Raven"? Why is* this *the meter I'm thinking in?*

She looks longingly at the television, but it's too late. The first, fat raindrop has fallen from the storm cloud of her creativity, and that cloud is threatening to open whether she's ready or not. She backtracks out of the room and up the stairs, then hurries to her desk, where her notebook and pen still sit from the night before. Conscious thought falls away. The words pour out of her.

She writes poem after poem, four in all, occasionally pausing to spin in her chair and look behind her, certain the feeling of being watched she keeps experiencing will turn out to be the ghost of Sarah Whitman—she's too content in this moment to fear Aidan Vesper turning up, as she had before—but each time she turns, the only eye upon her is the moon beyond the balcony doors, moving silently through the star-crusted sky. When she's done, a dull ache pulses in her palm and her mind alights from one thought to the next with the bouncy changeability of a butterfly among wildflowers. The clock reads 4:00 a.m. She goes to the bathroom, chugs ice-cold water from the tap, and falls into bed.

Her dreams are full of dark, disturbing imagery: a black-clad figure holding a woman in white against a towering, moss-covered gravestone. A ghost-white woman holding the bloodied corpse of a raven. A woman whose visage has been replaced by a ream of parchment paper on which lines of poetry are being written with a knife-sharp quill by an unseen hand.

Finally, after what seems like hours of cemeteries blanketed by mist and marigold-colored leaves, of specters rising from ghostly, whispering seas, Saoirse's mind goes blank. She sleeps in an endless, noiseless expanse of blackness and is still sleeping long after the sun rises.

Chapter 13

Saoirse's still a little groggy when she arrives at the Providence Animal Rescue League the next morning. Lucretia and Roberto are waiting for her by the counter, and a woman whose name tag identifies her as Heather leads them down a corridor to a room where eight curious cats blink at them from behind the glass of their respective enclosures.

"They're all so cute!" Lucretia jumps up and down, holding her hands up like little paws.

Roberto smacks her arm lightly. "There are empty cages, Lucretia. Be careful, or they'll put you up for adoption too." He turns to Heather. "Don't worry, anyone that took her home would bring her back within the week."

Heather smiles good-naturedly, then turns to address Saoirse. "I'll let you get acquainted with the animals and be back in a few minutes."

"Thanks," Saoirse says and watches Heather walk out before turning back to the wall of enclosures.

"Five black ones," Lucretia says. "I told you black cats were the hardest to place. Though, Midnight is the only entirely black one. Aww, but his little card says he has diabetes!"

Saoirse stares at Midnight. Adopting a cat with diabetes would be a lot of work. But Saoirse knows how it feels to be discounted due to a diagnosis. "Hello, Midnight," she whispers.

"Now that we're ensconced within the privacy of Catdom," Roberto says, "are you going to tell us why you look so exhausted?"

Saoirse turns to face him, momentarily forgetting her feline audience. "Believe it or not, I was writing."

"Oh. My. Gosh. Yes, Saoirse!" Lucretia hugs her. "You're over your block, then? And I'm sorry, but I have to ask, was it whatever happened during the séance that unblocked you?"

Saoirse shrugs. "Maybe? I'm still not entirely sure what happened during the séance. But after everyone left that night, I went upstairs, and a poem poured right out of me."

Lucretia grabs her arm. "Wait, a poem? Didn't you used to write cozy mystery novels? I didn't know you wrote poetry too."

"I didn't. At least, not seriously. I mean, I had some notebooks filled with poems from over the years, but they were nothing I ever bothered to show anyone."

Lucretia and Roberto exchange a glance.

"What?" Saoirse looks back and forth between the two of them. "What is it?"

Lucretia busies herself looking into the cubby where a cat named Bubba has rolled onto his back and is pawing at the air. When she looks over again, there is something in her face that Saoirse has never seen before. It's something a little bit teasing and a little bit scared.

"I mean, you can't tell me it didn't occur to you. What a weird coincidence it is that Sarah was a poet, and now, after the longest dry spell in the history of your writing, you come back, more prolific than ever *and* writing poetry? That's gnarly. Out there. Isn't that out there, Roberto?"

Roberto gives Saoirse a pointed look. "You know how much I hate agreeing with her, but Lucretia's right."

Saoirse turns back to Midnight, feigning nonchalance. "If you two are going to make such a big deal about my return to writing, then I totally shouldn't tell you who I had tea with yesterday."

"You should," Roberto says, grabbing Saoirse's elbow and turning her toward him. "And you will. You'll tell us right this instant."

"Emmit freakin' Powell. I guess he's a professor with Brown's MFA program. He ran into me on campus there, at a career fair. Literally.

He bowled me over, then asked to take me to Carr Haus to make it up to me."

Roberto's eyes practically bug out of his head. "Um, duh, that he's a professor with Brown's MFA program. He's also one of the most amazing writers to come out of the twenty-first century. Do you know he's technically a horror writer? Now, his agent and the people at his publishing house don't market him as such, because horror is genre fiction, and genre fiction is smut to be looked down upon by book snobs everywhere. But you cannot convince me that *Vulture Eyes* is anything but revolutionary, transcendent literary horror. The guy is a modern-day Edgar Allan Poe!"

Saoirse freezes at the comparison, but Roberto doesn't notice and continues, "*Vulture Eyes* is astonishingly terrifying but also gorgeous and lyrical and heartbreaking. Oh my god, Saoirse, I can't believe you got to sit down with him. Did you talk about writing? Did he say anything about where he got the idea for *Vulture Eyes*? Some of those passages where the protagonist was trying to escape his guilt by any means possible were written as if they'd really happened! And did he reveal anything about his next novel?"

Saoirse hasn't heard Roberto say so much in a single breath since she met him. "We did talk about writing. But mostly, we talked about death."

"Death?" Lucretia looks worried. "Did you bring it up or did he?"

"He did, I think. Or, maybe it was me? I can't remember. That's what the whole conversation was like. Like I couldn't tell where my thoughts ended and his began."

"Oh, shit," Roberto breathes. "So you guys hit it off?"

"We started to." Midnight holds a paw up to the glass, and Saoirse presses a finger to the little black pad. "But then he got all weird on me. I'm talking *Play Misty for Me* level of weirdness."

"Seriously?" Roberto says, then stops, looking confused. "Wait, isn't *Play Misty for Me* about a *woman* who gets all obsessive and stalkerish?"

"Come on, Roberto," Lucretia chastises. "Don't be so rigid in your obsessive stalker gender stereotypes."

"Right, whatever. But what exactly did he do?"

Footsteps sound in the corridor outside. "He told me he gets premonitions," Saoirse says, "and that he had a premonition he was going to run into me, or something. That something momentous—on par with the idea for his first novel—was going to happen, and then he met me." The door opens, and Heather walks into the room.

"Saoirse," Roberto says with deadly seriousness, "please, for the love of Mother Earth, and of great literature, you *must* see this man again. It's Emmit Powell! The guy is a goddamn genius. Of course he's going to be eccentric."

"I think Roberto has a crush on him," Lucretia teases. She smiles and winks at Heather, who gives her a confused smile in return.

"*Of course I have a crush on him,*" Roberto shouts. "He's Emmit freakin' Powell, as Saoirse herself accurately described when she told us they had lunch. I'd date him in a second."

"It was tea," Saoirse clarifies.

"He does seem really cool," Lucretia offers. "Did you get his number?"

"Can we talk about this later?" Saoirse asks. She nods in Heather's direction.

"Have you decided on a cat who would be a good fit for you, Ms. White?" Heather asks. "Or did you want to interact with a few of them before making your decision?"

Lucretia starts to say something, but Saoirse holds up her hand. "I don't think that will be necessary." She gestures to Midnight. "This little guy and I have a connection."

Heather nods cautiously. "Do you have experience caring for a cat with diabetes?"

"I'm sure I can figure it out." Sensing she needs to say more to convince the shelter worker, Saoirse adds, "I'm currently in a position where

I can afford to step away from work for a bit, so I have the resources and the time."

Heather smiles. "That sounds like a great fit for Midnight. Let's go back to my office. After a few more questions and some paperwork, Travis will give you a crash course in low-carbohydrate diets and fast-acting insulin therapy."

Lucretia hooks her arm into Roberto's and forces him around in a little circle. Roberto tries to rebuff her but can't help himself and breaks into a smile. Saoirse shakes her head in mock exasperation and ushers them toward the corridor.

"Great timing by the way," Heather says as she closes the door behind them.

"Were there others interested in adopting Midnight?"

"I just meant it's almost Halloween. Isn't there a spooky story about a black cat that's really famous? I read it in high school. By that guy who wrote a lot of spooky stories, what's his name again . . . ?"

Saoirse, Roberto, and Lucretia exchange a look.

"Edgar Allan Poe?" Roberto offers wryly.

Chapter 14

After a tedious trek home lugging the cat carrier—Roberto and Lucretia insisted they walk so they could further analyze her decision not to take Emmit's phone number—the black cat settles himself into the house on Benefit Street with far less fanfare than Saoirse anticipated. She sets up the litter box and dishes of water and cat food she'd ordered—along with a volume of Sarah Whitman's poetry—from Amazon, smiling as Midnight finds a patch of sunlight in which to curl up.

He's not completely at ease with her and his new surroundings, but she can tell it won't take long. Heather had said the reason he'd been surrendered had nothing to do with behavior or temperament; his owners had simply grown tired of the daily tasks associated with managing his diabetes. They'd told the shelter when they dropped him off that Midnight was four years old.

A cat, she thinks, still not quite believing she'd gone from casual mention to full-on pet ownership in less than a week. *Writing again. Friends. And at least a cursory attempt at finding a new job.* Despite the past continuing to weigh down on her like a suffocating blanket and the fear that Aidan is going to turn up at any moment, she's doing all right. *I guess moving back to Providence was the right idea.*

That's why it's so irritating when she can't shake Emmit Powell from her mind. Were Lucretia and Roberto right? Had she been shortsighted in refusing his phone number? Sure, he'd lied about running into her on the sidewalk, claiming it was an accident. And she can't forget the weirdness he'd displayed at the Ath and Carr Haus, regardless of having spun those interactions so that *she* came across as the weird one.

But he was also the most captivating person she'd met since . . . well, since Jonathan. She hates to admit it, but it's the truth. *Yeah, and look how well that turned out for us both,* Jonathan says from her head.

"Shut up," she says aloud. Midnight lifts his head from the floor and looks at her curiously, ears twitching. "Sorry," she says in a soothing voice. She paces the kitchen.

"Should I have taken his number?" she asks the cat. "I would have been the one with all the control. Like when I took Mia's, Lucretia's, and Roberto's numbers before inviting them back for the séance. The decision to call them had been in my hands." *Great,* she thinks. *You've gone from arguing with your dead husband to asking for advice from a cat.*

The house seems claustrophobic and stuffy. Regardless of whether it was the right decision to refuse Emmit's number, there's nothing she can do about it now. *Except maybe get out of this house and get some fresh air.*

She turns her attention back to Midnight. "What about your name?" she asks. "Midnight? Is that what you'd like me to call you?"

With his coal-black fur and glittering eyes, it's about as inventive as calling him Cat. Lucretia's vote had been for Catterina, but Saoirse's hesitant to encourage additional connections to the past; this house, this city, the sun-dappled alcoves in the library, they're enough of a portal to Edgar and Sarah. Naming her new housemate Catterina—though she'd seen when perusing articles on Poe and Whitman that Poe's own cat had been tortoiseshell, not black—might be akin to speaking Bloody Mary three times into a darkened mirror: an explicit invitation to the deceased to come on in.

But . . . there *is* the Poe story Heather referred to. Saoirse grabs her phone and googles "black cat story, Edgar Allan Poe." And there it is, the black cat of the eponymous tale: Pluto. Poe's work seems a safer bet than a detail from his actual life. And Pluto is a cleverer moniker than Midnight, taking the endless night sky analogy a step further.

"Pluto?" she asks the cat, watching with amusement the quick, twitchy jerk of his tail. "Do you like that?" She walks over to him and lays a hand on his back. He's purring, so she takes this as an acquiescence. "All right. Pluto it is. Pluto, I've got to get out of here for a bit. Take a walk. Clear my head." *Of Jonathan,* she doesn't add. "You could probably use some alone time anyway. Get used to the lay of the land without me breathing down your neck."

Pluto stares. His tail twitches again. Saoirse rattles the food in the bowl so he remembers where it is, grabs her jacket, and steps out into the autumn sun. Across the street, on a neighbor's porch, a resin tombstone warns visitors to BEWARE. From an adjacent porch, cornstalks rustle in the breeze. A quick look around tells her hers is the only house on the block not yet decorated for Halloween, and there's only one more week until the thirty-first.

"Pumpkin shopping it is," she says to the empty street.

It was better when you were talking to the cat, Jonathan taunts.

Ignoring him, Saoirse looks in the opposite direction of Brown's campus and the Athenæum, but she's loath to seek out a new grocery store when she's already familiar with the Main Street Trader Joe's. She heads south on Benefit Street, telling herself she will not, under any circumstances, let her unease—or is it her excitement?—about running into a certain Pulitzer Prize–winning novelist dictate her actions.

By the time she reaches Trader Joe's, she's forgotten all about Emmit Powell and is calculating the logistics of carrying a planter of maroon mums the mile-walk home. It's only when she hears a deep but lilting voice, friendly and thoughtful in equal measure, that she puts the palm-size pumpkin she is clutching down and turns toward the registers.

Twenty feet away, at the self-checkout, a man is inserting a credit card into the reader. A prepackaged salad and a bottle of iced tea are on the ledge by his elbow, waiting to be placed into the reusable shopping bag slung over his arm.

"No major calamities today, Janice," the man says to the fiftysomething woman charged with keeping an eye on the area. "I'll master these self-checkout registers yet."

The woman throws her head back in laughter. "I don't doubt it, Mr. Powell. In fact, it's been a few weeks since you've needed me to bail you out with my magic key card."

No. Saoirse's hands are cold and her muscles frozen. *No way. I fell asleep in the living room and am dreaming.* Saoirse spins around, her purse knocking into the pumpkins on the table. She manages to catch the two that go rolling before they drop to the floor. A thought intervenes before she can sprint for the frozen foods section: *This is insanity. He's buying a salad. He isn't stalking you.*

Maybe not. But this has gone far beyond coincidence and into the realm of statistical impossibility.

Maybe it's time to accept Emmit's theory that you two are predestined to have some sort of relationship, Jonathan says mockingly from inside her head. She resists the urge to respond and slowly turns back toward the registers.

Emmit has bagged his tea and salad and is giving Janice a salute as he makes his way toward the door. Saoirse follows at a walk until he gets to the exit, then jogs after him as he disappears through the door.

Outside, Emmit turns in the direction Saoirse came from a mere ten minutes before. She considers calling out, but she's only a few strides away. In another moment, she's caught up to him and reaches out to grab the sleeve of his soft wool jacket. He stops. Turns. Saoirse can't help it. At the sight of his wide, smooth forehead and bushy eyebrows, she smiles and says, "I thought about barreling into you on the sidewalk like you did to me, but I didn't want you to drop your expensive salad."

Emmit gawks. He looks down at his shopping bag then back up at her.

"Don't you dare ask if I'm following you," Saoirse says. "The only reason I came up to you is *because* of your goddamn premonition. I'm still not sure I believe in it, but it's getting harder and harder to explain why we keep running into each other."

Emmit studies her face, still not saying a word, then drops his gaze to her empty hands.

"I came for a pumpkin," Saoirse says. "I saw you before I could finish picking one out."

Emmit nods, and when he smiles, any lingering doubt over whether it was prudent to approach him melts away. *Don't turn into an idiotic, lust-sick puppy,* she thinks. *Even Jonathan was considerate and charming when he was courting you.* But then Emmit is angling himself toward her so that she can link her arm with his, and they are walking away from the supermarket.

"Where are we going?" Saoirse asks.

"I was supposed to be leaving for the airport," Emmit says. "Like every Sunday afternoon, I come to Trader Joe's and get a—sometimes healthy, sometimes not—dinner, drive to T. F. Green, and take the hour-and-a-half flight back to Baltimore, where I crash into bed before the start of another week."

Saoirse looks at the cars lining the street, though, of course, she has no idea what Emmit drives. "So, you're going to the airport?"

"Not anymore," he says and pulls her closer to him. "Now I'm going to the Farmer's Daughter to get you a proper pumpkin."

Saoirse tries to think of an excuse, a reason why she cannot get into a car with this man she does not know and go to some farm she's never heard of. But nothing comes. So she allows herself to be led, to enjoy the sunshine on her face and the company of a man who thinks it's worth missing a flight to spend the afternoon with her.

Chapter 15

They walk the streets of Providence, arm in arm, until Saoirse can't help herself, and asks, "If you skip your flight, won't you miss work tomorrow?"

Emmit looks down at her, and a wisp of dark hair falls across his forehead. "The classes I teach at Johns Hopkins are Tuesdays and Wednesdays, so all I'll really miss is an extra day of staring at a blank screen and pulling my hair out." He turns right onto Waterman Street. "I'll call the airline later and rebook for tomorrow. Or maybe I won't. I suppose it depends on how long this little pumpkin-procuring excursion takes." He winks, and Saoirse feels her body grow warm.

Emmit stops in front of a luxury apartment building and releases her arm to dig in his pocket. A moment later, he unlocks the sleek gray sports car in front of them.

Saoirse stares at the car, feeling her eyebrows climb toward her hairline. "This is what you use to drive the ten miles back and forth to the airport?" She's not quite able to keep the cynicism from her voice.

Emmit gives her a sheepish look. "At the risk of sounding like an asshole, I had to spend my book deal money on something. I hate public transportation, but I live in two different cities, so I bought myself a car here and, well, the same one in Baltimore." He laughs. "I haven't been traveling much post-COVID, my apartments are subsidized by Brown and Johns Hopkins, respectively, and aside from good booze and the occasional edible, I don't have what one might call expensive taste."

"Says the guy with twin Mercedes," Saoirse laughs, but she feels unmoored. The past fifteen minutes have been so unexpected, so surreal, she wonders yet again if she's actually asleep in the living room of 88 Benefit Street, immersed in a dream while Pluto purrs on her stomach. "What was the name of the place you said we were going to?"

"The Farmer's Daughter. One of my graduate students turned me on to it last year. It's in South Kingstown. You'll love it."

Pretty confident for a guy who's had one conversation with you, Jonathan sneers. *Are you really getting into a car with this stranger?*

Saoirse grits her teeth. *This is Emmit Powell,* she responds silently. *Pulitzer Prize–winning novelist.* Even if he does turn out to be nothing more than a womanizer with over-the-top pickup lines, he isn't going to murder her. Saoirse slides into the passenger side and buckles her seat belt.

You're strapped in now, Jonathan warns, *literally and figuratively.*

Exactly, she thinks back defiantly. *Might as well enjoy the ride.*

"Once we get off I-95, the drive is really scenic," Emmit says. "And there are pumpkins at the Farmer's Daughter in colors you won't find at Trader Joe's."

Saoirse marvels at the way he jumps from casual to contemplative in the space of a single sentence. As if the shades of pumpkins have moved him in some profound, gratifying way.

"Is that so?" She's careful not to meet his earnestness with sarcasm. "Well, I'm excited." They drive for several minutes in silence.

They're almost to the highway when Emmit glances at her. "I'd resigned myself to never seeing you again. What have you been up to since I saw you last?"

"Writing," she says, surprised by how quickly she answers him, how quickly he's elicited her trust. "Four poems in a single evening. It's wild, because I was never much of a poet."

"More like a mystery novelist," Emmit says. She stares at him hard, and he grins at her. "Did you think I wasn't going to look you up on

Goodreads after you told me you were a writer? I saw the series you did with Ballantine. It was pretty successful."

She blushes. "That's generous," she says. "Especially coming from—"

He cuts her off with a raised hand. "Don't say what you are about to say. I happened to write something that, for whatever reason, appealed to both the critics and the masses. Talent is talent, and aside from the handful—and I mean handful—of geniuses, those literary giants that captivate us all, most talent at the Big Five publishing level is comparable. The fact that *Vulture Eyes* sold as many copies as it did does not mean it was any better than *Sugar and Splice*."

Saoirse barks out a little laugh. "Um, of course it does. But I'm touched you know the name of one of my books."

"Not just one," he says. "After *Sugar and Splice* was *Science Doesn't Take Whisks*, followed by *We Knead to Keep Our Ion You*." Emmit smacks the steering wheel. "*Sugar and Splice* was delightful!"

"You read it?"

"I did. And let me tell you, a baker and a scientist who team up to solve murders is far more enjoyable than a man driven to madness by guilt so intense it becomes corporeal. If I didn't write *Vulture Eyes*, I'd never want to read it."

Saoirse stares out the windshield. "The woman who wrote those novels was a different person," she says. "One who was amused by lighthearted things."

"And then your husband died, and the idea of writing another installment in the series sounded as enjoyable as being gnawed on by rats or eviscerated by a swinging pendulum."

"That sounds about right."

Emmit allows his eyes to stray from the road for a moment to observe her. "You said at Carr Haus you'd already stopped writing before your husband's death. So your metamorphosis from commercial writer to death-obsessed poet has been much longer in the making."

One side of his mouth raises in its lopsided grin. "Speaking of your dark, death-obsessed poetry, when do I get to read it?"

"I'm not sure I'm ready for anyone to see this stuff. You're right that it's dark. Dark and disturbing."

"I like dark. I *live* in the dark. I don't care if it's on another planet from the *Sugar and Splice* series. I'd love to read more of your work."

Saoirse's cheeks feel warm. Emmit Powell wants to read *her* work? She sits in silence, a twinge in her chest. A good one, though—not the tightness she experiences when she's overexerted herself or missed a day of medication.

Emmit steers them around the curve adjacent to Thurbers Avenue, and the horizon beyond the highway darkens. "That looks sufficiently ominous," he says, frowning.

Saoirse stays quiet as raindrops spatter the windshield.

"I'm not averse to pumpkin picking in the rain," Emmit adds, "but neither of us is dressed for inclement weather." His frown deepens. "And I don't have an umbrella. Should we turn around?"

"I guess?" Saoirse responds, trying to hide her disappointment.

"Unless . . . you're hungry?" Emmit asks.

Saoirse's eyes flick to the back seat.

"Forget the salad. Do you know any restaurants around here?"

"I moved back less than two weeks ago, remember?" She looks out the window for a telltale building or landmark—not that she would remember anything from her sporadic ventures off Brown's campus more than a decade ago. "I have no idea."

The rain increases from a few splattering drops to a downpour.

"I'm getting off here," Emmit says, jerking his chin at an upcoming exit and slowing. It's cute, how worried he is. But she's a little uneasy herself. The visibility is terrible, and the rain is not letting up. Halfway down the ramp, the visibility improves, and Saoirse relaxes slightly. Emmit takes a left.

"What town are we in?" Saoirse asks.

"No idea. Maybe Cranston?" Emmit's knuckles loosen around the steering wheel. "It looks like we're coming to a little stretch of civilization now." He pulls into a small public lot next to a strip of shops and restaurants. "There's a place right there," he says, pointing. He reaches over, grabs her hand, and squeezes it, then gives a wistful glance over his shoulder. "I can't believe I don't have my damn umbrella."

Hand tingling from his touch, mind reeling from this unexpected adventure she's somehow found herself on, Saoirse shrugs. "It'll be fine. We'll make a run for it."

Emmit chuckles, staring at the rain, which is coming down in sheets. "I like your optimism." They grab their respective door handles simultaneously.

The rain has turned the late-October afternoon cold. Saoirse pulls her coat tighter around her as she runs for the restaurant. They're drenched by the time they reach the overhang and both laughing hysterically. Together, rainwater dripping in their eyes, they inspect the menu on the glass-encased bulletin board by the door.

"This looks great," Saoirse says.

"Ditto," Emmit replies, "though I'm basing my acquiescence entirely on their wine selection. I'm not normally a big drinker, but this rain makes me want to warm my bones from the inside out." He gives her a calculating look. "Are you a drinker?"

Saoirse hesitates. What to say to this? *Who could be, watching their husband mix everything from scotch to IPAs with his Ambien and Adderall, intent on self-medicating his stress away.* Or, *I am, as long as I err on the side of extreme moderation, so as to not upset the delicate balance of my own prescriptions?*

"Sort of," she says, and Emmit cocks his head, his expression indicating this is something he will return to later. But then his eyes jump from her face to the bulletin board again, and his mouth curls into a grin.

Saoirse follows his gaze to a piece of paper tacked to the side of the dessert menu. At the sight of the words there, a cool sensation passes along the back of her neck, as if a spider has skittered over the skin there. A spider . . . or a fly.

She reads the words a second time, and then a third, and each time she does, the image in her brain grows sharper. Sharper, but no more comprehensible. It's of Sarah Helen Whitman sitting in an alcove in the Athenæum, reading from a notebook to the man who has recently become her fiancé. Reading her poetry aloud to Edgar Allan Poe.

"What time is it?" Saoirse asks warily.

"Twenty of six." Emmit's eyes glint with the tiny drops of rainwater caught in his lashes. "I'm not going to say this is a sign."

Saoirse scoffs.

"But, I mean, this is a sign, right? It's got to be a sign."

She shakes her head. "The rain is sign enough that we should eat here. Let's go in."

Emmit opens the door. Saoirse looks one final time at the piece of paper, willing the words to change or to disappear. They remain:

Open Mic Night: POETRY! PROSE! MUSIC!
Regale us with your creative endeavors!
Too shy? Regale us with someone else's!
Every Sunday, 6 to 8 p.m.

Chapter 16

The entryway where Emmit helps her out of her coat is awash with low amber lighting. Saoirse shivers and resists the urge to wring out her hair. When she looks up, she finds Emmit is gazing at her with undisguised longing. He pulls her into an embrace, but steps back as quickly as he grabbed her, his hands coming to rest on her shoulders, where he rubs her up and down to warm her.

"Better?" he asks.

Saoirse nods, not trusting herself to speak.

"Good." He smiles. Saoirse feels as if she could fall into that smile, but then he's pushing open the door, one hand on her lower back, and she wants to pinch herself, or else imagine that the hand is Jonathan's, anything to keep from falling under his spell. "Come on," he says. "Let's get inside where it's really warm."

To their left is a dining room, LED candles flickering from the tables' white linen centers. To the right is a lounge packed tightly with high tops. The bar faces the typical row of stools to its front, but is backed against another high counter that's open to the kitchen. Beyond the bar, a small stage twinkles with lights. At the sight of the microphone, nerves rush through Saoirse's midsection. Why did the sign have to call out poetry and prose in addition to music, as if Emmit was right and it was some sort of portent? Better yet, why couldn't the restaurant not have had an open mic at all?

"We could have stumbled on a hell of a lot worse," Emmit says.

Saoirse murmurs an agreement just as the hostess acknowledges them. "Two?" she asks from behind a menu-strewn counter.

"Please," Emmit replies.

"Dining room or lounge?"

"Lounge," Emmit answers enthusiastically. "We want to be close to the open-mic action, should inspiration strike."

Saoirse starts to protest, but the hostess has picked up menus and is leading them in that direction, saying, "Of course. Right this way."

No sooner are they settled at a cozy two-top than a waitress appears to take their drink order. Emmit raises an eyebrow at Saoirse. "Shall we split a bottle of wine?"

Saoirse should be arranging a seven-dollar pumpkin on her front stoop and lamenting her decision not to trek home with an armload of mums. Instead, one of the country's greatest authors is asking her to split a bottle of wine, a man who's been making a habit of catering to her every whim, and who seems thrilled at the prospect of simply talking with her, of reading at an open-mic night—what Jonathan used to call the writerly equivalent of foreplay—and really getting to know her.

Is that what he's thrilled by? the voice of her disillusioned, dream-killing husband asks. *Or are you being obtuse? I mean, clearly he's too good to be true. I should know. On top of that, you're not a drinker. Not since your diagnosis.*

One glass of wine won't kill me, she thinks, then shakes her head to quiet the voice—not Jonathan's but her own—that reminds her: *it might.* To Emmit, she says, "Sure. Maybe a pinot noir?"

Emmit chooses one, hands the waitress the wine list, and takes a sip of water from the glass the bus girl has just filled. "I have to admit," he says when the waitress has walked away. "My brain is reeling." He checks his watch. "My flight for Baltimore would have taken off in the last twenty minutes."

Saoirse nods. "I'm right there with you in the 'reeling brain' department."

From across the table, Emmit stares into her eyes, and Saoirse is transported back to the Athenæum, when his penetrating gaze froze her at the top of the stairs like a rabbit in the headlights of a careening semi. She swallows. "It's nice, though," she says.

Are you sure about that? Jonathan asks.

"Really nice," she adds emphatically, hoping to shut her dead husband up.

The waitress appears with the wine, and Emmit gestures to Saoirse's glass, where the woman pours several ounces of deep-red liquid. Saoirse lifts the glass to her lips, feeling self-conscious. Jonathan had always been the one who determined what and when they would drink. "It's great," she says quickly. The waitress fills their glasses. When they're alone again, Saoirse wraps her fingers around the stem but doesn't move to take another sip. Emmit lifts his glass and angles it toward her.

"Cheers to meeting someone where they're at," he says. "No preconceived notions of significance or hidden meaning. No baggage or expectations."

"To meeting someone where they're at," Saoirse echoes and takes a long, luxuriant pull from her glass, reveling in the tart warmth as it coats her throat and spreads across her insides. It's been so long since she's allowed herself this small indulgence.

When she places the glass back on the table, Emmit is staring again. His lips are wet from the wine, and his dark hair hangs over his forehead on one side. He would look so much like Jonathan it would be frightening if not for the interest, the excitement, in his eyes. For the second half of their ten-year marriage, Jonathan looked at Saoirse the way he would someone whose feelings he considered himself unobligated to consider. A maid, or a therapist. Or maybe some sort of kitchen appliance: a mere object that he used to go about his day.

"Do you know what you're going to order?" she asks, trying to lighten the mood.

Emmit leans across the table. "Who cares what we're getting to eat. I want to know what you're going to read up on that stage."

"That's easy," Saoirse laughs. "I'm not reading anything at all."

Emmit blinks and shakes his head, the left corner of his mouth lifting in that crooked smile she's coming to know well.

"What about you?" she asks pointedly. "You've been blocked too. Are you telling me you're going to go up there on a wing and a prayer and freestyle something new?"

Emmit leans forward farther, and she's treated to another flash of his endearingly crooked smile. She wishes the wine wasn't drawing attention to his perfectly smooth, perfectly full lips.

"Oh, no," he says matter-of-factly. "I'll just read a bit of Edgar Allan Poe."

Saoirse feels the color drain from her face. She never mentioned anything about Poe or Whitman to Emmit at the coffee shop. Not the house she's moved into or people's fascination with it; neither did she tell him about stumbling onto the Ath exhibit. But before she can say as much, the waitress is there, asking what they'd like to eat. Emmit nods for Saoirse to go first, and she mumbles out the name of a pasta dish with a side of broccoli rabe. Emmit orders chicken parmigiana.

When the waitress has left them, Saoirse leans into the table so hard, water sloshes over the lip of her glass. "Okay, what the hell is going on? Why did you say Edgar Allan Poe?"

Emmit scrunches his face, and she sees for the first time that there are dimples in his cheeks. There's also a small cleft in his chin that deepens when he's thinking . . . or confused, as he appears to be now.

"I know it's weird," he says. "An established writer reading someone else's work. We used to do it all the time at the one open mic in Woodsto—" He stops. "In college. Poe's my go-to for public readings when I don't have anything original prepared." Emmit pauses. "In fact," he adds, "Poe's sort of my go-to for any challenge in writing. I feel like following an author's recipe for success to a T—an author whose success has only grown with time—can only benefit a modern writer in establishing their own legacy." He pauses again, and she knows he's taking in her flushed skin, the way her hand is shaking ever so slightly as she reaches for her wine. "Is that okay?" he asks. "Have you been personally victimized by 'The Raven' or something? What's wrong?"

Saoirse gulps wine from her glass, medication be damned. The figures of Poe, Jonathan, and Emmit flash through her mind, the spectral wave ebbing and flowing over the course of the séance, covering her ceiling with disembodied features, writhing insects, flickering faces.

"It's just . . . I live in Sarah Helen Whitman's old house," she says. "And ever since I moved back to Providence, the number of Poe-themed coincidences I've experienced has been uncanny."

Emmit stares at her, mouth open. "You live at 88 Benefit Street? So, let me get this straight, you moved here from—" He stops. "Where did you move here from?"

"New Jersey."

"New Jersey, and you moved into what was originally 50 Benefit, then 76, when owned by Sarah's mother, Anna Power? *You live in Sarah Helen Whitman's house?* You've got to be kidding me."

Saoirse laughs a little bitterly, thinking of how this declaration elicited similar disbelief from Roberto, Lucretia, and Mia the night she moved in. "I live at 88 Benefit Street. It was the first fully furnished house that appealed to me when I did a search for rental properties in Providence last spring. If I had known living here would be so interesting to so many people, I would have hit the thumbs-down icon on the goddamn listing!"

Would she have, though? Sure, Poe and Whitman popping up everywhere is beyond strange, but if she hadn't moved into the old red house overlooking the graveyard, she wouldn't have met Roberto, Mia, or Lucretia. She wouldn't have adopted Pluto. And she wouldn't have been the recipient of the Brown career fair flyer that resulted in Emmit and her running into one another.

Saoirse sighs. "I guess I don't mean that. The house is gorgeous, and its historical significance is inspiring. It's just wild how Poe and Whitman are still so intriguing, one hundred and seventy-five years later."

Emmit lifts the bottle of wine. "Have you read Whitman's work?"

He refills his glass, then hers. Saoirse's too distracted by their conversation to stop him. She says, "I hadn't before a week or so ago. But once several, uh, fans, I guess you could call them, enlightened me as to where I was living, I did a deep dive into her poetry. She was incredibly talented. I love 'Summer's Call to the Little Orphan,' and the satirical verse she composed for a suffragist banquet, 'Woman's Sphere.'"

"I'm partial to the valentine she wrote for Poe in 1848, months before she met him, addressed in the character of his famous raven," Emmit says. He takes three long sips from his glass. They're going to need a second bottle before the food arrives.

You *can't have any more wine,* she chastises herself, *and Emmit has to drive back to Providence.* Already, her thinking is a little bouncy, as if each thought is a rock in a river, and she's jumping from one to the next to get across. Still . . . it's nice to let go a little, to not feel imprisoned by her demons, by her depression. She hasn't seen a single fly since before coming upon Emmit in the grocery store earlier that afternoon.

"Did you say *fans* clued you in as to where you are living?" Emmit asks, interrupting her reverie. "Let me guess, some kids came to your house after one of the Providence Ghost Tours, asking if they could see where the grand poetess once lived?"

"God, no," Saoirse exclaims, almost choking on her wine. "At least not yet. I didn't realize that was a thing that might happen." She shakes her head, takes another sip. "It was a trio of writers who . . ." She decides to tell him about Lucretia, Mia, and Roberto without admitting that they'd functioned as her unexpected welcoming committee. "Well, I guess before I moved in, they had a bit of a history accessing the house without a key. Some weird little trick paneling along the walkout basement. I still need to examine it myself. They stopped by my first night in the house, wanting to meet the new inhabitant. They're really nice."

"So nice that they've been breaking into your house?" Emmit asks with a smile she can't quite read.

Saoirse shrugs. "They're interested in Whitman as a historical figure. And yes, they are nice. A little weird, I suppose, but, hey, aren't all us writers?"

Emmit's mouth drops open in mock outrage, and she smacks his arm. "Anyway, Lucretia, Roberto, Mia, and I, we've become friends. They've been good for me, helping me get out of the house, commit to making plans, stuff like that."

Emmit frowns. "I didn't realize you were struggling with that sort of thing," he says quietly. "No judgment, of course. Believe me, I get it." He reaches for her hand, stroking it with his thumb, then releases her and clasps his hands together in his lap. "Just be careful, okay. Some writers are weirder than others. I'd hate to see you open up to these people only to find out they've been using you."

Saoirse wants to say that this isn't Lucretia, with her vegan, gluten-free cupcakes. Neither is it Roberto; though he'd teased her about cleaning the basement stairs, she remembers the genuine concern on his face, his comment that they had to get her back into writing to save her from her depression. Mia was touched when Saoirse agreed to adopt a cat from her favorite rescue, and Saoirse can tell there aren't too many people with whom Mia shares her time and ideas. Before she can challenge Emmit's warning, however, their waitress appears with their entrées.

The conversation is abandoned for cutlery and talk of how good the first bites are. So, Saoirse is surprised when, a few minutes later, Emmit reaches across the table and grabs her arm. "I just realized something. You moved into Sarah Whitman's house after a long bout of writer's block, and now you're not only writing again, but writing poetry? And fantastic poetry, at that?"

Saoirse swallows a bite of pasta, trying to ignore the similarities between what Emmit's said and Lucretia's words at the shelter earlier that morning. "Who says my poetry is fantastic?"

"I can tell from the earnestness with which you insist you don't want me to read it."

As if to punctuate this statement, a woman walks onto the stage. Saoirse looks around to see that every table in the lounge has filled while she and Emmit have been talking and drinking wine.

"Welcome," the woman says, "to the lounge at Buon Appetito and to our weekly open mic." The diners cheer politely, though there are a few whoops of more enthusiastic applause. "There's a sign-up sheet at the hostess station," the woman continues, "but we usually operate on a 'jump up and go for it' kind of policy."

Emmit nudges her foot under the table. "Since I'm not reading my own work, I'll queue things up for you."

"No, you won't," Saoirse warns.

He smiles, and that smile stays with her as he makes his way to the stage.

She wants to shout after him, *I'll pour my poems into your ears if you want to hear them,* and is immediately shocked by the intensity of this compulsion. Still, the image of it fills her with excitement, giving Emmit Powell all her words, tracing them onto his skin with her tongue.

As if to highlight her descent into madness, Jonathan chimes in from the depths of her skull:

You've lost it. The Saoirse of just two days ago would hate you for falling for another man, for any man, so fast.

She doesn't bother replying. It feels too good to embrace the rush of dopamine, the high of surging norepinephrine. It's too tempting to believe that, this time, she's in the right fairy tale. Not one where she's at the mercy of her opportunistic father or locked in a tower by her ogreish husband. Saoirse catches their waitress's eye and lifts their empty bottle of wine. *Yes,* she says with a nod of her head, *we would like another.*

"Don't judge me," she whisper-hisses at Jonathan. Mercifully, he stays silent.

Emmit joins the woman onstage and takes the microphone. "Thank you." Though he seems to address the crowd, he stares directly at Saoirse. "I'm Emmit Powell, writer-in-residence at Johns Hopkins and a creative writing professor at Brown University. My novel, *Vulture*

Eyes, won the Pulitzer Prize for fiction a few years back. Despite these perceived accolades—and while I'd love the opportunity to regale you all with a little Edgar Allan Poe while you dine—I'm here to introduce"—he gestures in her direction—"Miss Saoirse White."

A chorus of *Nos!* and *What the hells?* sound in Saoirse's head. Despite his grandstanding, she hadn't thought he was going to do it. Hadn't *wanted* him to do it. But the only thing worse than reading would be to get onstage and not have anything to read, so she fumbles for her cell phone—amazing how much a few glasses of wine after not drinking for so long have affected her—opens her photos app, and navigates to one of the poems she wrote last night.

"Saoirse's poetry is both moving and disarmingly candid. I know you'll enjoy listening to her tonight."

The expression on his face is one she's never seen before: pride and lust, like some mix of a literary colleague and the stranger from the top floor of the Athenæum . . . a stranger who's becoming less and less unknown to her at every turn. Clearly, he's just being nice, since he doesn't know the first thing about her poetry. Nice and *wildly* presumptuous. Though, despite her anger, doesn't something else flutter inside her? Excitement? Self-respect at her newfound prowess and prolificacy? More of a thrill at being alive than she's experienced in years?

There's no time for further contemplation, however, because Emmit is gesturing for her to join him.

"Please help me welcome her to the stage."

Chapter 17

Saoirse steps in front of the audience with a mixture of resigned control and little-girl fear. She takes the microphone from Emmit, manages a weak smile at the crowd, and tests the mic: "My name is Saoirse White. I used to write cozy mystery novels, but I've recently become something of a poet."

Emmit, who's made his way back to their table, whistles and claps his hands. Saoirse unlocks her phone and zooms in on the image of her notebook, the lines marred with smears of ink and a few—but not many—cross-outs.

"I'll get right to it." She clears her throat, willing herself to exude more confidence than she feels. "This is called 'The Weight of Birds.'" From her position on the stage, she can see the waitress approaching Emmit, but the woman fails to gain his attention and leaves the wine on the table without having him taste it. It's the intensity with which Emmit stares at her, waiting, that gives Saoirse the strength to begin.

She reads the first stanza with slight hesitation, but by the time she starts the second, her voice has taken on the quality of a professional, Sarah Whitman onstage at the suffragist banquet, reshaping judgments with each provocative metaphor and slick rhetorical question:

"What to do with a cracked egg
when it is empty?
Where to put the pieces of the shells that once held

the thing you swore you'd treasure most in this world
but which now contains nothing but disappointment
and regret,
an empty repository to hold
tears that shoot from your eyes like filoplumes,
pain like talons clipped too far into the quick,
and the blood your heart still pumps,
having no one to tell it
that the ghosts of birds do not bleed?"

By the poem's closing lines, after Saoirse has recalled the pain she felt not when writing the words but during the events that inspired the words in the first place—"Weight is the endless night. / A night where birdsong is lost / to sleeping throats / and children are lost / to angry husbands, / whose words become speech bubbles / out of which whole flocks / spring forth."—she feels she could take flight herself. She reads the final stanza in a voice both as plaintive as the purr of a starling and as sharp as a vulture's beak:

"If a whip-poor-will calls out
in an empty forest,
does its trill fill the bellies
of every woman who wished to
feed off the expectations of others?
Or does the sound merely disappear?
If I call out
in an empty marriage
does my cry calcify
and deposit itself onto the outermost membrane,
an eggshell stronger than steel to those
screaming for life from outside it
but liable to break from the inside

by a breath so silenced
it's rendered as light as a feather?"

Saoirse thinks the crowd cheers, but she sees only Emmit.

Brava, he mouths at her.

She's walking to him, winding through the high tops. When she reaches their table, he stands and pulls her to him. He is kissing her before she can think, before she can say anything, before she can react. She is stunned, and then she is kissing him back.

The room falls away. The applause is superfluous. The world, as she knows it, disappears.

∞

The door to the hotel room smashes against the wall as their bodies knock against it. They kiss, Saoirse grabbing the sides of Emmit's face, feeling the smoothness of his cheeks, holding him, pulling herself against him. His hands are in her hair, on her neck, his fingers brushing against her skin, soft wisps of his hair tickling her forehead. Then the door slams shut, and they are ensconced behind the walls of this room on the top floor of a Hilton, or perhaps it's a Marriott; she's already forgotten which chain occupied the lot closest to the restaurant when they stumbled out of it, giggling like teenagers, drunk and railing against the weather.

Emmit has thrown his coat to the floor and is ripping off hers. She is pushed up against some low and inconveniently placed piece of furniture. He grabs her face again, and she is breathing hard through the kissing, letting out little gasps of pleasure. A mirror behind her slides noisily on its hook as her back knocks up against it.

He pulls away, stares into her eyes. She runs a hand over his cheek, feels the dampness there, wants to lick the remnants of rain off him with her tongue. "What?" she whispers, when he continues to stare.

A flash of the crooked smile. He's unsure of himself, which makes him even more attractive. "No, it's just . . . maybe it's too much. Too fast."

"Oh, wow," she says, and her hand drops from his face to his shoulder then trails heavily down his chest. "I didn't think that was something guys typically said." She steps away from him, toward the door. "Do you want me to run downstairs, get us some more wine?" She's not sure why she says this. Emmit seems merely to be making sure she's okay with what's happening, not wishing he had another drink. The last thing she wants is to leave this room, to be anywhere but with him. She wants more of him. More. And more. And more. Still, she feels an overwhelming need to relieve his anxiety, perhaps to assuage her own.

She turns back and gestures to where shadows still darken the room. "Or, maybe there's a minibar?"

The nervous smile again. A breath of disbelieving laughter. He steps deeper into the room, into the shadows, then turns and sinks down onto the bed. He looks at her in a way that is carnal and sweet and pleading. "No," he says, chest rising. Falling. Saoirse swears she can hear his heart beating. "Just you. I just want you."

She can't think. Cannot breathe for the pure longing for him. She sucks in a hot, desperate breath and goes to him. He stands before she can fall onto him, scoops her up and turns, lowering her onto the bed.

His kisses are like a rush of air after being suffocated. Relief. Release from everything that's been in her head for nine months. For nine years. She's taking her clothes off, helping him with his. He keeps flashing her that irresistible half smile, as if it's a nervous tic. It makes her want to sit back and study him, memorize his every mannerism, if only this wasn't at odds with her physical need to be against him, part of him, as close to him as humanly possible.

They melt into one another. Her hands are in his hair, and it is soft, so much softer than she would have imagined. Everything about him is unexpected and wonderful and warm, and that's before his kisses travel elsewhere on her body, and the strange, warm glow from some building across the street streaming in through the window lights his face as if he were an actor in a movie, highlighting his perfect skin and his perfect lips and his perfect hair. The moments stretch, and the night takes on the quality of a dream, but it's so much better than a dream because it's shared, he is in the dream with her, experiencing the same nighttime logic, floating in this bubble of wine and lust and warmth and . . . something. Something more. She can't, won't, put her finger on it, but it's close to perfection. As close as she's ever been. It's a dream within a dream, a dream in the poetic sense of the word. Magic. Euphoria. Transcendence.

She gives in to the bliss. Again.

And again.

And again.

Chapter 18

When Saoirse wakes, she is unsure of where she is until she sees Emmit's serene, sleeping face on the pillow beside her, realizes the artificial light from across the street has been replaced by sunlight. She has a moment of panic; everything is too bright, too stark, and she's painfully thirsty. After a stumbling lunge to draw the curtains, and a shaky trip to the bathroom for a glass of water, she returns to the bed, though the panic refuses to dissipate. When he wakes, will the dream of the night before be ruined? Will he be regretful? Was she a conquest, now complete? Or worse yet, a mistake to be forgotten?

Emmit stirs and opens his eyes. He appears to experience none of the disorientation or fear she did upon waking. Rather, his gaze jumps from the empty pillow next to him to where Saoirse sits at the edge of the bed and, once he's found her, he smiles contentedly.

"Hi," he says.

"Hi."

He reaches for her, pulls her into him, and she falls into the cocoon of his arms. She refrains from asking him if he wants coffee, asking him how soon he needs to leave to rebook his flight to Baltimore. If this is the last time she will lie with him, she wants to enjoy it.

But then he is kissing her neck, his arms slipping down her body, and they are tangled up in a re-creation of the night before. It no longer seems like morning, but rather as if the night has reclaimed them: the clock has stopped ticking, and the patterns of light on the floor do not move because the sun never changes position in the sky.

When they are done, he leans over her, smooths her hair away from her face. "Should I go out to get us some tea?" he asks.

She props herself up against the pillows. "Don't you have to make arrangements to get back to Baltimore?"

He sits up as well and pulls her closer. "I haven't missed a day of work at Johns Hopkins since I started teaching there." He fake-coughs into his hand. "But after three long years, I think COVID finally caught up with me." He smiles and winks at her. "I'll call the department head later today and tell him."

She studies his face, not sure if he's serious, too afraid to get her hopes up if he isn't. "Can you do that?"

He laughs. "Of course I can do that. But more importantly, I want to do that." He kisses her hard. "What were you planning on getting up to today, Miss White?"

What *had* she planned to do today? She has no idea. She can't really remember anything before the moment, after she read her poem, when Emmit pulled her into his arms and kissed her. Laundry was likely on the agenda, as was another session of job hunting. How exciting.

I was going to spend time with Pluto, she thinks guiltily, relieved she'd had the wherewithal to text Lucretia when they'd left the restaurant and ask if she minded spending the night at her house—after shooting out an *I'm fine, love you,* in response to her mother's string of messages checking in on her. Lucretia had texted back that it wasn't a problem, and she would head to Saoirse's place right away, but Saoirse dreads having to come clean about what her "emergency" had really been. She still can't believe she allowed herself to get so drunk.

"Nothing in particular," Saoirse says to Emmit, because he's waiting for her answer. "I should get home soon, though. I told you I adopted a cat, remember?"

"Of course I remember. And I totally understand." He rubs his chin. "I mean . . . ," he starts but trails off.

"What?"

"I don't want to impose or be like the people you mentioned last night, staking out your famous house, but if you did want to spend time together today, I'd be happy to come to your place. You know, make sure Pluto's okay."

Saoirse raises an eyebrow. "You're worried about Pluto."

"Of course," he says. "This has nothing to do with wanting to spend as much time with you as possible. I want to ensure Pluto is settling in, that he knows you haven't abandoned him. It's not that I want to follow you to your place of residence. Where you live. Where your bedroom—and, it stands to reason, your bed—is."

He buries his face in her chest, and she laughs, then lifts his chin. "I am on board with the idea of you coming back to the house with me. Oh, and with tea," she adds. She's not sure it's the best idea after last night, but it might seem weird if she turned him down, and she doesn't want to get into why she shouldn't have caffeine after so much alcohol. Plus, she *is* hungover. Once she gets home, it'll be nothing but lots of water and low-sodium food. And her medication, of course. She *must* stay consistent with that.

Emmit lets out a delighted whoop before kissing her, then disentangles himself from the sheets. He motions for her to follow him to the bathroom, where he starts the shower. The water clears some of the fuzziness from her head, and she stays in even after Emmit steps out from under the steaming spray. When she finally emerges from the bathroom, there are two to-go cups on the dresser.

"I got you a chai with oat milk," he says. "I didn't know if I could assume your caffeine habits from a single order at Carr Haus, but I took a chance."

"You assumed correctly," she says and takes a small sip. "Thank you." She finishes dressing, surprised it's not more awkward than it is to be naked in front of him. For a moment, as they're leaving the hotel room, Saoirse feels like she's leaving a little piece of herself behind. Then Emmit takes her hand, and the feeling clears like dandelion seeds in a gale. By the time they're on their way back to the city, Saoirse realizes that the lightness she feels when she's with Emmit is familiar. It's the way she used to feel all the time. Before the depression. Before Jonathan. Or, at least, not since the very beginning with Jonathan.

When she's with Emmit, she feels like herself.

Chapter 19

It's disorienting to arrive at 88 Benefit Street so quickly after leaving the restaurant parking lot. Saoirse feels as if they spent the night on a space station or an island—or at least in some distant part of the state—not fifteen minutes from her house. She unlocks the front door and leads Emmit through the foyer to the kitchen. There's a note on the table, and for a second, Saoirse feels a sharp, irrational burst of fear—*Aidan broke in! Aidan found me!*—before she remembers Lucretia spent the night:

I slept in the guest room . . . threw the sheets in the wash but didn't run it. I'll be home today . . . call me when you're back. I hope everything's okay!!!!!!!!!!!!

Pluto was an angel. I gave him his insulin this morning . . . glad I stuck around for the demonstration at the shelter! -Lu

Guilt shoots through Saoirse as she bends to pet Pluto, who is weaving around her ankles, though he seems none the worse for having spent the first night in his new home without her. She straightens—vowing to do better by her new housemate—slips the note into a drawer, and turns to find Emmit examining the woodwork around the kitchen doorframe.

"I can't believe it," he says.

"Can't believe what?"

"That Edgar Allan Poe spent time in this house. That Sarah Whitman lived here. You can feel it, can't you?" He closes his eyes. "Like, an aura. Something of historical significance happened here."

Saoirse continues staring at him another moment, then closes her eyes as well. Does she feel something? It's hard to tell; she's still getting used to feeling anything at all. She hears Emmit walk out of the kitchen and cross the hallway, and she opens her eyes to follow him. He has one hand on the rail above the three short steps to the walkout and is preparing to start down.

"No!" Saoirse says, and he pulls his hand back, surprised. "Sorry," Saoirse says. "It's just, it's a mess down there. Mostly stuff that belongs to the landlord."

She feels guilty for lying, but she can't remember if she pulled the rug over the trapdoor, and she doesn't want Emmit to find the basement. She's not ready to explain the black-clothed table and pillar candles, the belief—Mia, Roberto, and Lucretia's, but isn't her own now too?—that they commune with Sarah Whitman via a weekly séance. She'd like to have spent more than a single night with him before she admits she may owe her newfound poetic abilities, in part, to Emmit's own face, along with the faces of Poe and Saoirse's dead husband, projected onto her basement ceiling, during some sort of magic tea–induced hallucination.

"Sorry," she says again. "Let me show you the rest of the house."

Emmit fawns over the antique furniture and gothic atmosphere, and spends an inordinate amount of time analyzing the living room fireplace brickwork. She ends the tour at the door of her bedroom. "I'm going to put on fresh clothes," she says. Then adds, "You can come in if you'd like." She changes in the walk-in closet, and when she emerges, Emmit is on the balcony, looking down onto Saint John's Cathedral. She slides open the door and joins him on the small platform.

"I never knew how well you could see the cemetery from the third floor of the house," he says, more to himself than to her.

"At first, I thought it might be creepy, living so close to a graveyard," Saoirse says. "I mean, this house is practically on top of it. But

the more time I spend out here, the more peaceful I find it. It's like—"
She stops, embarrassed. Emmit turns to her.

"Like what?"

"It's stupid, but sometimes when I sit here, I feel like it's the mid-1800s. Like by viewing the world from this balcony, I've opened some portal to the past. The feeling has gone so far as to prompt me to go inside, walk downstairs, and cut across the yard to the cemetery. I'm always surprised—and a little disappointed—when I see the lichen covering the tombstones and cracks in the granite, the carvings all but worn away."

"How exquisite would that be," Emmit says, "to time travel with so little fanfare? It feels greedy, thinking that way, since we have the luxury of so many wonderful words from that period. We can time travel with all the ease of picking up a collection of Poe's stories or Whitman's poems. If anything, it's the way their words bring us back so effortlessly that makes me feel we deserve more." He takes her hand, brings it to his lips, and kisses each of her fingers, then turns and stares down at the cemetery again.

"When was the last time you tried it?" he asks.

"I'm sorry?"

"When was the last time you walked down to the graveyard, hoping to end up in 1848?"

"Oh," she laughs. "I don't know. A couple of days ago, maybe."

"Should we try it now? Regardless of what century we arrive in, I'd love to see some of the markers up close. I know this isn't the graveyard that featured so heavily in Poe and Whitman's romance. But I also know Poe first saw Whitman here, tending her rose garden, and the fact that I'm staring at that very rose garden right now makes the Goth English major still residing inside me a little giddy."

Saoirse shrugs. "Okay. Let's go." Then, unable to ignore her curiosity, she adds, "A *graveyard* featured heavily in Poe and Whitman's romance?" She must have missed this in her research.

"Swan Point. They strolled among the graves together during their courtship. Many believe it was in that cemetery where Poe proposed to Whitman. She talks about the proposal in one of her sonnets, and it's obvious she's describing Swan Point."

They descend through the house, Saoirse deliberately exiting from the front door and walking around to avoid the walkout. Saint John's Cathedral looms over them on their left. With regard to her comment about traveling to the past, Saoirse feels less foolish with every step. It does feel like leaving the normal world behind when she ducks under the low-hanging branches of a massive elm or steps onto the cracked marker of a weaving stone path. The air feels different in the forgotten graveyard. Still, but expectant. Surrounded by dwellings, buildings, churches, yet an island unto itself.

Emmit walks through the rows of markers with quiet reverence. Saoirse kneels beside an ogee headstone she hadn't noticed on any of her previous excursions. After brushing away a bit of dirt, she can read the inscription:

In Memory of Henrietta
Daughter of Samuel & Rofebellah Chace
Died Oct. 27, 1773, Aged 1 Day

There are more words at the bottom of the stone, but they are impossible to make out. Saoirse stands, not wanting to think about Jonathan, but she can't help but ponder what words they might have put on their child's headstone had she given him what he'd wanted.

Or what words might have ended up on hers.

She is pulled from her morbid thoughts by Emmit's hand on her arm. "You feel it, too, don't you?"

She knows what he means, but she wants to hear him say it.

"There's a vastness to this place that extends far beyond the perimeter of the actual graveyard. It's like we're standing on something undiscovered. Something that, if we could see it, would shock us far more than the bones and hair and teeth of the bodies buried here, far more than scraps of muslin fabric and dirt-encrusted diamonds."

This is more than Emmit agreeing that being in this cemetery feels like going back in time. His words feel hyperbolic; she's not sure she can get behind the idea that they're standing on anything other than one of countless small, private graveyards scattered across America. Still, he's so earnest, she can't help but nod. They walk toward her yard, Emmit lost in thought, half smiling as his eyes linger on each moss-covered marker.

Back in the small patch of grass behind the house, Emmit inspects the winterberry and echinacea stalks before moving to the storied rosebushes.

"How green of a thumb do you have?" he asks.

Saoirse winces. "My gardening skills start and end with houseplants."

"These rosebushes don't need much. Just a little pruning before winter so they're in the best possible shape come spring." He smiles. "I could help you if you'd like. My mother was an avid gardener."

Saoirse starts to open her mouth, but Emmit blushes. "Not that she ever got to teach me, of course. But my uncle always said she loved her gardens. As a teen, when I was going through a bit of a 'phase,' as my uncle called it, I grew plants to feel closer to her." He smirks. "Sometimes they were even the ones you gazed upon instead of the ones you rolled up and smoked."

He drops to his knees and brushes at the soil along the base of one of the thorny bushes. "It's a little late in the fall to fertilize. They'd use that energy to struggle against the first frost of the year, which could be any day now."

"Don't worry," Saoirse says. "I didn't move here from Jersey with bags of fertilizer in tow." Hadn't Emmit hinted at wanting to come here for a very specific purpose? Not that she isn't enjoying their time *out* of the bedroom, but she's not sure how—or why—the focus has turned to gardening. Emmit must realize, too, that he's lost her a little. He drops his gaze and shakes his head, hands still in the dirt.

"Sorry. I guess I'm more like those Whitman groupies you told me about than I care to admit. It's just—" He stops, frowns, and looks down. He moves his fingers back and forth as if he's lost something, then digs his hand deeper and scoops up a handful of loamy soil. He sifts it, purses his lips, and digs deeper.

"What are you—" Saoirse starts, but something falls to the ground with the next handful of soil Emmit sifts. He grabs it, brushes the object off, and brings it up to his face for closer inspection.

"I can't believe it." His voice is breathless, incredulous. He climbs to his feet. "I felt something in the dirt, and this was it! I can't believe . . ." He trails off, digs in his pocket for his phone, and jabs away at the screen for several seconds. Whatever he's found is pressed into the palm of his right hand. "Holy shit," he says a moment later. "Come here. I can't believe it. You *have* to see this."

She walks to him, but he holds out his phone rather than the mystery object. "Read this," he says. "And tell me if I'm completely out there." He points to a paragraph halfway down the page. It's a Wikipedia entry. Sarah Helen Whitman's Wikipedia entry.

Saoirse gives him a curious look but takes the phone.

> Whitman was friends with Margaret Fuller and other intellectuals in New England. She became interested in transcendentalism through this social group and after hearing Ralph Waldo Emerson lecture in Boston, Massachusetts and in Providence. She also became interested in science, mesmerism, and the occult. She had a penchant for wearing black and a coffin-shaped charm around her neck and may have practiced séances in her home on Sundays, attempting to communicate with the dead.

"I've read this before," she says when she's finished. "A few days after I discovered where I was living."

"You read the part about the charm she wore?" Emmit asks.

"Yes."

Emmit opens his right hand. In it lies a charm the size of a grass-hopper. It is dirt-caked but intact, its shape unmistakable. It is a tiny coffin, carved from some sort of dark metal. Tin, maybe, or iron.

"You found that?" Saoirse asks, now sounding as incredulous as Emmit. "Under the rosebushes? In my backyard?"

"Yes," Emmit breathes out, then laughs. "Under the rosebushes. In your backyard!"

"I don't believe it."

"I know! It's absolutely amazing."

Saoirse makes a face. "No, I mean, I really don't believe it. It couldn't be hers. Not after a hundred and seventy-five years. That Wikipedia article is public knowledge. Someone probably came here wearing that necklace as part of some ridiculous cosplay, and it fell off their neck. Somewhere online exists a collection of photographs in which two weirdos reenact the night Poe first saw Whitman. I bet there's a lot of dramatic swooning involved, and no small amount of cleavage."

Saoirse thinks she's speaking reason and so is surprised by how crest-fallen Emmit appears. "No way," he says. "Though, I won't deny that many a cosplay of that nature has probably taken place. Can I bring this to someone, my contact in the historical society, for their appraisal?"

Saoirse shrugs. "Sure. Of course. Let me know if you find out anything."

Emmit pulls his wallet from his pocket and places the charm in a zippered compartment. Then, without warning, he takes her head in his hands and kisses her deeply. When he pulls away, Saoirse's heart is pounding so wildly, she can feel it in her throat.

Emmit smiles at her, the nervous half smile that allows her to glimpse the mischievous boy he might have been. "Now, should we go inside and get to what we came here for?" he asks.

Chapter 20

Night is creeping against the windows when Saoirse wakes from a dreamless sleep. Emmit had left just before she'd succumbed to a nap—after spending the rest of the morning and all of the afternoon together in bed—with a promise he'd call her that evening. She raises her arms toward the ceiling and rolls her neck against the pillow, but freezes when the door to her bedroom opens with a squeak of hinges.

"Emmit?" It *must* be Emmit. She won't let herself entertain the idea that it could be Aidan. Though, did Emmit lock the door when he left? Had she instructed him to? *Stupid!* She can't get so distracted by this relationship that she forgets about Aidan and his resolve to find her.

Pluto noses the door all the way open and strides in, looking happier to see her than she deserves, and Saoirse breathes a sigh of relief. She hasn't paid the cat nearly as much attention as she'd planned to only that morning.

"Come," she says and pats the bed. Pluto jumps up, plops beside her, and purrs as she scratches his twitching ears. "Tonight, we will work on getting to know one another better. This bed has your name all over it. As does the armchair in the office. And the couch downstairs."

Pluto purrs more deeply and shuts his eyes. Still scratching him with one hand, Saoirse reaches for her phone. There are five unread messages, all from Lucretia:

Heeeey.

Where you at?

Helloooo . . . sorry to be a pain, but I'm dying to hear what went on yesterday.

You better be dead and writing poetry with Sarah for how long it's been without answering me.

IF YOU'RE NOT DEAD I'M GOING TO KILL YOU MYSELF.

Saoirse thumbs the cursor into place at the bottom of the screen and quickly taps out a message:

I'm SO sorry. I owe you an explanation, to be certain. I'm not too keen on leaving Pluto alone again . . . want to come over and I'll tell you everything?

The response comes a moment later:

Sure. But I'm with Roberto and Mia. Lol. Can they come too?

Saoirse is surprised by the lack of aversion she feels at the thought of having additional company. She must be less depressed than usual, to be fine with more than one human encounter in a single day. *Or wanting to distract myself from whether Emmit will call.*
She writes:

Are you hungry? There's a Thai place down the road I've been meaning to try. We can order take-out.

Lucretia responds:

Sounds great! See you in twenty.

Saoirse stands and checks herself in the mirror. She looks like she spent the day in bed. She looks hungover. She chugs a glass of water and forces herself into the shower. By the time she dresses and walks downstairs, she feels better. She scrolls through the Thai menu online but can't focus. She's too busy wondering how she's going to tell her friends she spent the night—and the entire next day—with Emmit Powell.

Her phone buzzes, and she checks it, thinking it will be Lucretia telling her they're here, until she remembers Lucretia doesn't carry her phone with her. Emmit's name, which he saved in her phone before leaving, parades across the screen.

A flutter of excitement turns her hands shaky. *I cannot let myself get this flustered over a man I just met.* The counterthought comes instantly: *I'm allowed to. I deserve to have a little fun, to have a man fawn over me. No, to have a man treat me like an equal.*

And that was it, when it came right down to it. Over the entirety of the twenty-four hours she and Emmit spent together, it wasn't the lust with which he kissed her, the way he stared into her eyes, or the way he moaned her name in bed. It was that he listened. Cared about her ideas. Felt she had something worthwhile to write about. To say. For all his remarkable insight and brilliance, he felt her ideas were as worthwhile as his own.

And not subject to erasure as their connection to one another deepened.

The phone is still ringing, and she swipes to answer it, eyeing the door as if her friends might come bursting through without knocking.

"Hi."

"Hi there," Emmit says, and the sound of his voice is both familiar and surprising in a way that makes her body ache. "What are you doing?"

"I'm—" she pauses. *Thinking about you?* She can't say that. "Just trying to decide what to have for dinner."

"I could help with that decision," he says, "if you wanted some company."

A bolt of longing crackles through her. "That sounds amazing," she says. "And I would have loved to see you, but I already have company. Or I'm about to."

There's a moment of silence. Emmit says quietly, "Oh. I'm sorry. I didn't realize." Is there disappointment in his voice? Or something more? It can't be jealousy. Can it?

"It's those friends I was telling you about. Roberto, Lucretia, and Mia. We're getting Thai food and hanging out."

"Could you cancel?"

Saoirse hesitates. "I really can't. Plus, only Lucretia and Robert have cell phones, and they don't even carry them."

"Of course, no worries." His tone is understanding. She's obviously imagined whatever negative emotion she thought she detected. "Thai food sounds fun."

"I'd invite you to come by, but . . ." Saoirse trails off, checking the door again. "I mean . . . I don't know." She laughs lightly, hoping he understands what she's getting at: they had sex for the first time last night . . . it's a little too soon to introduce him to her friends. "It might be kind of weird," she adds, in case he still doesn't get it.

"Of course." He laughs too. "Absolutely. Totally weird. Well, have fun."

"Yeah. Thanks. And Emmit?"

"Yes, Saoirse?"

"I had a really great time with you today. And last night. I certainly don't want you to get in trouble with work or anything, but I'm glad you didn't fly to Baltimore." She pauses. "You didn't get in trouble, did you?"

"Oh, god no. They said take all the time I need to get better."

"From COVID," Saoirse clarifies.

"From COVID." Emmit chuckles. "I couldn't exactly tell them what I was really stricken with, now could I?"

"And what's that?"

"I think you know."

They are both quiet for several seconds. Saoirse has to work to make sure her heavy breathing doesn't get picked up by the phone's speaker.

"I'm in Providence for the rest of the week now," Emmit says. "Can I see you again?"

Yes! Right now! Just let me send Lucretia, Roberto, and Mia away. Or, at the very least, let me see you as soon as they leave! "Maybe Wednesday," she says, going for breezy and noncommittal.

"How about tomorrow?" Emmit counters.

"Oh." She pretends to think it over. "Okay. I can make tomorrow work."

"What would you like to do?"

Saoirse hears footsteps on the stoop. A knock comes a moment later. "Shit."

"Everything okay?"

"No. I mean, yes, but my friends just showed up."

"I see. Well, how about you think on it. Whatever you want to do, we'll do. I'll pick you up at ten."

"In the morning?"

"Is that all right?"

"So, a day date?"

"I was thinking a *whole*-day date. We'll do something fun and Providencey, then get dinner in Federal Hill."

The knocking on the door becomes a bang. "Saoirse! Hellooooo!" Lucretia singsongs from the stoop.

She covers the speaker and calls, "One second." Then, to Emmit: "That sounds wonderful."

"See you soon, then. Goodbye, Saoirse."

"Goodbye, Emmit." Saoirse ends the call.

When she opens the door, Roberto and Lucretia are crowded on the top step, Mia a few paces behind them. Saoirse stares at the place where there should be a pumpkin and laughs.

Roberto arches an eyebrow. "What's so funny?"

"Nothing. Come in." Roberto and Lucretia give her a simultaneous half hug, then march inside.

Mia comes quietly up the stairs and fixes Saoirse with a thoughtful smile. "How are you?"

"I'm fine," Saoirse replies. "So is Pluto. I'm glad you're getting to meet him."

Mia crosses the threshold. Saoirse shuts the door behind her.

Lucretia and Roberto have already dropped their coats on the foyer settee and gone to the living room, where Pluto is lounging before the fireplace.

"He's even cuter than I remember," Roberto says, petting the cat's ears flat against his head. "And I remember him being pretty goddamn cute."

"He's so chill," Saoirse says. "He acts like he's lived here forever."

Mia studies Saoirse. "Lucretia mentioned you were called away last night. I guess it's a good thing Pluto *is* so easygoing, since Lu had to give him his insulin."

Mia doesn't look angry or annoyed, just curious. Likely she's getting right to the point rather than being critical, as Saoirse finds more and more that Mia seems inclined to do.

"How about we call in the food, and I'll tell you everything?"

There are murmurs of agreement. It takes less than five minutes to finalize the order and make the call. When Saoirse sits in one of the chairs by the fireplace, three pairs of eyes land on her from the settee behind the coffee table.

"Ready when you are," Roberto says.

Why does it feel like, in the short time she's known them, she's been in the hot seat more than once, called upon to explain what she's seen or felt or what she's been doing? Though, that's not entirely fair. Their first interaction was practically an interrogation, with Saoirse playing the part of disgruntled detective. She shifts in her chair, then opens her mouth to tell her story.

She's surprised by how few interruptions there are. Only once does Lucretia elicit a smack from Roberto to quell her excited squealing. Throughout Saoirse's monologue, Mia sits very still, betraying no emotion. When Saoirse's finished, she stares at the trio anxiously. "And, um, he called right before you guys got here to make plans for tomorrow," she adds. "So, there's that."

Roberto speaks first. "So, what you're saying is, you owe your new-found happiness to me for insisting you give Emmit Powell a chance."

It's Lucretia's turn to sock him. "That wasn't *your* advice! It was both of ours! And it's not like she took it, anyway. She ran into him unexpectedly. The universe intervened and made it happen."

"Saoirse could have turned her back on the universe's plan for a third time, waited for Emmit to leave the grocery store, and walked home with her pumpkin," Roberto says.

"Oooh, I can't believe it," Lucretia squeals, ignoring Roberto. "I can't believe that not only has your experience with Sarah at the séance gotten you writing again, but now you're having your very own Poe-Whitmanian whirlwind romance!"

Saoirse's mouth drops open. "My very own what?"

Before Lucretia can respond, Roberto chimes in. "I hate to agree with her, but Lu's right. I mean, you checked out a book of Poe's letters to Whitman, right? You must have read about the longing, the passion, the depth of his love for her, practically overnight."

"Just because I started seeing someone who happens to be a writer after moving into Sarah Whitman's house doesn't mean—"

"And writing poetry," Lucretia breaks in. "You're seeing someone who happens to be a writer after moving into Sarah Whitman's house *and writing poetry.*" Lucretia looks at Mia excitedly. "There's definitely some sort of echo going on. Right, Mia?"

"A residual haunting," Mia says from the arm of the settee, at the exact moment Saoirse thinks it herself. "The Stone Tape Theory."

Lucretia sucks in a breath.

"Oh my gosh," Roberto says. "That's exactly what this is."

"What the hell is the Stone Tape Theory?" Saoirse asks.

Mia tucks a strand of hair behind one ear. Her part is as knife-sharp and perfect as always. She wears no makeup but for a hot-pink shade of lipstick that turns her unblemished face paler than Lucretia's. "The Stone Tape Theory is the speculation that ghosts and hauntings are analogous to tape recordings, and that mental impressions during emotional events can be projected in the form of energy, 'recorded' onto rocks or other items, and 'replayed' under certain conditions."

Roberto is nodding. "The idea was inspired by the views of nineteenth-century intellectualists and psychic researchers, like Eleanor Sidgwick and Edmund Gurney," he says. "But it really entered the public consciousness after the BBC aired a ghost story one Christmas in—I think it was 1972—called, fittingly, 'The Stone Tape.' I've heard it before, and it's pretty creepy."

Saoirse stares back and forth between Roberto and Mia, equal parts disbelieving and transfixed.

"Sersh," Lucretia says, "is it okay if I tell them what we talked about at the coffee shop? I haven't said anything yet, because I wasn't sure if you wanted me to share it."

"If she didn't want you to share it, putting her on the spot isn't the best way to get an honest response," Roberto needles. Lucretia shoots him a dirty look, but Saoirse is already nodding, and the creases of worry disappear from Roberto's forehead.

"Saoirse's husband passed away nine months ago," Lucretia says, "from a heart attack."

"Oh my god," Roberto says. "I'm so sorry."

"I am too," Mia says, so quietly Saoirse almost doesn't hear her.

Saoirse nods once in acknowledgment, and Lucretia continues. "So, her husband passes away, and she moves into Sarah's house. Sarah was married prior to meeting Edgar Allan Poe, too, to John Winslow Whitman. John died in 1833; he and Sarah never had children, though there were many of the couple's friends in New England who said John wanted children."

Saoirse grips the sides of her chair, denying the whirlwind of emotions coursing through her.

"The Stone Tape Theory posits that environmental elements are capable of storing traces of human thoughts or emotions, that spoken words leave permanent impressions in the air, though they become inaudible over time," Lucretia says. "It's also thought to be connected to the concept of 'place memory.' Think about it: you meet a celebrated author, Emmit Powell, while living in the house of the woman who attracted the attention of America's greatest writer, poet, editor, and literary critic. Even Emmit's initials are the same as Poe's." She shoots Saoirse a look. "You don't happen to know his middle name, do you?"

Saoirse shakes her head impatiently.

"Anyway," Lucretia capitulates, "the last major nineteenth-century idea associated with the Stone Tape Theory is psychometry, the belief that it's possible to obtain knowledge about the history associated with an object through physical contact with it. Being in this house *is like a study in psychometry*. You're placing your very feet where Sarah Whitman walked while projecting the same frequency of energy she must have held within her. Widowed and alone, gifted and flirting with transcendentalism. I mean, gosh, the only thing you're missing is Sarah's tragically romantic and chronic heart condition."

Saoirse's body grows Arctic-cold, but Lucretia is bouncing up and down and looking at Mia. "I told you giving her a little nudge before the séance was the right idea," she says. "It got her writing again! It helped tip the scales from psychometry into a full-blown residual haunting!"

Mia's expression grows wary. "Lucretia, I don't think—"

"What nudge?" Saoirse asks.

"Right, sorry," Lucretia says quickly. "I shouldn't—"

"When's the food getting here?" Roberto says, standing up and looking toward the living room door.

"What nudge?" Saoirse says, loud enough to silence everyone else.

Mia sighs. She looks at Lucretia and raises an eyebrow. "Well, you've got to tell her now."

Lucretia remains silent.

"Tell me what?" Saoirse demands.

It's Lucretia's turn to sigh. She turns to Saoirse, guilt wrinkling her face. "I sort of included LSD in the cupcakes I made for the séance last week," she says meekly. "It was the equivalent of a microdose in each, so that's why you came down so quickly. It's also why you felt great just a few minutes later. It helps open the mind and expand the consciousness."

Saoirse's mouth hangs open. "You drugged us?" she asks disbelievingly.

"Oh, not me," Roberto says in a tone that indicates he knows better. "I'm far too distrustful of Lucretia's baking skills to eat anything she makes."

Saoirse looks at Mia, who shrugs. "I don't eat chocolate," she says matter-of-factly.

Lucretia smiles sheepishly. "I'm sorry. I meant to tell you, but then you seemed so anxious to get the séance started, and I know how stressed you've been, and I've done a ton of research into microdosing, and I felt like it would help you get over your block, and it's totally not dangerous if you take it—"

"Without a heart condition," Saoirse says, bringing a hand to her chest.

Lucretia pauses, looking confused. "I'm sorry?"

"LSD is not dangerous if you take it without a heart condition," Saoirse says again. The words *Get out!* are poised on her tongue, but somehow she swallows them. She wants to hear what Lucretia has to say.

Lucretia glances at Roberto, then at Mia, then back to Saoirse. "I don't understand. Sarah Whitman's condition was—"

"I'm not talking about Sarah Whitman." Saoirse heaves a deep sigh and shakes her head. "I'm talking about me. Maybe there's something to your residual haunting theory, after all, because I have cardiomyopathy. I'm on a host of medications. Water pills, potassium, Entresto, not to mention antidepressants." She looks at Lucretia. "And in addition to the meds, I try to limit my caffeine, alcohol, *and hallucinogen* intake."

Saoirse brings a loosely closed fist up, taps her thumb to her chest, and looks at each of the three shocked faces in turn. "So, I guess I'm not missing Sarah's tragically romantic and ultimately chronic heart condition, after all."

Chapter 21

Lucretia, Mia, and Roberto continue to stare at her without speaking. Mia is the first to break the silence. "When were you diagnosed?"

Saoirse rubs her temples. "Seven years ago. About two years after Jonathan and I were married." She can't say anything else about that time, the nightmare her diagnosis led to. She won't. "Now that I know how to manage it, it's not that big of a deal," she says. "I get dizzy or lightheaded if I try to work out, but I've never been much into sports. My doctor back in Jersey reviewed my medications regularly, and I was honest with her about how well I was complying with my treatment." She glares at Lucretia. "But I wasn't typically being slipped unregulated hallucinogens without my knowledge."

Lucretia looks as if she's going to be sick, and Saoirse is opening her mouth to berate her further when a knock comes at the door. "That would be the food," Saoirse says dryly.

Lucretia looks down at the floor then back at Saoirse. Tears well in her dark eyes, magnified by her thick glasses. "I'm so sorry. I'll pay for the food, and we'll leave," she whispers. When Saoirse says nothing, Lucretia stands. Mia and Roberto get up to follow.

"Wait," Saoirse says when Lucretia's at the living room door. Before she can think about what she's doing, she continues, "You don't have to go. I'm not happy about what you did, but against all odds, it turned out okay. My physical health is fine, and, well"—she lets out a disbelieving chuckle—"it apparently worked, because I'm writing again. Better than ever, in fact."

Lucretia grips the doorframe. "You're not mad?"

"Oh, I'm mad. And I'm never eating anything that comes from your kitchen ever again. But—" She sighs. "Like I said, everything turned out okay." She looks at each of them in turn. "And I like you weirdos." The shock of Lucretia's admission has Saoirse feeling bold. "I like the séances. I like who I am when I'm around you." She doesn't say she hasn't had real friends since before Jonathan, doesn't say she hasn't had her own personality with which to make friends since their wedding.

Lucretia expels a huge sigh of relief. "Oh god. Thank you, Saoirse. Thank you for not being too angry with me. I promise you, I did it out of love. And I won't do anything like that ever again. No more secrets."

Saoirse looks down at her lap. If they're committing to no more secrets, she should do the same. But before she can consider saying more, Mia pushes past Lucretia in the doorway. "I'm going to pay for the food before the delivery guy decides there's no one here and takes off."

Once they're situated around the kitchen table with various cartons, Saoirse considers returning to the previous conversation, considers telling her friends the whole truth. But where would she even begin? *Hey, do you want to hear what happened after I was diagnosed with cardiomyopathy? Do you want to know what my husband did when I told him I didn't want to risk having children with a heart condition?*

Mia looks up from her curry. "You're seeing Emmit tomorrow?"

Saoirse recalibrates her thoughts. "I am. He told me we could do whatever I wanted to in the city. Any ideas?"

Mia ignores her question. "What's he like? Aside from being really into you, which is great, of course."

Saoirse puts down her fork. "He's thoughtful, in an almost preternatural way. Intelligent, obviously. And intuitive, even putting aside all that premonition bullshit. He's confident but not arrogant." She takes a sip from a can of seltzer. "Why?"

"No reason."

Roberto scoffs. "Like Mia ever pries into anything without reason." He looks at Mia. "But seriously, why *do* you ask? What *could* Emmit Powell be like, other than a literary genius?"

Mia glowers at him. "It won't mean anything at this juncture of their relationship."

"What won't?" Saoirse pushes.

Mia studies her. "Have you ever googled him?" she asks.

Roberto scoffs again. "Who hasn't?"

Saoirse ignores Roberto. "Maybe when I read *Vulture Eyes* last year? I can't remember. But not after meeting him this past week. Why?"

Mia sighs as if something is paining her, and annoyance flashes through Saoirse like electricity. "No more secrets, right?" she says. "If you have something to say, Mia, please, say it."

"If you *were* to google him," Mia says slowly, as if against her better judgment, "you'd be met with all the things you might expect. A Wikipedia page touting his writing credentials, descriptions of his work, a bibliography. You wouldn't see a ton of details beneath the headings of 'early life' or 'personal life,' but that's not out of the ordinary." Mia pauses, and Saoirse resists the urge to shout, *Get to the point!*

"But if you google, say, 'Does Emmit Powell look familiar?' or 'Is Emmit Powell a pen name?'" Mia continues, "you'll find some increasingly odd entries. A blog post by an independent horror author who swears she was in a writing group twenty years ago with a man who looked like Emmit Powell but whose name was Willem Thomas. References to a series of now-deleted tweets that attempt to discover if 'Emmit Powell' is a pen name, to no avail. Reference to another series of now-deleted tweets by a reporter from *Entertainment Weekly* attempting to track down Emmit's aunt and uncle, also to no avail."

Saoirse doesn't know what to say, but it doesn't matter; Lucretia speaks first: "Maybe Emmit Powell *is* a pen name. What's the big deal?"

"The big deal is, he's said in numerous interviews that he doesn't use a pen name."

Saoirse shakes her head, wondering if the bewilderment she feels is written on her face. "When did you do all this googling anyway? I only just told you I'd spent time with him."

Mia waves her hand. "Lucretia said he ran into you on Brown's campus this past Saturday."

"And you immediately cyberstalked him?" Saoirse pushes her chair back and stands. She never expected one of her new friends to leave her feeling like she does after a conversation with her father: Exposed. Foolish. Attacked. "Why are you acting like he's some sort of criminal with something to hide?"

Mia levels her gaze at Saoirse. "I didn't."

"You didn't what?"

"Cyberstalk him."

"You just said—"

Mia cuts her off. "I didn't google him to find out the things I just told you. I knew them already. From a woman named Josephine Martin. She was a student in Brown's Literary Arts program last year. Emmit was her professor. The instant Lucretia told me you'd gone to Carr Haus with Emmit, I recalled what Josephine told me about her MFA last year."

With a sinking feeling in her stomach, Saoirse sits back down.

"Josephine didn't want any MFA; she wanted an MFA from Brown, and she applied five years in a row until she got in. Her first semester was, in her words, 'like a dream,' and she felt like she was making tremendous progress. Then, her second semester began, and she was paired with her new mentor." Mia pauses and smooths her already-sleek hair.

"Josephine and I don't know each other well," Mia continues. "We met at a Halloween party of Roberto's."

"I throw a killer Halloween party," Roberto adds in a stage whisper.

Mia rolls her eyes. "Anyway, Josephine and I talked that night and realized we had similar interests, explored similar themes in our work.

We stayed in touch, beta reading for one another occasionally. When I asked her to exchange work with me last year, she said she would look at what I had, but had nothing to send in return because she'd stopped writing.

"I asked her what had happened. She wrote to me about her second semester mentor, Emmit Powell. Except, he wasn't Emmit Powell, Josephine said, and because she knew that, she wasn't invited back. A letter she received from the dean said it was due to the lack of growth she'd shown, but Josephine swore that wasn't the case."

Saoirse wraps her fingers around the seltzer can and squeezes. "She knew that he wasn't Emmit Powell. What the hell does that mean?"

Maddeningly, Mia nods, as if acknowledging the bizarreness of the story she is telling. "Josephine had been in Providence for the five years she'd spent applying to Brown. Working in restaurants, honing her writing. But she was from Virginia. She'd gone to high school at a place called Massanutten Academy, a military school in Woodstock. Apparently, Massanutten is one of two private schools in what has the distinction of being the biggest hick town in Virginia."

"Meee-ahhh." The singsong voice Roberto uses barely covers his impatience. "What does any of this have to do with Saoirse's new boy toy?"

Mia gives Saoirse an apologetic look. "Josephine swore to me that the man whose novel won a Pulitzer Prize, the man who was mentoring her at Brown, was Willem Thomas, someone she went to high school with at Massanutten Academy.

"There'd been some drama with him and another girl at the school—something about Emmit, or, Willem, pushing this girl further than she'd wanted to go in the relationship because it inspired him to write more meaningful poetry—but Josephine said it was mainly gossip, had hardly reached the level of scandal. He was a nerdy Goth kid, nothing more, nothing less. At least, she'd always thought he was nothing more, until she found herself sitting across from him at Brown.

"She didn't say anything right away, just continued with their one-on-one sessions. She wondered if she could somehow be mistaken—his hair was fuller and darker, his skin clear and his eyebrows more sculpted than in high school—but eventually she couldn't deny it. At one of their sessions, she said something along the lines of, 'Willem, I know it's you, but don't worry, I get it. If I had your talent, I wouldn't want to be associated with our white-trash town either.'

"She said Emmit smiled strangely at her but didn't confirm or deny what she said. They completed their session, and not long after, Josephine received that letter. In addition to 'not showing growth,' the letter claimed one of her professors had cited 'severe derivativeness and increasing ineptitude as a writer.'"

There's silence for several seconds. *No way any of this is true,* Saoirse thinks. Then, *Please don't let it be.* She grits her teeth. "So, I'm supposed to stop seeing Emmit because some girl you barely know thinks that Emmit is a hick from Virginia in disguise?"

"No," Mia says. "That's not what I'm saying. I would never tell you to stop seeing him. To stop seeing anyone. You're an adult, and you've been through a lot. You deserve to make a new life for yourself. You deserve to be happy. I just wanted you to know what I know. That, maybe, he is not who he says he is. And to be careful."

"Emmit said things like this happened a lot," Saoirse says. She knows she's being irrationally defensive, but every nerve in her body is tingling, electric, utterly on edge; for, if Emmit *has* been hiding something from her, it means she must face two terrible truths: Jonathan—with his mocking, derisive, maddeningly *prudent* observations—has been right all along, and the quiet, half-buried voice of her own, the one that says she should have listened to her dead husband, is intuitive rather than belittling.

"What happens a lot?" Mia asks, looking confused.

"That students tried weird things all the time to get into the program," Saoirse clarified. "How do you know this Josephine girl was even a student at Brown? How do you know she's not some crazy ex, or just plain crazy? And speaking of crazy, let's say she's right. That Emmit really is Willem Thomas, who graduated from Hicksville, USA. So what if he wants to shed that identity and start fresh? Do you think the *New York Times* or *USA Today* would pay as much attention to a man whose formative experiences growing up included—or was likely even limited to—tipping cows?"

"But if that were the case, why not just admit to it?" Mia asks. "And swear Josephine to secrecy? Why expel her from the program? Why punish her?"

"It seems less a punishment than a threat," Roberto says, then shoots Saoirse a regretful look. "Like, 'Admit you know who I am, and see what happens.'"

Saoirse feels her frustration growing. But is it frustration with Mia or with herself? Has she known Emmit isn't who he appears to be all along and has been trying to prove otherwise? If so, to whom? Herself? Her dead husband? How ludicrous is that?

The thought makes her even more indignant, and she spits out, "So Emmit is in the business of threatening his students? That sounds like some conspiracy theory bullshit to me." She glares at Mia, knowing she shouldn't verbalize the thought forming in her mind, but she feels cornered. "Or like the hypervigilant-bordering-on-paranoid opinion of someone who's been burned by a shitty partner in the past."

She feels horrible the minute the words leave her mouth. Mia closes her to-go container and looks up. Rather than anger, there's sorrow on her face, or maybe worry. "If that's the case, would it be so bad?"

It's worse that Mia has met her lash-out with kindness. Lucretia's eyes are on her as well, but when Saoirse turns to look at her, there's nothing to indicate she's upset with Saoirse for bringing up Mia's past.

"I'm sorry," Mia continues. "I'm sure it's nothing. It's just that, if the situation were reversed, I feel like you'd have wanted me to know. Especially considering the weirdness with which this whole thing started: seeing him at the Ath and the coffee shop, his overall intensity. I'm just trying to look out for you. We're friends."

Are we? Saoirse wants to ask. *Does a friend dump all over another's happiness at the very moment they've grasped it?* But there's still nothing but concern on Mia's face, and Saoirse feels her frustration, her defensiveness, diminishing, then disappearing altogether. Of course Mia's only looking out for her. How could she be so nasty in return? And Mia's right; if Saoirse had known something like what this Josephine girl had said, she would have said something too.

"It's okay," Saoirse says. "I'm not going to say anything to him, but I'll keep my guard up. Who knows, if there's anything to tell, maybe he'll relay it without me even asking. Until then, I am going to keep seeing him. I think it's good for me. It feels good."

They clean up and move back to the living room, where Lucretia and Saoirse talk about writing and take turns throwing a little mouse toy with a bell inside for Pluto. Mia plucks one of the leather-bound gold-leaf books from the shelves in the corner and thumbs through it, and Roberto lies on the settee and closes his eyes. Eventually, he stirs, stands, and yawns dramatically.

"Time for bed," Roberto says. "If you two leave with me, I'll walk you home. Any later, and you're on your own." The two women stand without argument and follow Roberto to the foyer, Saoirse trailing— and yawning herself—behind.

They leave with hugs and farewells. No mention of heart conditions, residual hauntings, or literary identity fraud. When she's shut and locked the door and climbed the stairs, Saoirse checks her phone. Almost midnight. Too late, now, to be tempted to call Emmit, though that doesn't stop her from wondering what he's doing. After washing up, she checks her phone again and feels a jolt at the sight of a new text message. She opens the app and feels another, stronger jolt: the text is from Emmit, and it's long.

. . . thy beauty is to me
Like those Nicéan barks of yore,
That gently, o'er a perfumed sea,
The weary, way-worn wanderer bore
To his own native shore.
On desperate seas long wont to roam,
Thy hyacinth hair, thy classic face,
Thy Naiad airs have brought me home
To the glory that was Greece,
And the grandeur that was Rome.
Lo! in yon brilliant window-niche
How statue-like I see thee stand,
The agate lamp within thy hand!
Ah, Psyche, from the regions which
Are Holy-Land!
I long to see you again, to kiss your face
To hold your hand.
I think it's time for you and I
To slip between the gravestones
And back in time.

Though she knows the first part of the poem is Poe's "To Helen," a quick Google search tells her the last lines were composed by Emmit. *Using another man's words to prove his love to you,* Jonathan whispers from her head. *And you've somehow convinced yourself that the man is not a liar?*

Saoirse doesn't dignify this with a response, though Jonathan's words linger longer than she'd like. Eventually, she forces them away, like a gust of wind dispersing a tower of chimney smoke. The thought that clears her mind enough for sleep is that it doesn't matter if Emmit Powell really is Willem Thomas from Virginia. Not if she's going to keep seeing him.

For she, Saoirse White, carries a secret far larger than a duplicitous name.

Chapter 22

Saoirse spends the morning plotting out an itinerary for her "all-day date" with Emmit and writing poetry while she waits for him to pick her up. The time passes pleasantly, except for the feeling of being watched from the corners of the quiet house. Once, when she turns around, she thinks she catches a fleeting glimpse of white, like the trailing wisp of one of Sarah's oft-worn scarves. And on several occasions, a strange knocking comes from the direction of the secret passage into the house.

You will *listen to what I have to say.* She hears the words Aidan spoke after Jonathan's funeral in her head. *And you will look at the text message Jonathan sent me that night, right before you*— Saoirse digs her pen into the paper, refusing to let her mind finish that statement. She recalls her own words to Aidan in the cemetery: "Jonathan died of a heart attack. The autopsy confirmed it." The autopsy *confirmed* it.

When Emmit's gray Mercedes pulls up, Aidan's threats leave Saoirse's head and Mia's warning enters it: *He is not who he says he is.* But then Emmit is getting out and coming up the steps and kissing her as passionately as she's ever been kissed, dipping her low and exploring her mouth so hungrily she can barely breathe. When he pulls away, Saoirse sees an explosion of twinkling dust like stars.

"Did you decide where you'd like to go?" Emmit asks, but his voice is low and thick. There's undisguised longing in his face and an intensity that—she already knows from experience—must be burned out of him.

One hand is on the small of her back, the other on her waist. They are both breathing as if their bodies are on fire.

"I was thinking—" Saoirse starts. "I thought—" But she doesn't want to say what she was thinking, doesn't want to utter the words that will result in them walking down the stoop and into the car. She wants only to be led inside and up the stairs, wants him to draw the shades and peel off her clothes, wants to take him into her until the sun no longer has control of the sky.

Emmit reads this desire within her as if it's words on a page. Inside, they fall atop the peach settee while golden late-morning light streams in from the sidelights, patterning their bodies like the ridges of seashells or ripples in the sand after the tide rolls out.

At lunchtime, they order curry dishes and rice paper rolls from the same Thai place Saoirse ordered from the night before. They eat in bed, make love again, read poetry to one another, coo over Pluto whenever the black cat enters the room, pick at leftovers, make love a third time, talk about writing. When the light coming in from the balcony turns the shadows in her bedroom long and toothy, Saoirse reaches for her phone and checks the time.

"Oh my god. It's almost six o'clock."

"So?" Emmit smiles at her lazily.

"So we've been in this bedroom for eight hours! How is that even possible?" She rolls onto her back and stares at the ceiling. "This whole day feels like one long dream."

"Those who dream by day are cognizant of many things which escape those who dream only by night," Emmit says.

Saoirse props herself up on one elbow. "Did you just quote Poe at me?"

Emmit smiles. "Guilty."

She flops back onto the pillow and lets out a groan. Emmit leans over her, tracing circles on her stomach, his dark hair falling across his forehead. "I have the feeling," Saoirse says, "that as long as I'm living in this house and spending time with you, Lucretia, Roberto, and Mia"—she strains to plant a kiss on his lips—"I'm doomed to a never-ending barrage of all things Poe and Whitman."

"Is that so bad?" Emmit asks. "Culture today, *society* today, is so vapid and recycled and terrible. TikTok and the Kardashians. AI-generated blog content. AI-generated *fiction*. God help us. Oftentimes, I wonder how *Vulture Eyes* even sold as many copies as it did. It doesn't seem like there are many people left in this country who read anything that doesn't come as the caption to a fifteen-second dance craze video." He grips her by the shoulders and lifts her up. "We should embrace this unexpected umbilical cord to the past. This house, the cemetery out there, this wonderful, historic city—we should embrace all of it."

He releases her shoulders and smacks the bed excitedly. "That's it!"

"What's it?"

"If we want to embrace Providence, I have just the thing." He jumps off the bed and sorts through their clothes on the floor. He lays her sweater, underclothes, and pants on the bed before stepping into his boxers and jeans and shrugging into a white linen shirt. Despite staring at him for the better part of eight hours, Saoirse lets her eyes run up and down him yet again.

How are you here? she wants to ask. *How did my life go from being so empty, so haunted, to being so exciting?* She hates that this change is attributed to a man, feels she's become the epitome of the woman she always hated: the one who gets a boyfriend and all her problems disappear.

That's not what this is, Jonathan says. *Because you are still you. Everything you've done is still inside you, waiting to rear its ugly head.*

It's going to have to do its rearing later, Saoirse hisses silently. *Because right now, I have a date.* To hell with Jonathan's cynicism; she'll enjoy her newfound happiness just to spite him. To Emmit, she says, "And how do you suggest we 'embrace Providence'?"

He pats her clothes, and she crawls forward and plucks her bra from the pile. "Remember when I mentioned the Providence Ghost Tours?" he asks.

Saoirse has her sweater over her head and is wiggling into her pants. "Sort of."

Emmit smacks his forehead with the palm of his hand. "I told *you* to decide what we were going to do today, and here I am stealing the show."

Saoirse shrugs and smooths her hair. "I didn't have anything all that spectacular in mind. Just walking around the city, seeing the sights." It's not entirely untrue. She'd planned to suggest they visit the John Brown House and maybe another museum if they could fit it in. But she could ask Roberto to give her a tour of his place of employment another time.

"If you want to see the sights," Emmit says, "a ghost tour is a legit, if less conventional, way to do it. I'm friends with Courtney, the woman who owns the company. Let me see if there are any openings tonight. After that, we'll get dinner near the tour's last stop? Does that sound okay?"

"It sounds great," Saoirse says, and again, while it's not an outright lie, it's not the truth either. Between the séance last week and all the talk of Poe and Whitman, she can do without ghosts for a while. Though, putting a nice long stroll between their multicourse Thai lunch and another meal doesn't sound like the worst idea.

"Okay then," Emmit says a moment later, slipping his phone into his pocket. "There're two openings on a tour that leaves at seven. We can be ready to go by then, right?"

Saoirse agrees, and Emmit stands on the balcony while Saoirse reapplies her makeup. He stays upstairs while she tests Pluto's blood sugar and injects him with the necessary level of insulin into the fat at the back of his neck. She hears Emmit on the steps as she's filling Pluto's food bowl.

"You ready?" he asks from the foyer.

"Almost." She places the food on the floor beside the water bowl, and Pluto brushes against her legs. "I'll see you in just a few hours," she says to the purring cat. She goes to the sink and rinses out the cat food can.

"Serrr-shaaah!" Emmit calls.

"Just need to wash my hands."

As she grabs for a dish towel, she catches sight of her myriad heart medications and antidepressant in the crack of an open cabinet. *I didn't take any of my meds!* She reaches for the bottles, opens them quickly, and counts out the pills—oval white and sky-blue ones, yellow-and-orange capsules. *When's the last time I missed a dose?* She can't remember, but she certainly doesn't want to start now. It could be disastrous. She throws the pills into her mouth and sips water directly from the faucet to wash them down.

Emmit sticks his head through the doorway into the kitchen, and Saoirse steps in front of the dish drainer, not wanting him to see the telltale orange bottles. She wipes her mouth with the back of her hand.

"We only have ten minutes to walk there," he says.

"I'm ready," she insists and smiles. When Emmit turns back toward the foyer, she returns the bottles to the shelf and closes the cabinet. Giving Pluto a final pat, she steps out into the coming twilight of the clear October night.

Chapter 23

Emmit stops at his Mercedes before they leave, riffling through the glove compartment. The walk to the park at Prospect Terrace on Congdon Street takes a little over five minutes. They arrive in time for introductions and directives from their tour guide, Stacy.

After checking her phone to make sure everyone's arrived, Stacy turns in the opposite direction from which Saoirse and Emmit have come. "All right, everyone. Our tour has officially started. Onward, to what we in the biz still refer to as the Biltmore Hotel."

Saoirse and Emmit match their strides to the half dozen or so other participants on the ghost walk. Saoirse wishes she'd thought to bring a pair of gloves. It's much colder than when she had initially planned to be out with Emmit, nine hours earlier.

"Are you excited?" Emmit asks.

"Sure," Saoirse replies. "This is cool."

"Are you scared?" He grins.

Saoirse feels her mouth lift into a half smile that mirrors the one Emmit so often wears. "It takes an awful lot to scare me these days."

"Fair enough," Emmit says, "though, just in case, I packed us a little liquid courage." He's staring at her, gauging her reaction. When she raises an eyebrow, Emmit slips a hand into his jacket pocket and pulls out a flask. Saoirse feels a little drop in her stomach. Emmit unscrews the top and drinks, then holds it out to her, the cleft in his chin deepening.

The drop in her stomach rollercoasters into a rise of anger, but she derails it. She can't be upset; Emmit doesn't know about her heart condition. He doesn't know because she hasn't told him. She meant what she said the other night at the restaurant: she was a "sort of" drinker in that she'd never had a problem with it. Not like Jonathan had. And because she'd had a conservative approach toward drinking before her diagnosis, not overdrinking with her heart condition hadn't required much of a transition.

Emmit is still holding the flask in her direction, and she takes it from his hand. She's always so careful with her health; a few sips of whatever is in the flask isn't going to kill her. She sips, wincing at the burn in her throat, and sputters as she hands it back.

"What is that? Gasoline?"

"Brandy." He takes another sip. "It *is* a little strong. Next time, I'll mix it with eggnog."

"Next time?" Saoirse scrunches her face. "Do ghost tours whip you into a partying frenzy or something?"

"Eggnog is criminally underrated," Emmit says. "We're embracing Providence's past tonight, aren't we? Eggnog was the drink of gentlemen and women throughout the nineteenth century."

Saoirse forces a little laugh, but already her heart rate is increasing, and she feels the alcohol traveling through her, heating up her muscles, her skin, her veins. Emmit returns the flask to his pocket and grabs her hand, and she relaxes slightly and smiles. With his fingers entwined in hers, she can forget about eggnog and brandy.

Their first stop is the Graduate Hotel, built in 1922 and formerly known as the Biltmore. Saoirse listens to Stacy's anecdotes about the hotel's famous guests and unexplained deaths, a flood in 1954, a plague of lawsuits, unpaid debt, and an eleventh-hour rescue from demolition. Stacy is delving into how these events resulted in the hotel's various unquiet spirits, when Emmit slips the flask out of his pocket again.

Jonathan speaks up instantly: *So much for Emmit not being a big drinker. Looks like you picked another winner, huh?*

Before Saoirse can decline the flask, Emmit thrusts it into her hand. Her heart rate ratchets up another notch, though whether from the brandy she's already consumed or her rising unease, she can't be certain. Emmit is staring at her expectantly, and a dozen excuses, explanations, and retorts spring to her mind. Rather than utter any one of them, she takes another swig, the large letters—B.I.L.T.M.O.R.E.—atop the eighteen-story hotel glowing red in her periphery.

He takes the flask back and glances at the other tour patrons. Stacy is explaining to a young woman how the hotel's famous glass elevator is now—according to a plaque on its brass door—for time travel only. Emmit flashes her a grin, but his eyes look a little clouded. Saoirse feels her own eyes drooping a little, and the traveling warmth of the alcohol moves to her stomach. There's a fuzziness around the edges of her vision and a looseness to her shoulders. She shakes her head, trying to clear her thoughts, and they follow Stacy and the rest of the tour-goers down the sidewalk.

A half mile later, they're on Brown's campus, with Stacy introducing the building before them as University Hall. The tour guide gestures animatedly as she says, "It's haunted by the ghosts of the American soldiers treated here when the building was used as a hospital during the Revolutionary War."

"I remember this," Saoirse says to Emmit, trying to get their date back on track. "We used to scare each other with stories of ghostly soldiers roaming the halls."

Stacy is fielding questions from the group when Emmit jams his hand in his pocket yet again. Saoirse's stomach sinks at the same moment her heart rate rises. But this time, Emmit doesn't come out with the flask. He's clutching something obscured by his closed fist. He leans in close, breath hot against her ear.

"I have an idea," he whispers. He pushes something smooth and oval-shaped into her hand. She looks down. It's a capsule, clear and flimsy; she can press the sides of it together with her fingers, see the light-brown powder shifting beneath the pressure. Quickly, she hands the capsule back to him.

"What is it?" she asks over the noise of Jonathan in her brain, cackling something about how wildly she's misjudged this man. Emmit regards her hungrily, and despite her fear and incredulity, her face grows warm under his gaze, the way it had that morning when he kissed her on her stoop.

"Nothing crazy," Emmit says. "And one hundred percent safe. Just something to liven up this tour a bit. To liven up our"—he grabs her and pulls her close—"feelings for one another too. I only ever get them from the same person, and I trust him like my own brother."

Saoirse glances around at their little group. A middle-aged woman with a Lizzie Borden House tote slung over one arm. A twentysomething man pleading with Stacy to admit whether she's seen a Revolutionary War–era ghost herself. A college-aged couple snapping photos in front of a set of stairs leading up to the large brick hall. Saoirse turns back to Emmit.

"Why?" she asks, genuinely puzzled. Why do they need something to liven the experience up? The tour was his idea, and it's more interesting than Saoirse anticipated. Is Emmit so bored that he needs a synthetic mood boost, or is something else going on?

Something . . . like . . . addiction? Jonathan asks. *Something like what you accused me of at the end but never offered to help me with?*

Shut up, Saoirse thinks back. *Shut up and let me think.*

"Why what?" Emmit asks.

"Why *drugs*?"

Emmit looks around, but everyone's listening to Stacy, who's launched into another story about ghosts on Brown's campus. He turns back to her, and before Saoirse knows what is happening, he is slipping his hands beneath her jacket and under her sweater, then running his palms up her sides and sliding his fingers under her bra. He kneads her flesh, and Saoirse struggles to remain standing, the muscles in her legs turning to jelly.

He turns her body away from where Stacy is standing so that anyone regarding them would think they're engaged in an innocent embrace. When he pulls away, his mouth jumps up in that maddening half smile, and Saoirse realizes it's as much a nervous tic as it is an endearing expression. He dips her back over the sidewalk and kisses her again, parting her lips with his tongue, one hand still on her breasts while the other holds her up. She grows dizzy. Thoughts fly out of her head.

After he rights her, he lifts a hand, a pair of brown-powder capsules between his fingers. He takes one, places the other on her tongue, removes the flask from his pocket, and swigs from it, then presses that to her mouth too.

"You want to know why?" he asks. "Because I want to do everything with you. I want to experience everything with you. I . . ." He stops and puffs out a little breath, as if even he can't believe the things his desire for her has him doing and saying. A tuft of hair hangs over his forehead. He looks at Saoirse from under it, eyes wet with emotion, with lust. "I am in awe of you. Being with you is like being bathed in an electric light. If we were to part right now, never to see each other again, I'd be a better person for having met you. For having lain with you. For having heard one single line of your poetry."

Saoirse struggles to retain the last breath of air in her lungs. The capsule still sits on her tongue. *Do not swallow this. Do not fall under his spell. Anyone can say words that are pretty.*

But not everyone *can* say words that are so pretty, so captivating, and that's a major part of Emmit's appeal. Though . . . speaking of pretty words, why do the ones he's just uttered sound so familiar? Did she read them somewhere? In the book she took out from the Athenæum of Poe's letters to Whitman? So . . . a second instance of Emmit serenading her with another man's poetry. Still, the warning in her head—whether Jonathan's or her own—doesn't matter. She feels the exact moment in which she fails to heed the warning. Feels the exact moment in which she falls.

Saoirse closes her mouth, wraps her fingers around the flask, and washes the capsule down with the acrid brandy. She takes Emmit's face in her cold hands and kisses him. Whatever he's given her will be an experience, and it will be an experience they can share together. The contents of the capsule can't be much more dangerous than the antidepressants she already mixes with her heart medication every day.

Stacy leads the group toward Benefit Street, and it occurs to Saoirse that her own house may very well be their next stop. The thought is like a shimmery length of ribbon that unspools from her grasp. She no longer feels the cold of the October evening, and Emmit's hand in hers is like a lifeline, making her feel equal parts elated and invincible.

So much for Mia's heads-up, Jonathan says from a shadowy corner of her mind. *You're jumping into this with all the caution of a skydiver with a glitchy parachute.*

This time, she does issue her dead husband a response: *Did you ever think that maybe my relationship with you inoculated me from another toxic, dangerous situation? I suffered so much at your hands. The universe couldn't possibly have delivered to me anything other than a good person, who treats me with equality and respect. Not after the monster I endured. Not after you.*

There's a chuckle from that same dark recess of her mind, and Saoirse can see Jonathan, his smug expression, his arms around his torso as if he's wrapped himself in a hug: *You and I both know that's not how the universe works.*

Saoirse's so lost in the conversation, in her flighty, tipsy, floaty thoughts, she almost walks into the woman in front of her before Emmit pulls her back. The rest of the tour group stands on the sidewalk, peering up at a butter-yellow Colonial. There's a steep set of steps leading up to a fence painted the same shade of yellow; the grounds beyond the fence are overgrown and weed-choked. Saoirse blinks. Are the grounds also veiled in a layer of strange, billowy mist . . . or is that the by-product of her dreamlike vision?

"135 Benefit Street. The Shunned House," Stacy says theatrically. "Built around 1763 and inhabited by Howard Phillip Lovecraft's aunt Lillian in 1919 when she worked as a companion to a Mrs. H. C. Babbit. Lovecraft based his infamous story on a house in New Jersey, but felt the tangled ivy and unnaturally steep roof of the house before you lent itself to the idea of being 'corpse-fed,' and so crafted his story with the Babbit House as its basis."

At the words *corpse-fed*, a sensation like the brush of insect legs travels up Saoirse's spine.

"From our vantage point here," Stacy continues, "the Shunned House appears to be three floors. However, if you look around the side of the house, you'll see the first floor is a walkout basement. The plot of Lovecraft's story revolves around the *actual* basement, which would mean the area *under* this level"—she gestures at the windows in front of them, then lowers her voice—"the area that's completely underground. This is where the narrator and his uncle attempt to discover the source of a strange yellow vapor, or 'corpse-light,' but find death, decay, and an unspeakable monster for their troubles. Lovecraft wrote in a letter to a friend that the house's image would come up throughout his life with renewed vividness. And with good reason. The latent horror of this house has captivated the city's imagination for a century."

There are whispered murmurings of excitement, and several hands go up.

"I'm happy to take questions," Stacy says, "but let's do so as we walk, because our next stop is just ahead, and I need to be mindful of the time. We don't want to be out in this city too long after dark." She punctuates this statement with a boom of vampiric laughter. The group follows her up the sidewalk and away from the looming yellow house.

Saoirse starts after them, feeling like she's outside of her own body, when a yank comes on the hem of her coat so hard, she stumbles. Emmit catches her, pulls her close, and takes her chin in his hand. He kisses her, then pulls away and orients her head so that she's looking up at the Shunned House's wide, slanted roof.

"I've got another idea." His words tickle her ear, and in an instant, she's turned on, his proximity pushing her body to the brink, igniting her imagination, and she feels, suddenly, like she could write a poem while he's inside her, that she could conjure the cadence of it inside his head, and he would, in turn, speak the words aloud.

"What's your idea?" she responds, and her words run together slightly.

Emmit pulls his hips into hers and grips her jawbone tighter. "We're going inside," he says. "We'll find an unlocked window or an open door, and we're going to find out just what otherworldly phenomenon Lovecraft intuited in the basement."

Chapter 24

Saoirse sees the words escaping Emmit's mouth as if in a cartoon speech bubble, but it takes a moment to register their implications. She shakes her head, throwing his hand off her face in the process, and blinks up at him, then at the yellow house, which glows in the moonlight, recalling Stacy's words about the noxious vapor in the basement of Lovecraft's story.

"We're going . . . inside this house?" she asks. "Without a key?"

Emmit laughs, shoots a quick look at the vanishing tour group, and pulls her up the first couple of concrete stairs. "We are. Come on, it'll be fun."

Saoirse casts a wild look at the darkened windows. "How do you know someone doesn't live here?"

But Emmit is already leading her across the scrubby crabgrass. "For one thing, look at this yard." His voice eases the sharp sting of her panic. "And for another, friends of mine knocked on the door last Halloween and said that no one answered."

"Those don't strike me as nearly strong enough reasons," Saoirse says, but they're circling the back of the house toward a storm door dotted with black mold and rusted hinges. The windows along the back of the house are as dark as the street-facing ones. Saoirse wants to protest more earnestly, but there hasn't been a single sign of life anywhere on the property. She follows Emmit to the storm door and watches as he pushes it open to try the knob of the heavier wooden door behind it.

"Locked," Emmit says and turns toward the tree line. His eyes scan the yard, squinting as he looks for something in the swirling mist. Even tipsy as she is, all fuzzy-headed and floaty, Saoirse has a bad feeling about this. It's not the thought of getting caught that bothers her; it's that they will find a way in, that they'll actually have to venture inside. Whatever drug she took is probably making her paranoid, but she doesn't want to imagine what might be waiting for them inside this house, doesn't want to see what lies, forgotten but no less hungry, in the shadow-saturated corridors of the basement. Her heart pounds like a machine on the brink of collapse, and this exacerbates her paranoia and fear.

The crash against the door is so loud, Saoirse lets out a little yelp. She turns to find Emmit grinning, a large rock in his hands, the rusted knob dangling from its socket and the door hanging open several inches.

"Whoa," Saoirse says, but something inside her shifts, as if the drug has only now fully integrated into her system. Her fear lessens, and her paranoia is ethereal, like a bird whose call she can hear from the surrounding trees but cannot see.

What would she be doing right now if she wasn't here with Emmit? Streaming endless, mindless episodes of shows she didn't care about, splayed across the couch and pretending to job hunt, pretending to care about her future? Pretending she isn't still damaged or that she's healed from the trauma of what her life has become? That she isn't far more affected by what Jonathan did to her than she cares to admit? Instead, she's on this adventure, experiencing something, forging a connection. Engaging with life. Engaging with another human. Visualizing a future for herself that doesn't consist of depression and guilt and grief and regret. Of illness and of conversations in her mind with her dead, relentless husband.

Emmit grips her hand, bringing Saoirse back to the present. Together, they step over the threshold. They stand for a moment, listening for sounds that mean they're not alone in the house, but nothing comes.

"Come on," Emmit whispers, and she follows him down a long hallway. At the end, they come to a large dusty room, empty of everything but a wide brick fireplace and a set of built-in bookshelves. "Abandoned," he says excitedly. "I knew it. *I knew it!*"

"But *why* is it abandoned?" Saoirse asks. "It's a nice house." She squints at him. His excitement seems greater than it should be, like breaking in wasn't a spur-of-the-moment decision on a spur-of-the-moment ghost tour, but like he's been hoping to get inside this house for a long, long time.

"I have my theories. Let's keep looking around."

They traipse in and out of rooms on the ground floor: a kitchen, a bathroom, several bedrooms, and what appears to have been a parlor, though, without furniture, it's hard to tell for certain. Despite the perpetual emptiness of the rooms, muslin curtains—yellowed to the point where they match the house's exterior—still hang from all the windows. The curtains let gauzy moonlight into the rooms, or perhaps it's the orangey glow from nearby streetlamps. A trip to the second floor reveals more rooms with curtains but no furniture. In a third-floor room at the back of the house, Emmit stops short in the doorway with a gasp.

"What?" Saoirse says, trying to see around him. "What is it?"

He moves to the side, revealing a cobweb-draped rocking chair. It's child sized. Creepy. Saoirse expects it to move on its own in a nonexistent breeze at any moment. "The previous owners must have forgotten it," she says, trying to downplay the wrongness of this lone piece of furniture in an otherwise empty house.

"Then sit in it," Emmit says.

"Huh?"

Emmit turns to her in the doorway. "Sit in it. I dare you."

His expression is mischievous, playful. A chill shoots up her back at the thought of sitting in a chair that'd be at home in a film about a possessed doll, but Saoirse forces herself to shrug and crosses the room. The floorboards creak beneath her feet as if she's making her way through a haunted house . . . the kind where you pay money for admission and the sound effects are drowned out only by the teenagers' screams.

When she reaches the chair, she brushes a layer of dust from one arm and turns back to Emmit. "Just an old abandoned chair," she assures him. Or is she assuring herself? Because . . . why does the room suddenly feel as if it's holding its breath? Saoirse's heart stutters, and she looks to her right. An open closet yawns from the darkness. *Please be empty,* Saoirse thinks, but the closet cuts into the wall beyond the opening, and it's impossible to see into its farthest recesses.

"Did you hear something?" Emmit whispers.

Saoirse turns halfway in his direction, then decides she doesn't want to turn her back on the closet. "I don't think so," she whispers back. But isn't there a noise? Just quiet enough to where she can't decide if it's real or if her fear is playing tricks on her. A scratching from the back of the closet. Like claws on a paint-peeled wall. Like something creeping closer to the closet's doorframe, ready to peer around it, to confront her, to show its face to the sickly yellow glow of the moon through the muslin-cloaked windows.

Saoirse shakes her head, clearing the fear as if it's cobwebs, half wishing she hadn't taken the capsule Emmit had given her, half-relieved that she had.

"Well?" Emmit asks. "Are you going to sit?"

"Yes," she hisses. This is so dumb. Why is he daring her to do this, anyway? But perhaps the better question is: Why is she scared? It's just an empty house on the same street she lives on. There's nothing in the closet—or the basement, for that matter. The biggest threat in their immediate future is neighbors noting the busted door and calling the police, not some monstrous creature secreting a fungus ooze. Saoirse brushes several cobwebs from the seat, turns, and plops down in the chair.

"See," she says smugly to Emmit. "The tour guide had it wrong, and so did Lovecraft. There's nothing cursed about this pla—"

The unearthly chittering starts from behind her before she can finish her sentence, filling her ears within the space of one dangerously painful heartbeat. Saoirse bolts from the chair with a strangled cry but stumbles over the left runner. She catches sight of Emmit, sees that his face is a mask of shock and terror. But before she can lunge in his direction, the creature—no, creatures, for there are half a dozen of them—are all around her: dark, grotesque shapes that scrabble like monstrous hybrids of miniature humans and bulbous, hulking-shouldered things, as if creatures meant for the sea had severed previously fused appendages and have now waddled from the black depths across pale, uneven mounds of sand. Saoirse's vision goes dark around the edges. The sound of Emmit yelling is very far away. Squeezing her eyes shut, Saoirse drops to her knees on the gritty, cobweb-dusted floor.

Chapter 25

Pulse thudding like the entirety of Brown's marching band resides within her rib cage, Saoirse covers her head with her elbows and tries—with her last ounce of rational thought—to keep her bladder from releasing. She is going to die in this ridiculous house, this shunned house, this two-bit tourist attraction, die like Jonathan from a mixture of hubris and a stupid, failed heart! With her ears covered by her arms as they are, sounds are muffled. Saoirse could be convinced she's underwater. Still—muffled sound aside—after a moment, she thinks the shrieking has stopped. Saoirse moves her elbows half an inch away from her head; Emmit is—calmly, almost robotically—calling her name. Slowly, she lifts her head and stares up at him, still standing in the doorway.

For a moment, Emmit does nothing but stare back at her, dark eyes wide, the hair that falls over one side of his forehead more disheveled than normal. Then, one side of his mouth pulls up in a crooked smile, and he is chuckling. Saoirse continues to stare, and Emmit laughs harder. In a few more seconds, he's bending over and placing his hands on his knees. He tries to speak, but he's laughing too hard to form the words.

"Wha—" she tries, but her tongue won't move properly. Her body feels heavy from the downswing of adrenaline. "What is so funny?" she finally manages. "Where'd they go? The creatures—" She throws a quick, terrified glance over her shoulder. "Where were they? *What* were they?"

"They were raccoons!" Emmit shouts, then drops to the ground himself. He crawls toward her, tears streaming from his eyes as he laughs, so hard he can barely catch his breath. A frisson of siren-red anger shoots up from Saoirse's stomach, but it explodes into a dozen lighter-colored streaks that unfurl within her body like falling stars. Mostly, she feels relief. *Raccoons? Were they really just raccoons?* And she starts to laugh too. The capsule she swallowed not forty-five minutes before has not worn off, and as she laughs, she feels those pastel streaks of relief mix with waves of euphoria and lingering terror. It's a veritable roller coaster, one with no room to be purely angry, purely relieved, purely anything.

When Emmit reaches her, he grabs her shoulder and pulls her into him, and the two of them are rolling on the grime-coated floor, howling like hyenas. She's still laughing when he kisses her. His tongue against hers makes her giddy with longing, convinces her that breaking into this house was the best idea they could have had. She rolls on top of him and kisses him hard, rips his jacket off and then hers.

They lay the jackets on the floor, strip the rest of their clothes off, and the shunned house falls away. Once, for the briefest of moments, Saoirse wonders if those abstract, waddling creatures really were raccoons, or something more sinister, less of this world. But in the next moment, the thought is lost, to bliss, to lust, to the joy of being alive, diseased heart or not. Alive and—against all odds, after what she went through with Jonathan—spending time with this electrifying, offbeat, alluring man. A man who seems, more and more, to be bringing out a more exhilarating—and terrifying—side of herself.

∞

They are dressed and back downstairs, heading toward the back door and the cool autumn night, when Emmit ducks out of the main hallway and into another.

"What are you doing?" Saoirse asks in a loud whisper. "I thought we were getting out of here." Their tryst upstairs went a long way toward eliminating the unease she feels in this house, but the effects of the brandy and capsule have worn off enough for her to feel hungry and a little on edge. And who's to say the raccoons won't return, lumber-waddling back to what is undoubtedly the site of their nest. But Emmit neither answers nor reappears.

"Hey," she says again, then sighs and steps into the lightless hallway. Like the three shallow steps at the back of 88 Benefit, this hallway is the passage to the walkout basement. As she enters the space and scans the floor, she sees the Shunned House shares another architectural design with 88 Benefit: there's a trapdoor at the center of the room. Emmit's nowhere to be seen, and the trapdoor is a huge mouth that's hanging open.

"Emmit!" she calls, more exasperated this time. Still no response. Irritated, Saoirse creeps toward the door. She peers into the gloom, but it's too dark to see what's at the bottom of the stairs. She holds her breath and listens, but not a sound comes from the yawning expanse below.

"Emmit?"

From a long, long way off, she hears Emmit's voice call back, "Saoirse, you have to see this!"

"No, thank you," she starts to respond, but then there's a crash, like timber and stones falling from a great height, from where Emmit's voice had seemed to come. The subsequent silence sends chills—like the legs of myriad insects—skittering across Saoirse's shoulders. A fly buzzes up from the alcove, and she follows its haphazard progression with her eyes, intent on determining if it materialized from the dark labyrinth of the basement or the darker recesses of her mind. She's not sure which would be worse.

"Emmit?" she tries one more time, pushing the fly from her thoughts. Silence. She curses, reaches for her phone in her jacket pocket, and engages its flashlight. Blinking away the remnants of booze and drugs and swallowing her rising dread—*this is not like when I found Jonathan, this is not like when I found Jonathan*—Saoirse makes her way down the stairs.

The steps creak as if she's disturbing the dreams of whatever sleeps beneath them. At the bottom, she aims the flashlight to the left and is met with a crumbling, dust-whitened brick wall. The air is humid and dank, and there's a strange, heavy odor, like leaf-rot after a storm.

"Emmit," she calls, forcing herself to keep walking. Would he dare to tease her after the terror she experienced in the upstairs bedroom? *Tell me something, Saoirse,* Jonathan says from her head, and she groans. "I don't need input from you at present," she whispers, but he will not be ignored.

How well do you know this man? Jonathan's tone is arrogant. *Better than you knew me after years of being married? Of course not. And yet, look at what you say I did. Look at what our relationship disintegrated into. And we had history together. If there's something evil in this basement, do you think you are safe? Do you think he'll save you?* A pause, and then, *Are you sure the evil thing down here isn't him?*

"Shut up," she warns, running the flashlight's beam along the brick wall as it extends out before her.

You could disappear down here, Jonathan adds, *and no one would ever find you.*

No, the her-part of her brain retorts. *That won't happen. I* do *know Emmit. We bared our souls to one another. He didn't go back to Baltimore this week so he could stay with me. He's not playing me. He's not after anything.* Then, the thing she's been unwilling to admit even to herself unfurls like a rose under a midnight moon: *I think he's falling in love with me.*

The room she traverses is far, far longer than the floor plan of the house should allow. The concrete floor has changed to dirt and a strange, heavy dust, the particles of which mix with the wet air, making it difficult to breathe. The room narrows considerably until, the next time she looks away from the flashlight beam, she finds herself in less of a room than a corridor. The ceiling is no longer the same wide expanse it was when she descended the stairs, but has dropped down at either side to form something of an archway.

"No way," she whispers and starts to turn around. She will not be the idiot in a horror movie, walking foolishly to her own demise. But then Emmit's voice rings out, bouncing disorientingly off the walls:

"Saoirse!"

"Emmit!" she yells back. "Where *are* you?"

"Down here," he calls. "You have to see this!"

She speeds up, though every cell in her body is screaming at her to turn around. "Are you okay? I heard something crash."

As if to solidify her point, a second crash comes. A cloud of dust plumes up ahead in the beam of her flashlight. She starts to jog toward it, but when she reaches the scene, she still can't see Emmit anywhere in the settling debris.

And that's when a hand grabs her ankle. She shrieks and tries to jump back, but the hand holds her in place. "Get off me, get off me!" She kicks her leg and gasps for breath, but there's a second level of fear vibrating beneath her panic, beneath the terror of being grabbed, like her fear has its own subterranean lair beneath a walkout basement. She drops into that secondary fear as abruptly as plunging through an unseen opening in the floorboards: *This stress on top of alcohol and drugs cannot be good for my heart.*

"Let go!" she shrieks, squinting into the black hole from which the hand extends. A head appears beside the arm, and Emmit is there, struggling to climb out of the hole.

"Saoirse," he croaks, "it's me. Stop kicking, and help me out of here."

For the second time that night, Saoirse, too weak to stand, drops to her knees on the ground. Emmit looks at her strangely, eyes glinting, a smirk at one corner of his mouth, as if he knows a delicious, terrible secret. "Jesus Christ, Emmit," she exclaims, catching her breath. "Was that the crash I heard? Did you *fall* down there? Are you okay?"

"I . . . I think so," he replies, and the smirk disappears. Likely, she'd imagined it in the first place. "There are boxes or something down here. I fell onto one of them. It blocked my fall, but I shouldn't stand on it too much longer. It's pretty unsteady."

Saoirse grips his hands, and Emmit worms his way up. "Why the hell did you come down here in the first place?" she asks.

"I had to see where Lovecraft's story was set," he says and brushes dust and chips of wood from the collar of his jacket. "Where it was *actually* set. Dumb, I know. But once I was down here"—he pauses and gestures around them—"I had to see how far it goes. I'm not high anymore. Well, not *that* high. But it's not my imagination, right? This basement, it goes way beyond the foundation of the house."

As Emmit continues talking about the inexplicable construction, Saoirse leads him back in the direction of the basement stairs. "It's not your imagination. The rooms *do* extend too far to make sense within the framework of the house. But I don't need any more raccoons, and I don't need you falling into any more holes in the floor. If you want to investigate, why don't you contact that friend of yours with the historical society? Find out about the Shunned House from the safety of street level?"

They've reached the bottom of the stairs, and Saoirse brushes more dust from Emmit's jacket. Emmit blinks and flexes his fingers, as if returning to himself.

"For now," Saoirse continues, "how about we get out of here? Maybe get some dinner?"

"That's a great idea," he says. "And, Saoirse? I'm sorry for dragging you down here. It's just, once I started walking into the, well, abyss, for lack of a better word, I couldn't help myself. We were there! In the very place that inspired Lovecraft! I started thinking"—he stops and smiles at Saoirse a little sheepishly—"that it might inspire me too." He moves closer to her, his expression earnest. Then, in a tone of reverent disbelief, he says, "I think it *did* inspire me."

Saoirse takes his hand. "That's great," she says, leading him up the stairs. At the top, she closes the trapdoor, then shepherds him across the walkout basement and into the hallway. She's desperate to be outside, away from the heavy stench of mold that makes it hard to breathe, that makes her heart thud painfully in her chest. She's desperate to suck in lungfuls of fresh, cold air. "And I want to hear all about it. Just as soon as we walk out the back door, prop that big rock in front of it to keep it closed, and get the hell out of this creepy old house."

Chapter 26

The next morning, Saoirse lingers in bed, staring out the balcony slider at the brilliant swath of leaves in shades from dandelion to cider. Emmit left earlier than she expected, citing the need to head into his office to work on story critiques for several mentees. But Saoirse doubts this. His urgency, she thinks, has more to do with the inspiration he claims visited him the previous evening than with returning papers while he's out, recovering from his fictitious bout of COVID.

Emmit didn't say much over dinner regarding the nature of this inspiration, only that—while far from the fully formed idea he received prior to embarking upon *Vulture Eyes*—it was the beginning of something special. Saoirse didn't question whether his excitement was misplaced, though she can't see how anything from that damp, disgusting basement could translate to something of literary merit.

Still, he seemed hopeful to the point where she chose to ignore the two bottles of wine he drank with dinner, invigorated so that his eyes remained bright and alert even after Saoirse grew tired. He was energetic on the walk home, and after they fell into the front door of 88 Benefit, up the stairs, and into her bedroom, his thirst for her was endless, his need for her touch and attention exhausting her, his demand for her reciprocation and synchronicity almost sending her over the edge.

Saoirse remains tired even after the full night's sleep, drained from the drug and alcohol consumption. She still can't believe the woman last night sipping from a flask and swallowing unidentified powder-filled capsules was her.

Easy to fall down the rabbit hole of substances, isn't it? Jonathan asks. *Even with a bum heart.*

Saoirse ignores him.

Vowing to get back on track with her health, she goes to the kitchen to put the kettle on and search for her computer. Despite these distractions, despite her attempts to focus on the fun she's had with Emmit, or the seeds of an idea for a new poem, the only thought that continues to present itself is the one she's trying to dodge most vehemently: *I might not be anything like Jonathan. But might Emmit be a little more like my late husband than I first thought?*

No. That isn't it. They're just in that early stage of relationships, when everything is new and full of potential. It's normal to let loose a little more than normal, to rely on a bit of liquid courage to let down one's inhibitions. Emmit is *not* like Jonathan. He can't be.

But it's not just the substance use—abuse?—that reminds you of me, is it? Jonathan asks. *That night you were having dinner with your friends . . . Emmit didn't just sound disappointed when you weren't free, he sounded jealous. I didn't even get jealous of you spending time with other people.*

"No," Saoirse says aloud. "You were jealous of my insistence on maintaining a life, on maintaining an identity, separate from you. You wanted to strip me of my autonomy, to control—no, obliterate—my very life. I'll take Emmit's disappointment over your abuse any day of the week."

That's a little dramatic, Jonathan says.

"It isn't."

Really? I mean, I still don't even buy the little meet-cute as it supposedly happened. Emmit, worrying you were stalking him? It was an act meant to turn you away from your original suspicions. You and I both know Emmit saw you in the Athenæum that day, followed you home, and has orchestrated every subsequent run-in.

Saoirse opens her laptop angrily. "Will you get out of my head! Why won't you disappear already, shut up and leave me alone?"

Oh, Saoirse, Saoirse. You know why I won't leave. It's simple, really. Poetic. My voice is the disembodied heart beneath the floorboards, and I'm going to keep on beating till I drive you mad.

Any lingering motivation to check job postings dissipates. She pushes her laptop across the table, leaves the kitchen, and wanders into the living room. She will not continue arguing with someone who's not really there, whether that's the ghost of her dead husband or a fragment of her own splintered brain. She sits on the settee and opens a notebook on the coffee table. She wants the peace that comes with writing but doesn't want to be alone to achieve it. She's considering going for a walk to shake some ideas loose when her cell phone rings.

"How'd you like to engage in a little mysticism for mysticism's sake?" Roberto asks after Saoirse's accepted the call.

"Huh?"

"Just a little transcendentalist humor. Writing. How would you like to get together to do some writing?"

"You have great timing. That sounds perfect right about now." She pauses. Something about Roberto's opening comment was sticking for her, like a spot she couldn't rub clean. "What was the whole mysticism humor thing again?" she asks.

Roberto chuckles. "Oh, it was nothing. Just a dig at ol' Poe."

"Poe?" Saoirse feels a chill, like moth wings, at the back of her neck.

"Poe couldn't stand transcendentalists. Wrote a whole story that was a thinly veiled critique of those responsible for the movement. Thought their 'mysticism' and symbolism turned their poetry into the flattest kind of prose."

She can practically hear Roberto shrugging, but her mind is churning, contemplating what he's said. Odd, that Poe despised those individuals with whom his fiancée would have surrounded herself. A strange parallel, since Emmit has been lukewarm, at best, whenever Saoirse's mentioned her transcendentalist friends.

"Anyway, where do you want to meet?" Roberto asks.

She shakes her head to clear her thoughts. "How about Carr Haus?" *Who am I? Just last week, all I wanted was to curl up under a blanket of Paxil.*

Paxil. Entresto. She shoots a look toward the kitchen then down at her phone. Ten o'clock. Wherever she and Roberto end up going, she needs to take her medication before leaving the house. She promised herself she was going to start making her health a priority, and here she is, an hour late taking her meds. Not only that, but she needs to find a cardiologist and psychiatrist now that she's settled in Providence. Her New Jersey providers won't prescribe to her indefinitely. She's worked too hard finding the perfect balance of drug interactions to risk having a lapse in her treatment.

"What was that?" she asks, coming back to the present yet again. "Sorry, I zoned out for a second."

"I saaaid," he starts, drawing the words out, "let's skip Carr Haus. That's not even a you-and-Lucretia place anymore, it's a you-and-Emmit one."

"Oh, please," she says, mock-irritably. "But fine, no Carr Haus. What do you suggest?"

"How about the Ath?"

Saoirse freezes.

"Saoirse? You still there?"

"Yes. Sorry. I'm here." She can't be weird about the Ath; Roberto will ask too many questions. "That sounds fine."

"Meet you there in twenty?"

"See you then." Saoirse hangs up, takes her medication, and is about to head out when her phone dings again. Thinking it's Roberto, Saoirse eyes the screen, but the text is from an unknown number. She opens the message:

It's Aidan. Why'd you block my number? I'm going to find you, Saoirse. I'm GOING to talk to you. Just respond, agree to meet, and make this easier on everyone.

Saoirse throws the phone across the room. She is trembling. Aidan didn't say *agree to meet somewhere in Providence*, so it's possible he still doesn't know she's here. But he got *another* new phone, which means he's going to start texting her relentlessly again. She wants to call Roberto back and cancel, but she also doesn't want to be alone, so she forces herself to grab her bag and leave the house. She walks the ten blocks between 88 Benefit Street and the Athenæum looking over her shoulder every few steps.

Ten minutes later, still jumpy, Saoirse stands before the trickling fountain. Her eyes roam over the carved granite leaves and elongated letters. A fly whizzes past her right ear, then doubles back and circles her left one.

"Buzz *off*," Saoirse hisses, and swats the air so hard that she misjudges her proximity to the fountain. The back of her hand smashes into the thick granite, and her brain goes blank from the pain. She doubles over, sucking air through gritted teeth. Something warm snakes over her fingers, and Saoirse looks down to find the skin along her knuckles is raw and broken; the deepest scrape oozes blood.

After several deep breaths, she forces herself to straighten. The stream of fountain water fills her vision like a mirage. Unthinkingly, she jabs her hand forward and lets the cold water run over the bruised tendons and aching bones. It flows into the series of scrapes, washing the blood down the scalloped stonework and into the lower basin. When she pulls her hand away, more pink-tinged water runs off her fingers to disappear into the cracks of the city sidewalk. *Once you drink from the fountain, you can never leave,* the couple walking down the sidewalk told her just one week ago.

Drinking it would be one thing, Jonathan says, *but what does the legend say about filtering the water straight into your bloodstream?*

Saoirse whimpers and shakes excess water from her skin. The throbbing has lessened to a dull ache. She looks one way then the other—no Aidan, and no one has witnessed her run-in with the fountain. Saoirse rubs her palm across the leg of her jeans and starts up the stairs.

As she reaches the library entrance, Roberto calls out from behind her. "Hey! You beat me here."

She waits while he jogs up the stairs, more grateful to see him than she'd expected, and they enter together. Saoirse focuses on Roberto's easy gait and the casual way he greets the librarians rather than the vivid memories of spending time with Jonathan at the Ath now joining her anxiety over the text from Aidan. That those memories are all pleasant, coupled with the knowledge of what her and Jonathan's relationship would become, causes a dissonance that nags at her as persistently as her injured hand.

She wonders what Roberto would say if she told him about her husband. She *always* wonders what people would say if they knew the truth of how Jonathan had changed from a normal, fun-to-be-around guy to the veritable prison guard he'd become. *Why didn't you just leave?* she imagines they'd ask. That question simultaneously infuriates and demoralizes her. *Imagine the frog in the pot of boiling water,* she can see herself saying. *Then imagine that, during the first few instances of the water warming by a few degrees, the frog was also systematically belittled, worn down, stripped of its agency, and gaslit out of taking the very remedies that could have motivated it to escape. Do you see now? Do you see why leaving wasn't only not an option, it was as likely as starting a little frog pond on the dark side of the moon?*

"We could see if the Art Room's available," Roberto muses.

"No," Saoirse says quickly. Too quickly. She needs to stop letting her mind wander before Roberto starts to question her sanity. Still, the last thing she wants is Leila Rondin finding her near a table of artifacts for an upcoming exhibit. "One of the alcoves is fine."

When they reach the second floor, Roberto turns left. He passes the first alcove and veers into the second. Saoirse follows, wishing she'd insisted on meeting at Carr Haus, after all. She takes in the multipaned windows, the bust on the sill, the straight-backed chair pushed neatly against the empty desk.

Saoirse's been in this alcove before. It's the alcove with the best light, according to Leila Rondin. The alcove in which, two days before their planned Christmas Day wedding, Edgar and Sarah were sitting when Sarah was handed a note telling her that Poe had broken his promise of sobriety.

She thinks of Emmit and his affinity for Poe, his irresistible lopsided smile, the way he listens to every word she says, encourages every thought she has. The way he treats her poetry like it's some sort of magic. Then, the lopsided smile turns sinister, and she sees him tipping back the silver flask. Handing her the small capsule stuffed with suspicious brown powder. Beckoning to her after smashing the door of the Shunned House in the yellowy light of a waxing gibbous moon.

You're having your very own Poe-Whitmanian whirlwind romance, Lucretia had said, and Roberto had agreed, claiming *the longing, the passion, the depth of his love for her, practically overnight* was on par with Emmit's feelings for Saoirse. Everything feels too orchestrated, a little too much like Saoirse is acting out a role in a play. The relationship is too exciting, too full of meaning, too significant. Serendipitous. The past couple of days, her every action feels like it could be an echo of Sarah's. And Emmit? Were his actions an echo of Edgar's?

"Does this work?" Roberto asks, interrupting the madness swirling around her head.

Saoirse forces a smile and nods. She slides across from him at the desk and pulls out a notebook. The framed drawing of a pen-and-ink raven above their heads reflects the light from the alcove across the open-air space of the second floor. Saoirse wishes she had a bottle of water, feels a little fuzzy-headed.

It's because you're letting Emmit inside your head now, like you once did me, Jonathan whispers.

Saoirse and Roberto settle into a comfortable silence, broken only by the flip of Roberto's pages. Saoirse stares at her own notebook for several minutes but can't clear the static from her brain. After ten minutes without writing a word, she pushes her chair back and stands.

"I'm going to take a walk." She's thinking of something to add, something about needing to look for inspiration, but Roberto is already nodding.

"Sounds good," he mumbles, pen flying.

Saoirse wanders around the second floor but sees no glass enclosures or well-lit display cases. It's almost the end of October; the exhibit Leila Rondin had been curating should be up now. When an authoritative woman walks by with a stack of books cradled in her arms, Saoirse taps her on the elbow. "Excuse me," she says, "can you tell me where the Poe-Whitman exhibit is located?"

The woman leads her downstairs and to the right of the main entrance, kitty-corner to the children's wing. Saoirse thanks the woman, and she nods and disappears. The exhibit is small—much smaller than she expected—a mere three glass cabinets of artifacts, the most prominent being a parchment featuring Poe's signature. There are early newspaper printings and contemporary parodies of "The Raven," a print of "Le Corbeau" by French modernist painter Édouard Manet, inscribed to Sarah Whitman by poet and critic Stéphane Mallarmé. Saoirse spots several first editions, some memorabilia of Poe's, and, finally, a portrait of Sarah.

It's different from any of the portraits she's seen, a daguerreotype taken—according to the plaque beside it—by Providence photographer Joseph White and depicting his subject in profile, her dark-brown hair peeking past her accustomed headwear: a black veil and ribbon tied in a bow under her chin. The plaque also states that Sarah, "or Helen, as she was known to her friends," was fifty-three at the time the photograph was taken.

Saoirse stares at the woman before her—the whispers of Jonathan, Aidan, and Emmit that had swirled through her mind since entering the library falling away.

Too long benighted man has had his way.
Indignant woman turns and stands at bay.

The lines materialize in her head as if delivered on the wings of a raven. Though, was it possible this was something she'd read before and was merely recalling? More lines arrive just as swiftly:

Old proverbs tell us when the world was new,
And men and women had not much to do,
Adam was wont to delve and Eve to spin;
His work was out of doors and hers within.
But Adam seized the distaff and the spindle,
And Eve beheld her occupation dwindle.

Saoirse steps back from the exhibit, the lines cutting serpentine patterns through her head. She makes her way back to the staircase as if she's a sleepwalker—new words, new rhymes, spinning themselves around her like smoke.

At the top of the stairs, she turns left past an empty alcove. She's two stacks away from Roberto, from her empty, waiting notebook. But after another step, she stops, forced to a standstill by the words in her brain, the poem's final line presenting itself along with a shiver that runs up her spine and cascades along her neck. It's not the shiver of scuttling spiders or the unpleasant prickle of fly legs. This is a sensation of delight and exhilaration, and the fingers of her right hand twitch, anxious to transfer the odd, alien words from her head to the page.

She moves forward another step. A noise comes from Roberto's alcove, like he's sliding his chair back from the desk. Saoirse looks up at the exact moment a figure steps out from the stack on her right, blocking her path. A hand goes to her neck, brushes her collarbone to grip her shoulder, and Saoirse feels herself pushed backward, past the last two stacks she passed, into the farthest corner of the library, feels her shoulder blades press up against cold metal shelving and smells the chemical compounds of the glue, the ink, the paper of the hundreds of books that surround her. The arm against her chest is firm and unmoving.

Saoirse's heartbeat skyrockets. She is back in the graveyard with Aidan Vesper, beneath the weeping willows. All the lovely lines of poetry disappear from her head.

Chapter 27

"Emmit," she breathes when she sees it's him and not Aidan who has backed her into the corner. "What the hell are you doing?" She jerks her chin at the stacks. "What the hell are you doing here?"

The crooked smile animates his lips, but the expression seems nervous, his normal mannerisms pressurized, like he's pure carbonation, about to explode. He brushes a lock of hair away from his forehead, and Saoirse stares at him, full of dismay and incredulity at his actions. She grits her teeth and says in an angry whisper, "Seriously, what are you doing here?"

"I always come to the Athenæum to write on Wednesdays," he says, and there's something in his voice she can't place. "So, imagine my surprise when I looked up from my work and saw . . ." One side of his mouth jumps up again, the movement automatic, agitated. His eyes flick to the right, and he turns his head slightly, as if checking to see if anyone is behind them. Saoirse follows his gaze to the alcove she was in earlier, to where she imagines Roberto sits still, pen in hand, working away. ". . . you with another man," Emmit finishes.

So that was the note in his voice she didn't recognize: jealousy. And here she'd insisted to Jonathan that Emmit was above this. "You've got to be kidding," she whispers. "I'm with Roberto. *Roberto*, one of the three writer friends I told you about. The ones I've been spending time with since moving here." She narrows her eyes. Is this really another instance of her and Emmit ending up in the same place at the same time? Or did he follow her here? And what exactly is he accusing her of?

"*Did* you tell me?" Emmit asks. His voice is low and measured. "I don't remember you saying anything about a Roberto. Maybe you didn't mention their names, and I just assumed all three of your new friends were female?"

He emphasizes *new* as if to point out that new friends couldn't possibly be close ones. Saoirse tries stepping back, but there's nowhere to go. "Whether I told you or not," she says, "you know I'm allowed to hang out with whomever I want to, right? Male or female?" She looks out across the library, then back at Emmit. "Were you really at the Ath, or did you follow us here?"

For a second, Emmit looks properly chastised. Then his eyes search her face again, more intently. "So, this guy hangs out with you and two other women all the time?" he whispers, ignoring her last question. "Is he gay?"

A flash of white-hot light explodes behind Saoirse's eyes. Her heartbeat jumps from a trot to a gallop, and she puts the heels of her hands on Emmit's shoulders and tries to push him away.

"Well, is he?" Emmit presses, undeterred by the shove or her anger. For someone whose build isn't particularly muscular, he's far stronger than she expected.

"Not that your arrogance deserves a response, but yes, Roberto is gay. He also doesn't ask me ridiculous questions or confront me in public places when I'm writing." She whirls away from Emmit and steps toward the aisle, then stops and says, "You're way out of line right now."

She makes herself sound disgusted, but what she's feeling is something far more primal. Something she does not want to admit she's feeling. His turning up like this, his jealousy, the physical intimidation, the manipulation. What she's feeling is the first thin, spiky tendrils of fear.

She gets two steps out of the stacks when Emmit grabs her again. This time his touch is gentle. He pulls her toward him, into an embrace.

"You're right," he says into her ear, his breath warm against her skin, and she hates herself for wanting him, right here in the corner of the library, wanting him to take her the way he did in the hotel room, in her bedroom, in the Shunned House.

"Saoirse, I'm so sorry. Jesus, I don't know what I was thinking, what came over me. It's just, I was writing, working on that new idea that came to me last night with you, that came to me *because* of you, and I looked up and saw you with someone else, and I just saw red." He pulls away and stares into her eyes. He smiles at her fully but in a pleading, apologetic way. When she doesn't return the smile, he says, more desperately, "I promise I didn't follow you. I always write here on Wednesdays, I swear it."

The lie zigzags through her brain like lightning, and her heart pounds wildly. Saoirse rips her hands away from his. "I thought you were in Baltimore on Wednesdays." She shakes her head, feeling sick. "You told me you're in Baltimore every week, Mondays, Tuesdays, and Wednesdays." Should she call out for Roberto? Or yell for one of the librarians? Ask that they call security?

But Emmit is closing his eyes and murmuring to himself, like he's forgotten some key piece of information, not like he's been caught in an outright lie. "Of course," he says evenly, as if trying to calm a spooked horse. "Of course you're right. I meant that, before I accepted the position at Johns Hopkins but had already become a professor at Brown, I wrote here every Wednesday. And today . . . I mean, gosh, Sersh, it's been a whirlwind. Last night with you, it broke apart something inside me. It tore down the block! I wrote all night, and I've been writing—feverishly, fantastically—right in that alcove across the way"—he gestures across the open air of the second floor—"since the Ath opened this morning. And none of it would have happened without you! It's like I knew it would be, from my premonition. You are my momentous thing; you are the catalyst. You are the Whitman to my Poe, the Sarah behind my 'To Helen.'"

Saoirse takes a breath, tries to quell the canter of her heart. Could he be telling the truth? "I'm glad you're writing," she whispers. "But you sound manic. You're scaring me. And regardless of how excited you are to be over your block, that doesn't give you the right to give me the third degree about who I'm here with. And it doesn't give you the right to ask anything like what you did about Roberto."

He grabs her shoulders again and rubs her arms in slow, rhythmic circles. "You're right. I'm so sorry. I don't know what came over me. I haven't slept. I haven't eaten. I've had way too much caffeine. Please, forgive me. Of course you can spend time with whomever you want. Of course you can *do* whatever you want. I feel so lucky to have met you, and—"

Saoirse holds up a hand. "Wait a minute. You feel so lucky to have met me because you like me, or so lucky to have met me because I'm the thing that's gotten you writing again?"

He pulls her close to him again. "*Of course* it's because I like you." His eyes do not blink as they stare into hers. "You *know* that what's between us is real," he continues. "You know it. I know you've felt it. It doesn't feel like we've known each other a matter of days. It feels like a lifetime. Like when we stepped into that graveyard behind your house, we did go back in time, then forward again, but all the while, we were together."

He trails the back of one hand down the side of her face. Her skin pulses with electricity. "And I think you know that I don't just like you, Saoirse." His mouth jumps into an anxious half smile. "I'm falling in love with you." He slides the hand caressing her face behind her head and pulls her into him.

Their kiss is long and hard and breathless. It steals the strength from her legs. When he pulls away, Saoirse sees how tired and wrung out he is. How jumpy and forlorn and desperate for her to forgive him. Maybe his behavior *is* due to a sleepless night, a morning of caffeine and frantic writing. And after the evening they had last night, full of sex and brandy and powder-filled capsules, anyone would be a little erratic.

He's holding her face with one hand and biting his bottom lip. He's waiting for her to say something, but she can't. Between the kiss and the admission, and with the silence of the library pressing in around them, she's too overwhelmed to say it back. Or, is it that, in the wake of Emmit's recent behavior, she knows saying *I love you too* would be untrue?

He kisses her again, and slides his hands up the sides of her shirt. She gives in to his touch, then, remembering where they are, ends the kiss and pushes him away. "I have to go," she whispers. "Roberto's going to wonder what happened to me."

Emmit's smile slips, but he recovers quickly. "Of course. Though, we *are* in the library where Sarah and Edgar courted one another. It's practically made for romance."

Saoirse groans and slides past him. "Enough from the original Goth English major quoting Joyce from the back of the lecture hall. I have to get back. Not just because I'm being rude, but because I have to get some words onto the page." Emmit looks like a lost, sad puppy, so she gives him another quick kiss and whispers in his ear, "I'll call you later. Maybe we can get dinner?"

He nods. "That would be fantastic. And Saoirse. I really am sorry."

She watches him hurry down the stairs, then smooths her hair and the hem of her shirt, and starts toward the third alcove from the back wall.

Roberto barely looks up when she slips into the seat across from him. She tries to focus, to recall the earlier words of the strange, old-fashioned poem that had come to her while standing across from Sarah Whitman's portrait, but the lines remain hazy, like mist curling from the surface of a glassy lake.

She's about to give up when Emmit's face flashes through her mind, the way he'd looked when he'd tried to keep her from leaving, the hint of something naked and dangerous in his eyes. As she considers their interaction, a new poem takes shape. It's razor-sharp and venomous, full of shedding insect skins and carnivorous mantids, chitinous wings patterned with owl eyes—an impressive feat of mimicry meant to fool potential predators—and of parasitic vines that twist around the mortal pillars of men's earthly souls.

Saoirse composes and considers, slamming metric frameworks around stanzas like tiny prisons, her pen catching up to, then surpassing, the speed of Roberto's. She could almost believe Emmit's appearance in the stacks was the product of her imagination, if not for the taste of him on her lips, the feel of his hands on her sides, and the way his presence bleeds into every word she carves—like the indentation of an insect—onto the page.

Chapter 28

When Saoirse returns from the Ath, she retrieves her phone from behind the settee and blocks the number from which Aidan texted her. She and Emmit don't end up getting dinner because Emmit is too immersed in his writing, and Saoirse finds this is fine with her . . . maybe even preferable. She spends that night and the next morning rearranging—then editing—her new poem. At noon, she takes a break, gently shooing Pluto from her lap before heading to the kitchen, where she takes her meds, drinks a glass of water, and makes a salad.

You need more than your current scripts, water, and a few vegetables, she reminds herself. *You've got to get set up with a new cardiologist and psychiatrist.* She has a few refills left, but she wants, *needs,* to be proactive. *I'll call my old doctors in New Jersey this afternoon and ask for recommendations in the city.*

With medications on her mind, she prepares a dose of insulin and tests Pluto's blood sugar. His values are better than she expects, better than they've been on any of the previous days he's been with her. She caps the unneeded syringe and almost slips it into the pocket of her sweatshirt before remembering it has to be stored in the fridge. After depositing it on a shelf next to the oat milk, she retrieves a little bell toy scented with catnip from under the table and tosses it toward the foyer, sending Pluto scampering after it.

Throwing the ball back and forth for the frisky cat, Saoirse's thoughts turn to Emmit. She's conflicted about his behavior at the library yesterday, and she's still unsure how she managed to convince Roberto everything was fine when she returned to the alcove. They'd stayed at the Ath another two hours and planned to write again together next week, but several times, Saoirse caught Roberto looking at her strangely, as if he'd heard more of the commotion from a few alcoves away than he was letting on.

She's still lamenting the loss of the poem she'd crafted in her head upon seeing the daguerreotype of Sarah. The poem she'd written after her interaction with Emmit wasn't nearly as good; she realized that this morning, trying to mold it into something salvageable. It wasn't just the time spent fielding Emmit's heated questions that had caused her to lose the initial poem, nor the brief delay in transcribing the newly conceived lines. It was the way he'd accused her without saying the words, then launched into an explanation of his glorious return to writing. It *wasn't* the interruption, like she'd initially thought; it was his manic, needy energy that—like a black hole—had sucked the poem right out of her head.

She looks up, realizing the ball is in her hand, and Pluto is staring at her expectantly. She lifts her hand to throw it again, but before she can do so, her cell phone rings from the counter. A knot of fear forms in her stomach. *Did Aidan get another burner phone already?*

But when she sees the name on the screen, her fear changes to a sinking, shameful dread. She wants to toss the phone back behind the settee. But she knows if she puts off the call, he'll only call again. She lifts the phone, steels herself, and presses accept.

"Hi, Dad."

"Saoirse. About time that we spoke."

She closes her eyes. "I've been meaning to text you."

"I don't do the whole texting thing. You know that." He says the word *texting* like it's a fly he's discovered in his ice cream. "Anyhow, I assume you're settled in. Have you found a job yet?"

She walks into the living room and collapses onto the settee. Pluto jumps up beside her, and she weaves her fingers through the fur at the scruff of his neck. The action comforts her enough to swallow an acerbic remark. "Not yet." She makes her tone as light as possible. "But I went to a career fair at Brown over the weekend. I have a few prospects to follow up on this week."

"This week? Saoirse, it's already Thursday."

"I've been busy," she says, trying to sound matter-of-fact rather than defensive.

"Doing what? Not wasting your time writing, I hope. Saoirse, I told you, once you lost your agent, that career path was a dead end. Even when you had that woman in your corner, those baking mysteries, well, they weren't the type of book you'd expect a Brown graduate to write. Likely why they didn't bring in a whole lot of cash."

Saoirse's muscles stiffen, but none of this, coming from her father, is surprising. "I have been writing, actually. Not for an agent but for myself." She tells herself not to say this next part, that it will invite more criticism and too many questions, but old habits die hard, and despite never having had her father's approval, she still desires it, and isn't above seeking it through channels both grotesquely reliable and undoubtedly sexist. "And I've been seeing someone. He's a professor at Brown and a renowned novelist. Emmit Powell. Have you heard of him?"

There's a short silence, and then her father says, "I haven't, but I'll look him up, see if I've read anything he's written." Another pause. "While I'd much prefer to hear you'd found a job, it wouldn't be the worst thing for you to get married again. It pains me that you lost Jonathan. He was such a good man. He would have made a fine father, and you would have been a good mother to his children."

His reaction to her being in a new relationship and his comments about Jonathan *despite* Saoirse having told him what had happened are like a knife in her side. "We've been over this," she says through gritted teeth. Though, had they, technically, if her father always refused to listen? She decides to try again. "Even if Jonathan hadn't died, we could have never been parents. The doctors were very clear that, with my condition, my chances of dying during childbirth were extremely high. And cardiomyopathy is the leading cause of serious complications and death *during* pregnancy."

"Nonsense," her father says. "They can manage anything at the big-city hospitals these days. And I know better than anyone how, if you do the right things, the disease doesn't have to dictate your life."

She balls her hands into fists to stop the tremors in her fingers. *Right, because having cardiomyopathy as a near-seventy-year-old man is the same as having it as a woman of childbearing age.* "Even if they could have," she says, as if speaking to a toddler, "I told Jonathan that any joy associated with having a child was not enough to make me want to undertake the risks. It was bad enough he blamed me for his inability to become a father, but that you can't seem to understand why I wouldn't want to risk my own life for that of an unborn child's is . . . well, it's devastating. It's like you're saying you'd prefer a future grandchild over your present daughter."

Her father huffs out a disgruntled breath. "I'm sorry you feel that way," he says, "since that's not at all how I meant it. Anyway, I'm glad you're dating someone new. I just googled him; he appears to be very successful. I bet prenatal care for someone with your condition has come a long way since you and Jonathan were trying. Maybe the opportunity for you to have a family has had new life breathed into it by this Emmit character."

A scream rips loose in Saoirse's head. How had she not seen, once they'd been married for a few years and Jonathan's true nature started emerging, that he was exactly like her father? She covers the speaker and sucks in a shaky breath, then puts the phone back to her ear. "It was nice talking to you, Dad, but I have to go. I'm sending out some résumés and applications now, so I need to concentrate. Have a nice day."

"Please remember, Saoirse, I'm only this hard on you because I care. My success as a father is entirely dependent on you being able to take care of yourself, and on having someone to pass on your legacy to. You can't do either of those things without a job or a man."

"Bye, Dad," Saoirse says and hangs up. She's about to throw the phone across the room for the second time in two days when she sees the red notification above her messages. Despite her staggering anger, she sends a hasty response to her mother: *I'm okay. No bad dreams, no flashbacks. Trying to live in the moment. Love you too.* She stands, but her legs feel like the brittle stalks of a rosebush and her heart—goddamn her heart. It beats like a horse fleeing a bolt of lightning.

Saoirse steps around the coffee table, but her eyes fill with tears. The Zuber panels, with their scenes of lush forest and thick canopy leaves, melt into one another, until her vision swims green, like flooded watercolors. She lurches into the foyer, not sure where she's going, needing only to move, to run away from her thoughts, from the words of her father, from her past.

The door handle spins uselessly, her hand too wet with the tears she's wiped from her eyes, and she is trapped inside this house. Trapped inside her mind. She drags her palm across her jeans and grips the handle more firmly. In the moment after throwing open the door, she is blinded by the afternoon sun. Before she can shield her eyes, a figure steps onto the stoop, blocking the light.

And then Emmit is there, taking her tear-stained face in his hands. His eyes are heavy with concern, and his mouth is twisted in an expression of love and longing. He throws his arms around her, then reaches up to stroke her hair. Her head is pressed into his chest, and the smell of him relaxes her. "Everything's going to be okay," he says, and she wants to laugh with relief.

Though, the longer they stand there, through the hammering of her heart and the spinning of her thoughts, despite her messed up head and her haunted soul and her misgivings about her and Emmit's relationship and her anger at her father, despite the past and the love she once had for Jonathan—a love that was weaponized—and the love she thinks she has for this man holding her now, on this whitewashed stoop that once belonged to a woman who held the heart of another mysterious, macabre man, the more his words don't sound like a lie at all.

They sound like a promise.

Chapter 29

Two hours later, she's told Emmit about her heart condition, how she'd been afraid to tell him—how she's *always* afraid to tell someone new, terrified they'll judge her, assume that the disease is somehow her fault—and how her diagnosis kick-started the dissolution of her marriage, how Jonathan wanted something from her that she couldn't give him. And while she didn't divulge how Jonathan's retribution had manifested, she told him that what he had taken from her cost close to everything.

Most importantly, she told him how, before coming to this city, to this house, before meeting her new friends and adopting Pluto, before writing again, and finding him, she didn't think she'd ever shake off the chains of what Jonathan had done to her.

"I had no intention of opening up to anyone, romantically"—*or, especially, sexually,* she thinks but doesn't say—"ever again." She sniffles, and then she lets out a little bark of disbelieving laughter. "I'm still not even completely sure how *this*"—she gestures back and forth between the two of them—"happened." Emmit smiles but says nothing. He seems content to let the "this" she's referring to speak for itself.

They are in the living room, Saoirse holding a cup of now-lukewarm tea Emmit had made her and contemplating his reactions to what she's told him, how he berated himself for giving her drugs and alcohol—*It doesn't matter that you didn't tell me about your diagnosis, I shouldn't have offered you pills anyway!*—and how he sat quietly, staring into the empty fireplace, when she summarized some of Jonathan's less heinous offenses. The whole afternoon, his support, is almost enough to make her forget that he'd simply shown up on her doorstep. Almost.

She places her tea on the coffee table. "Emmit, why were you at my house? When I was upset and opened the door, you were already here."

The crooked smile animates his face. "I had to bring you something," he says. He digs into his pocket and comes out with a navy velvet jewelry box. Saoirse's body goes cold. Emmit opens it, and she exhales a quiet breath of relief. Of course there wouldn't have been an engagement ring in the box. That would have been too impulsive, even for Emmit. There's something small and flat nestled against the velvet partition. Emmit's fingers obscure the object, but a moment later, a silvery-gray charm dangles from the end of a chain in front of her face.

"Is that—" she starts, catching sight of the charm's unusual shape.

"It is," Emmit replies and releases the clasp. "And you're never going to believe this, but I was right. This charm is at least one hundred and seventy-seven years old."

Saoirse looks at him, eyes wide. "So, it's hers, then. Sarah's. Is that what you're telling me?"

Emmit shrugs, but there's reverent disbelief on his face, as if he cannot believe it either. "Levi, my contact with the historical society, he connected me to the antiques appraiser they use. They confirmed the jewelry's age and authenticity. As for whether it was Sarah's, my inclination is to go with the simplest explanation. Sarah was known to wear a coffin charm around her neck. The charm was not recovered with her posthumous belongings, and neither has it been held with her papers at the Athenæum or in any other museum. We were on her former property when we found it." He shrugs again. "If the coffin fits, I guess you should wear it?"

"But," Saoirse says, bringing her hand to her throat as Emmit clasps the charm around her neck, "surely your friend felt this had historical significance. Why isn't it in a museum now?"

Emmit's mouth twitches mischievously, and he narrows his eyes. "Levi's a good writer but often too busy to send out his work. I helped him cut through some red tape a few months back and get a story of his published in *Granta*. He owed me a favor." He moves from his seat beside her on the settee, slides onto the coffee table, and looks at her appraisingly. "Do you like it? Because it suits you. That's why I was coming over here. Because I couldn't wait to see what you looked like wearing it."

Saoirse fingers the charm at her throat again. For a moment—just a moment—she thinks she hears the antique phone from the séance ringing in the basement. *Are you here, Sarah?* Saoirse wants to ask. *Is this your necklace? And if so, are you okay with me wearing it?*

"It's beautiful," she admits. "But don't you think—"

Emmit shushes her. "I think it's meant to be on your neck. Much more so than on some cold shelf in a museum."

"Isn't it a little—" *Macabre?* she thinks. "Strange?" she asks instead.

"There is no exquisite beauty without some strangeness in the proportion."

She has a feeling this is a quote from a poem of Poe's in which the narrator moons over one sad-faced, ill-fated maiden or another. Who *else* would Emmit be quoting? She's starting to wonder if his interest in Poe is more like an obsession. "Okay," she says. "Well, thank you. It's unlike any gift I've ever been given."

Emmit beams. "I'm glad you like it." For someone as masterful with words as Emmit is, Saoirse's surprised he doesn't realize that this isn't what she said.

Saoirse fidgets, trying to ignore the unnatural feel of the chain around her neck. "How's the writing been coming?" she asks, anxious to move on from both her troubled past and the necklace.

He shakes his head, eyes cast downward, and laughs in a way that suggests it's going better than he ever could have imagined. "I wrote eight thousand words last night," he says. He takes her hand and pulls her up from the settee. "Saoirse, this novel is going to be better than

Vulture Eyes. And I don't just think that. I *know* it. Though, I'm a long way from sending it off to my editor for a second opinion." He starts toward the door from the living room to the back hallway but stops halfway and turns to face her. "Or, a third opinion, I guess I should say. I'm hoping that, once it's finished, you'll be the first one to read it."

"I'd be happy to," she says. She stands, follows him out of the living room, and up the stairs. At the top, Emmit turns in the direction of her bedroom.

"The writing, it's like air," he says. "Like water. Like *you*. It sustains me."

Inside her room, he passes her bed and walks to the slider. He opens it, steps onto the balcony, and gestures for her to join him. Together, they look out at the darkening sky and the lights popping on all over the city.

The statue on the dome of the statehouse glints like liquid gold, and a pair of crows caw harshly from the trees above the cemetery still clinging to the last of their leaves. Emmit takes her hand. "Saoirse," he says, and at the twinge in his voice, she looks up into his face. There's no flash of the half smile, no jumping eyebrows. "Can I ask you something? Something else about your marriage?"

Chapter 30

Saoirse refrains from flinching and tries to smile. "Okay."

"It's just that, Jonathan was wrong to pressure you about having a baby after you'd shared your feelings with him, don't get me wrong. But do you—"

"I didn't just 'share my feelings with him,'" Saoirse says, cutting him off, then forces herself to take a breath. If Emmit wants to discuss her marriage in more depth, she will not get upset or angry. He's asking because he wants to know her. Truly know her. Because he cares.

"It's not like he and I never discussed it," she says more slowly, relieved she's gotten control of herself. "It's not like I waited until after we got married to drop this bomb on him that I didn't want children. Even before I was diagnosed, I was lukewarm on the subject, and he knew I didn't want to risk *dying* in order to have a baby." Emmit is studying her intently, hanging on her every word, so she continues.

"*Six years* after we were married, he brought it up again. By then, there were a million other things wrong with our relationship. I thought he was joking. I hadn't wanted to risk death by having a baby with Jonathan when things were *good*. Why would I give up my life so that a man who treated me like an empty vessel for his ideas could have a child? After enduring years of his bullshit, he was lowering me to the status of a breeding cow to be sent to the slaughterhouse when he was through with me? No, thank you.

"I dragged him to doctors' offices. I made him listen to the statistics. At this point, some part of me must have thought something of our relationship could be salvaged. I was still trying to make him see reason. But he wouldn't let up. Eventually, it started feeling like he didn't care whether I lived or died. The only thing that mattered to him was that I submitted to his desire to have a child."

She pauses and looks out over the tombstones in the cathedral's burial ground, thinks, as she often did back then, of her name carved into a slab of enduring granite, whether Jonathan would bring their child to the cemetery in which she was laid to rest. She shudders, and Emmit wraps his arms around her.

"I'm so sorry," he says. "That must have been awful. And then, to have Jonathan pass from a heart condition of his own. You must have felt—" He doesn't finish.

Saoirse barks out a bitter laugh. "It's hard to have sympathy for a man who asked the things he did of me. Harder still, to have sympathy for someone whose own selfish refusal to admit he'd formed a reliance on a dangerous mix of medication led to his heart stopping, especially when you've worked every day for as long as you can remember on keeping your own heart beating. It was so frustrating, Jonathan's drug use. Such a waste. He wasn't even really an addict. He was more of a perfectionist. His own worst enemy. Taking too much Adderall during the day to maximize his performance at work followed by handfuls of Ambien to get to sleep at night." She stares out over the graveyard. She will not cry again. She hadn't said anything to Emmit of Jonathan's actual death when they'd spoken downstairs.

"Will you tell me?"

Saoirse looks up at Emmit sharply. "Tell you what?"

"About finding his body?"

Saoirse shudders. "Why would you want to hear about a thing like that?"

Emmit shrugs. "Because it's something you went through, something that brings pain to your soul. And I want to know your soul, every inch of it, even the darkest parts."

Saoirse closes her eyes and is transported back. She feels the cold of the January night, the weight of her suitcase in her hand. She feels the electricity in the air, feels the anticipation of the thing to come in her bones. In her teeth.

"I'd been to visit my mother," she says, combating her apprehension by telling herself she'll only have to tell him this once, and then they will never speak of it again. "In Connecticut. I was supposed to go from Wednesday to Sunday morning, but I stayed later than expected, and it was close to ten p.m. on Sunday, maybe even eleven, when I'd driven back. It's strange, because I remember everything else about that night except the time. It was like time had ceased to exist in preparation for what I was about to find.

"I came in through the front door, but the house was dark, so I figured Jonathan was asleep. I started to bring my suitcase up the stairs but stopped one step up. I stood there, listening. Trying to figure out what it was I was hearing. And then, two big black flies buzzed by me, circling my face, whizzing around my ears, my hair.

"I swatted them away. I've always hated flies. But I didn't go upstairs. Because I thought I heard more buzzing, farther off. I stood in the foyer, one foot on the first stair, still just listening. I was exhausted from traveling. I remember wanting to drag my suitcase up to my office—I was sleeping there by that point, in a daybed—slip into some comfortable clothes, and crawl into bed.

"Instead, another fly flew past my head and landed on the railing. I watched it crawl in the dim glow shining in from the porch light, its tiny legs and giant eyes twitching, and for the first time since entering the house, I felt afraid. 'Jonathan?' I called. There was no answer, so I dropped my suitcase and turned away from the stairs.

"The silence persisted, but the quiet felt hollow. Like a bell had rung somewhere in the house and its echo still lingered. The sounds of my feet on the floor were like drumbeats intended to awaken an ancient curse. Halfway across the foyer, more flies buzzed around me. A smell I hadn't noticed while near the staircase became evident then. Something sweet and rank. Spoiled fruit or the sludgy water at the bottom of a vase of flowers left too long without rinsing.

"I crept through the rooms on the ground floor, but there was nothing in the kitchen, living room, or dining room. I looked out the back window toward the yard, wondering if something had died out there, close to the house. A foolish thought, since it was January, and none of the windows were open. Another fly buzzed close to my ear. It's funny, because the sound of a fly buzzing has always made me break out in goose bumps. I can't explain why. But in that moment, it wasn't the fly that caused the chill that spread over my entire body. The only room left to explore was Jonathan's office, and some deep, primal part of me knew what I would find.

"His door was shut, and the smell seeping from the cracks around it was so thick I thought I would choke. The feeling grew, then, the knowing, that once I opened that door, I would never be the same. A fly crawled over my hand as I reached for the knob, and my mind went blank, dissociating from the fear, my body on autopilot.

"I pushed the door open. He was lying under the window. His face was bloated and black. A highball glass must have broken in his hand when he fell. There was blood. So much blood from just a slice across his palm. And the flies. God, the flies. He'd been dead since Thursday, the night after I left. He'd been lying there for three whole days."

Saoirse peels her eyes from the gravestones below them and turns to look at Emmit. "I still see them, you know. The flies. I've never told anyone that. Not my friends. Not my mother. Not my psychiatrist or the cognitive behavioral therapist assigned to 'guide me through the trauma narrative.' I see them all the time. Sometimes they're real. Sometimes . . ." She trails off, eyes unfocused.

"It *is* a response to the trauma," Emmit says softly. "You have such a quiet, creative soul. There's no way you could have gone through all that without suffering some negative consequences. I'm sure that, in time, the flies will go away."

She nods but isn't really listening. She's too busy feeling out the new, lighter way her breath rises and falls in her chest. It feels good to have told someone. No, it feels good to have told Emmit. He's understanding, supportive. Perhaps she could have even told him a little more.

"And thank you for sharing that with me, Saoirse," Emmit says. "I know it couldn't have been easy." He cups her face, then trails his hand around to the back of her neck. He squeezes the taut muscles there and bends to kiss her.

"What did you want to ask me?" she says.

"What do you mean?"

"Before I told you everything just now, you said, *Jonathan was wrong to pressure you about having a baby after you'd shared your feelings with him, don't get me wrong.* But then I cut you off. Don't get you wrong about what?"

Now it's Emmit's turn to stare out at the tombstones. The sun has traveled farther west, and the shadows in the cemetery are long. "I was just going to ask, in the most nonjudgmental way possible, do you ever regret not trying to have a baby? And I mean that sincerely, not in the way your father might ask it, or because I agree with Jonathan. Your reasons are your reasons, and they're valid even if they weren't completely justifiable, which they are. I'm just curious as to whether you still think it was the right decision."

Saoirse forces down a slew of reflexive urges: to pull away from him, to shout in his face, to widen her eyes in disbelief. She manages to say without too much force, "Of course I don't regret it. Forty percent of pregnant women with cardiomyopathy succumb to heart attack, heart failure, abnormal heart rhythm, or death. *Forty percent.* Those seem like high enough odds to be at peace with a child-free lifestyle." Despite her best efforts, she still sounds defensive. Emmit isn't finished.

"I get that, and I completely agree. I'm just wondering, have you ever thought about how things might be different?"

"If I'd agreed to get pregnant?" This time, incredulity weaves its way into every word.

"Well, yes. Or, agreed to try. Maybe Jonathan would still be alive."

Saoirse squeezes her eyes so tightly that stars explode across the backs of her lids. "No, Emmit, I haven't thought about whether my decision to remain childless might have somehow resulted in my husband's death, rather than the cardiac arrest from a near-lethal combination of alcohol and drugs, like the coroner said. But please explain to me how it might have. Because without a decent explanation, it sounds pretty fucking bad. It sounds dismissive and shitty and one-sided, and misogynistic, and I *know* that's not how you meant to sound. Right? *Right?*"

She backed him into the corner of the balcony as she spoke, but rather than hold up his hands in mock surrender or engage in some other weak cop-out behavior, he places his hands on her shoulders and stares into her eyes.

"I'm *not* saying you were to blame," Emmit says. His voice is calm and even. One half of his mouth jumps up in its usual tic. "I mean, honestly, Saoirse, you know me. Of course that's not what I'm saying. You know me, so you know I'm going to push you on this, at least a little. Why do we write? To push past death. Why do we live? To push past death. I just want you to open up to me. To talk to me more deeply than you have any other human. Maybe more deeply than you have to yourself.

"You were right to do what you did. If I were you, I would have done the same. I wouldn't have wanted to try for a baby if there was even a ten percent chance I could die. I mean, isn't the rate of maternal mortality in healthy women in the US less than one percent? I'm on your side here. But the new book I'm working on is all about choices. And regret. I was just curious as to whether you'd ever wished you'd at least explored other options, in a philosophical sense."

In a philosophical sense. Can she divorce her very painful memory from a philosophical question? She isn't sure. And is he really pushing her on this because of some theme he wants to explore in the new book? She wants to turn away from him and walk inside. She wants to end this conversation. But some small part of her brain hasn't yet reconciled the reality of the last few days, of being with Emmit, from the radicality of *sleeping with Pulitzer Prize–winning novelist Emmit Powell.* And another part of her brain is stuck on the words Emmit spoke just yesterday: *I'm falling in love with you.*

"I don't regret not trying to have a baby with Jonathan," she says slowly. "Do I wish things had been different? Maybe. But only if a *lot* of things had been different, and where does one draw the line on their 'I-wishes'?"

She can sense Emmit's about to ask her to clarify, so she continues, "I wish I'd never married Jonathan. Or else, I wish I'd married Jonathan and he hadn't turned out to be such a bastard. And if he hadn't been such a bastard, I wish I'd never inherited cardiomyopathy from my asshole of a father. I guess I wish I'd never inherited cardiomyopathy, regardless. But if Jonathan hadn't turned out to be such a bastard and I was healthy, I wish I'd tried to get pregnant. I wish, in a perfect world, a different world, I was a mother.

"So, to answer your 'philosophical' question, yes, I wish I'd been able to carry a healthy baby safely to term, to have a family with a wonderful man who respected and loved me and treated me as an equal. But if some benevolent god or drunk jinn is handing out wishes, I'll take infinite resources and unending inspiration too. Maybe my own private island."

She turns to Emmit again, who's staring at her as if considering a painting he can't quite make sense of. In a tone that is tired rather than angry, she asks, "Is that what you meant by your question? Is that what you wanted to hear?"

Emmit turns back toward the cityscape and chews his lip. That he's considering her question is obvious, trying to determine whether her response has, in fact, satisfied his sympathetic? . . . academic? . . . curiosity. She tries not to mind that the most intimate and painful pieces of her life seem to be fodder for the ongoing brainstorming process of Emmit's new novel.

His probing *could* be akin to their first conversation together at Carr Haus, and their exploration of whether death is the end-all, be-all topic writers set out to explore. It's the same sort of deepening of their relationship, the same sharing of intimate information. But if she's merely been "sharing intimate information" for the past twenty minutes, why does she feel as if the deepest parts of herself have been invaded? Why does she feel raw and used and exposed?

She watches as Emmit looks out over the Providence skyline. He never answered her question, but he's clearly contemplating what she's told him. Is he doing so as her lover, her partner, internalizing her trauma to know her better and to be there for her in the future, or as a novelist, conceptualizing, categorizing, and fictionalizing her pain?

Saoirse studies Emmit's face, feeling like if she could discover the answer to that one question, she'd know whether she should move forward with their relationship. *Say something,* she thinks. *Anything.* And though the internal command goes unheeded, one side of Emmit's mouth curls into the smallest of satisfied smiles.

Chapter 31

It's late afternoon on Friday when the wall phone rings in the kitchen. Saoirse steps over Pluto lapping water from his silver dish to answer it.

"Saoirse, hi, you're there," Emmit says. "I called your cell a few times, but you didn't answer, so I figured I'd try the house phone."

She suppresses a sigh. Why had she given him the house number? "Sorry about that. My cell must be upstairs." It's not a lie; she's been avoiding her phone, dreading the inevitable moment when a message appears from another unknown number, and Aidan is that much closer to telling her what he knows, to relaying what was in Jonathan's final text.

On top of this, Saoirse's exhausted, having expended most of her energy over the last twenty hours or so wondering what to do about Emmit. The whirlwind ups and downs of the past week play on a loop inside her head. She's too uncertain of his motives, too undecided as to whether she should throw herself into the relationship even harder or tell him she needs a break.

"No worries," Emmit says. "I understand. We've seen a lot of each other this week." He chuckles, and she imagines the half smile flashing across his face. "But, as usual, I can't stop thinking about you. Do you want to get together tonight?"

So you can mine my soul for dark shit to write about? "To do what?" she asks.

"I don't know. Dinner. A movie. Whatever you'd like."

"I need to take it easy on drinking and eating out," Saoirse says. "You know, watch my salt intake, monitor my fluids."

"Of course. We could stay in. I'll cook for you."

A quiet night in with him does sound nice, but it is Friday, after all. "I'd like that, but I actually have plans this evening." She's not sure why she didn't say this to begin with, but something about denying Emmit outright felt . . . not dangerous—of course not anything that extreme—but unpleasant. Anxiety-producing.

"Oh?"

"With Roberto, Lucretia, and Mia. We . . ." She hasn't told him about the séances, but after her admissions the night before, it seems silly to lie. Still, she laughs, trying to downplay the strangeness of what she's about to say. "We've sort of been holding séances in my basement."

There's silence on the other end. Then Emmit says, "Wait, you're kidding. Whose idea was this? Has anything ever happened at one?"

Saoirse laughs again. "No. Well, not really. I had a bit of a strange experience—I've only been to one, mind you—but that was probably because I convinced myself beforehand something weird was going to happen." She's not admitting to the microdose of LSD hidden in Lucretia's cupcakes; Emmit would never want her seeing the three writers again.

"What happened, exactly?" He sounds breathless with excitement, the way he did in the Shunned House when they discovered the length of the basement exceeded the perimeter of its walls.

Through the phone, Saoirse hears the sliding sound she associates with an opening drawer and the telltale click of a pen. *Is he writing this down?* Her earlier suspicions return to her. She swallows but says nothing.

"Saoirse? Come on, you have to tell me."

"I actually need to get going, Emmit. Another time."

"Wait, hold on a minute. I know this is forward of me, but I can't help it. A séance in the basement of Sarah Whitman's house when she herself was a spiritualist? I have to come. If you told your friends you invited me, I'm sure they wouldn't mind."

Forward is an understatement, she wants to say. *Out of line is a much more apt description.* "I can't, Emmit, sorry, but these séances are totally Mia's thing. She barely let *me* into the circle, so I don't want to overstep." Before he can protest, she continues, "I'll call you when we're finished. If it's not too late, maybe you can come over then?" She bristles at her weakness, at keeping open the possibility of seeing him, of softening the blow of denying him. She realizes, too, that in the week since they've been seeing one another, he's never invited her to his place.

"Sure, okay," Emmit says, but it's clear from his tone he's annoyed. "I should get back to the novel anyway. I do hope you call, though. I miss you."

"I miss you too. Bye, Emmit." She hangs up before he can say anything to change her mind. The way, last night on the balcony, he pushed her to speak of things she'd have been happy to never speak of again weighs on her mind. She *does* miss him; she's felt more alive with Emmit this last week than she has in the last five years. But even as she craves his touch, a quiet voice inside her head—not Jonathan's—warns her that she cannot trust him. And to pay more attention to those flutters of fear she's experienced several times over the past few days.

He is not who he says he is.

Saoirse walks upstairs to get dressed for the séance but is drawn to the balcony by the twilight mist swirling around the lichen-covered gravestones. Fingering the coffin-shaped charm around her neck, she steps outside and recalls how Emmit looked last night, standing in this very same spot. It occurs to her suddenly that she recognized the expression that had come over his face when she'd shared those terrible details from her past. It was the same way he looked when she found him in the basement of the Shunned House. All glinting eyes and a mouth hardly able to keep closed around the secrets—or squirming insects—it held.

It was the way he appeared to her on the ceiling of her basement, in the vision she had of him during her first séance.

Chapter 32

Lucretia, Roberto, and Mia arrive with their usual whirlwind of controlled chaos. Lucretia places the black drawstring bag on the floor of the foyer, drops to her knees, and scratches Pluto beneath the chin. Mia drapes her long black coat over the peach settee and asks Saoirse if she can use the bathroom. Roberto kisses her on both cheeks, then holds her by the shoulders and studies her face, concern bunching his thick eyebrows.

"How are you doing?" he asks. "Is everything okay?"

"Of course," Saoirse lies. "Why wouldn't it be?"

Mia returns from the bathroom. "Did you tell her yet?" she asks.

Saoirse looks from Roberto to Lucretia. "Tell me what?"

Mia purses her lips at the others, then says to Saoirse, "We're switching the ritual up. Rather than a séance, Lucretia brought her cards."

"She's actually great with them," Roberto says. "I know it seems like she wouldn't be. That she'd squeal over every card she flipped and the readings would be all 'oh-my-gosh, you got the Death card' drama queen central, but her mom was a professional reader. Lucretia grew up with this shit."

"Card reading," Saoirse says. "You mean, tarot?"

"Tarot. Oracle. Runes. Pendulum magic. She does it all."

Saoirse raises an eyebrow at Lucretia, who smiles shyly and shrugs.

"What do you think, Saoirse?" Mia asks. "Are you down?"

"Let's do it." She leads them through the living room, to the hall-way, and down the short flight of steps. Before she reaches the trapdoor, something hits her.

"You know, no one ever showed me the secret way into the walkout basement." Her phone buzzes in her pocket, distracting her. She pulls it out, and a text message parades across the screen. Emmit.

Don't forget to call.

Then, a second message, this one from her mother.

Just wanted to check in, make sure you're seeing the sunshine beyond the shadows . . . and that there's still no word from any of Jonathan's friends.

"You're right," Roberto says when Saoirse's stuffed her phone into her pocket without responding. He walks to wood paneling along the left wall and hooks his thumbs beneath the shallow overhang. "You place your hands here, then yank up while pulling forward simulta-neously." He does so, but nothing happens. Roberto grunts. "You do have to pull up kind of hard to get it to—" He tries again but, again, nothing happens.

"What the hell?" He examines the area beneath the overhang. "That's weird. There's something stuck here. Like putty." Lucretia joins him, bends to see what he's looking at, then takes off one of her many bracelets and scrapes it beneath the wood. A long strip of beige-colored putty comes loose, and the panel immediately falls forward. Lucretia and Roberto jump to either side as it crashes to the floor. They exchange looks, then turn to Saoirse and Mia.

"What's going on?" Saoirse asks. "Did you guys—"

"We did *not* put this putty there," Lucretia says. "It's like the panel has gotten looser since we last used it. The putty was keeping it in place."

"Maybe the putty was always there and you just didn't realize it?" Saoirse asks.

Lucretia looks worried. "Maybe," she agrees skeptically.

"I think it's safe to say that I'll be calling a contractor come Monday. Someone who can tighten everything up as well as install a lock." Mia, Lucretia, and Roberto all nod. Roberto raises the panel, takes the putty from Lucretia, and returns it beneath the overhang. The panel stays in place. Saoirse takes a deep breath and pulls up the trapdoor.

Downstairs, the air feels cooler than usual. They each go to the seat they sat in the previous week. Lucretia unpacks a few additional candles and a long wooden box with etchings of the moon phases carved into the top. The silver paint of the moons' surfaces shimmers in the light from the candles Roberto's lighting.

"So, we each get a turn and then"—Saoirse looks at Lucretia—"you do a reading for yourself?"

Lucretia chuckles. "I pull cards for myself three times a day. When I'm in Sarah's house, I only do readings for others."

"Was Sarah into tarot?" Saoirse asks.

Lucretia smiles. "She held weekly séances, wrote trance-inspired poetry, and published articles on spiritualism in the *New York Tribune*. What do you think?"

Lucretia shuffles three different decks of cards, and they stare at one another, no one sure who should begin.

"Mia should go first," Roberto says, turning to face her. "You've been trying to figure out whether it's time to leave PETA."

Saoirse has numerous follow-up questions. Why does Mia want to leave? What's been going on with her work? She's been so self-involved lately she's made zero effort to reach out to Mia. Between coffee and writing dates, she's strengthened her relationships with Roberto and Lucretia, but ever since Mia told her not to let down her guard with Emmit, Saoirse's been cold toward the other woman.

Now, considering how Emmit's been behaving, Saoirse feels guilty for discounting Mia's warning, and Mia herself. She sits back, prepared to pay attention to whatever details are revealed through her reading. But Mia glances at Saoirse, then back at Roberto, and shakes her head.

"I don't need a five of swords to tell me I'm stuck between two undesirable options and headed for conflict. No, Lucretia reads my cards all the time. I think Saoirse should go." Her dark eyes flick toward Saoirse again. "Go ahead, Saoirse. Clear your mind. Focus your intentions. And ask Lucretia—or, really, Sarah—your most pressing question."

Despite feeling, mere seconds earlier, that she's been unfair to Mia, a jolt of annoyance pulses through Saoirse. Her most pressing question could only be one thing. Should she lie? Ask something more benign? Less intimate? A draft of cool air passes through the room and she shivers, resisting the urge to pull the sleeves of her sweater down.

Lucretia is staring at her expectantly. "Once you ask your question," she says, "I'll choose whether traditional tarot, oracle, or an animal deck is best for helping you with the answer."

Saoirse nods. Even colder now, she does yank down the sleeves of her sweater. Avoiding Mia's penetrating gaze, Saoirse forces a smile at Lucretia and says, "Okay."

"Okay."

"Great."

Lucretia hesitates. "I'm ready when you are. Unless you need more time." A pause. "Do you need more time?"

Saoirse grips her chair. "No. Sorry, I'm ready. My question is—" She sees Emmit's charming half smile in her mind. She hopes she isn't making a mistake. "My question is: Is Emmit Powell in love with me, or is he using me for some unknown—but potentially nefarious—purpose?"

She's not sure why she added the "potentially nefarious" part, but it's too late to take it back. To their credit, none of the others so much as raise an eyebrow, let alone gasp or comment on her question. Lucretia nods once and moves a hand to the tarot deck, but she doesn't lift the cards. Rather, her tattooed, black-polished fingers hover there.

"You know," she says, "I think I'm going to meet a loaded question such as this with an arsenal of tools rather than just one." She lifts each deck and moves them by her left elbow. Then, she cuts each deck three times, restacks, and one by one, flips the top card of each deck face up in front of Saoirse. Saoirse stares at the cards, having no idea what to make of them.

"Okay," Lucretia says a moment later, but stops when a noise comes from behind them. It sounds like a cough, and it repeats several times, but each time the noise comes, it changes location, like whatever's making the sound is floating around the room. The candles flicker, but Saoirse tells herself it's because all four of them are shifting in their seats, turning to look at the walls, the ceiling, one another.

"What is that?" Roberto whispers.

"Just the house settling," Mia says. "Go on, Lucretia."

"Right." Lucretia smiles reassuringly and picks up the card on Saoirse's right. A massive, menacing bird glares from its center. The gray wings extending from its body are so muscular and hulking, they appear concave, like twin, shallow parachutes. A slate-black double crest crowns its head, and its eyes are like two black marbles against the whitish-gray feathers of its face.

"The harpy eagle," Lucretia says. "Signifying truth. Truth that just might swoop down like a giant bird and pluck you out of the river." She glances at Saoirse, who nods at her to continue. "Like the harpy—the half-human and half-bird personification of storm winds in Greek and Roman mythology—the truth you're seeking is frightening and painful, but it can also be glorious and liberating." Lucretia catches Saoirse's eyes. "If you let it."

Before Saoirse can respond, the strange cough comes again. This time, it's moved behind Mia, and a moment after it's begun, the cough evolves into a scream. It's a woman's scream, but muffled and throaty, as if coming to them from beneath layers of dirt and silt and rock and as if the woman screaming has had her vocal cords cut. It's eerie and unsettling, and chills shoot up Saoirse's back and down her arms.

"Seriously," Roberto says. "What the hell *is that*?"

"It sounds like it's coming from the other side of the walls," Lucretia whispers.

"That doesn't make any sense," Mia hisses. "The only thing on the other side of walls in a basement is dirt."

Saoirse thinks of the way the basement of the Shunned House extended beyond any perimeter that made sense. She thinks, too, of the alcove Emmit plummeted into—caught only by the wooden planks, or box, or whatever it had been—and wonders if there'd been even more traversable passage beyond it, but she doesn't say anything.

"Maybe something got trapped *in* the walls," Roberto says. "That happens with mice all the time."

Lucretia rolls her eyes. "What kind of mouse makes a noise like that?"

Roberto sits back in his chair. They continue to listen, but the scream has dissipated, or else whatever was making it moved farther away. Lucretia catches Saoirse's eye again. "Ready to go on?" Saoirse wants to say no, but nods.

Lucretia holds the middle card several inches above the table, then barks out a small laugh. "You're going to think I'm messing with you, but this particular oracle deck deals with archetypes, and you got 'The Poet.' This card is representative of deep emotional creativity and"—she pauses, glances at Mia and then at Roberto, as if wanting them to vouch for her in some way, to assure Saoirse that she knows what she's doing—"the drive to find our truth."

"Truth," Saoirse repeats. "The poet and the eagle, both urging me to find the truth."

Lucretia holds the card up a few more seconds, and Saoirse studies the silhouetted torso, the two shadowy hands clutching a full moon, the explosion of black birds where the figure's head should be but what instead looks like a mountain, the birds' fanned wings pressed against a pink and orange and cerulean sky like buttons into clay.

"Last card," Lucretia says and holds it up. It seems benign enough: a gray-and-white pencil sketch of a woman, long hair cascading around her upturned face. There are seven pieces of glass falling toward her, but the woman doesn't appear concerned; rather, there's something sensual about her expression and posture, as if she's welcoming the shards to rain down upon her the way she would the touch of a lover. Four plum-colored rivulets run vertically across her body, but upward, as if they were painted at her waist and then the image was turned upside down. They cover one wrist, an exposed breast, one shoulder, and the ends of a few locks of hair. At the bottom of the card are the words: *Seven of Cups.*

"This is a card of illusion. Of dreams, transitions, and mystery," Lucretia says. "It indicates that you must bring yourself out of the land of aspiration and into the real world. It warns against indulging in wishful thinking. More specifically, it speaks to the dangers of illusion where temptation is concerned. What you want, what you have, it may not lead to happiness. You are being led from your ideal path—whether that's health, wellness, or personal fulfillment. Seven cups once held positive feelings, a positive relationship, a wealth of creativity. But those cups are shards of glass now. They are en route to your eyes, and they will blind you."

Saoirse opens her mouth, but it's not really to respond; she has no idea what to say. It doesn't matter, though, because a response comes anyway. From far, far off, somewhere deep in the dirt beyond the walls of the basement, or perhaps from some other plane, a mental impression from another era forged and projected outward in time, recorded onto the rocks beneath the soil, recorded when the rocks were *still above* the soil, onto stone, *a stone tape*, only to be replayed for them tonight, lit by these candles at this table, the grating, gravelly, impossible, tortured scream comes again.

Chapter 33

She tries to relax after they've left, bringing a cup of chamomile tea to the living room and collapsing onto the settee, planning to fall asleep there, loath to climb the stairs to her bedroom, to lie on sheets that smell of Emmit, to breathe in air that still holds echoes of their whispered confessions. Pluto curls atop the knit blanket she's draped over herself, and she tries to lose herself in the softness of his fur, concentrating only on the way his ears fold under the weight of her fingers, how his black nose twitches when she rubs a specific spot on his neck.

But the inexplicable scream from beyond the basement, the plum-colored rivulets dripping—skyward—over the Seven of Cups, the silhouetted torso that extends, not into a head but a mountain, expanding further still into an explosion of frantic birds, these things flip through her mind like a deck of cards.

The truth. That's what the cards urged me to do. Search for the truth. She looks up and finds her computer balanced on the arm of the settee. Careful not to disturb Pluto, she reaches for it, pulls it into her lap. First, she opens the text from her mother and responds:

Let's catch up tomorrow. Sorry I've been distant but everything's fine. I love you. No contact from any of J's friends.

She hates how long it's been since she's talked to her, longs to be beneath a blanket in her mother's cozy living room in Connecticut, encased within the cocoon of her perpetual love and safety. But she also doesn't want to hear the worry in her mother's voice, dreads that one day that worry will shift to resentment or disappointment. And there's no sense adding to that worry with news about Aidan. Her mother can't protect her should Aidan come. Pushing these thoughts aside, she opens a browser and navigates to Wikipedia. She types Emmit's name into the search bar and reads the entry while chewing on her lip:

> Emmit Albert Powell (born January 30, 1982, in Boston, MA) is an American writer, poet, editor, and literary critic who is best known for his Pulitzer Prize–winning novel, *Vulture Eyes* (2021). He is widely credited as the most commercially successful author since those of the Romanticism period to meld horror fiction with literary themes and structure. His second novel sold for a seven-figure sum, at auction, and was the highest advance paid to a noncelebrity author in the last ten years.

Nothing troubling or out of the ordinary, though she'd forgotten just how lucrative his second-book deal had been. And Saoirse imagines Shirley Jackson would roll over in her grave at the idea of Emmit being the most successful post-Romantic author to write literary horror. Her eyes jump to the second paragraph:

> Powell was born in Boston, the second child of lawyer David and homemaker Elizabeth "Bess" Powell. His father abandoned the family in 1983, and when his mother died the following year, Powell was taken in by Sebastian and Linda Parker of Richmond, Virginia. They never formally adopted him, but he was with them well into young adulthood. He attended the University of Virginia and graduated in 2004 despite

arguing with his uncle over what Powell has described in interviews as "artistic incongruities"; "he wanted me to leave school with a diploma, and I thought he was condemning my creativity to an early grave," Powell told a reporter for the *New York Times* in 2020.

Condemning my creativity to an early grave. Hadn't Emmit said that exact thing during their first conversation at the coffee shop? Were those the words of a celebrated writer, relaying how he felt about an uncomfortable situation, or the canned response of an actor repeating lines memorized from a script? And if so, a script for what? For being an author? For being a *successful* author?

Something shifts in Saoirse's brain, some connection not previously made. She pulls up the Wikipedia bio for Edgar Allan Poe, the same one she read a few days after arriving in Providence, wanting to reacquaint herself with the famous writer. She drags the browser with Emmit's bio to the right, and when the screen splits, she adds the Poe bio to its left. Her eyes flick to Emmit's bio as she reads the general and early life facts about Poe, the pit in the center of her stomach growing deeper with every word:

> Edgar Allan Poe (January 19, 1809–October 7, 1849) was an American writer, poet, editor, and literary critic who is best known for his poetry and short stories, particularly his tales of mystery and the macabre. He is widely regarded as a central figure of Romanticism in the United States, and of American literature. He is the first well-known American writer to earn a living through writing alone, resulting in a financially difficult life and career.
>
> Poe was born in Boston, the second child of actors David and Elizabeth "Eliza" Poe. His father abandoned the family in 1810, and when his mother died

the following year, Poe was taken in by John and Frances Allan of Richmond, Virginia. They never formally adopted him, but he was with them well into young adulthood. He attended the University of Virginia but left after a year due to lack of money. He quarreled with John Allan over the funds for his education, and his gambling debts.

How many coincidences before the similarities between two people became an impossibility? "It's *already* an impossibility," Saoirse whispers out loud to the empty room. "Even some of the wording in the write-ups is the same."

Residual haunting? Jonathan asks, his voice a little mocking. *Or something less supernatural—but far shadier?*

Swallowing her dread, she opens a third browser, fingers hovering over the keyboard, then types: *Is Emmit Powell really Willem Thomas?*

She doesn't find anything at first, but then she sees the blog Mia mentioned, on a website belonging to a horror writer named Piper Kirby. Saoirse reads the post, but aside from alleging she was in a writing group in the early 2000s with Willem Thomas/Emmit Powell, Kirby's claims were far from outrageous. Saoirse can find none of the other sites or references Mia talked about, so she returns to Kirby's blog. She skims the entries over the last several years until she sees one entitled: *RIP Matilda: The Death of an Aspiring Poet.* Saoirse clicks it and begins to read:

> The world lost a shining beacon of light this past Saturday when Matilda Eliza Crabb tragically took her own life in her hometown of Woodstock, Virginia. I knew Matilda for years; the same friends from Massanutten Academy—the only other high school in Woodstock besides my alma mater, Central High School—that had hooked me up with my first writers'

critique group had been close with Matilda. She never joined our group, but I saw her post often on social media of poetry acceptances . . . as well as the occasional announcement that she was being admitted to yet another mental health facility. As sad as this is to type, people knew for years that Matilda was unhappy; her trauma and deep-rooted self-esteem issues were sewn into every line of poetry she ever wrote.

I caught up with some other Massanutten alumni on social media, and they told me a horrific story . . . that Matilda had been involved in high school with Willem Thomas—the same Willem Thomas whom I believe is actually Em**t P**ell (I have to star out part of his name, otherwise I'll be contacted by the legal dept. of his publishing house again with another cease and desist!)—and that he'd done something to her over the course of their relationship. Something no one could ever totally get a handle on, for Matilda would never say, but which changed Matilda irrevocably, from a sweet, happy-go-lucky kid to a tragic, dangerously underweight, chronically ill, and ultimately doomed young woman.

I've tried to get the former Massanutten writing group members to listen to my theories about Willem/ Em**t—he was in our group back in the day for Christ's sake!—but it's like none of them care enough to believe me, or even look into it. Same with any newspaper I've ever contacted. So, in the interim between now and the day that I pray Matilda will have justice, I will leave this post here. Let it be the toll of a bell for a spirit flown forever!

Saoirse's stomach roils. First one fat, black fly, then another, dive-bombs past her face. The young woman Josephine had told Mia about. The young woman Emmit—if he really was Willem Thomas—had chewed up and spit out during their relationship. She'd killed herself. But why? And did Emmit really have something to do with it? Had what he'd done to her in high school resulted in Matilda's decision to end her life?

Saoirse clicks on the "Contact" page of Piper's website, cursor hovering over the first field of the form. But before she can decide if she wants to do this, if she wants to actually reach out to this woman and hear her crazy theories, there's a pounding at the front door.

Saoirse freezes. Emmit, at her door, meeting her newfound wariness with an unannounced visit to her house. Suddenly, Saoirse is more than wary. She's more than annoyed. She's furious. Emmit is ruining everything, proving Jonathan right, proving he's too good to be true. She stomps across the living room, through the foyer, and yanks open the front door.

But it's not Emmit on the stoop, backlit by the streetlights, his shadow spilling across the threshold and into the foyer, as if he's already entered, already forced himself into her home.

It's Aidan Vesper. His lips are pinched. He's wearing the same black trench coat from the graveyard and holding what looks like a burner phone in one hand.

And the look on his face is one of grim satisfaction that they are finally, after all this time, going to have their talk.

Chapter 34

At first, Saoirse thinks she speaks. She thinks she says his name, threatens him in her take-no-prisoners voice, demands he get off her stoop. It takes her a moment to realize she's made no sound, that she's simply stared at this specter from her past, this link to her husband, as stunned and unnerved as if she were seeing a ghost.

"Aidan," she finally whispers. "Wh-why . . . What are you doing here?"

It happens so fast she can't do anything. One moment, Aidan is on the stoop, staring back at her, and the next, he's shoved past her into the house. Fear shoots up her spine and down her limbs. Her fingers tingle with adrenaline. She scuttles backward, hits the wall of the foyer, and turns, ready to run. The front door bangs against the frame, closing them off from the outside world, but doesn't latch.

"Saoirse, wait! I'm not going to hurt you. I'm sorry I barged in here, but this is insane. *The way you've been avoiding me* is insane."

Saoirse pauses. "How did you find me?"

He has the good grace to look sheepish. "Your MyChart medical records. I wasn't supposed to access it, ethically speaking, but as a doctor in the same network, I was able to look up the address change you filed with your cardiologist." Saoirse gapes at him, and Aidan raises his hands. "I'm sorry, it's just . . . we have to talk."

"No," Saoirse says. She tries to shout the word, but it comes out half wail, half sob. "No, we don't."

"Just listen," Aidan insists. "I understand. I know everything. You can't run anymore. You don't have to. You found Jonathan's body, right? That's what you told the police. That you came home after spending four days at your mother's house, and he was already dead. But I got a text from Jonathan. The night he died. He said your car had just pulled into the driveway *and you were home!*"

Saoirse shakes her head. "No. That's not true. It's a mistake. Maybe he thought I was, but I wasn't. I stayed in Connecticut."

Aidan advances on her, his shoulders hulking in the narrow black coat, eyes fixed intently on hers. "Don't you understand? I know he wanted to have a baby, and you didn't. I know what was going on. *I'm an obstetrician*, Saoirse. Jonathan was confiding in me. I don't get why you—" He pauses, groans. "Oh, god. It makes me sick."

He lunges at her, and Saoirse's vision goes dark around the edges. She screams, ducks. The cherrywood stand falls, sending the potted fern crashing to the ground in an explosion of dirt and terra-cotta. Aidan wheels around, a startled expression on his face. But before Saoirse can run through the front door, it's flying open. Emmit rushes into the foyer and grabs Aidan around the waist, tackling him to the ground.

"Get the fuck out of here," Emmit growls, lifting Aidan toward the open door and tossing him through it. When Aidan stumbles onto the stoop, Emmit pushes him again, and Aidan falls to the sidewalk. "I'm calling the police."

"Please don't do that," Aidan cries, at the same time Saoirse says, "No." She can't let Emmit call the police, can't have anyone else knowing what Aidan knows.

Emmit looks back and forth between them, his expression hard.

Please, Saoirse mouths to him.

Emmit relents. "Get the fuck out of here," he says again. When Aidan scrambles to his feet and jogs off, Emmit slams and locks the door. "Are you okay?" he asks. He is staring at her like he can't quite believe what he's just seen. And why should he? Angry men don't usually barge through the front doors of women's houses. Women who live alone. Women who harbor secrets. "Who the hell was that?" he asks.

"A friend of Jonathan," Saoirse says quietly.

"What did he want?"

"I have no idea," she lies. Because she does know now. She knows what she's feared since that moment under the willows in Rosedale Cemetery. "He just got aggressive out of nowhere," she adds, when Emmit's eyes continue to bore into her.

Finally, he turns from her to shoot a look of disgust at the locked door. "I should have called the police. We shouldn't have let him get away."

Maybe we shouldn't *have let him get away.* The thought fills her with renewed dread. *It's been almost ten months, and Aidan hasn't given up yet. How much longer until he does something drastic? Something from which there's no coming back?*

Saoirse closes her eyes. She doesn't want to think about this now. It's too much for one night. It's too much for one lifetime. "I just want him gone," she says. Even to her own ears, she sounds exhausted. "And now I want to go to bed." She opens her eyes and looks at Emmit. "What were you doing here, by the way?"

His mouth jumps up in a nervous twitch. "What do you mean?"

"I mean, while it was certainly advantageous that you were here, we didn't have plans to see each other tonight." She *is* grateful he was here, that much is true, but Saoirse can't quite wrap her head around having to deal with Emmit at present. She may not want to think about Aidan, but she has to. Has to come up with some sort of plan. Has to speak with her mother.

Emmit expels a puff of air. "I needed to see you tonight. More than I ever have before. It was urgent."

"Are you okay?" she asks, then regrets it. She has a feeling she knows what this is, and it unnerves her. The wrongness surrounding him has been growing since the moment Lucretia turned over those three cards. No, her dread has been growing for much, much longer than that.

How have I been so blind to who Emmit Powell is? But even as she poses the question, she knows the answer. Because she wanted to be blind. Wanted to be swept off her feet. After years with Jonathan, worrying about nothing but self-preservation, she wanted to be reckless. To believe herself the princess in the fairy tale, destined for her happily ever after, when all along, she's been the ill-fated maiden in a poem penned by Poe.

You are a scarred oak, Jonathan whispers, as if her own thoughts aren't damning enough. *And lightning is always drawn to a tree that's been leveled once already.*

"*I'm* okay," Emmit says, interrupting the voices in her head, "but my manuscript is not. I've lost my way with it. I've lost my way because I've lost my way with you."

His tone worms under Saoirse's skin. It's not just the lack of emotion but a lack of concern *for her emotions.* A blatant disregard for the guilt trip he's attempting to lay on her, even after what she just went through with Aidan. And she can't help but worry that Emmit is exhibiting this behavior in increasingly frightening regularity as he discovers he can't bend her to his will, can't get her to do exactly what he wants.

You know that tone, Jonathan says. *It's been a while since you've heard it, but you know it all the same. It's the dehumanizing one. The one that says my whims are more important than your personhood.*

"Emmit," she says slowly, as if speaking to a coyote she's stumbled across on a trail and is trying to back away from, unscathed, "I really am tired. It's been a long day. A long week. I'm shaken up over what just happened, and I want to go to bed. I'm sorry your writing isn't going well right now. But I'm sure things will improve."

Emmit stamps his foot. "But I was with you when the idea came to me. I was with you, talking with you, when everything solidified. I need to stay with you, stay close to you, to keep the momentum going. That much is obvious, don't you think?" Emmit pauses. "I haven't told you this yet, but now I have to. You know how I requested an extension? My publisher didn't take it well. Not at all. They've threatened legal action if I don't deliver this book by the agreed-upon deadline."

This is certainly unexpected. Emmit is his publisher's golden boy. Piper Kirby's words come back to her—*I have to star out part of his name, otherwise I'll be contacted by the legal dept. of his publishing house again with another cease and desist!* Might they be sick of dealing with Emmit? Despite this thought, the reflex to give Emmit what he wants flutters through her.

But just as quickly, it's replaced by rage so sharp she tastes it. It's the same dead-earth taste of leaves she felt in her mouth when she arrived in Providence. The rot of something that had once been beautiful. She is not married to this man. Not literally, not figuratively. "That's not my problem," she says, and the words are a flush of cold water, driving out the awful taste.

"Not your problem?" Emmit's face drains of color before two small splotches appear in his cheeks. "What the hell is that supposed to mean?"

Saoirse shuts her eyes. "It means exactly what I said. Your manuscript is not due tomorrow, threats of legal action or not. It's midnight. My late husband's best friend just broke into my house. I told you I need sleep. Your next line is, 'Good night, Saoirse.'"

There's an extended silence. The red splotches in his cheeks grow darker. Then, in a voice so low and rough, it sounds more like a growl, Emmit says, "This isn't like you."

"Excuse me?"

"This isn't like you. Blowing me off? Being sarcastic? Your job is to support me."

"My job?" Saoirse balls her hands into fists to keep from shouting. "You know what, Emmit, that's the problem. You say, 'This isn't like me.' *That's because you don't know me.* Not really. We've had sex. We bared our souls to one another. But we've been seeing each other for a week. A *week*." She sighs. "I'm done, Emmit. *We're* done here." She resists the urge to turn her back on him right there and run up the stairs.

"Done?" Emmit's voice is shrill. "What do you mean, done?"

"I mean—" Panic ripples through her. Is she ending the first thing that's made her feel whole in as long as she can remember? That thing that's made her feel undamaged? Worthwhile? That writing, that life, is worth living?

She closes her eyes again, hard. She thinks of her new friends, eccentric as they might be, and of her diabetic cat. Maybe she's no more damaged than they are. Maybe it's time to see past the illusion, the magical thinking, the temptation. To turn away from the shards of glass raining down into her eyes.

"What I mean, Emmit," she starts again, renewed confidence in her voice, "is that we're not going to see each other anymore."

Emmit's hands fly up to either side. "No. No, Saoirse, no, don't say that." It's a command, but it's the old Emmit saying it, the sweet one. The one who warmed her at the front of the restaurant on their first, impromptu date. The one whose half smiles make her weak with longing. The one who would never say something as enraging as *Your job is to support me.*

But she will no longer listen to this man, who slips on personas as easily as choosing poems from an endless volume of verse. "I'm sorry," she says. "I had hoped this was something different. But I won't lose myself again. I—" Her voice cracks, and she swallows. "I can't," she finishes. Then, more forcefully, she says, "Maybe you're losing yourself too. You missed work. We broke into a house. I'm drinking too much. We took drugs together. Now, this." She gestures between them. "The way you're speaking to me. No. It all ends here. Tonight."

"You can't do this," Emmit says and reaches for her.

She pulls back. "I *can.* And the fact that you're saying I can't makes me all the surer I'm making the right decision."

"No. No, Saoirse, we have something here. Please. You must feel it. I know you feel it. We're meant for each other. We make each other better."

"Do we? Or are you using me to make yourself better?"

"You and I . . . this is . . . supernatural in its rightness. We are following in the footsteps of Poe and Whitman, literally and figuratively: walking where they walked, feeding off the echo of their artistic energy, their carnal energy. It's like their spirits have possessed us, have elevated us, and you want to sever that connection?"

Saoirse sets her jaw. "If that's how you want to frame things, then think of this as our moment in the alcove of the Athenæum, the moment in which Sarah discovered Poe's drinking and called off their wedding." Her tone is harsh and full of finality. "Goodbye, Emmit." She unlocks the front door and holds it open. To her surprise, though he opens his mouth to speak again, he says nothing and walks out the door. Slowly, Saoirse shuts the door, locks it, and walks, like a woman in a trance, to the living room, where she collapses onto the settee.

Pluto jumps up onto the arm and tilts his head. She focuses on him, his little face. Studies the way the length of his whiskers varies so she doesn't have to think about everything that has just occurred. She stands and walks to the kitchen. Forcing herself to abandon thoughts of Emmit and Aidan, she prepares a dose of insulin then gathers the glucometer, test strips, lancing device, and cotton ball. Back in the living room, the brilliant colors of the Zuber panels smear into one another, and she blinks away tears.

"Sorry, little guy," she says to Pluto as she uses the lancing device to prick a vein in his ear. He doesn't flinch, just closes his eyes, tolerating the routine procedure. A moment later, the glucometer displays a reading that renders the insulin dose unnecessary. It's silly, but this makes her feel a little better. That Pluto is settling in so well and his condition is stable is a far greater achievement than some whirlwind relationship with a narcissistic writer. She scoops Pluto up. Holding a cotton ball against the inside of his ear, she walks toward the hallway, wanting nothing more than to climb into bed.

As Saoirse places a foot on the first stair, a noise comes from outside. A glass bottle, exploding against the pavement. She stands another moment, foot poised, temples throbbing. Listening. When no other sound comes, she continues up the stairs. Aidan is gone. Emmit is gone. There are lots of people on the streets at night. Lots of noise. Soon, these sounds will fade beneath a cloak of sleep. Her mind will be wiped clean as thoroughly as a stretch of pavement dotted with dogwood blossoms after a summer rain.

She will not think of Emmit Powell as she lies, restless, in bed. She will not think of Aidan Vesper. Of Poe. Or Jonathan.

She will not think of Emmit Powell as she dreams.

Chapter 35

She is on the floor of a cavernous house, a thin white dress clinging to her skin like a sheet of mist. She knows she is dreaming, but this does nothing to alleviate her nauseating fear. Something is coming for her. No—something already has her. She looks up to where the cathedral ceiling extends into a dizzying dissolution of shadows. A tap-tap-tap comes from one of the windows, but each time she turns to find the source, the tapping changes location. No matter where she looks, no matter how she turns, there are more windows behind her.

She spins, desperate to find her way out. The floor drips like candle wax down the walls. Like the world's most disorienting elevator, the entire giant room lowers. The floor stops, but the ceiling continues its downward trajectory. Eventually, the ceiling stops, too, until the grand, creepy hall has melted into a subterranean lair. The walls are stone. The floor is dirt. The smoky-prismed chandelier hanging from the ceiling has morphed into a thick, draping mass of cobwebs.

The setting of her dream is not the basement of the Shunned House, but it's not *not* that basement either. It certainly smells the same. Strange, she can smell the house in a dream. The air is so thick she can barely breathe, and not just with the stench of black mold and wet cement. There's something harsher there, too, more astringent. Something chemical that she tastes so palpably, it makes her eyes water. She imagines the smooth muscle of her esophagus burning.

The lair is lit by a single lantern that swings from a ceiling of dirt and root. She's no longer beneath a house, then, but fully underground. Behind her is a set of stone stairs so thick with ash, she'd leave footprints if she were to walk up them. Though, there will be no opportunity to test this theory; whatever egress used to exist at the top of the stairs has been boarded up with concrete.

Ahead, however, is an alcove. The only potential chance of escape. As she creeps toward it, she recalls how Emmit fell into a shallow pit beneath the Shunned House, the fear she felt when he grabbed her ankle. Would she find him here, too, in this menacing, underground dreamscape?

One hand on the crumbling wall, Saoirse peers into the blackness. When nothing emerges from the depths, she drops to her knees and reaches forward with one hand. While the floor does indeed drop off, she feels something about a foot down from where she's kneeling. There is neither flashlight nor candle with which to illuminate the darkness, but as she stares, the space brightens enough for her to see what's before her, in that strange bending of reality that so many dreams take.

The object in the alcove is a coffin, gleaming and polished and wholly at odds with the dust and grime of the lair. She wants to look away. She wants to run away, but she can only trail her fingers over the coolness of the wood. She knows—with the same certainty with which she knows her name—that, should she open it, she'll find her own pale corpse, wearing the same white cotton dress she wears now, lying on maroon velvet, her waxy fingers intertwined and resting on her stomach.

It's a realization so cliché, she wants to shout at her subconscious, *This is the best you can come up with?* But despite her belief that she knows the way this dream ends, she is powerless to stop herself from following the script.

She leans forward onto the coffin, testing its ability to hold her weight. When it does not go crashing to the ground, she flattens her body against the lid and feels around with her feet for the floor.

She finds it about three feet down, so that when she slides to a stand beside the coffin, the lid is just below her chest. She hooks her fingers under the latch, steels her muscles for the wood's weight, and throws open the lid. Time flickers, and for an instant, she is not in this alcove. For an instant, she is somewhere else. Then, the coffin is open, and she is staring at the body inside it.

It is not her. She was wrong. The faces flicker so fast, there's no opportunity to identify the corpse as any one individual: It's Jonathan. It's Poe. It's Emmit. Now Jonathan again. The supine form is the same obscene, flickering vision of madness from the first séance. The mouth opens, but the image continues to stutter, and Saoirse sees the horrible, writhing insect mouth again. The flickering increases to the point where the movement smooths out, and three different mouths speak the same word:

"Miiiiiiinnnnnnne."

Saoirse is so paralyzed, staring into that gaping mouth, considering the implications of that word, she reacts too slowly to the raising arms. The specter, no, *specters*—the writer who haunts her, the dead husband who almost ruined her, and the man who has manipulated her affections—reach up, grab Saoirse around the torso, and pull her down.

Down, down, down into the madness.

Chapter 36

There's a scream in her throat, but it's strangled by the realization that, despite awakening, the rough fingers of the specter still dig into her arms. Saoirse struggles, but the fingers dig in harder. Not fingers. Ropes.

She is tied to a chair.

Sleep paralysis, she thinks. *That's why I can't move. I'm in my bed, and this is some weird extension of the dream.* But if she *is* in her bed, where's the diffuse glow from the streetlamp outside the balcony door? Where is the silvery light of the moon, bisected by the point of Saint John's Cathedral? She blinks, straining her eyes against the darkness, which sets off the pain in her head. A low moan escapes her, but it's interrupted by the striking of a match.

Every ounce of blood in her body turns to ice.

Fiery light materializes at the center of her vision, small at first, then growing as the match is held to the kerosene wick of a lantern. Hulking shoulders grow around the lantern like wings.

"Aidan?" Her voice is a croak. But the figure is too broad, too muscular, to be Aidan Vesper. Saoirse raises her gaze to the face above the shoulders, lit not just with the glow of the candlelight, but with an expression she knows as well as she knows anything in Providence. A tuft of dark hair across the forehead. Warm brown eyes. A jumpy half smile.

"Emmit. What is this? What's going on?"

The left half of his mouth jumps up again. Her conversation with him before she fell asleep, before the dream, returns to her. She'd ended things with him. Is he trying to teach her a lesson? Her head hurts too much to settle on any one explanation.

She looks around at the room in which she's trapped, and her skin rises in gooseflesh. A subterranean lair. Walls of stone, a floor of dirt and dust, a ceiling hanging with cobwebs, and the air thick with the stench of black mold and wet cement. *I'm in my dream.* But this is real. Emmit is real. The rope digging into her flesh *is real.* The astringent, chemical taste is there in her throat as well. *Chloroform.*

She's not in her dream; her dream was reality.

"You drugged me," she says. She looks around. There's the lantern hanging from a ceiling of dirt and root. Not beneath a house but beneath the earth. Saoirse manages to turn just enough to see the stone stairs thick with dust. Just like her dream, the top of the stairs has been boarded up with concrete.

And before her, between where she's restrained and where Emmit stands, is an alcove.

Panic wells within her, so intense it feels like she's sinking into a pool of water and will drown. Conscious thought is eclipsed by animalistic terror, and she pulls against the ropes, but no matter how she twists against them, they do not shift or give even a fraction.

Emmit shakes his head. "It won't do you any good to struggle."

She hears the words, but they have no meaning. She cannot fight through the wild landscape of her mind, the way her heart knocks in her chest like a specimen trapped beneath a bell jar.

"I'm hoping that, once you hear what I want," Emmit continues, "you'll realize struggling will only make things worse."

This time, something connects. *Worse. He said worse. You cannot make this worse, Saoirse.* Still, she's not ready to hear the horrific thing Emmit wants. "Where are we?" she asks instead. Despite the adrenaline coursing through her, her tongue is sluggish.

"I'm not going to answer that."

"Why?"

"Because I don't want you to panic."

Too late, she thinks and pulls harder against the ropes, but her muscles already burn with exhaustion. Likely the aftereffects of the drug. "How long are you going to keep me here?" she asks.

"I'm not sure. I guess that depends on you."

Her heartbeat hurts within her chest, and she thinks, *I had to put off getting a new cardiologist, didn't I?* The thought is so mundane, and yet so ironic, Saoirse wants to laugh. She takes a deep, shaky breath. "What do you want from me?"

"To continue being my other half," he says. "I don't think you understand how special what we have is, Saoirse." He pauses. "Have you heard of residual hauntings?"

Now, she does laugh. She can't help it. "The Stone Tape theory, right?" she says, a note of hysteria in her voice. "That ghosts are tape recordings, and that mental impressions during events can be projected as energy and 'recorded' onto certain objects?" She's not sure why she's answering him. Maybe it's a defense mechanism, her brain forcing her body to react as if she is having a normal conversation with a normal person, so that her heart doesn't up and quit on her that very second.

"I'm impressed," Emmit says. "Though, not surprised. You are special, Saoirse. Not just intelligent, but intuitive. Feeling. You see things differently. You're ahead of your time. Sarah Whitman was ahead of her time. As was Poe, of course. And I'm ahead of mine. It's remarkable enough when *one* person emerges from an era with a view and a talent that can change the world. But for two people to come out of that same time period? And then to find each other? That relationship *must* be cultivated. It cannot be ignored."

She wants to cry. She wants to scream. She wants to spit in the dirt at his feet. But what she does is nod, feigning a calmness she does not feel. She's not sure her heart can take it otherwise, and it helps that she is utterly exhausted.

"Case in point," Emmit continues, "over the time you and I have been together, I've written two-thirds of what is destined to become not just the next great American novel, but the next evolution in literature. The way Poe pushed the envelope on what was considered groundbreaking work in the 1800s. But I cannot go on without you. Something clicked when you and I found each other. We've fulfilled a void that was lingering in this city, haunting Benefit Street. And now that it's been fulfilled, it cannot be undone."

She struggles to smooth her shallow breathing, not wanting Emmit to see the starkness of her lingering terror. "You need me," she says. "So let me go. We'll keep doing what we were doing."

Some mix of sadness and disappointment touches Emmit's features, amplified by the flickering glow of the lantern. He shakes his head and clucks his tongue.

The cornered-animal panic returns with the intensity of a seizure. *He took me from my bed. He carried me somewhere in*—she looks down to discover she wears a thin white dress like the one from her dream . . . this, along with the metal coffin pendant around her neck—*and brought me to the basement of some abandoned house.* Saoirse's eyes rove over the stone and wood and brick, the dirt and dust and decay. Is she in the Shunned House? Somewhere beyond the passages they traveled the night they broke in?

A burst of hope, like a dandelion from scorched earth, blooms in her center. If she is beneath the Shunned House, the Providence Ghost Tour will go by. Pedestrians will line the street. She'll scream. They'll have to hear her.

You don't know whether it's night or day, Jonathan taunts. *You have no way of knowing when anyone will be out there, if you're even beneath Benefit Street. Plus, if you scream now, you'll only piss him off. Best to keep him talking.*

Saoirse forces her lips into some grotesque facsimile of a smile. Emmit is clearly crazy, so she should pacify him, right? Or does pacifying crazy men make things worse? "Of course we'll go back to what we were doing before," she ventures. "I wasn't breaking up with you. I just thought we needed a little break. I thought you needed a break. So you could focus on your writing. I didn't realize that you—"

"Don't do that."

"Don't do what?" So, crazy, but sharp enough to resent pacification. She should have known; Emmit's crazy and obsessive, but he's also preternaturally insightful and observant.

No, she insists. *There's nothing preternatural about him. He's a man. Don't build him up in your mind to anything more than that.* Despite this pep talk, Saoirse's crying now, silent tears streaming down her cheeks, heart ratcheting up to resume its previous wild beating. "My medicine, Emmit," she whispers. "I'll die down here without it."

"You won't." His tone is so emotionless and matter-of-fact, so *final,* Saoirse thinks she might faint. "You must understand that I can't take the chance of trusting you, of trying to move on with you, only to have you run away. Or worse."

Saoirse's breath hitches in her chest. "So, what then? You keep me . . . wherever I am, and come down here to . . . rape me? Play house? How on earth does that help you write the next evolution of literature?"

Saoirse's stomach turns as Emmit's mouth jumps into a half smile of excitement. "That's what's so amazing about having *you,*" he says. "That you fulfill the other half of this partnership. Like Sarah and Edgar. Doing *anything* with you is enough to inspire me. So, yes, I'll come here to continue our relationship, but if you refuse me, there are other ways to get from you what I need.

"I learned this in the Shunned House, when the raccoons ran out of that closet. And again, downstairs in the basement. Your fear is pure. You've seen death. You have death beating inside your body. An ex-husband who is nothing but bones. A faulty heart. Your fear itself is inspiration."

Saoirse's tears devolve into sobs. She's getting an unobstructed view into Emmit's psyche, and what she's finding there, in the dark, is far worse than any airless, lightless space below the earth. "Please, just let me go. I'll keep being your Sarah. I'll do whatever you want. I just can't be down here. I can't *breathe* down here." She looks around, the reality of her situation causing her thoughts to short-circuit. Where will she sleep? Go to the bathroom? What will she eat?

No. It's the voice that usually retaliates against Jonathan in her head. *The only thing you need to determine is how to get out of here. And you will figure that out. You just need him to leave, to give you some time alone.* She tries yet again to control her breathing.

"There's an energy in this city," Emmit says. "A residual haunting in the truest sense of the phrase. The city requires it of you. I require it of you. For my work. What would the world have been without Poe, without the legacy he left behind? He came from nothing—from fucking *nothing*!—and catapulted himself to greatness."

She wants to shout at him, tell him one stupid novel does not catapult him to Poe-like status. That he cannot stand on Poe's back—or hers—to create a legacy. But now he's walking toward her. Saoirse bucks against the ropes and tries to slide the chair away from him, but it's bolted to the floor.

"Get away from me. Get away!"

"Don't make this harder than it needs to be," he says, and his expression is that sad, disappointed one again. He removes a bottle from his back pocket and a rag from a front one. He soaks the rag in the chloroform. "I'm sorry, but I have to move you."

Before she can ask what that means, the rag covers her face. She tries not to breathe. Tries not to think of what a chemical like chloroform might be doing to her already taxed heart. Then she thinks, *Maybe it's best to die now . . .*

. . . and takes a long, deep, shuddering inhale.

Chapter 37

When she comes to, Saoirse remembers every detail of her kidnapping and imprisonment in an instant, with none of those precious moments of forgetting that sometimes occur when waking after a trauma. It's dark to the point of blindness again, but the pressure of the ropes around her arms is gone. She tests the air, tests her muscles, and feels solid ground beneath her.

She's *on* the ground. Unrestrained. Saoirse pushes herself onto her elbows and feels around her, yelping when her hand hits something hard. Tentatively, she reaches out, finds what feels like cool metal, something long and cylindrical. There's a button. She presses it, and the world erupts with light.

The flashlight illuminates a space terrifying in its vastness; Saoirse has the sense that she's in a labyrinth the size of a football field. The smell is no better than the first prison, only different: earth and the wriggling bodies of worms rather than dampness and mold. Even with the brightness of the flashlight's bulb, the beam is swallowed by the yawning darkness, like a pebble dropped off a cliff. Something scuttles over her hand, and Saoirse suppresses a shriek.

She shakes the spider away and scrabbles to her feet, batting at roots that hang above her. The walls and ceiling are composed of stacked stone, with stone pillars that crisscross and arch over her head, but the earth has pushed through the cracks and crevices of these materials so persistently, they are almost completely overgrown. The effect is dizzying, like an autostereogram, an artificial tunnel that becomes a lair of subterranean fauna when viewed with the correct vergence. Saoirse shivers, and sweeps the flashlight over the walls, following the progression of the stone arches and taking small steps forward, unsure if she's ready to see just how far her prison extends.

She's gone about twenty paces when she finds a giant stone slab that looks to be set into the larger frame of the stone wall, not a part of it. Though the labyrinth feels impenetrable, she knows it can't be. Emmit got her in here. There must be a way out. Could this stone slab be it? She props the flashlight against the wall and stands with her feet spread wide, then places her hands on the stone.

A wave of lightheadedness assails her. She is weak with hunger and feeling the effects of the chloroform, lethargic and disoriented. Or perhaps it's something worse . . . something to do with her heart, the lack of beta blocker medication and her antidepressant. How long until she really feels the effects of being off her medication?

Twenty-four hours, most likely, Jonathan says. *Forty-eight at the most.*

"I will *not* be down here that long," she says aloud. No sense replying to Jonathan in her head. She presses her hands more firmly against the stone, but the slab is too heavy to be mobile. There's no way this is how Emmit got her in here. She retrieves the flashlight and continues feeling her way along the stone until the wall turns to dirt. Saoirse digs her fingers into the loam, but it's more compact than she expected.

She continues trailing her hand along the wall until the corner of something sharp snags against her palm. She aims her flashlight at the spot but doesn't see anything. She feels around again, trying to find the edge she felt a moment ago. When she does locate it, she finds the dirt is packed so thickly she has to chop at the sediment with her flashlight.

Enough filth falls away so that Saoirse can make out the shape of the object in the soil. Her mind stutters at what—horrifyingly, unbelievably—she thinks she's seeing. Her heart thuds in her chest like a gong, and she lurches back, but this only makes things worse. Seeing the wall of dirt from several feet back allows her brain to make sense of the big picture, to parse what she's discovered in the soil. It makes sense. As much sense as this nightmare can possibly make.

The hard edge in the soil is the corner of a casket. Buried so long, it's as much a part of the dirt in which it lies as the rocks and worms. The room she is in is not an extended basement. It's not a subterranean chamber. It's not a dungeon or a lair.

It's a catacomb.

A catacomb that must exist directly adjacent to a cemetery.

Nausea roils in Saoirse's stomach, and she drops the flashlight to put her hands on her knees, breathing hard, more terrified of fainting—and falling unconscious again—than of facing this horrifying reality. The *bastard*. He left her in a catacomb. She's as good as buried alive down here.

No. Again, the adamant refusal. If she submits to her fear, to her fate, she might as well fashion a noose out of a hanging root or throw herself into the slab of stone now. She will not die down here. He told her he'd be back. He wants her to go on as if she's in love with him. Wants her to be the Sarah to his Edgar. The muse to his enigmatic, tortured, artistic genius. If it means her life will be extended long enough to figure out how to get out of here, she'll do it.

Saoirse sinks to the ground against the root-choked wall. Trapped underground by her once-lover, a Pulitzer Prize–winning, nationally beloved author. A strangled laugh escapes her. How could she have been so stupid?

You really didn't learn your lesson, did you? Jonathan asks.

"Shut up," she says. "Shut up, shut up, shut up."

She's without her medication. Without a weapon. Without food or water or even a blanket. Without people who will be looking for her, and—here, she becomes overwhelmed with sadness—the ability to take care of Pluto. Without a single thing but this gossamer-thin dress and her own wits.

But this isn't true. Not completely. She has one more thing. Something she's kept from Emmit, for all their long talks over dinners and in her bedroom. For all their commitment to baring their souls and knowing one another on a molecular level. She has what is perhaps the greatest weapon of all.

She has a secret. A secret that reminds her of what she's capable of when her back's against the wall.

∞

Emmit rouses her from a sleep she hadn't expected to be granted with a single "Saoirse?" rather than a shriek of stone against stone or the groan of a trapdoor lifting out of the ceiling.

"Hi there," he says, laying a blanket by her feet and a bottle of water beside it. Saoirse grabs the water, unscrews the top, and takes long, desperate sips. When she's drunk two-thirds of the bottle, it occurs to her to save the rest. *But who knows if he'll leave it when he goes?* She finishes it and tosses the empty bottle on the floor.

"You can keep this," he says, gesturing at the blanket, "so long as you behave. Like I told you, this can be like it was"—he nods vaguely toward the surface—"up there. Or, should you refuse to keep up your end of our relationship, it will be a very, very different experience for you. You've proven unequally valuable to my craft; I won't hesitate to subject you to experiences like those you had beneath the Shunned House if it keeps me writing. Do you understand?"

She nods. Her stomach cramps with the water she's just poured into it.

"Come here."

She freezes. Now? He means, now? Keep up her end of the relationship this minute? *What did you think?* Jonathan asks. *He was going to wait until you'd acclimated?*

"I—" Saoirse says.

Emmit shoots her a look. "Are we going to have a problem?"

She shakes her head. She remembers this feeling, this unadulterated rage she must conquer so it appears she's no more bothered than a woman being asked to repeat herself rather than one about to be assaulted.

Emmit lays the blanket on the floor as if preparing for a picnic. He sits and pats the fabric beside him. Saoirse swallows her volcanic anger and crawls forward to sit beside him.

She keeps her eyes very wide, afraid if she blinks, the tears will come. Emmit strokes her face. "I've missed you," he says.

Saoirse thought that, despite her fear and horror, she might feel the ghost of their previous connection. Some glimmer of familiarity. But there's only fear and horror. And hatred.

That sounds familiar, Jonathan says.

It should, she thinks back. *The trio of emotions that dominated our marriage.*

"Come closer," Emmit whispers, and pulls her down onto the blanket. She feels the ground beneath her head, the blanket a mere wisp of protection against its firmness. Emmit stares into her eyes. "Didn't I tell you?" he says. She smells the faint hint of chai obscured by toothpaste and the lingering remnants of aftershave. "That you're my momentous, soul-crushingly significant thing?"

He kisses her.

Though she hears them buzzing all around her, feels their legs walking over her skin in the same oppressive way Emmit's tongue explores her mouth, Saoirse does not open her eyes to the flies that swarm the cave like a plague.

Chapter 38

Saoirse lies on her back in the darkness and counts the beats of her heart, mercifully alone. Once again, she has no idea how Emmit took leave of the chamber. When he'd finished, he incapacitated her with another chloroform-soaked rag. Saoirse thinks back over her many hours and conversations with him, wondering at what point she should have known he was a monster. At what point she should have run. She shouldn't have gone with him to the coffee shop. She'd been right about him manipulating her to believe he'd thought she was stalking him. He'd had her in his sights all along. Maybe if she hadn't gone to the career fair, it wouldn't have been so easy for him. As it stands, she's a fly who's thrown herself onto his web.

Saoirse struggles to her feet and walks across the vast tunnel, turning the flashlight on every twenty steps to orient herself. She stops where the walls change from stone to concrete, then again when they shift to dirt. She examines the ground beneath the casket; the dirt she forced out of the wall is imperceptible. She looks back across the expanse of the catacomb, aiming the flashlight at the blanket Emmit left. That blanket is not quite the farthest point from where the catacomb meets the cemetery, but it's close. If she did claw a hole through the dirt, it would take Emmit a while to notice. He might never notice. Until she escaped like Andy Dufresne beneath Shawshank Prison. She, too, could be gone like a fart in the wind. Saoirse swallows a manic laugh.

She turns the metal body over in her hand. What would be worse? To chip away the dirt with the flashlight and risk breaking it, or not dig at all? Even if she doesn't use the flashlight as a battering ram, it will die eventually. She'll dig, then. It's decided.

You're screwed no matter what, Jonathan whispers, like a worm in her ear. *You dig, you won't hear him coming. Even if he doesn't catch you in the act, he'll see you're filthy. On the other hand, you don't dig, you die down here anyway.*

"Didn't I tell you to shut up?" Saoirse asks. She puts a hand to her chest, then pushes away the thought that the work will raise her heart rate as inevitably as Jonathan's voice.

She falls into a monotonous routine: a hundred whacks with the flashlight's head, a whispered prayer that she hasn't knocked the filament loose or dented the battery compartment, then a press of its dirt-smeared rubber button. While light streams from its lens, she examines her progress, then kills the flashlight and starts the process over. After an unknown number of one-hundred-whack sets, she increases the number to five hundred, not wanting to wear out the battery.

The work is worse than she anticipated: endless motion with no immediate gain, shot through with the knowledge that her survival depended on digging upward through ten feet—or maybe more . . . please, God, not more—of 150-year-old grave dirt, then—eventually, somehow—crawling up onto the flimsy casket and digging some more.

She sweats and curses. She screams and cries. She pauses to rest her heart and quell the stuttering of a brain that, more and more, feels the absence of its beta blockers and Paxil. She tears strips from the hem of her dress and wraps them around her hands, then tears another strip and wraps it around the handle of the flashlight. She rests with her back against the dirt wall. *I will not doze off. I will not doze off. I will not doze—*

She's ripped from sleep by a scream that erupts through the catacomb, echoing around her like a surround sound. Saoirse fumbles for the flashlight as the scream comes again. She recognizes it. It's the sound from her basement, the sound that interrupted her tarot reading. It's an unearthly, tortured sound, poetry ripped straight from hell, and it mirrors the scream Saoirse's heard in her own head since she woke up in this nightmare.

"Sarah?" Saoirse calls out, feeling less foolish than on the other times she called out to the former mistress of 88 Benefit Street. "Is that you?" Down here, where the idolatry of men's genius is held above a woman's right to live, the poet's ghost may just appear. The beam of Saoirse's flashlight roves over the walls, but the source of the scream does not appear. The next time the scream comes, it is far off, as if the screamer has moved to another chamber, dragging its pain. Its chains. Its secrets.

Saoirse forces her tired body across the catacomb, cleans herself as best she can with the underside of the blanket, then lays the blanket flat. She instructs her mind to allow her to sleep lightly, begs her brain to attune itself to the slightest of sounds. Then, she sleeps.

∞

A thump. Light. Another thump, this one with a scrape of gravel at the end of it, as if someone has jumped off a curb and landed on asphalt sprinkled with a thin layer of gravel. Saoirse stirs. Her hands smart from the torn calluses she suffered while wielding the flashlight as a shovel, and the muscles in her arms and neck creak like rusty hinges. She sits up fast and finds Emmit staring at her from several feet away. She prays his lantern won't illuminate the dirt on her arms or stains on the fabric of the thin white dress.

Emmit holds up a silver bucket, then walks it to the opposite wall. Saoirse's cheeks burn with indignation despite how badly she needs to relieve her bladder. Emmit walks toward her again, but passes her on the blanket, and heads toward what Saoirse thinks of as the northern tip of the catacomb, despite having no way of knowing north from south in this underground prison. "I'll give you some privacy," he says, and Saoirse hates herself for the gratitude she feels as she hurries to the bucket. When she's done, she returns to the blanket. Emmit meets her there.

He wipes her cheek, then her brow, and Saoirse waits for the accusation. But none comes. He kisses her, squeezes her shoulder, then lowers himself to the blanket, pushing her down along with him.

"Your mother sent you a text," he says, and it hits Saoirse only now that Emmit has her phone. That she told him, once upon a time, how most of her communication with her parents consists of brief check-ins via text. That he knows her transcendentalist friends don't carry cell phones. And that Saoirse rarely—if ever—posts on social media. Shards of dread crystallize in her stomach like stalagmites.

"She's sent you a lot of texts, actually," Emmit clarifies.

"What did you say to her?"

"I pretended I was you, of course, and that I was fine. Still seeing the new boyfriend. Still writing. She sounded happy for you. She sounds like a very nice woman. I'd like to meet her someday."

"About that," Saoirse starts, knowing she must choose her next words very carefully. "You're smart, Emmit. And you're not delusional. You must know you can't keep me down here forever. The texts will only appease my family for so long. My mom, my friends, the landlord when my rent's past due . . . someone will come looking for me."

He waves a hand. "I'll pay your rent."

She holds his gaze, careful to avoid staring at the lantern, not wanting to compromise her vision for even a second. "That's not the point. You know this arrangement can't go on forever." Emmit looks thoughtful, and Saoirse takes this as a sign to push forward. "And what if the new novel is everything your editor hoped for in a follow-up to *Vulture Eyes?* Are you going to risk losing that momentum by leaving me to die down here? Or is your plan to bring me back up into the world as if nothing happened and continue our relationship there?

"And if that *is* the case," Saoirse says, unable to stop now, her voice rising in volume, "why wait? Why not go back to the way things were right now? I'll stay at 88 Benefit Street. You could even move in with me." She forces a smile as she rattles off one lie after another. She needs him to believe her. She needs to get out of this tomb. Then, she can call the police. Run screaming down the street. Get as far away from Emmit as possible.

Emmit is studying her. "To be honest," he says, "I don't know what I'm going to do long term. But I don't think it will matter."

The air in Saoirse's lungs disappears. "What do you mean?"

"The exact number is debated, but it took Poe somewhere around one hundred and fifty works to achieve literary greatness. Sixty-five poems, nine essays, a single novel, a handful of novellas, one play, and seventy short stories. I figure I can keep you here long enough to create a similar body of work."

Saoirse's brain stutters. *He aims to keep me down here until he's written enough fiction to support an entire career?* Her breath threatens to choke her, and she starts inhaling in little gasps. Her fear is so all-consuming, she feels sick, the adrenaline pumping through her muscles so heightened that she is nauseated. Her mouth fills with saliva. White dots of light fall at the edges of her vision.

But despite the fear and the nausea, the wild panic at needing to run but having nowhere to go, one emotion rises above everything, one blazing, undeniable reality that turns the adrenaline into fire and her spotty vision into clarity. Anger. Anger so pure and all-consuming, Saoirse could smash every inch of time-hardened dirt in this catacomb to powder.

Careful, Jonathan warns. *Getting angry with me only made me resent you.*

A bubble of laughter escapes Saoirse's throat. *God forbid we upset the man who plans to kill me.*

Emmit's eyes narrow. "What's so funny?" His tone is inquisitive, as if they're back in the lounge the night of the rainstorm, sharing secrets.

Last chance to keep your mouth shut, Jonathan warns.

Saoirse cocks her head at Emmit. "You know it doesn't work like that, right?"

"Doesn't work like what?"

"Life. Literature. The world. You can't churn out fiction similar to Poe's in size, theme, subject matter, whatever, and expect to achieve a similar reception. It's madness." Something occurs to her, and she stares harder at Emmit, amazed. "You haven't just been trying to churn out work like Poe's, have you? You've tried *to become him.* That's what Mia was hinting at. Your MFA student. Josephine Martin. She knew you were Willem Thomas. You changed your name. You took on Poe's bio as your own."

Emmit's eyes flash with something dangerous. She shouldn't have mentioned Josephine. But, in her rage, she wants to hurt him. Even if it's just the smallest fraction of the amount he's hurt her.

"As for the work, it's not just that we live in a different world from the one in which Poe sold 'The Raven' to the *Evening Mirror,* and *nevermore* was on the lips of every man, woman, and child in the country. Not just that anyone with a cell phone and a self-published novel can become a sensation via BookTok. It's that, when it comes right down to it, you're not as talented as Edgar Allan Poe." She can't be sure, not in the lantern light, but she thinks Emmit's face has gone pale.

"You may have won a Pulitzer, but in a few years, no one will remember your name or your work. You'll be nothing." She laughs at the irony of what she's about to say. "Emmit Powell, nevermore."

She steels herself for his rage, maybe even his violence. What she does not expect is the look of appreciation, almost fascination, on his face.

"This is why I love you," he says, and Saoirse feels herself deflate. "This is why I need you. It's not your imprisonment in a catacomb that's interesting; it's how you react to it, how you are dealing with the trauma. Your view of the world is unparalleled."

Emmit's mouth tics, jumping into a half smile once, twice, three times. "*You* are all I need to write great things. If I cannot derive inspiration from your connection to Sarah, from our residual haunting across the centuries, I will find it in other ways. If I can't have your love, I will take your fear."

Saoirse's body goes cold. She wills herself not to cry. "I won't give you that either," she says. But inside, her body pulses with terror as thick as sludge.

Emmit throws his head back and laughs. "Of course you will. Poe's work is timeless not because of its subject matter—dead girls, plagues, and evil cats are a dime a dozen in horror fiction—but because of *the way* he writes about these things. His exploration of death, its physical signs, the effects of decomposition, premature burial, the reanimation of the dead, mourning lost love . . . I can explore these things too. *With you.* You will be my muse, whether you like it or not. And down here, no one can hear you scream."

Emmit reaches out and caresses her cheek. "Oh, saintly soul that should have been thy bride, you have death upon your eyes." Saoirse jerks away, and he laughs again. "The death of a beautiful woman really is the most poetical topic in the world." He shakes his head. "I wish I could say you'll enjoy what's in store."

He reaches in his pocket and produces the bottle of chloroform and a rumpled rag like a magician. "When it's over," he says solemnly, "I'll compose the most beautiful of burial rites. An anthem for the queenliest dead that ever died so young."

Saoirse scrambles to her feet, but Emmit grabs her by the hair. Pain burns along her scalp, but she pulls against his grip. In an instant, the chemical-soaked rag is pressed to her face.

"A dirge for you, Saoirse," Emmit breathes into her ear. "No longer my Sarah, but my Lenore. My Ligeia. My Annabel Lee."

Saoirse's heart stutters. The smell of chloroform engulfs her. The sounds in the catacombs devolve to the pull of a night-tide. The wind in the clouds. The moon in a dream.

And Saoirse slips down, down, down. Farther down than she's ever been. As close to death as a Sabbath song. As close as an atom forged in a star.

Into her kingdom by the sea.

Chapter 39

When Saoirse was a child, her mother—worried she wouldn't experience all the whims and fancies of a happy childhood without a sibling—spent every Saturday morning from May to October with Saoirse in the woods surrounding their backyard, a canvas bag of gardening tools and mason jars with holes poked through the tops at the ready, a song on her lips and joy on her face. It was these outings that were the foundation of Saoirse believing her mother was the best, most reliable person she knew.

They'd dig for worms in the rich garden soil by the property line, then venture into the pine trees, the summer sun filtered through endless, crisscrossing boughs and massive squirrel nests, their footsteps muffled by last year's needle-fall and by their excitement for the unknown.

Saoirse's favorite game was to find the biggest rock her ten-year-old arms could manage. She'd curl her fingers under its edges, reveling in the way the soil slid beneath her nails, feeling like she knew, even then, the way the words to describe the sensation curled into rhymes and stanzas in her head. Her mother would count backward from ten, and when she reached one, Saoirse would lift the rock, squealing with anticipation, while her mother scooped creepy-crawly, many-legged things into the open mouths of their jars.

Later, running through the woods with her mother, Saoirse would catch the pad of her finger in the thorn of a nearby rosebush or a net of interwoven briars. Forgetting about the dirt beneath her nails, she'd place a finger in her mouth to suck the wound. Blood and dirt would mingle into something bitter and heady but not entirely unpleasant. It was the taste of long, lazy days with her mother, just the two of them, and all the secrets of nature and the words and images and stories that intermingled in Saoirse's mind.

The taste in her mouth now is like that, but without any of the happy associations. Saoirse reaches for her face, but the trajectory of her hands is blocked by something, her knuckles whapping against the hard, flat barrier, and when she reaches up, she feels the wood, unyielding and expansive, six inches from her face. She attempts to push up on her elbows, but her forehead smashes into the wood, and she falls back, little white lights exploding across her vision. Those stars are the only light there is; she's in utter blackness, utter silence, the dirt not only on her tongue but in the back of her throat, crunching between her molars, the smell of it in her nostrils, and she tries to spit it out, but there's nowhere to turn, no reprieve from the taste and the darkness, and she feels as if she's drowning.

He buried me, she thinks wildly, incredulously, and she waits for Jonathan to say something smart, something cutting, but no such remark comes. She's alone with her terrified thoughts and her quivering, useless muscles, and she's in a goddamn coffin. How did Emmit even go about orchestrating such a thing? Surely he couldn't have had an open grave freshly dug and waiting for her.

Saoirse freezes. Surely he *couldn't* have had a grave freshly dug and waiting. Who did she lay with in this coffin? No. *No.* That would be too much, even for Emmit, even after hearing the things she's heard. She must be in some cardboard box, in some makeshift hole Emmit dug a few feet below the surface. It's not an actual grave. It can't be. If she can manage to push the lid open, she'll find a few inches of loose dirt are all that separate her from freedom. All that hold her in this claustrophobic nightmare.

But as she presses her hands to the wood above her a second time, she becomes cognizant of the surface on which she lies. She'd thought it was flat. It *is* flat. But there's something on top of the bottom board, beneath her supine body. Against her brain's desperate directives, her fingers walk themselves over the surface. Jonathan's voice finally sounds in her skull: *You won't survive this. Not the being-buried part, but the stress and fear, the horrific discovery you're about to make. Your heart won't be able to take it.*

Reflexively, she agrees with him: *Don't make this worse,* she instructs herself. *Concentrate on the board above you, on busting that open. For the love of sunlight and of living and of the breathing, beautiful world, do not explore what's below.* But it's like her fingers have a mind of their own.

She feels the dry, desiccated fabric first, the crinkly texture of what might be centuries-old lace. Below that is something hard and knobby. Like twigs. Like bones. She counts. One. Two. Three. Four. Five. Then backtracks, to the fourth digit. Feels the circular object there, bisected by ridged metal teeth clamping down on the cold, hard centerpiece. It's impossible to tell whether the ring features a diamond or a small stone.

The hyperventilating starts then. In a matter of seconds, she feels as if her lungs have shrunk to the size of quarters. She pulls her hands back into fists and pummels the wood above her. Her panic is good for something; her thrusts are manic, fueled by the instinct to survive, to breathe. The wood splinters, chips and dust falling into her eyes, into her mouth, as she screams.

And she is screaming. She hadn't realized it before, but she is screaming, and her heart is pounding in her temples, her throat, her chest, her stomach, in her fists as she pounds and pounds the wood. She's pummeling Emmit, pummeling Jonathan, and Aidan, punching herself for her stupidity and gullibility, screeching as she rails against her weak heart and her weaker mind, her desire to have tried again for love, for a life. She screams, and she jams her fists at the casket, and the debris hitting her face and neck becomes less slivers of wood and more chunks of dirt and tiny pebbles and dried bits of branches and other detritus from the earth.

She turns her head and spits great mouthfuls of dirt over her shoulder, then sucks in what she hopes will be clear air, but dirt still floods in—more dirt, and more dirt, and then she's broken free from the casket, pushing the remaining jagged edges of wood out of her face, but the dirt floods over her in rivulets now, and she can no longer scream at all, her mouth too full of the earth, of sorrow and regret.

Like a flash of lightning, the epitaph from the Athenæum's fountain explodes in her mind: COME HITHER EVERY ONE THAT THIRSTETH. She drank from the fountain. She will never leave Providence. She will be buried in this city.

She almost stops struggling then, but with a final burst of strength, she makes a wide, sweeping motion with her arms, a drowning swimmer desperate to break the surface. She gets her legs beneath her, despite the endless avalanche of dirt, but her feet catch in the rags of the corpse who's been so unceremoniously disturbed, the corpse whose grave—if Emmit gets his way—would be one shared for all eternity.

And she *would* have shared a grave with this quiet skeleton, interred forever in Providence, had the dirt above the coffin not been so recently tilled by Emmit by virtue of needing to deposit Saoirse within it. Saoirse's route of ingress has become her saving egress, the dirt unpacked and uneven enough to allow her to flail her way to freedom. She feels the cool, open air with her left hand first, grabs for it like a rope, finds harder ground beside the gravesite, and scrambles upward on what's left of the dilapidated coffin. Her starving lungs burn and consciousness dips. She cannot pass out now. Just three more seconds.

She forces her left knee up through cascading dirt in conjunction with the opposite arm. Her fingers close around something—a still-intact side of the casket, perhaps, or a root; it doesn't matter which, it only matters that its existence allows her to make one final push for the surface. Her nose and mouth come clear of the earth, and she gasps in air. Saoirse stays like this, face partially unburied, simply breathing, content with this small gift, unbothered that the rest of her body is still encased in dirt. She doesn't even open her eyes, just breathes, feeling the oxygen relieve her muscles of their near-fatal burden, calm the thrashing of her overtaxed heart.

When her lungs have ceased their volcanic burning, she wriggles up farther, blinks the dirt from her eyes, and looks around as much as she can without being able to turn her neck. It's a surreal sensation, being eye level with the base of so many tombstones, like she's at the center of a city, staring up at blocks of skyscrapers the same steel-gray, the inscriptions like darkened windows or recessed moldings.

She's about to laugh—or cry—with relief when it occurs to her that Emmit must be watching. Did he expect her to break free? Would he have pulled her out himself if she hadn't? Either way, he's not going to let her get away now. She wriggles from the grave, pulling herself onto her forearms, then her stomach, ending in a wobbly-legged crouch. *Do I scream and hope someone hears me?* she asks herself, or maybe Jonathan. *Or make a run for it now?*

A branch snaps behind her, and she lurches forward, blinking wildly in the dark. She spins, trying to determine where the graveyard's exit is, but there are too many trees, their branches like hands waiting to pluck her from the ground like a flower, blocking her line of vision. She darts from one line of tombstones to the next, panic rising, dread rising, a scream rising, and she wants to cry that, after years of taking care of herself, of taking her medication even when things with Jonathan were at their worst, this is how it's going to happen, this is how her heart will stop beating for good. Somehow, she pushes past the terror, past the despair, and runs, gaining speed despite her steadily increasing pulse, and even when her foot catches the base of a thick square headstone, and she falls to her knees, she is back on her feet and running again in an instant. Up ahead is a long stone wall, and beyond that is a street. A streetlight shines a circle of orange onto the pavement like a halo. Beyond that, something gold—like a reflective ghost—glints in the distance.

"Help," she calls out, but her voice is a croak, her throat too scratchy from the dirt she swallowed. She sucks in a breath. "Hel—"

The word, the world, all the air is cut off when something hits her in the chest. Saoirse's feet fly out from under her, and she hits the ground on her back with the force of a brick wall stopping a semi. Along with the air from her lungs, every hope of freedom she'd harbored whooshes from her body as Emmit steps out from behind a tree trunk, rubbing his arm where he'd used it to end her desperate sprint.

She tries to scream, but his hand is over her mouth, and then it's the chloroform and the blackness, and she's gone, into the sulfurous current, into the dim lake of Auber, her heart beating to ash, her memories treacherous, her path no longer even a nebulous luster but merely a dust plume in the night, in the misty mid-region of some Poe-penned place.

And she disappears. Into the ghoul-haunted woodland of Weir.

Chapter 40

He is there when she wakes, watching as she rolls to her side, the filthy dress hanging in tatters at her elbows. She looks up and into the eyes of a man she thought, once, she knew. Her own eyes fill with tears.

"Please," she says. "Please, if you're going to do this, at least give me my medication." She puts a hand to her chest. "I won't survive another . . ." She trails off, shaking her head.

Emmit shakes his head, too, in disagreement. "I can't do that," he says. "Don't you see? How you responded to being buried alive? I waited, in the graveyard. I watched you break the surface; I saw your determination, your desperation. There aren't many who can say they've witnessed something so primal, so raw."

"Go to hell," she whispers.

"It was like I could hear your thoughts," he says quietly. "As you crouched there, weighing your options, considering your chances. It was . . . beautiful. Like watching someone in the window of a burning building deciding whether they should jump."

She cannot look at him, this person who does unspeakable things in service of his self-perceived genius. "You're sick," she whispers. "Maybe if you got some help, you could get better, continue writing. But if you commit to this, what you're doing to me, eventually you'll get caught."

A charming smile animates one half of his face. "I told you I only need you alive while I compile enough work to sustain my career. If you keep giving me gold like back in the cemetery, that won't be long."

Saoirse pulls away from him and covers her face. She is weeping, yes, but more than that, something's occurred to her, the last thing she noticed before Emmit stepped out from behind the tree, derailing her escape. She doesn't want him watching her as she considers what he's said: *If you keep giving me gold like back in the cemetery.* And that's it. That was what she saw. Gold. Glinting like an out-of-place orb in the distance.

She'd thought she was dizzy from lack of oxygen, but that wasn't it. The gold was the gilded bronze statue—Rhode Island's Independent Man, meant to embody the spirit of freedom—atop the statehouse. The statue just past Saint John's Cathedral. The statue she's seen every day off her balcony since moving to Benefit Street. Which means Emmit *is* keeping her beneath Benefit Street!

Saoirse's heart swells at the realization. She hasn't been driven to another state or dragged to some remote site in the woods. If she can get to the right chamber, find the right tunnel, she might be close enough to a street or dwelling where someone could hear her pounding. Her screaming. She just has to bide her time . . . and keep her newfound knowledge from Emmit.

Saoirse composes herself, hardening the protracted sobs into a bitter laugh.

"Something funny?" Emmit asks.

"Just your logic. If you think you can withhold my medications and I won't keel over in the middle of one of your fear experiments, you're wrong. The joke will be on you."

"You don't give yourself enough credit," he says. "The woman I fell in love with is too strong to give up. Too strong and far too stubborn."

Some macabre part of her hopes she goes into cardiac arrest right then. But the bigger part of her is ready to fight, to ensure Emmit never adds another manuscript to his literary canon. "Are we through here?" she asks. "I'm ready to be chloroformed so you can leave and I can go to sleep." The sarcasm is meant to be a shield, but there's a waver in her voice she can't disguise. Emmit might think she's bluffing in her entreaty to be given her meds, but she doesn't believe her heart has too many more instances of being chloroformed left in its bank.

Emmit opens his mouth, then closes it. He gives her the half smile and a little shrug. "I suppose it is that time. I need to write while the details of tonight are still fresh. Not to mention finish planning the next test of your endurance."

He digs the rag and bottle out of his pocket and leans toward her. Under the guise of a dramatic recoil, Saoirse sucks in a massive intake of air and holds her breath. Emmit presses the rag to her nose and mouth. Her heart pounds, and her lungs burn, but Saoirse moves her chest up and down, as if she's breathing in the chemical. Emmit must sense something is amiss, because he presses the rag to her face even harder. She lets out several puffs of air opposite the feigned inhalations. When every bit of air in her lungs has been expelled, Saoirse lets her body go limp.

Emmit continues to hold the rag over her face, and Saoirse starts to panic. *He knows I'm faking; he's not going to stop. He's going to hold this rag over my face until I have to breathe again!* She resigns herself to another stint of drug-induced blackness and prepares her body for the shock of the chemical stink in her nostrils, but the rag is removed. Emmit takes her by the shoulders and lowers her to the ground. Saoirse senses more than hears him turn away.

Her brain is screaming for her to suck in oxygen like a sprinter at the end of a race, but she manages a series of slow, shallow breaths in time with Emmit's footsteps. When she feels he's a safe enough distance away, she opens her eyes. Everything depends on seeing how he gets out of the catacomb.

Though the lantern light has diminished along with Emmit's shadowy form, Saoirse sees him pull something from the waistband of his jeans. With a flick of his wrist, the object extends, then extends even further as he pulls each segment out of the previous one with a coinciding click. In a matter of seconds, he's holding a two-foot pole that, with a final click, boasts a rubber knob on one end. Saoirse inhales a bit too loudly, and Emmit whips around.

She snaps her eyes shut and freezes. *No, no, no, don't look over here, don't bring the chloroform back, please, god, no, I am begging you, keep doing what you're doing . . .*

Three, five, seven seconds pass, and she hears the scrape of metal against stone. Saoirse opens her eyes in time to see Emmit fish a length of wire down from the arched stone ceiling, wrap his hand in his shirt sleeve, and yank the wire down to reveal an ancient-looking wood-and-rope ladder that unfurls in a series of jerky thumps. The final step stops a few inches from the ground. She closes her eyes again, worried he's going to take one last look at her before going up the stairs. When she opens them, Emmit's left foot is disappearing into the ceiling. He reaches down and pulls the ladder up, each step making a muffled thump as he stacks the layers on top of one another.

Saoirse is plunged into darkness. She takes several deep, replenishing breaths, hardly daring to believe she's avoided another chloroform-induced blackout. It's not the victory she hoped for, however; not now that she's seen the way out might as well be on the moon. There's no way to reach the wire; she's not even sure she'd be able to discern which stone the wire is tucked behind. She fears Emmit's left her without a flashlight, but after a moment of panicked groping, her fingers find the metal cylinder.

Turning the flashlight on, Saoirse walks to the spot from where Emmit ascended the hidden ladder. She shines the beam along each stone in the archway, once, twice, three times. Finally, on the fourth swoop, she sees it: a half-inch piece of wire barely visible at the top of a particularly cracked stone.

That wire is the way out. But without the expandable baton Emmit took with him, how can she reach it? She moves the flashlight back and forth, examining this new prison more closely. Stone. Dust. More stone. Concrete blocks. The tattered dress on her back. The flashlight in her hands. She turns, reilluminating the place where stone becomes concrete, then jogs over to stand beside it. She inspects the concrete. The grout that was used to bind the blocks together must be as old as the catacomb itself. She scrapes it with a fingernail, watching it turn to dust that disappears as it falls to the floor. She wraps a finger in the fabric of her dress and scrapes at the grout harder.

A few larger chunks break away, but even buffered by fabric, her nail aches with the effort. Saoirse turns the flashlight off and bangs at the space between the blocks of concrete with its handle.

When she turns the flashlight back on, she can't believe her eyes. Almost all the grout connecting the two blocks has been knocked free. But she can't use the flashlight as a sledgehammer. If it breaks, knocking out enough blocks to reach the wire won't matter. She won't be able to see anything in the blackness without a flashlight. Saoirse looks around for something with which to scratch out the gravel. Desperately, she runs her hands over her body, across the flimsy fabric of the dress, as if a hidden pocket might reveal itself.

"Goddamn you, Emmit," she says. "A flashlight and a stupid dress? That's all I get?" Her hands reach the neckline of the fabric, and she grips it, enraged by her helplessness. And that's when her fingers bump against the pendant at her throat.

The pendant. Sarah's coffin pendant. Sarah's *metal* coffin pendant. Small, but shaped like a tiny spade. She unclasps the necklace and positions the pendant along the top portion of the block to the left. With five long, scraping motions, the grout disintegrates. She moves the pendant to the left line of grout, and counts five more, then does the same at the bottom. The grout here is thicker, but she's still able to scrape it out.

Holding the flashlight under her arm, she grabs the concrete block with two hands and wiggles it. It moves, and not just a few millimeters, but several inches. She places the flashlight on the ground and shakes the block back and forth with manic, frenzied movements. A moment later, the block jumps from its place in the wall like something alive.

Saoirse stares at the block by her feet, so pleased with this small victory, she lets out a quiet, incredulous laugh. She picks up the flashlight, shines it at the ceiling, then back at the block, gauging how many she will need. It's about ten feet to the ceiling, and the blocks are— she measures with her finger—about nine inches wide. She'll need eleven to reach the top, then one less for each stack beside it, descending to one, if she wants to make a staircase, which, stability-wise, is really her only option. So, sixty-six blocks in all.

She stares at the concrete wall, her mind brimming with defiance and determination despite the job before her.

"All right, you concrete bitch," she whispers. "Time to fall."

Chapter 41

The throbbing in her fingertips starts first, followed by a headache that blooms behind her eyes like forsythia, yellow and draping and pungent. The staccato tremors of her heart are constant, so Saoirse ignores them. She removes blocks with an intensity that would scare her had it been applied to any other endeavor prior to being held prisoner in a lightless dungeon. Time passes as both a trickle from a dying fountain and a deluge from a broken dam. She does not expend energy trying to determine the number of hours that pass, or why some blocks are liberated quickly while others will not part from their house of dust and ruin at all.

For those blocks that don't loosen after scraping the grout twenty times, Saoirse cuts her losses and moves on. The ratio of blocks that are jarred free versus those that remain in place is about two to one. It's easiest, of course, to liberate blocks adjacent to one another as opposed to moving to a fresh expanse of wall. Saoirse goes long, long stretches without turning on the flashlight. She grows used to working in the dark and—aside from the scrape of the pendant—the silence, a world as black and soundless as the bottom of an ocean. Everything but the muscles in her arms and the metal in her hands and the numbers in her head ceases to exist.

Finally, pushing away a powerful—but not irrational—fear that Emmit's snuck up behind her while she worked, Saoirse switches on the flashlight. She'd lost count of the number of blocks that'd dropped to the catacomb floor, and when she sees a massive pile stretching along the wall, she can't help but cry out in shock and joy. There are sixty blocks, intact and sturdy-looking, and one that's cracked down the middle. Motivation renewed, she turns the flashlight off and goes back to work, this time keeping count. A few minutes later, there are six additional blocks on the ground.

She lays the flashlight on one half of the cracked block, illuminating her path across the catacomb. She picks up the first block, stacks it on a second, and runs them over to where Emmit disappeared into the ceiling, stacking them beneath the visible length of wire. Two at a time she transports the blocks, stacking them in a narrow but sturdy staircase. Her stomach twists with hunger, and once, she has to wait for a spell of lightheadedness to pass. When the last block is in place, she puts a foot on the bottom stair. She doesn't have time to examine each level for gaps or weaknesses; Emmit could return at any moment.

Bare toes gripping the concrete, she moves with more balance and dexterity than her weak muscles should warrant. After seven blocks, she looks up. At this height, she can see that the bottom portion of the wire is a loop, about as wide as her fist. If she were taller, or didn't need her hands to grip the blocks above her, she'd have no problem grabbing the loop and pulling the wire downward. As it stands, she needs to climb higher. Saoirse lifts her left foot and ascends another block. Her muscles are trembling now, and the concrete staircase feels less and less steady the closer she gets to the top.

You're going to fall, Jonathan says matter-of-factly from inside her head. Or, has the voice come from *outside* it? Saoirse glances left and then right, her jackrabbiting heart somehow increasing in speed. Is Emmit here? Did he come in through another entrance? But no, it was—without a doubt—the voice of her dead husband.

"Jonathan?" she calls softly. The word is as shaky as her muscles.

For a moment, there is only silence. Then, Jonathan's voice, in conjunction with a flash of movement in the shadows, comes from the left of the catacomb, clear and loud and full of bravado: "Yes, dear wife?"

Saoirse gasps, and her hands peel away from the block she clutches. For one infinite moment, she flails, and it seems as if she'll be able to return her hands to the makeshift staircase. Then the block beneath her left foot shifts, and she's falling, falling, down, a bird pitched from the sky with wings that were clipped one too many times and never grew back.

Saoirse lies on the ground, oblivious to everything but pain and the pulse of her heart in her ears. After several agonizing moments, she tests her bruised and throbbing body. Mercifully, nothing seems broken. When she's able to get to her feet, she limps across the catacomb for the flashlight. Tracking the beam around the perimeter tells her she's alone. No Emmit. No Jonathan.

She half expects a smart remark from her trickster husband, but nothing comes. She considers whether hallucinations—auditory or otherwise—are a symptom of rapid withdrawal from antidepressants, but it's been too long since she first went on them to remember the details of tapering off. She shines the flashlight at the loop of wire and feels something drip down her arm and over her hand.

A long gash from wrist to forearm glistens, the strip of skin alongside it ragged. Blood pools in the wound, and she tears at the hem of her dress, planning to wrap her arm with it, but stops. She looks back up at the wire. She looks down at her arm again. She looks at the flashlight, and her plan comes together.

In a flash, she pulls the tattered dress over her head and stands, naked and shivering. She ties the wrist of one sleeve closed and drops the flashlight into the armhole. The light in the catacomb is muted now, filtered through sheer muslin fabric. Saoirse can see just enough to make her way to the staircase.

She ties the sleeves around her neck to keep her hands free and places a foot on the first block, planning to follow the same path up. Before she can do so, the scream comes. Not far off, but here. In this chamber. Hands shaking, Saoirse aims the filtered beam around the catacomb. Nothing . . . nothing. Had she imagined the scream the way she'd imagined her husband's voice? But then there's movement in the outermost ring of the flashlight beam. Heart in her throat, Saoirse repositions the light, illuminating the ghost that haunts her.

The creature opens its mouth, and out of it pours a scream of primal rage. Despite the low light, Saoirse sees the animal's large pointed ears and its matted rust-red fur. She sees the cut of its ribs, like another set of teeth, as if the fox's body itself has become a mouth, desperate to devour. To take what it can. And despite her fear, Saoirse feels overcome with sadness. It was Emmit's opening of these catacombs that caused the fox to become trapped. She knows it like she knows her own name.

They lock eyes for several moments before the fox raises its delicately boned face to the ceiling and screams again. With tears in her eyes, Saoirse says, "I'm so sorry. I'm *going* to get out of here, and then they'll exhume these tunnels. There'll be a chance for you to get out." She forces herself to break eye contact but whispers, "A chance to be free." These final words are more to herself than the trapped animal. Saoirse starts back up the steps.

At the top, she unties the sleeves from around her neck and takes the portion of fabric containing the flashlight into her right hand. She'll have one chance to throw it through the loop in the wire and catch some part of the weighted sleeve on its way back down. She can't lose her footing. She can't miss the loop. She can't drop the flashlight.

You were never much of an ath—Jonathan starts to say from her head, but she doesn't wait for him to finish. The flashlight is already leaving her hands, time slowing as she watches it sail toward the loop, a bull's-eye of just four, maybe five, inches across. She might be inclined to think herself lucky when the glowing sleeve arcs perfectly through the wire, but to be lucky would be to have never found herself in these catacombs at all.

The rest of the dress trails spectrally behind the flashlight, a dutiful ghost to be delivered into Saoirse's waiting hands. She catches the heaviest portion of her moving target, one hand clamping down over the wire before it can liberate itself from the fabric and spring back up and out of her reach.

Saoirse stands there momentarily, hardly daring to move, to breathe. Then, she ties the fabric around her neck, yanks the wire down, and the wood-and-rope ladder unfurls itself in the same series of jerky thumps it had when Emmit accessed it. She realizes it's going to upset the bottom portion of her staircase in time to grab the rope and swing herself onto the middle step. The last two steps knock the concrete foundation askew and, like a too-tall Jenga tower, the tower falls, crashing in on itself into a pile of upended blocks and dust.

The rope ladder sways, and Saoirse clings to it. She half expects to see the fox in the muted, bobbing beam of the flashlight, but the creature is gone. She starts for the top, her promise to find help echoing in her head, her excitement at escaping this chamber tempered only by her apprehension of what she'll find above.

As she pulls herself through the hole and onto a dirt floor, the knot around her neck comes loose. Saoirse grasps the hem of the fabric just before it slides back through the hole. With shaking fingers, she yanks the flashlight from the sleeve, pulls the dress back on, and shines the beam into the yawning chamber before her, Alice coming out of the rabbit hole into a garden of dust and stone.

Saoirse's heart plummets. She's exchanged one impenetrable catacomb for another. But then she sees that this chamber extends into an actual tunnel. Aware of how much time has passed since Emmit last chloroformed her, sick with dread that she'll run into him as soon as she steps into the tunnel, Saoirse throws a final glance at the hole from which she's emerged, pats the flashlight reverentially, and starts forward.

Into the unknown.

Chapter 42

She walks through the spiderwebs and the silence until she comes to a three-way fork. Choosing the middle passage, she walks some more.

Interesting choice, Jonathan comments. He's been inclined to remain between the walls of her skull since her fall. *It's not like you have any way of knowing where you're going.*

"*You* were always the indecisive one," Saoirse responds aloud. "*I'm* the one who made a choice and stuck with it, no matter the consequences." She's almost annoyed he refrains from breaking free from her, wishes she could face him head-on when she says this, even if what appeared before her was a specter horrifying to behold. She wants him to remember how she didn't back down despite the traumatizing pressure, that she didn't give him what he wanted just because he wanted it.

The flashlight dims, and Saoirse stops. She presses the button, plunging the cave into darkness, and closes her eyes. "Please," she says, every heartbeat driving force into this single word. When she turns the flashlight on and opens her eyes, the beam is strong again. "Thank you. Just a little longer."

A few strides later, Saoirse wonders if the flashlight dimmed at all. How many days have passed since her last dose of medication? Enough to produce corporeal dead husbands? Flickering lights? "Keep it together," she mutters. "You can do this."

You know, Jonathan says, and Saoirse groans. *Maybe when you fell off that ladder of blocks, you hit your head. Maybe you're lying on the ground, bleeding out. Or maybe you never made it out of that grave Emmit dug for you. It seems far more likely you suffocated on all that grave dirt than that you dug yourself to freedom. This whole thing—me, your escape from the lower catacomb—could be nothing more than a hallucination produced by your dying brain as you return to the stars.*

Saoirse considers this for a moment. "Did you see things?" she asks. "When you were dying?"

The voice in her head is quiet for a long time. Then, finally, very, very softly, it says, *You know what I saw.* After that, Jonathan is quiet.

Saoirse comes to another split, the tunnel separating into two narrower passages. She pauses, cocks her head. Down the passage to the left . . . is that a sound? She listens, but nothing more comes. The presence of sound might mean Emmit, but Saoirse remembers the conclusion she came to after her premature burial. The golden glint of the statehouse statue, her likely proximity to Benefit Street, her own house. The presence of sound might mean Emmit . . . but it might mean other people. It might mean help. Saoirse starts down the left-hand passage.

After several minutes of walking in the dark with only her labored breathing to accompany her, she hears it again. Something like a chant, accompanied by distant drumming. She quickens her pace, but the sounds stops as quickly as it started. Twenty strides farther and she hears it again. As she hurries forward, the sound grows in volume. Saoirse runs, forcing herself to hold in her cry for help until she can be sure it isn't Emmit. Up ahead is a wall, and though she's out of breath, Saoirse sprints for it. She presses her hands to the stone, then holds her ear against the wall. The drumming continues. Saoirse's about to call out when a muffled—but familiar—voice rises from behind the stone.

"Whitman House, we reach back through time to your one true inhabitant. We ask for your help. Our friend took up residence within you and sought to uncover the truth through words. Now, she is missing. We need your ability to *see*. We need you to call the Divine Poet. What has Emmit Powell done with Saoirse White?" Mia speaks a line from one of Sarah's poems, and the voices of Roberto and Lucretia join in.

"I'm here!" Saoirse shouts. "Right here! In the wall! Mia, Roberto, Lucretia, help! I'm in the catacomb. He's trapped me in here! He . . . he buried me!"

There is the briefest of silences, and then a squeal. Saoirse would know that squeal anywhere.

"Saoirse, oh my god." Lucretia's words are a shrill, incredulous crescendo. "Is that really you? How do we get to you? How do we get you out of there?"

"I don't know!" Saoirse yells, wanting to cry from an overwhelming mix of happiness and frustration. Her friends are holding a séance to find her. People are looking for her. People care. She tries to think, too stressed and dehydrated, her mind tripping over bad ideas and false starts, having no idea how to instruct them to find her. "The Shunned House!" she cries suddenly. "The basement of the Shunned House! There's an alcove in the floor. That's where he took—"

The hand clamps over her mouth with such force, Saoirse bites a chunk out of her tongue. She tries to scream, to make some sort of noise, but Emmit holds her too tightly. Saoirse thrusts her thigh back between his legs, and Emmit grunts in pain.

"Saoirse!" It's Lucretia again. "What's happening?"

Roberto's voice comes next. "My god, he's in there with her. He's got her. Saoirse, we're coming! We're going to get you out of there!"

The muffled sounds of chairs moving and people running reach her ears, followed by bumps and knocks on the other side of the stone. "Maybe it's a trick wall," she hears Roberto say. Already, however, her friends' voices are farther away. Emmit hauls her back toward the catacomb, her bare feet dragging on the ground, and she considers Jonathan's words again: *This whole thing could be nothing more than a hallucination produced by your dying brain as you return to the stars.*

At this point, you should be so lucky, Jonathan quips.

Saoirse keens with hopelessness. Her heart rate rises, falls, then rises again, the thuds against her rib cage growing increasingly erratic. She squirms and clutches for her chest, but Emmit's arms around her torso are in her way. Finally, he stops dragging her, releases her arms, and stands her upright before him, as if he's about to scold an uncooperative child.

"You could have ruined everything!" Emmit gasps. "What were you—" He stops when he sees she's trying to speak. He sighs dramatically, Goth English major to the last. "What is it, Saoirse?" His tone is impatient, almost sarcastic. "What do you want to say?"

Saoirse drops to her knees, rolls onto her side, and writhes, gasping and clutching her chest. Her hands flutter. The movement within her rib cage is unceasing and unprecedented: white-hot lava that bubbles up from the glassy-iced cauldron of her rib cage. "Heart attack," she croaks. "Heart . . . attack."

Emmit's expression is confused, then skeptical. Finally, when he sees what she can only imagine is all the color drain from her face, his eyes—those eyes she stared into as they made love, walked the graveyard and the streets of Providence, as they talked of writing and death and living and love—open wide, not in concern but in anger and disbelief.

"Are you—" he starts, but it's too late. The grays and blacks and browns of the catacomb drop away until the world is an overexposed photograph, inverted, more white than dark. Everything is hot and bright and so, so white.

"I—" she says but can't continue and rolls onto her back, head lolling against the ground. Gravel digs into her neck, the backs of her arms, and the pain blooms outward like little explosions of wildflowers that cover her brain, bathing her thoughts in fragrance, soft petals, velvety leaves. The sensations converge, and a stanza unfurls in her mind:

> The poet sleeps, and pansies bloom
> Beside her far, provident tomb;
> The turf is heaped above her bed;
> The stone is moldering at her head;
> But each fair creature of her dream,
> Transferred to daylight's common beam,

Lives the charmed life that waneth never,
A Beauty and a Joy forever.

She's not sure if it's hers or a memory of some distant verse. Sarah's, perhaps, dropped into her head by the ghostly poet whom she feels standing over her even now. Saoirse smiles through the pain and closes her eyes. Tears patter the ground like heartbeats.

Whether hers or Sarah's, the words are beautiful. She will miss beautiful words. She hadn't realized they could exist down here. In the catacombs.

And if they can exist here, then they will exist wherever she's on her way to now, falling from the sky like raindrops to jewel her hair, droplets that contain multitudes . . . entire worlds.

Chapter 43

"*Shh.* You're all right. You're all right. Did you really think I was going to let you die?"

Saoirse stirs, unsure if the voice is in her head or her ears. Her body feels like sheets of layered gauze, porous and flimsy, liable to float away in a breeze. She flexes her fingers, trying to determine if she is, in fact, alive, or if her tortures have extended into death.

"You were *not* having a heart attack," Emmit says, and Saoirse opens her eyes. "Just a little bout of anxiety, by my reckoning."

The light is strange—bluish, and not diffuse, but a bright streak that falls behind Emmit's crouched form. He follows her gaze. "Your flashlight died, and I don't have my phone on me. I was writing when I got one of my feelings. *Something momentously significant is happening, Emmit,* it said. I knew I had to check on you that very minute, not wait. On the way out the door, I grabbed this stupid blue flashlight, and, well, here we are."

Saoirse swallows, and this simple act causes the pain in her chest to expand outward in all directions. It feels as if every rib is broken and her lungs are full of stones. "Not anxiety," she chokes out. "Heart attack. Need a hospital."

"Don't be so dramatic. And besides, I can't take you out of here now. You made sure of that when you yelled out to your friends. They're probably at the police station this very second. I need to secure you somewhere temporary and get home before the inevitable officer arrives at my door." He pauses. "No, I won't go home. I'll go to the Ath. Where I've been working on my novel all evening."

Saoirse is having trouble focusing. Her friends are at the police station? What friends? Why? And Emmit's a writer? Is that how she met him? She blinks, trying to grasp on to the edges of her thoughts, but nothing registers. Nothing but the pain and shortness of breath.

"Now that you know for sure where I've been keeping you," Emmit says, "you have to admit how remarkable it is." His expression is reverent. "Who would have ever believed the basement from Lovecraft's Shunned House *was real*, uncovered by Poe during one of his visits to Rhode Island?" Emmit laughs. "I read about it on the website of a Poe-fan-turned-collector. At an auction at the Ath, he came into possession of a map of Benefit Street, published in 1846. There were notes in the margins that matched Poe's handwriting, notes that cited the location of the basement with a single, scribbled word: *portal*.

"It kills me that the Athenæum staff wouldn't have thoroughly examined anything from that time period before auctioning it off; Poe spent a good deal of time there when he was courting Sarah, and was known to have signed his poem 'Ulalume' in the library's copy of the *American Review*." Emmit laughs again and shakes his head, as if tickled by his own good fortune.

The unnatural glow of the flashlight's blue glare behind Emmit turns his face into a shadow-saturated jack-o-lantern. Saoirse's fear comes back to her, pushing the memories of the last several days out of the basement of her mind.

"It makes perfect sense when you think about it," Emmit continues. "That Poe's interest in the house on Benefit Street wasn't limited to his infatuation with Sarah. That he'd uncovered a series of catacombs beneath the city and that Sarah's home contained one of the easiest points of ingress. That 'The Premature Burial' and 'The Cask of Amontillado' took their inspiration from Poe's real-life adventures.

"There were whispers of slave tunnels beneath College Hill over the years, but when no one could prove their existence, the rumors were attributed to drain tunnels. It's so easy to assume all the mysteries of the world have been uncovered; it takes but a single person with a specific set of interests for a connection to be made." He gives her a look like, *Wouldn't you agree?* Saoirse does not—cannot—respond.

Emmit sighs. "I refused to abandon the theory of a network of underground tunnels," he continues. "I located several references to a catacomb in the annals of Saint John's Cathedral. When I considered this in conjunction with Poe's interest in burials and graveyards—and with Lovecraft's Shunned House, not even a quarter of a mile from the cathedral—I knew there was something to it, but the entrance to the tunnels eluded me. That is, until you moved into 88 Benefit Street. Into Sarah's house.

"I was watching the house, as I had so many nights before, contemplating where the entrance to the catacombs could be, certain the answer lay inside, that Sarah Whitman, and Poe's obsession with her, was the key. And then you pulled up in your dusty little Mazda, and I saw you step out onto the street, a timid little bird but possessed of a palpable strength. I fell for you as utterly as Edgar did Sarah, watching her tend her garden by the light of the moon."

Saoirse's lucid now. Though, while her brain stitches the details of Emmit's confession into a macabre tapestry, her heart threatens to unravel, arteries and ventricles severed like thread against teeth.

"You were the key to unlocking the energy, the history, of the house. Your arrival in Providence initiated the residual haunting. The more I pursued you, the stronger our connection to the past became. Oh, and thanks for telling me about the trick paneling at the side of the house. That was crucial. Do you want to hear something hilarious? Your friends? The little séance circle they constructed? Their black-clothed table was directly over what I eventually discovered was the false floor. Once I found it and chiseled it free from almost two hundred years' worth of dust and grime, I needed only to slide the table back over the now-visible outline. You four sat right over it and never knew."

Saoirse winces.

"As for the second entrance," Emmit continues, "I'd searched the Shunned House before, but plunging through the floor the night I was with you convinced me to return the next day and pursue what was beyond it. But something followed me, some animal that got into the walkout. Maybe one of those damn raccoons." He shakes his head and chuckles. "So I didn't go too far. But I had what I needed. And the more I explored the catacombs, the more my embodiment of Poe solidified.

"Under the city's streets, I saw how his stories came to life. My ability to write grisly settings, my passion—so stymied after writing *Vulture Eyes*—was returning." One side of his mouth curls in a derisive smile. "Until you derailed everything. Twice."

"I'll die if you don't take me out of here," Saoirse whispers.

"You will die, my love. The queenliest dead that ever died so young. But not before I see you as the protagonist of Poe's—and soon to be my—greatest story of all." He scoops up the flashlight and aims the blue beam at her face. Saoirse drops her head and shields her eyes.

"Here." He tosses something at her. A tote bag, one of her own, from the closet of her bedroom. It hits her in the chest, and what little air she has whooshes from her lungs. "The help that you asked for. Clothes, water, some food. To lift your spirits—and your strength— while I finish crafting the climax of your story. I'll be back, my Helen." One hand goes into a pocket and comes out with a bottle and rag. "My soul, this night, shall come to you in dreams and speak to you those fervid thanks which my pen is powerless to utter."

"Please." Saoirse chokes the word out, not recognizing the voice as her own. It's a voice buried too long, a voice that doesn't know it has died. It's too late to hold her breath, to trick him as she did before. She's so weak. Emmit lowers the rag over her face like an eclipse.

Saoirse welcomes the black-winged annihilation. It's a painless burial. An eternal silence, everlasting blindness, without the desperation of searching, in the dark, for the moonglow beam of a solitary flashlight.

Chapter 44

Darkness, indeed. And it goes on forever.

She swims up from the depths, arriving at the surface of consciousness with the same necessity for air she'd had after being buried alive. Every muscle, every tendon, every cell in her body thrums with pain, screams—desperately, hollowly—to be allowed to rest. Despite this marrow-deep exhaustion, she's returned, delivered back to the crypt of her body. Back to the catacombs, with no knowledge of how to escape, no inkling as to which passage, which ceilinged archway, Emmit manipulated to take leave of her once more. She's left with nothing. Hopeless. Helpless.

No, not left with nothing: there's the tote Emmit threw at her before he left. She gropes until she finds the canvas straps. Inside is her flashlight, the same heavy metal one she's had all along. Might Emmit have replaced the batteries? There's no way to tell, but when she pushes the button, the beam comes to life. Ignoring the pain in her chest, she aims the flashlight into the tote.

At first, she sees only the water. Two bottles of it, the first of which she makes short work. She guzzles, but her stomach protests, the muscles cramping violently. She vomits, furious with herself for wasting such a precious commodity. She opens the second bottle, dizzy with the effort, and sips it slowly, one sip for every handful of minutes that pass. When her lightheadedness—if not her chest pain—lessens some, she returns to the tote.

The idea of food nauseates her. *Not a heart attack, huh?* she thinks bitterly. *Just a little bout of anxiety that's making me not want to eat, though I've had nothing for who knows how many days?* If she had to guess, she'd say it's been three days. But less time could have passed . . . or more.

Despite the intellectual knowledge of it, the certainty that she has, in fact, suffered a heart attack, she struggles to come to terms with it, this calamity she's worked to avoid the entirety of her adult life coming to pass. She tries to recall whether her cardiologist ever dispensed any advice should she think she was experiencing a heart attack, but, of course, it was only ever *Get yourself to the nearest emergency room immediately.* She wonders how long she has. Wonders if antidepressant withdrawal is exacerbating her weakened condition.

She forces herself to eat a handful of soda crackers—chewing slowly and methodically—and is surprised to discover she feels a bit better. Enough to continue riffling through the tote, slipping her hand into every crevice. Emmit clearly took pains to make sure there wasn't so much as a wayward pen left inside. There are the clothes, however; and they are *hers*—no more ridiculous, flowing white Victorian-era garb.

She peels the filthy garment over her head and dresses in the underwear, bra, soft black leggings, and black sweatshirt. By the time she's done, she is panting, sweat dampening her hair and neck. The walls of the catacomb swim before her, and she reaches out, but there's nothing to grab on to. She drops to her hands and knees, sucking in breath as if she's just cleared the finish line of a marathon.

A minute passes. Then another. Finally, Saoirse feels she can climb to her feet. She keeps her muscles taut despite the effort, afraid her legs will buckle and send her careening back to the ground.

As she stands, arms by her sides, spine rigid, the fingers of her right hand discern a small lump in the fabric of her leggings, near the midway point of her thigh. Her soft black leggings. Her favorite pair. They have a pocket meant to conceal a credit card or a house key on a jog. *Please be something I can use.* The object is long, like the pen she'd wished had been in her tote.

Saoirse slips her hand into the pocket and pulls out what's inside. She stares at the object, sure it's a joke. A mirage. What she holds is a syringe. A syringe of Pluto's insulin. A medication equally deadly to feline or human, when administered to someone without diabetes.

Saoirse drops to her knees again, keeping the syringe upright as she does. She'd been wearing these leggings when she'd last tested Pluto's blood sugar, after the breakup with Emmit and before she'd turned in for the night. Emmit had missed the thin cylinder when he'd scooped the leggings up from the floor and thrown them into the bag.

Saoirse chuckles, then cackles, unconcerned with what the laughter might be doing to her heart. She thinks of the unnamed narrator of "The Black Cat," brought to ruin by the eponymous Pluto, driven to madness as effectively as if by a beating heart beneath a floorboard. After ensuring the needle's cap is clamped tight, she returns the syringe to her pocket.

Armed with this new secret, she sips her water and nibbles crackers.

And, like a writer mapping an upcoming scene, she plans.

Chapter 45

The grind of stone against stone wakes her. Saoirse retreats to the right-hand wall of the catacomb, as far away from the sound of Emmit's return as she can get. She needs time to see from where he is entering, to see what he might carry in his hands. He said he would see her as the protagonist of Poe's—and his—greatest story of all, and she imagines him walking toward her with all manner of torture devices. The muscles in her chest tighten, but she thinks of the syringe in her pocket and wills herself to be calm.

"Serrrrr-shaaah," Emmit calls, materializing from behind a sheath of stone, scanning the chamber for her. She watches the wall behind him, the seamless way in which the stone doorway fits back into the frame. Emmit follows her gaze, then turns to her and smiles his charming half smile. "While a good magician never reveals the mechanism of a trick"—he pauses, cocks his head—"there's no reason not to let you in on the secret now." He slips his fingers into a groove, pulls upward, and the door swings open like a secret bookshelf in Holmes's library.

"Sometimes," he says, "the truth is right before us. A flyer on a foyer table. The ghost of a dead woman standing behind you as you write." He raises an eyebrow, as if to say, *Can you believe how brazen I've been?* Saoirse keeps her gaze—and her emotions—level, refusing to rise to the bait.

Emmit regards the empty bottles of water and sleeve of mostly eaten crackers. "I see you've taken advantage of my generosity. I knew all your talk about needing your medications was inflated. You're ready to take on the final endeavor, then? Your very own pit-and-the-pendulum conundrum, as it were."

She tries to recall the plot of "The Pit and the Pendulum." Something about darkened catacombs that are slowly illuminated and a prisoner exploring the area in which they're being held captive? Hasn't she been in "The Pit and the Pendulum" all along?

Emmit walks toward her, pulling a length of rope from the waistband of his jeans. "Scholars claim the first trip Poe ever made to Rhode Island was in 1845. 'The Pit and the Pendulum' was published in 1842. If Poe didn't discover the room containing the pit and the pendulum within these catacombs, then I can only assume he built it himself." He tilts his head, considering something. "It's actually more likely he built it himself, since he didn't base the elaborate torture scheme of the story on any parallels with the Spanish Inquisition, during which the tale is set. Conversely, the unnamed narrator must face his fate—either evisceration by the swinging, razor-edged pendulum or forced into a depthless pit by red-hot, advancing walls—separate from any historically accurate method of prisoner torture." Emmit comes a few steps closer, and Saoirse gauges the distance.

"It's a few chambers over," Emmit continues. "An exact match to what's described in the story: wooden frame facing the ceiling, a picture of Father Time above a foot-long pendulum."

He takes three quick steps toward her in time with the words "footlong pendulum." Saoirse's muscles twitch, but she stays crouched, refusing to envision pitch-black rooms or creaking pendulums swinging ever closer as they descend from ceiling to floor.

"I've placed a bucket of raw meat there," Emmit says casually, as if inviting her to dinner, "though I doubt the bait will draw the rats as effectively as it did in Poe's story. If it does, I imagine it's even more of a long shot that the rats will chew through the leather straps, allowing you to escape. That part of the story seems mere fiction to me. I'll give you the option, though, to fling yourself into the pit *before* I strap you to the board beneath the pendulum. That's the whole point of the exercise, of course. The way your mind works, the way you chew your way out of being backed into every corner . . . that's where my obsession lies. You remain my Muse even after refusing to serve my art the way Sarah served Edgar's."

Lunging from her crouch against the wall, Saoirse lobs the tote containing the remaining food at Emmit's head with one hand, gripping the flashlight with the other. Emmit cries out and ducks, and Saoirse darts past him, but he recovers quickly. He grabs for her, just missing her sweatshirt. Saoirse sprints for the stone frame, letting fear and adrenaline pump her arms and lift her feet. She reaches the door, slips her fingers into the horizontal groove the way she'd seen Emmit do, and pushes up and outward. The door swings forward, and Saoirse slips through, then pushes it shut behind her.

She was prepared to dash forward with only the flashlight to guide her, but there are sconces along the walls, lighting the chamber. Warm candlelight flickers against the stone like serpent tongues. She doesn't hesitate; her bare feet are already pounding the floor when Emmit bursts through the door behind her. Grit and gravel sting her feet and panic defibrillates her heart, but she does not slow.

The chamber narrows into a tunnel, and the sconces disappear. Even with the flashlight, it's like running through the blackest part of night with a rocky cliff looming ahead. Emmit's footsteps smack the tunnel floor behind her, and Saoirse tries to concentrate on her breath, to ignore intrusive thoughts of hidden pits and swinging pendulums. For all she knows, she's heading straight toward Emmit's final trap.

Better to die running. The moment she thinks it, Saoirse's steps become lighter. Her breath, too, comes easier, filling her lungs more completely than it had before. The tunnel is brighter, until Saoirse realizes it's because her vantage point has changed. She is floating above herself, watching a woman in a black sweatshirt and black leggings sprint for her life, watching herself—despite a failing heart and terrified mind—outrun her captor in a desperate bid for freedom, eyes wide in the inky dark, panicked but determined, exhausted but persevering.

If I die down here, Emmit will write a book based on my soul, on my spirit. I will endure through his words, through his awful, stolen take on my life. I cannot let that happen. I cannot. I have more things to say, more life to write. More life to live. Sarah Helen Whitman may be known because of her connection to Poe, but she lives on through her poetry. Edition after edition of her own words, printed and bound, circulated, proliferated. Celebrated.

I've survived too much to give up now. To give in to someone like him.

The floating-Saoirse beckons the running-Saoirse forward, who aims the flashlight to where the tunnel widens into another catacomb. A half circle of evenly spaced sconces lights the chamber ahead; Emmit must have come from this direction before. Saoirse bursts forward, into the chamber, where the stone walls of the tunnel are replaced with mildew-stained plywood and the haphazard zigzag of sagging boards.

The floating-Saoirse can see this is the area beyond the alcove below 135 Benefit Street, the one Emmit fell into during their felonious exploration of the Shunned House basement after defecting from the ghost tour. Someone had plans, once, for this space—it's like an abandoned construction site—but now the chamber is a collection of perilously leaning planks and swaying scaffolds, of sliding half-finished walls and yawning chasms in false floors.

Saoirse stops running and scans her surroundings. She's breathing hard, deciding whether she should find somewhere to hide or press forward. If she can locate the alcove, climb out of it, and make her way through the main portion of the Shunned House basement and up the stairs, she'll be street level, that much closer to rescue. But Emmit's right behind her. Hiding might be the only option there's time for.

Keep running, she begs herself, at the same moment the floating-Saoirse yells, *Hide!* and the furious voice of Jonathan shouts, *Give up! You don't deserve to live!*

Her two selves, cleaved by starvation and exhaustion, unite the moment Emmit bursts into the room. But the reintegration comes too late. He grabs a fistful of her hair with one hand, shouting incoherently, used up of all his pretty words.

With the other hand, he drops her to the ground like a fallen star.

Chapter 46

Saoirse's body smashes into the ground. The world goes white. A second later, Emmit is on top of her, pinning her with his thighs and holding her down with his hands. His fingers dig into the flesh of her underarms, and she's surprised to find that she can feel more pain, more torture, in this world of ceaseless tortures and myriad agonies.

Her flashlight lies on the floor where she dropped it. She and Emmit are spotlighted in its beam like actors in a play, poised to deliver their closing lines. Emmit's face is a twisted mix of rage and relief. He's breathing as heavily as she is. So heavily, in fact, it takes Saoirse a moment to realize his incoherent rambling has morphed into laughter.

"Every time," Emmit says, mouth jumping in a series of manic half smiles. "Every time I think you have nothing left, you give me more. You give me *this*."

Saoirse squirms beneath him, succeeding in moving her arms several inches closer to the lower half of her body. A thought occurs to her: How many hours had they spent in this position, him inside her, whispering into her ear, telling her how similar they were, how much he loved her? She wants to go back in time, take every moment of it back. She wants to make him feel her pain. She wants to kill him.

"Thank you," Emmit says.

Saoirse stares up at him, waiting.

"This last mad dash. Your refusal to give up. *Your belief that you were going to make it. This was better than my pit-and-the-pendulum* scheme. Now, when I kill you—and I do have to kill you, I hope you know that—I can be certain that I took everything. Every emotion. Every dream. Though—"

He pauses and runs the back of his hand down her cheek. Saoirse recoils and tries to turn away. Her arms move, like wings on a downswing, closer to her body a few more inches.

"I'd still like to carve you up a bit," he continues. "For my writing. For the details that will stay with me, that will inspire me, for years to come." He releases her arms and wraps his hands around her throat. "But I can do that after you're dead. Goodbye, Saoirse. My Helen."

"Wait," Saoirse says, and Emmit looks at her pityingly. "I have to know. Why me? Lucretia, Mia, they were getting into Sarah's house regularly for their séances. You had to have noticed. You had to have seen them. Or any of the dozens of women writers you mentored at Brown. Surely one of them could have been convinced to move into 88 Benefit Street, unoccupied and available to rent as it was the last five years. So, why me, Emmit? Why did you choose me?"

A tuft of dark hair falls over one eye. Emmit blinks, considering her, considering the question. Then he smiles. A massive, full-faced smile. "It's simple," he says. "Because despite your beautiful mind, your uniqueness, your intelligence, you had one unalterable factor I couldn't shy away from. Something that would soften you to me, no matter your strength. No matter what."

"Oh?" she says, urging him to keep talking, dropping her arms to her sides slowly, ever so slowly, every cell in her body at attention, praying her movements go unnoticed. "What factor was that?"

"Death," he says simply. "The death of your husband. It changed you. Weakened you. Made you into a different species from any other woman I've ever met. Ever seen. If the death of a beautiful woman is the most poetical topic in the world, then the torture of her soul is the second. You were like a tall, thorn-choked, dew-dazzled black rose in a sea of identical pale-pink ones. I knew this the night I first saw you, and it was confirmed for me during our first conversation at the coffeehouse."

"I see," she says. "And I see that you have to kill me. But before you do, I'd like to tell you a story."

Emmit scoffs but straightens slightly, his hands loosening around her throat. "A story?"

"One you've heard before. But only partly. You were missing the beginning. And the end. And, well, I had to change some parts in the middle too." She cocks her head. "It's the writer's right, you know. Taking a little artistic liberation."

Emmit looks at her as if she's surprised him yet again, as if he can't quite believe she's daring to speak when he's promised to silence her forever. He shrugs. "Okay. Tell me the real version of your story."

Saoirse closes her eyes. If this doesn't go the way she hopes, it'll be the last story she ever tells.

"Once," she begins, "there was a young woman who met a young man in Providence. They fell in love, and they were married. Things were good until they weren't. Things were good until the woman wouldn't fall in line. It wasn't just that she wanted a career, a voice, of her own. He'd allow her that. He was educated, after all, a self-proclaimed feminist. No, it's that she wanted him to care about her career, her voice, as much as she did his. She wanted him to care about—*to see*—her as a person, the way she, of course, saw him.

"Years passed, and the relationship became strained. The woman figured they were heading for divorce. But when she brought it up, the husband looked at her like she was mad. He said he thought they were ready to have a baby. He knew about her condition. The diagnosis that made becoming pregnant as risky as cliff jumping or cave diving. But the husband wouldn't let it go. He dragged her to every cardiologist in New Jersey and half of New York, as well as every obstetrician, including his best friend, Dr. Aidan Vesper. Hoping to get a different answer. A different probability. Some number, a set of odds, that would make her feel comfortable enough to move forward. That would make her change her mind.

"At first, the woman attended the appointments. She listened as every doctor said the same thing: 'It's feasible, but dicey. With a diagnosis of cardiomyopathy, delivering a healthy baby while remaining safe is a study in risk.' Eventually, the woman hit her breaking point. She told the husband the matter was closed. She would not attend another appointment, nor entertain any further conversations about getting pregnant. Maybe, she told him, if their relationship recovered from the strain it'd been under, they could look into adoption. But for the time being, he'd have to get used to the idea of being childless.

"That night, the husband acted like he accepted her decision. He bought a bottle of champagne and cooked dinner. He told her he wanted them to recover, that they were celebrating the next chapter, childless or not. She hadn't realized how much stress she'd been under, and she drank way more champagne than she'd normally allow herself. She woke up later to the husband on top of her. Finishing inside of her. If she wasn't going to give him what he wanted, he was going to take it. He made that perfectly clear.

"Why did the woman stay? Why didn't she tell someone what was going on? She was depressed, for one. She had long since stopped writing. And every day, the husband filled her head with the most horrible sentiments. She was evil. Debased. The very opposite of a woman. She was damaged goods, with her defective heart and her defective brain. That her mind was only as good as the stories it could no longer produce, her body as good as the child it couldn't create.

"He came into her bed for two years. Not every night. Not every week. But every month, unless he was particularly busy at work. The woman was drowning, dying, until, on a whim, she started seeing a new psychiatrist. With the help of this doctor—and an adjustment to her antidepressant, as well as birth control prescribed for hormone regulation that would help her mental state—the woman started feeling better. The husband's words stopped seeming like gospel. And then, one weekend, she went to her mother's home in Connecticut to regroup, planning to demand a divorce when she returned to her husband on Sunday."

Saoirse pauses, taking stock of Emmit's expression, the placement of his body on top of hers. He's engrossed in the story, sitting back now, not even trying to hold her upper body in place. She slides her right hand down to her thigh and slips her pointer and middle fingers into her pocket. Careful to keep every other muscle still, she pinches her fingers around the stopper of the syringe.

"She wasn't supposed to return until Sunday," Saoirse continues, "but after speaking with her mother, after committing to her plan, she hadn't wanted to wait." She looks hard into Emmit's eyes. "The woman came home Thursday evening. Not Sunday. *Thursday.* Around eleven p.m. Three days earlier than planned.

"I drove the three and a half hours back to Cedar Grove from Connecticut without stopping," Saoirse says, switching from third to first person unexpectedly, wanting Emmit to hear the *I*'s and *me*'s. "But when I got home, I almost lost my nerve. Rather than leave my suitcase and purse in the car, so that I could take off to a hotel after I told him, I brought them inside, terrified of what I was about to do. The walkway was ice-strewn and muddy. Snow clung to patches of grass around the yard. The key to the front door was cold in my hand. I took a final, deep breath and pushed open the door. The house was silent.

"I dropped my bag in the foyer and looked to the top of the stairs, thinking, *I could go up right now and get into bed. Wait until tomorrow to tell him I'm leaving.* Instead, I started down the hallway. Toward Jonathan's office.

"The door was closed, and the light that seeped from the cracks was molten amber. If he was at his desk, he'd be accompanied by a rocks glass of bourbon. He'd be volatile. I was walking into a trap. Still, I'd come too far to turn back now.

"The room smelled so strongly of whiskey it made me dizzy. Jonathan sat at his massive desk with his back to me. I cleared my throat, but he didn't turn. Intent on dissipating the sickly glow in the room, I moved toward the floor lamp, but my hand smacked against the shade, sending it wobbling. With excruciating slowness, Jonathan raised his head and turned, until he was looking right at me. 'You've come to tell me you're leaving, haven't you?' he asked. I closed my eyes.

"When I opened them, the office felt different. Warmer. No longer dangerous and silent but charged. Something waited for me. Something more than a house haunted with the sound of floorboards creaking beneath my husband's footsteps, on his way to me in the night. The warmth was the idea of my freedom. Of getting my life back. 'Yes. I want a divorce,' I said.

"He grabbed me in one lightning-fast movement, one hand wrapping around my throat, fingers not yet squeezing but the pressure heavy, the pads of his fingers pressing into the cords at the side of my neck. With the other hand, he reached for his bourbon, brought the glass to his mouth, and drained it. 'Why would I give you something *you* want when you won't give me what *I* want?' A prescription bottle peeked out from the pocket of his button-up shirt. I couldn't see the label, but I knew it was one of his 'nighttime meds': Ambien, perhaps. Or Valium. 'I'm not asking for something outlandish or unreasonable,' he continued. 'You're my wife. I want a child. Our purpose for being here becomes diluted if we cannot pass on our possessions, our wealth, our genes. It's not a difficult concept.'

"His eyes were bleary, despite the laser-sharp focus of his words. 'It's not that you *can't* give me what I want. That, I could understand. If you were physically unable to conceive, I'd have a different set of decisions to make. Maybe I'd leave you for a woman who could have children. Maybe I wouldn't. But that's not the situation we are in here, is it? It's that you're a selfish'—he poked me in the sternum—'brutish, difficult woman who refuses to give me what I want just because she thinks she can. And therefore, I will take—'

"He faltered. The expression on his face became bewildered, as if he'd belched among dinner company and was not quite sure how it had happened. 'I will take what is—' he tried to continue, but something was happening. He put a hand to his chest, and his mouth twisted. I knew that gesture. Knew that expression. But I didn't dare believe—

"He fell to his knees, clutched his chest, and grunted, then looked at me, wincing with pain. He managed to get out a single word. His voice was hoarse, like something that'd been buried for the darkest, coldest, and longest of the seasons.

"'. . . miiiiine,' he said."

Chapter 47

Saoirse hears the word echoing out into the future, across months and places, from the writhing mouths of specters and the lying mouths of lovers, blaring in her mind like a siren. It hasn't lost its volume. It hasn't lost its power. Emmit is staring at her, his face twisted in an expression of horror.

"He pleaded with me," Saoirse says. "'My phone,' he said. 'It's right there. Please, call an ambulance.' I remember the way his breath caught in his throat, the continuous heaving of his chest. But I didn't know where his phone was. I never looked for it. I never took my eyes off him. The man who held me prisoner in my own home. My own mind. Who would have traded my life for that of the baby he wanted on mere principle.

"He made one final attempt as he leaned, half-crumpled, against the side of his desk, his eyes pleading. The way mine had pleaded with him night after night after night for years. 'Call,' he whispered. 'Please, Saoirse. Please.' But I didn't. And do you know why, Emmit?"

Emmit flinches at being addressed. He shakes his head. As he does, Saoirse pulls the syringe from her pocket and flicks off the cap.

"Because this was my momentous, soul-crushingly significant thing," she says.

Emmit's eyes widen, and he pulls back as if he's been slapped.

Saoirse continues, "I watched him die, and I didn't call for help. Had I known he'd sent a text to Aidan—that's the man you kicked out of my house the night you kidnapped me—telling him I'd come home early, I would have deleted it." Saoirse stops. "I still can't figure why Aidan hasn't gone to the police." She shrugs one shoulder, using the movement to further move her arm into position.

"Anyway, after Jonathan died, I stayed in the house for three whole days while his body rotted." She tilts her head. "Most people think that flies don't appear on a corpse until a few days into decomposition, when the body starts to bloat. But did you know that blowflies and flesh flies often arrive on the scene within minutes after a person has died? They swarmed the office, the house, in droves, and I endured them, so that I could say he was dead when I found him." Slowly, she lifts the hand with the syringe. "He was dead when I found him," she adds thoughtfully. Her thumb thrums against the plunger. "Or, at least, he might as well have been. Twelve years earlier on a moonlight night in Providence . . . he was already dead to me."

Saoirse drives the syringe into the front of Emmit's thigh and slams the plunger down, dispensing every milliliter of its contents. Emmit howls and propels himself off Saoirse, rolling back onto a low stack of concrete slabs. Saoirse scrabbles backward, careful to steer clear of the holes in the floorboards. On a wide, somewhat sturdy-looking beam, she jumps to her feet.

Emmit clutches his thigh and struggles to stand. Already, his eyes are glassy. His muscles contract in a series of shudders. He tries to maneuver off the slab, but he can't figure the best way forward. He's surrounded by joists and noggings, no baseboard. To jump from his current position to an opposite joist would take dexterity and balance, and Emmit no longer has either.

He clambers to the farthest side of slab, where a frayed rope hangs out of reach. Before Saoirse can consider why this jump might seem like a better option to a man whose vision is blurring and whose hands are starting to tremor, Emmit leaps for it. He misses, falling toward a vertical alcove against the chamber's back wall. Through sheer luck, he lands on a thin piece of wood that juts across the space, keeping him from plunging to some subterranean level below. With slow, labored movements, Emmit pushes himself to a sitting position, blinking across the yawning expanse of empty space, the crisscrossed beams and haphazard piles of building material, the chaotic loops of rope and open walls.

Saoirse scans the area before the vertical alcove that culminates in a free fall. A thick sheet of wood siding leans against the already-nailed-in portion of the wall. She jumps over a beam to an actual floorboard, the one where her trusty flashlight still provides them the only light in the chamber. Careful not to kick the flashlight, she positions herself on the board and looks over to the slab.

"I was the one haunting you," Emmit says, the words slurring together.

Saoirse jerks at the sound of his voice, almost slipping off the floorboard. "What?"

"The preshents—*presence* in your house you thought was Sarah. I was the one watching while you wrote your stupid poetry. While you pretended to have something worthwhile to say. I read your words while you slept. They were amateurish. Cliché. That's why this didn't work. Why the residual haunting fell apart. I was a worthy successor to Poe, but your derivativeness couldn't hold a candle to Whitman."

His mouth tries to jump into its half smile, but the muscles spasm. He huffs out a little laugh, as if she only needs to wait and she'll get what's coming to her. "Your so-called poetry was garbage."

Saoirse moves to the sheet of wood, lifts it from the wall, and fits its edge into a groove along the ground. She slides it toward the opposite sheet, six feet across, stopping before she completely closes off the space. Emmit sees it then. What he hadn't seen before. That she can board him up in the wall of this chamber. That, with a few quick motions, he'll be trapped inside the bowels of the Shunned House with no one to hear him scream. If the fast-acting insulin coursing through his veins will even allow him to issue anything approaching a scream.

"And *you* made a grave misjudgment in the way you believed Jonathan's death changed me," Saoirse says. "I'm not different because of what Jonathan's death did to me." She makes sure Emmit's eyes are focused, makes sure he's seeing her when she says, "I'm different because of *what I did to cause Jonathan's death*."

She slides the board farther into place while Emmit gasps. She hears his nails scrape along the wall as he searches for something to grip, something to pull or throw open.

"Pleash, Seerrshh-ahh, don't do this. I'm shorry. I'm shor—sorry for all of it."

Listen to him, Jonathan screams. *Do you want to end up with another voice clamoring at you from inside your head? Do not do this.*

Saoirse drops her hands from the wall. Her heart gallops. "You know," she says, and there's something in her voice that causes Emmit to quiet, "I think the most poetical topic of all has got to be when the sociopathic, narcissistic, pompous man's plan to cause the death of a woman—beautiful or otherwise—is thwarted, when his plan against that woman becomes his very undoing."

She raises her hands, clasps the wood panel, and slides it another two inches to the right. Before she fits it firmly in place, she peers through the three-inch gap one final time. A wave of lightheadedness assails her, but not before she swears she sees Jonathan in the corner beside Emmit. Jonathan the way he looked the last time she saw him alive, crumpled against his desk. Emmit's skin is just as pale, and in addition to the trembling of his lips—no more self-aware, charming half smile—there's a look of bewilderment on his face. Sarah Whitman's accomplishments were never supposed to outshine—or outlast—Poe's.

"One more thing," Saoirse says. "Go fuck yourself. Both of you."

Emmit's panicked keening starts as Saoirse slides the board into place. She listens until the keening stops. She listens until his breathing slows. When several minutes pass without a sound, she picks up the flashlight and aims it at the tunnel that will take her to the main basement of the Shunned House. She follows the beam of light without looking back.

Without regret.

Chapter 48

Making her way out of the long-abandoned chamber takes more effort than Saoirse anticipated. Another tunnel separates the wall behind which Emmit remains—alone and silent—and the alcove he'd once plunged into, and by the time she reaches the recessed area, she is drenched with sweat, jittery from adrenal fatigue, and breathing in shallow, painful gasps.

She lowers herself onto the lip of mottled wood, pausing for a moment as another bout of lightheadedness hits. *So close,* she thinks automatically. *Can't give up now.* She places the flashlight beside her and rolls onto her stomach, legs dangling in the blackness. Her toes are still three feet from the ground; the jump will jolt her, and she readies herself for it. Before she can slide off the edge, she hears something from the direction of the tunnel, a shuffling and the panting of breath.

Saoirse freezes, then walks her fingers toward the flashlight, spinning its beam partway back toward the tunnel, illuminating its circular new-moon entrance by degrees. Why hadn't she kept the syringe? Maybe she could have used the needle as a weapon. Her breath is ragged, eyes wide as her pupils try to take in enough light to discern movement, to see the figure emerging from the tunnel before he sees her.

The soft pant of breath comes again, and the scrape of limbs against gravel. She walks her fingers back to the flashlight, this time curling them around the metal, turning the flashlight into a club. She ignores the erratic staccato of her heart. She holds her breath.

The strip of white floats into view, a ghostly hem swishing to the beat of footsteps, or else to unspoken rhymes in a poet's head. Saoirse stifles a gasp, accidentally jerking the flashlight. The beam bounces, elongating her view, turning the strip of white into an entire dress, hands extending from lace shirtsleeves, feet from ghostly hem, pale head and neck, spiral curls from a sheer, ruched bonnet.

"Sarah," Saoirse whispers, and the flashlight jerks. The specter—or vision . . . hallucination . . . whatever it is—disappears. No, not disappears. Changes. The strip of white compresses. The orientation shifts, from portrait to landscape.

The creature's head lowers over the white strip of fur on its chest as it steps into the widest crease of light, snout to the ground, tail held straight out behind it and eyes glowing. It raises its head to look at her, unblinking. For just a moment, its mouth opens, teeth bared in fear or warning or exhaustion. Saoirse readies herself for the animal's scream, but it doesn't come.

"I kept my promise," Saoirse whispers. "I'm almost out. I'm going to get help."

But the fox no longer looks distressed. Perhaps it has found its own way out, dug free from its own grave, found a path to the light. Perhaps it comes and goes as it pleases. The fox holds her gaze another moment, then turns and trots back the way it came. Saoirse looks to see if the creature turns into the Divine Poet yet again, but the change doesn't come. Maybe it had never occurred at all.

As if freed from some lingering spell, Saoirse pushes past her sluggishness and exhaustion, grabs the flashlight, and drops to the floor of the alcove. She crosses the space and finds the collapsed boards Emmit fell through the night they broke into the Shunned House. A coffin, she sees now. Empty, mercifully, but definitely a coffin. She steps onto its moldering sides and grips the floor above her, then shimmies up and out of the alcove. The dust and dankness of the Shunned House basement coalesce in the flashlight beam, and it's the most beautiful thing she's ever seen. Gathering all her strength, all her longing to breathe fresh air and see sunlight, Saoirse runs.

The stairs leading out of the basement come into view less than a minute later, and in her relief, she doesn't notice, at first, what Emmit's done. It's only when she reaches the base and prepares to climb out from this endless hell that she sees. The stairs are demolished, treads and stringers reduced to shards of wood and dust. It is the unclimbable staircase from her dream. A trail of breadcrumbs scattered to the wind. A sledgehammer lies a few feet away. Emmit must have worried Saoirse would find her way back to the Shunned House, and placed one final barrier between her and escape.

Saoirse's heart stutters. Her breath deserts her. *I'll climb the debris,* she thinks. *I won't let him keep me here.* But she can see—even through her panic—that what remains of the staircase falls far short of the threshold between basement and house. She can climb it, but it won't help her reach her destination. Her vision darkens. Her breath becomes an ocean, a tsunami, in her ears.

But something's cutting through that ocean. A gentler crest, a familiar one, spoken with force but also with kindness.

"Saoirse! We're here! Oh my god, are you okay? Can you climb? If you can, we can grab your hand!"

Saoirse looks up to see Lucretia and Roberto. Beyond them is Mia with rope and a flashlight. Her vision remains stained and murky, but it's not from the darkness anymore. It's from tears of gratitude for her friends.

Mia throws down the rope, and Saoirse navigates up the demolished staircase. At the top, she's still four feet below the frame of the trapdoor. Mia has tied the rope to something farther down the hall. She grabs Lucretia by the waist, and Roberto grabs Mia. The three of them lean forward until Lucretia's hand is a few inches away from Saoirse's. Using the rope to anchor herself, Saoirse reaches up for Lucretia's hand. Their fingers touch, then their palms, then Lucretia is grasping Saoirse with surprising strength, the many rings on her fingers digging into Saoirse's flesh.

"Jump!" Lucretia yells, at the same moment the rubble beneath Saoirse starts to tremble. She sucks in a breath, releases the rope, and jumps.

Lucretia pulls Saoirse up with the help of Mia and Roberto behind her. Saoirse dangles below the frame and over the precipice. Roberto reaches down and grasps her other hand, and he and Lucretia pull Saoirse up. They use even more force than is necessary, and Saoirse lands on top of them in a heap. They lie there, gasping and shaking, until Mia pulls Saoirse up and props her against the wall. She looks Saoirse over like a worried mother.

"Where are you hurt? What do you need?" she asks.

Saoirse closes her eyes, smiles, and shakes her head. "I'm okay. For now. But I had a heart attack. I need to get to a hospital."

Gently, Roberto takes Saoirse's chin in his hand and lifts her face so she's looking up at him. "Sersh," he says. "Where is Emmit? Do we need to worry about him appearing at any moment and causing mayhem?"

Saoirse closes her eyes again. "He . . . he tried to kill me. We struggled. I pushed him, and he fell into this space within the wall. An alcove." She looks at Mia, then at Lucretia. "He had Pluto's insulin. When I pushed him . . ." She trails off, eyes glazing over, then refocuses on her friends. "He fell on the syringe. He was out of it but still trying to come after me. I dragged a board over and fitted it into the wall so he couldn't get out."

Saoirse keeps looking from one pair of shocked, wide eyes to another. "When I left, he was sobbing. Begging me not to leave him." She looks down, then back up. Her eyes are hard and her jaw is set. "At least, that's what I'm going to tell the police. I'll tell you the real story later, when this whole thing is over."

Mia, Lucretia, and Roberto exchange glances. Lucretia shrugs. Mia nods.

Saoirse sags against the wall. "Thank you. For holding the séance. For looking for me. It made all the difference."

"It was Mia," Lucretia says. "Roberto and I wanted to go to the police. But Mia said they wouldn't believe us, that Emmit would be too charming, have everything too buttoned up, if they questioned him." She helps Saoirse sit up a little more. "She insisted we hold the séances. When you heard us? That was our third one. As soon as you said 'the Shunned House,' we came right here." She glances from Mia to Roberto. "Thank god we're all such nerds, and we knew exactly what you were referring to."

Saoirse looks to Mia. "Thank you," she whispers. "I guess the hypervigilant-bordering-on-paranoid opinion of someone who's been burned wasn't so bad, after all."

Mia smiles. "I guess not," she says. "And you're welcome. Those who've been hurt by the Emmit Powells of the world have to stick together." Mia pauses and tilts her head. "And, you know, despite Lucretia saying it was all me, someone else was looking for you. He came to your door before we went downstairs for the final séance. Aidan something? He told us he was worried about you, that he'd tried to talk with you a few days ago but got thrown out by a guy whom he'd seen lurking around your house earlier that evening."

"Aidan was . . . *worried* about me?" Saoirse says, then thinks, *That doesn't make sense. And,* of course, *Emmit was lurking outside my house.* She drops her head into her hands.

"We told him we knew all about the lurker and were on our way to do something about it that very minute," Lucretia says. "He seemed really concerned. Who is he?"

Saoirse lifts her head. "Someone from another life," she says. "And a story for another day." This whole time, had she misjudged Aidan? Misconstrued why he wanted to speak with her? Either way, she was going to find out. No more running. After catacombs and screaming foxes and being buried alive, facing questions from Jonathan's friend didn't seem that bad.

A moment passes in which no one speaks, then Roberto says, "We need to get out of here. I'm going out to the street to flag down a car, get them to call 911."

Saoirse reaches out, frantic. "No, don't leave. Don't any one of you leave me. We can call them from here."

The three exchange a look again.

"What?" Saoirse says. "What is it?"

"It's just that, we commune with the earth, remember?" Roberto says.

"Huh?"

"We're one with nature," Mia adds.

Saoirse gives her a blank stare.

"We don't have a cell phone with us," Lucretia says finally.

Saoirse looks from one face to another, at their kind, worried, ultimately relieved expressions, and bursts out laughing. "Right," she says. "Of course. Well, I guess we better get out and hail that car, then." She pauses, trying—and failing—to summon the energy to stand. "Can one of you help me up?"

"Of *course*," Lucretia says, placing emphasis on the final word like a disgruntled teenager. She scrambles up at the same time as Roberto. "Come *on*, Saoirse. We're transcendentalists, not monsters."

Epilogue

The pot of Earl Grey sends notes of honey and bergamot swirling through the sunbeam-streaked air of the kitchen. Saoirse is arranging cups and saucers beside a sugar bowl and creamer on a decorative wooden tray when the telephone rings. She smiles when she sees who's calling.

"Hi, Mom."

"Hi, honey," her mother says. "How are you?"

Saoirse pulls out a chair from the table and sinks into it. From her periphery, two orange prescription bottles gleam in the window's light from their shelf in the open cabinet. "Dr. Carrigan says everything looked really good at my last visit," Saoirse says. "She doesn't think there'll be any long-term damage."

She fingers the petals of a pink rose at the center of the table, listening for a voice, vain and sardonic—*You were a thorn-choked black rose in a sea of pale-pink ones*—but nothing comes. Saoirse closes her eyes. It'll take time to get used to the silence in her head; no echoes of Emmit, no guilt-induced commentary from her husband. "How are you?" she asks.

Her mother laughs. "Leave it to you to ask how I'm doing after all you've been through. I'm well. At a bit of a crossroads, however, hoping to get an answer on something."

"What's that?"

"How soon is too soon to visit you again?"

It's Saoirse's turn to laugh. "You were here last weekend." Her mother stays silent, and Saoirse chuckles again. "Come whenever you'd like. I'm happy to have you."

She thinks of how she held her mother at arm's length for most of her marriage to Jonathan. How she kept her distance from her even more aggressively after her mother had not only agreed but insisted that they say Saoirse had been in Connecticut the whole weekend, that she'd arrived home Sunday evening and found Jonathan dead, feeling the vise of guilt tighten around her heart at how she'd implicated her mother. How she'd implicated *only* her mother, the one person in her life she wished to spare pain. She doesn't feel that way anymore. Like Jonathan's voice in her head, that guilt has left. She refuses to make space for it, refuses to allow it in.

"You know," Saoirse says, reaching down to pet Pluto, "when I woke up in that grave and the dirt was everywhere—in my mouth, in my eyes—a memory came back to me, of running through the woods as a little girl, with you. How we climbed trees to peer into birds' nests and dug for worms." Saoirse pauses, her throat tightening. "You were with me every moment of my childhood after Dad turned his back on even weekend custody by moving out of state. You never showed one ounce of bitterness or regret for anything you did for me, any sacrifice you made."

The tears are coming now, streaming silently down her face. Saoirse swallows. "I think it was as much of a reason for not wanting to have a child as my heart condition was," she continues. "I am who I am because of my amazing, patient, compassionate, and levelheaded mother. And I know myself; I'd never have lived up to even half the mother you were."

Her mother is crying as well; Saoirse hears the muffled sounds through the phone. "You would have," her mother says, her voice cracking. "You would have been a fantastic mother, but I'm glad you didn't pursue it. It was too risky for you. I'm glad I have my daughter, and nothing is worth anything otherwise. Nothing."

Saoirse cannot speak through her tears.

"I know you have company this afternoon," her mother says after a moment. "I won't keep you. I just wanted to check in, and—"

"Come next weekend," Saoirse interrupts. "If that's good for you."

Another sniffle, and then she says, "That's perfect. I'll call you in a couple of days to make sure it still works with your schedule. I know you're on a writing deadline."

"The manuscript's not due for a few months."

"Who would have thought your old agent was looking for memoirs?" The slight disbelief in her mother's voice makes Saoirse smile; that slight disbelief is exactly how Saoirse feels.

"Who knew I had a memoir in me?"

Though, is it really a memoir? The police recovered Emmit Powell's body—no, Willem Thomas's, for "Emmit Powell" had indeed been a pen name, adopted to distance himself from not just his hometown but his transgressions against Matilda Crabb. Everything about Saoirse's story—the syringe Emmit had fallen on after brandishing it against Saoirse, the way she'd had to board him up in the alcove to escape—tracked, especially considering the horrific tortures he'd inflicted upon her. These are the parts of the story Saoirse will keep to herself. Or, rather, the parts she will keep between her and her mother, her and her closest friends.

After they've said their goodbyes and Saoirse's hung up the phone, she returns to the tea tray, adds the small vase of pink roses, and starts through the house. In the walkout, she lets her eyes stray briefly to the trapdoor. They haven't returned to the basement, haven't held a séance since Saoirse escaped the catacombs, but she thinks they will. She wants to, anyway. Wants to reach out to Sarah directly. To say thank you. Or, maybe, goodbye.

For now, her friends wait outdoors by the rosebushes on a new patio Saoirse convinced Diane to let her hire contractors to install. It's not as if Saoirse could forget what lies beneath Sarah Whitman's house, or much of Benefit Street, but the patio serves a purpose: it reminds

Saoirse to keep her focus on the world above, on the realm of sunlight and blooming flowers.

The moment Saoirse steps out of the walkout, Roberto runs up to take the tray from her.

"You didn't have to host us," he says. "We could have gone for coffee at Carr Haus."

"No way," Saoirse says. "You know I need every opportunity to use up all this tea you three have gifted me over the last nine months."

Lucretia gives Saoirse a long hug. Mia's gaze is on the rosebushes, but she turns to Saoirse after Lucretia releases her.

"How are you?"

Saoirse studies Mia's face, looking for any clue as to the woman's emotions, the thoughts swirling beneath the knife-slash part of her brown hair and the tranquil, sleepy eyes. Mia still hasn't opened up to Saoirse about her past. Not completely. But Saoirse thinks that will happen, too, in time. "Never better," Saoirse says, and Roberto chuckles. "Come on, make your tea while the water's hot."

While Roberto and Lucretia argue over whether it's unhealthy to drink caffeine in the afternoon, and Mia pours herself half a cup of Earl Grey, Saoirse stares beyond the rosebushes, to where the gravestones cast shadows on the spongy grass. The grave that Emmit desecrated to stage Saoirse's premature burial was repaired by the historical society. Grass has started sprouting from the expanse of fresh dirt.

"I spoke with Aidan yesterday," she starts, and three pairs of eyes fix on her. "He called to see how I was doing." She pauses, sighs. "I still can't believe I was so scared of what he knew of Jonathan's death, I never let him close enough to explain it. That he knew Jonathan had been abusing me for years and planned to keep the existence of Jonathan's last text message a secret as reparation for not confronting him."

"As he should," Mia says. "He's an obstetrician, for goodness' sake. I would think his code of ethics would have bound him to do *something* when he realized how hell-bent Jonathan was on having a baby regardless of the danger to you."

"Though, coming to check on you after realizing there was something weird about Emmit was sweet too," Lucretia chimes in. "Who knows . . . if we hadn't stormed the Shunned House, maybe Aidan would have been the one to save the day."

Mia shrugs, and Saoirse bites her lip to keep from smiling. She knows Mia is wary of Aidan, isn't keen on his simple promise to keep Saoirse's secret. But Saoirse doesn't fear Aidan any longer. Aidan's shared things with her, things about his relationship with her late husband, things that spoke to the imbalance of power between the two men. The secrets Jonathan forced Aidan to keep, from cheating to get into law school to siphoning money from the charity organizations he oversaw.

She looks to where Benefit Street intersects with Church and says softly, "It wasn't much of a surprise to find out Jonathan's manipulation extended well beyond me, into his relationship with Aidan."

There is silence, and then Roberto asks, "Wasn't the restoration crew here last week, working on the, um, grave Emmit disturbed?"

She nods. "I came out to see what they were doing. I guess part of me wanted to see the place I'd dug myself out of again. To view it in the light of day. A man started speaking with me. Mostly small talk—he had no idea who I was. Until he saw the pendant around my neck."

Saoirse reaches up to finger the metal coffin. It's never felt strange to continue wearing it. On the contrary, she likes what it reminds her of: Security. Resourcefulness. Escape.

"It was Levi Leland. Emmit's contact from the historical society. He told me the pendant I was wearing, the one Emmit"—Saoirse makes air quotes—"'found' there?" She points to the rosebushes. "It had been part of the Athenæum's Sarah Whitman collection since her death in 1878. Emmit made an appointment to see it with a member of the library's staff, then supposedly never showed. When the librarian returned to the Art Room, the pendant was missing.

"A staff member reported the theft to the police, but there were no leads, and of course, no one thought to suspect Pulitzer Prize–winning novelist Emmit Powell. He was questioned as a formality—why he had made the appointment, why he hadn't shown up, that kind of thing—but was quickly dismissed."

Saoirse pauses. "I thought Levi would ask for the necklace back, and I put my hand to my throat, ready to unclasp it, but he stopped me. 'I read about Emmit,' he said. 'What he did to you.' I nodded, surprised, and told him the pendant was how I escaped. 'You should keep it,' he said, and winked at me. 'Sarah would want you to have it.'"

"I still can't believe Emmit stole it in the first place," Lucretia says. "And pretended to find it in your rose garden to convince you that the two of you were manifesting magic, possessed by the spirits of Sarah Whitman and Edgar Allan Poe." She pauses, staring at Saoirse from under her long, dark lashes. "Did you believe him?" she asks gently.

Saoirse is quiet for a long time. Roberto pours her a cup of tea, adds a generous spoonful of honey, and pushes it across the table. She smiles and sips from it. Finally, she says, "I think a small part of me did." She waits to have to defend herself, to say she knows how stupid it sounds, but no such demands come.

"Why Poe, do you think?" Lucretia asks.

"What do you mean?" Roberto says.

"I mean, why did Emmit fixate on Poe's life and career for his authorial road map and cast Saoirse as his Sarah? Why not Sylvia Plath and Ted Hughes? Or Mary and Percy Shelley?"

Saoirse bites her lip. "Who knows? Pure chance? Bad luck? But whatever was inside him that made him believe this path was the only way to success, it was kicked into overdrive by his arrival in Providence, by his proximity to this house."

"It's hard," Mia says, "because there *was* a residual haunting that was happening."

Roberto looks from Mia to Saoirse and back again. "What do you mean?"

"I mean, it wasn't a coincidence Saoirse came to Providence. Sarah's energy called her here. Residual hauntings don't have to be negative."

Saoirse considers this. "She did get me writing again," she admits. "I knew all along it was her. It was never Emmit."

They are silent for several minutes until Lucretia starts riffling around in her purse. She comes out with a deck of tarot cards and slaps them onto the patio table.

"Who's up for a reading?" she asks. A glint of mischief lights her eyes behind the thick-framed glasses.

Roberto and Mia exchange glances. "Saoirse?" Roberto says. "I think it should be you."

Lucretia looks at Saoirse, and Saoirse nods. She watches the mesmerizing flick of Lucretia's fingers as she shuffles, the glint of her rings, then allows her gaze to wander, up the red siding of Sarah Whitman's house, along the boughs of the trees lining the graveyard, to the gold statue atop the statehouse, floating among the clouds.

She ponders what she will ask the cards. How long she'll live here? How long she'll call the people before her friends? Or should she ask whether the voice in her head will remain hers and hers alone? She's not sure. But she doesn't worry about it. In a moment, when Lucretia asks her to pose her question, that question will come. Because the voice inside her persists, crafting stanzas, forming paragraphs. Telling her story.

Hers, and hers alone.

AFTERWORD

No one questions an author's motivation in writing a book inspired by the works of Edgar Allan Poe—or based on Poe's life—but in case readers finish *Beneath the Poet's House* wondering, *Why Sarah Helen Whitman?*, let me start by stating that my depiction of the Divine Poet (a personally devised moniker, subsequently adopted by Mia, Lucretia, and Roberto) in this novel is accurate and unembellished. She was indeed an accomplished poet, essayist, and literary critic, known throughout Providence—and wider literary circles—for her keen intellect and, eventually, her thoughtfully penned defenses of once-fiancé Edgar Allan Poe. (See *Poe's Helen Remembers*, by John Carl Miller, for a thorough examination of these defenses, including unpublished correspondences between Whitman and John Henry Ingram, the latter of whom would pen Poe's vindicatory biography in 1880. It worked for Saoirse in gaining an appreciation for Whitman's writing as well as her admiration for the author of "The Raven" . . . I believe it will work for you too.)

Whitman was friends with women's rights advocate, fellow critic, and transcendentalist Margaret Fuller and the poet Mary E. Hewitt, and became interested in transcendentalism after attending the lectures of Ralph Waldo Emerson in Providence and Boston. Her passion for science, mesmerism, and the occult in *Beneath the Poet's House* were similarly unfabricated; while she typically dressed in black, wore a coffin-shaped pendant on a satin ribbon around her neck (though records indicate this pendant was dark wood, not metal), and held séances in her home on Benefit Street (on Saturday evenings or Sunday mornings, in lieu of church), her belief in the afterlife was careful and measured.

Whitman scorned the obvious charlatans and professed—in a letter to Ingram—the belief that occult sciences, while "dimly discerned and obscured by superstition," still covered "great truths." She attended the first ever recorded séance in Providence in September of 1850. And she cultivated these interests during a time where most of the population was enamored with industrialization and the accumulation of wealth. In other words, she was a fascinating, multifaceted, and purposeful individual, a woman who knew her own mind and surrounded herself with similarly idea-driven friends . . . and romantic interests.

In 1828, Whitman married John Winslow Whitman, a Boston lawyer with an occasionally scandalous reputation (he set fire to haystacks belonging to the president of Brown University, where he'd been a student, and served time at Leverett Street Jail for signing his name to a worthless note), and they were together until his death in 1833. As for Whitman and Poe, the details Saoirse digs up during her research into their courtship are taken straight from the history books: Poe had indeed seen Sarah Whitman for the first time in the backyard of 88 Benefit Street in 1845, tending her rose garden under a midnight moon, while walking with the poet Frances Sargent Osgood.

Three years later, on September 21, 1848, Poe met Sarah officially, again at 88 Benefit Street. The two shared the same birthday—January 19, though Sarah was six years Poe's senior—and a love of literary criticism, and began corresponding with one another, culminating in plans for what was to be an "immediate marriage" at the end of December that same year. Everything librarian Leila Rondin tells Saoirse in the Athenæum is factual as well, from Whitman's mother's—and friends'— dislike of the troubled writer to their short-lived engagement—and its dissolution, beginning in an alcove of the Ath when Whitman discovered he'd been drinking, and ending with Whitman holding an ether-soaked handkerchief to her nose at her home less than half a mile up the road.

Something unexpected I discovered when researching the heart condition Whitman treated with ether: there are no formal medical records diagnosing her with any actual heart abnormality; it's believed by some that the chest tightness and shortness of breath she experienced may have been an anxiety disorder. Even still, Whitman rarely went anywhere without her ether, and this perceived heart condition is likely why she never had children.

So, if so much of my portrayals of Whitman and Poe are accurate, where did I take liberties? Why, with what's *beneath the poet's house*, of course. While long-ago rumors of slave tunnels beneath College Hill are real, there are no catacombs snaking beneath the houses on Benefit Street, Saint John's Cathedral, or the adjacent cemetery. While Whitman's garnet-red abode and H. P. Lovecraft's Shunned House may be linked in many a reader's mind, they are *not* connected by trap-door-accessed, sconce-lit tunnels. Poe did, contrary to Emmit's villain-ous monologue, first arrive in Rhode Island in 1845, and "The Pit and the Pendulum" was published in 1842. While he *didn't* base the story on any parallels with the Spanish Inquisition, despite setting the tale there—to the confusion of many readers and critics—he also didn't base it on any real-life torture chamber . . . at least, not that I'm aware of; the room containing the pit and the pendulum with which Emmit threatens Saoirse is entirely of my own creation.

I also must admit that I've not had the pleasure of entering either 88 Benefit Street (which, as Emmit reminds us, was once 50 Benefit, then 76) or 135 Benefit Street, Lovecraft's Shunned House. Both are private residences and, from my understanding, 88 Benefit is indeed five separate apartments (as it was in this very manuscript, before archi-tecturally and historically savvy landlord Diane Hartnett renovated . . . no, *restored*, it to its original single-family residence). While you can embark upon a wonderful "Walking Tour of Poe's Providence," cour-tesy of tour guide and Poe/Whitman scholar Levi Leland (yes, Emmit's contact with the historical society is named for Mr. Leland, thanks to his indispensable contributions to my research), I hope readers of *Beneath the Poet's House* and fans of Poe and Whitman alike show the same (albeit difficult) restraint I had to in refraining from knocking on these historic doors in the hopes of stealing a glimpse into the past and these talented writers' lives.

As for the excerpts of poetry contained within the novel, the words Saoirse hears Mia, Lucretia, and Roberto chanting when she finds them in her basement ("Oft since thine earthly eyes have closed on mine, / Our souls, dim-wandering in the hall of dreams, / Hold mystic converse on the life divine, / By the still music of immortal streams") are the first stanza of one of Whitman's sonnets, published in her 1853 collection *Hours of Life, and Other Poems*, and commonly believed to be from a series relating to Edgar Allan Poe. During Saoirse's first séance, Mary recites, "Vainly my heart had with thy sorceries striven: / It had no refuge from thy love,—no Heaven / But in thy fatal presence;—from afar / It owned thy power and trembled like a star," which is the opening of Whitman's "To-" published in that same collection. And the lines that materialize in Saoirse's head as if "on the wings of a raven" are from a satirical essay Whitman composed for recitation at a suffragist banquet in Providence in 1871, "Woman's Sphere" (I like to think Saoirse was still experiencing the delayed effects of Lucretia's LSD-laced cupcakes when this verse occurs to her several weeks after coming across it during her initial internet sleuthing).

"I have pressed your letter again and again to my lips, sweetest Helen—bathing it in tears of joy, or of a 'divine despair'" is a line from one of Poe's letters to Whitman, penned October 1, 1848. And, of course, the text message with which Emmit attempts to woo Saoirse after their first two dates together is composed mostly of Poe's "To Helen," first published in *Poems* in 1831. Admittedly, I did add some of Emmit's signature flair to the end ("I long to see you again, to kiss your face / To hold your hand. / I think it's time for you and I / To slip between the gravestones / And back in time"). I think we can all agree that, despite his grandiose delusions, Emmit Powell's poetry falls far beneath the literary merit of Poe's. A similar sentiment is evoked when Emmit recites a stanza of "Night Piece" by James Joyce (*Poetry: A Magazine of Verse*, 1917) at Carr Haus.

Lastly, the stanza that unfurls in Saoirse's mind as she's suffering a heart attack ("The poet sleeps, and pansies bloom / Beside her far, provident tomb" . . .) are from Whitman's 1859 poem, "A Pansy from the Grave of Keats," slightly altered to fit a female speaker, and one of my personal favorites by a poet who penned countless nature, death, and myth-inspired verses (and I read them *all* over the course of researching this novel; see her posthumously published volume, *Poems*, published in 1879, or the *Scholar Select* edition of Whitman's collected works).

So, if after all these gorgeous verses and captivating biographical facts, all the moonlit roses and reverent dips into the inscrutabilities of Death, you're still asking, *Why Sarah Helen Whitman?*, then I'll leave you with this: because she of the coffin pendant and midnight-black dresses, she of nighttime gardening sessions and regular attempts to understand where the dead go, was as hauntingly intriguing as the lines of her delicate, decadent poetry. Because the house she once inhabited infuses mystery from every Federal-style window molding—bone white against the striking shade of red—as it sits, sentry-like, above Saint John's Cathedral and the silent, shadowy cemetery. And because, though no one can discount the macabre genius of Edgar Allan Poe, the woman who commanded his attention with her sharp wit—and sharper discernment—is just as deserving of contemplation, admiration, and indulgently eerie spin-off stories.

—Christa Carmen
November 15, 2023

ACKNOWLEDGMENTS

I'm incredibly grateful to the wonderful team at Thomas & Mercer for the opportunity to write this book. Thanks to associate publisher Gracie Doyle for her enthusiasm and insight, and to editor Charlotte Herscher for her discerning eye. It was especially fun—and helpful!—to discover all of Charlotte's personal connections to many of the places in *Beneath the Poet's House* along the way. Thank you to my steadfast and invaluable agent, Jill Marr; her excitement somehow seems to grow with each novel I write, and I can't wait to see where the next one takes us. And endless thanks to my circle of beta readers who are truly worth their weight in gold: Joshua Rex, Belicia Rhea, Allan Patch, and Levi Leland. Levi, additionally, for his depthless knowledge of Poe and Whitman, and Josh for his vault-like understanding of Providence . . . its historic rumors and hidden streets, how you can look between two tombstones and, suddenly, be transported to other worlds. Everyone who took the time to read this book in its early stages contributed something wholly indispensable to its creation, and that includes the Monday Night Write Group: Valerie B. Williams, Terry Emery, Ken Godfrey, Jessica McMahan, Stephen Cords, Larry Hinkle, John Buja, and Tom Deady. Special thanks as well to Sarah Itteilag for her review of the novel's medical aspects; her input was vital, and any errors with regard to the authenticity of these subjects are mine alone.

My sincerest thanks to Gwendolyn Kiste for our chats about both writing and life. She helped me reach the finish line of this novel in a way that was distinctly meaningful and utterly essential, a world beyond mere keyboard clicks and craft concepts. Thank you to Lauren Elise Daniels, queen of grounded advice; Elissa Sweet, empress of last-minute editing inquiries; and Aron Beauregard, king of taking control of one's writing career. Major thanks to Claire Cooney, Carlos Hernandez, Julia Rios, Lazaryn McLaughlin, and Nicole Gehman for their unwavering support. Thank you, as well, to Mary Robles, Belicia Rhea, and Jessica Wick for instilling in me the confidence that I can, in fact, write at least one decent piece of poetry.

Thank you to those amazing individuals who provided early praise for *Beneath the Poet's House*: Luanne Rice, Zoje Stage, Jess Lourey, Katrina Monroe, Vanessa Lillie, Jessa Maxwell, and Levi Leland; your generosity, kind words, and support mean the world.

Thank you to my parents, Jeanne and Rick Quattromani, for, as usual, *everything*, and my sister, Lauren Forenza, who's simply the best. And to every other exceptional, encouraging, endlessly-game-for-a-new-creepy-tale-from-yours-truly member of my family. To Christine Granfield and Jean Colistra for their eagerness to read newly finished drafts of my work. To Mirabel, for demanding all those long walks during which tangled plot points were unwound. And to my husband, who listened raptly as I went on and on about the John Hay Library's Poe–Whitman collection or the social reform work of Susan Hamond Barney across late nineteenth-century Rhode Island. Did he know that Sarah Whitman hated the bizarre red shade of the Benefit Street house? Or that Poe gave her a lock of his hair while they were courting? He did not, but he sure as hell knows now.

And thank you, finally, to my lovely daughter, Eleanor, a child held as rapt by "The Raven" and "Annabel Lee" as she is the Little Golden Books adaption of *Frozen* or *Moana*. She is as unique and spirited an individual as Sarah Whitman. My April-moon. She is my store of sweetness, my pearly orchard-bloom, who fills "with rose-light all the room."